Unfinished EX

A CALLOWAY BROTHERS NOVEL

samantha christy

Books Publishing Group

Saint Johns, FL 32259

Copyright © 2022 by Samantha Christy

All rights reserved, including the rights to reproduce this book or any portions thereof in any form whatsoever.

This is a work of fiction. Names, characters, places and incidents are either the product of the author's imagination or are used fictitiously, and any resemblance to actual persons, living or dead, business establishments, events or locales is entirely coincidental.

Cover designed by Coverluv

Cover model photo by WANDER AGUIAR

Cover model – Dane D.

Samantha Christy

Chapter One

Jaxon

I've always had a sixth sense. Or good intuition. Or some kind of inexplicable awareness. Ever since I was a kid, I've had it. Once when I was five, I told my parents I was going to have a little sister. Three weeks later, they told us Mom was pregnant with Addy. It happened again when I was thirteen. I knew Nicky was going to walk into my eighth-grade history class at the middle school. More than that, even before I kissed her behind the dugout that Friday night, I knew she was going to be my wife.

At eighteen, when a local child went missing, I was the one who found her alive, albeit hypothermic, out near old Joe Henson's cabin. I'm not sure why I looked there; my feet just took me.

The day I found out about my brother Chaz's death three years ago was the worst. I couldn't concentrate on anything. It was the strangest feeling. Cooper was his twin, but I was the one who 'felt' his death without really knowing it.

And now I've had a feeling all morning. Heisman knows I have. He's stuck close to me. He didn't even run after the stick I threw to him in the park after our run. Dogs have an even better sense of things than humans.

"What?" I ask him, as if he'll answer. I pull out my phone and reread the text from my oldest brother Tag. "He said he wanted to tell me something later." I cock my head, studying Heisman as he walks from tree to tree, picking his favorite toilet. "You think I should call him?"

He glances up at me as he pees, almost like he knows what I said.

Heisman isn't just my dog. He's my best friend. I know it's corny, but it's been true since the day I got the rambunctious golden retriever puppy from the pound two years ago—both of us rescuing each other in ways we couldn't possibly understand at the time. And call me crazy, but I actually do think he knows what I'm saying sometimes. And I swear he would speak if he could.

He trots over and licks my hand.

"You're right." I put away the phone. "I shouldn't call him. Whatever he has to tell me, we'll learn soon enough."

Still, this feeling—it's nagging at me. I look at the sky. No looming storm. We cross from the park to McQuaid Circle, and I glance down the street. Nothing to see here. Just the normal Friday evening activities: kids running toward Calloway Creek Park, adults carrying coffee from Ava Criss' Corner Coffee Shop. People coming and going from the eateries, the bookstore, and the flower shop.

I peek into Gigi's Flower Shop, the establishment owned and operated by Maddie Foster, Tag's girlfriend. She's at the counter helping a half dozen people. And her daughter, Gigi, is by her side. *Her daughter.* I still can't believe my brother, the playboy of Calloway Creek, has a girlfriend. One with a kid no less. The world has definitely shifted on its axis. Gigi spies me peeking through the window and happily waves to me. I smile and wave back. Because *I* actually like kids.

Heisman nudges me. He knows our routine. Home is our destination, and once we get there, he gets his treat, a large Milk-Bone.

My house is just around the corner. I love the fact that Heisman and I can take this walk every day. Along the way, I say hello to every person we pass, and Heisman greets every pet. Not in the same way. I smile or extend my hand, while my sidekick smells buttholes and sometimes noses.

I stop walking and contemplate turning the corner when we come to Tag's street. But somehow I know this feeling I have isn't about him. Heisman grunts. He's getting impatient. I reach down and pat his head. "Come on, buddy."

As we approach my house, something is off. Heisman usually runs ahead, excited about the impending treat he knows he'll receive. But he doesn't leave my side. I've heard dogs can sense when people are ill. They can smell tumors, and they can even tell when their owners are going to have a seizure.

"Are you trying to tell me I'm sick?" I ask, trying to think of the last time I've been in for a checkup.

He presses his weight against my leg.

"Shit. I'm dying, aren't I?"

He sits dutifully by my side at the gate by the front walk. I stare left and right and shake my head at the white picket fence in front of the perfect bungalow I bought for Nicky and me thinking it'd be a great place to raise kids. Yet now, Heisman and I are the only occupants, the second and third bedrooms sitting empty, if you don't count the piles of boxes I never got around to shipping to Oklahoma.

Why is that?

I open the gate for Heisman. He doesn't trot to the front door as usual. He's glued to my side. "Dude," I say. "If I'm going to keel over with a heart attack, just tell me now. Give me a sign."

He stares up at me with his innocent brown eyes.

"Some best friend you are."

I open the door, the weather stripping on the bottom edge sweeping the mail across the floor inside. I love that I live in a town where they still drop mail through slots in the front door. I lean down to pick up the mail and freeze.

My eyes focus on the official government return stamp on an envelope. Immediately, I know what it is. And it has me feeling like I could very well be having a coronary, because it feels like a fist is closing around my heart. I thought the envelope would be bigger, thicker, more significant somehow. After all, you'd think the end of my marriage would have arrived with more fanfare than a sixty-cent stamp.

I hold it and slump to the floor, my trusty friend ignoring the box of Milk-Bones on the foyer table. Heisman lies next to me and puts his head in my lap.

There are a million thoughts going through my head. But I only voice one of them. "Fuck."

Heisman isn't alarmed by my choice of words. I may not be the asshole that Tag is, or the grumpy daredevil that is our youngest brother, Cooper. But we all seem to have the same affliction when it comes to our vocabulary.

I turn the envelope over in my hand, wondering what my wife is doing. Did her envelope get delivered today? Is she thinking the same thing? That once we open them, that's it, we're done, it's over. Or should I say I'm wondering what my *ex-wife* is doing? Ex-wife. The air whooshes out of my lungs as swiftly as if I'd been sucker punched. Any fragmented flame of hope has been doused. Pain closes in, its weight crushing and claustrophobic.

Five years down the drain. Well, fourteen if you count the nine years we dated before we got married, the three years we lived together as husband and wife, and the two after she left me before the divorce became finalized.

The front door opens and Tag walks in.

"Don't you fucking knock?" I spit, well aware I'm not my usually sunny self.

He eyes me on the floor of the foyer and laughs. "I'd ask if your dog died, but I can see he's lying here looking as pathetic as you are. Did you have a hard run or something?"

I don't answer. I get up and throw the envelope on the table. Then I toss Heisman a Milk-Bone.

He doesn't go after it. I retrieve it and hold it in front of his snout. "It's okay, bud, take it."

Reluctantly, he does. He walks to the corner of the living room and plops down, giving me one last glance before he devours it.

"Oh, shit!" Tag says jubilantly behind me.

I spin to see him holding the envelope.

"Is this what I think it is?" A smile splits his face. "You're finally free of that lying, cheating bitch. We should celebrate." He pulls out his phone. "I'll have Cooper and Quinn meet us at Donovan's. Eight o'clock?"

He wants me to celebrate. Double fuck.

His finger lingers over his phone. "Who else should we invite? Lucas? Eric?"

"No, man. Just us."

"Got it. We'll make it a family celebration first. We'll organize something much bigger for your divorce party. It'll be epic. Hey, now we have two parties to plan."

"Two?"

"Your divorce celebration and my bachelor party."

I blink twice, replaying his words. I knew he and Maddie moved in together last month. Still, I wasn't expecting this. "You're engaged?"

"Asked her yesterday."

"Holy shit." I can't stop the motion of my head as it shakes back and forth. My brother, Tag Calloway, the guy voted in high school as most likely to never get married, is getting hitched. I push the jealousy down and try to be happy for him. I pat him on the back. "Congratulations, brother. Tonight's celebration should definitely be about you, not me."

"We can kill two birds. Two fucking years you've waited, Jax. The tramp left you in limbo for twenty-four months. You're finally free. That's worth tossing back a few shots, don't you think?"

Heisman and I lock eyes. He gets me. Even though he never met her, he sleeps in Nicky's spot on the bed every night. He knows everything. He knows my secrets. He knows I was the one who dragged my feet on the divorce. He knows I hold just as much responsibility for ruining our marriage as she does. He knows that although I should hate her, I can't.

How could I hate her when I still love her so goddamn much?

Tag's phone vibrates. "Cooper's in. And speaking of our homeless brother, maybe you should invite him to crash with you since it seems like he'll be in town for a while."

"He's living in his van. His very expensive decked-out, solar-paneled van that has more conveniences than my first apartment."

"Sheriff Niles issued him a ticket the other day when he parked overnight behind the bank."

"That asshole. Niles, not Coop."

"Maddie said he could park in the spare spot behind her shop, or maybe at the train station. People leave cars there overnight all the time."

"So why doesn't he do one of those?"

He laughs. "Do you not know our brother? Danger has become his middle name. Rules—he breaks them. Guidelines—he doesn't follow them. Laws—he thinks they don't apply to him."

"You're worried about him."

"Aren't you?"

"Lots of people do what he does. He's not the only crazy twenty-something who jumps off bridges and parachutes out of planes."

"It's more than that, and you know it. And surely it strikes you as odd that he didn't do anything nearly this idiotic until after Chaz died."

"You think he's got some morbid desire to join our dead brother? I think he's just found his passion. Plus, if you recall, Chaz died *because* they did something idiotic."

"Still, it couldn't hurt if you talk to him. You've always been the sensible, brainy one of the three of us."

"Brainy? You think because I teach horny adolescents all day that I'm brainy? You're the one who's kicking ass at his own business."

"He lived with me for a month, Jax. Never listened to a word I said. Tuned me out whenever I tried to get him to move back home."

"What makes you think I'd have more luck?"

He shrugs. "Power in numbers, bro. I've got Addy working on him, too. Few people can deny our little sister."

"Fine. I'll see if he wants to crash here. But I'm not going to force him to talk about anything he doesn't want to talk about."

"Fair enough." He heads for the door. "Eight o'clock."

I wave a hand after him. Then I look at the envelope from across the room, deciding I'm not going to open it. I won't give her that satisfaction.

"Come on, Heisman. Let's go watch the game."

He follows dutifully as I grab a cold beer and plop onto the couch. It only takes one swallow to know I'm going to need something much stronger.

~ ~ ~

"The first round is on me," Lissa says, serving us a tray of shots.

My brothers chuckle knowing Lissa has been after me since elementary school. She knows why we're here. Everyone does. When we arrived, Tag pushed open the pub doors and announced to the entire establishment that my divorce was final. And despite the fact that I've been dating Calista—*kind of*—for the past six months, Lissa seems to think there is renewed hope.

I lift my shot glass. "Thanks, Liss."

She goes back to waitressing but is always looking over when she passes.

"Tell me again why you never went there?" Cooper asks.

"She's too short," Tag says. "And she's got small tits."

I roll my eyes. "Her tits are fine. Breasts are breasts, man. As long as you can grab a handful, who the hell cares how big they are? And she's not too short. She's just… not my type."

Donny, the owner of the pub, comes over with a shot and a smile. He places the whiskey in front of me. "Cheers to Jaxon Calloway," he says boisterously. "The happiest time in any man's life is right after his first divorce."

Everyone at the surrounding tables laughs as I swallow the drink, playing along.

"I don't know," Tag says. "I'm pretty damn happy right now, and divorced is not something I plan on being."

"You think I planned this?" I bite. "You think I went into my marriage anticipating this would happen?"

"Maybe you should have," Cooper says. "She never made a secret of her career aspirations. I don't see why it would have come as a surprise that the woman wanted to go to Oklahoma and chase tornadoes."

"Because he thought it wasn't true," Tag says. "Or that chasing tornadoes was a metaphor."

I shake my head. "I knew she loved the weather. And I knew chances were she wouldn't get to follow her dreams if we stayed here in Calloway Creek. I guess I just thought—"

"You thought you'd get married, spout out a couple of kids, and her priorities would change."

"I don't know." I trace the rim of the shot glass. "Fuck."

Tag gets Lissa's attention. "My recently single brother here needs more alcohol." He turns to me. "We're supposed to be celebrating, not mourning, Jax."

Then why does this whole day feel like a fucking wake? "Yeah, I know."

A woman I don't recognize stops at our table. "Calloway? As in Calloway Creek? Does your family own this town?"

My brothers and I share a look. We're so tired of answering this question that we've considered changing our last name more than once over the years. "No, ma'am, we don't. Google the town name along with the name Lloyd McQuaid. It'll tell you everything you need to know about the infamous bet."

"As in who the rightful owners are," Hunter McQuaid shouts from the bar.

"Fuck you and your derelict brothers," Tag says in his usual eloquent manner.

Hunter salutes Tag with his middle finger. It's a back-and-forth we've perfected with the McQuaid brothers over the years. Our family feud belongs to our ancestors, but I think we keep it going for sport.

Calista and her friends walk into the pub and take a booth across the room. She doesn't see me. Any normal guy who has been kind-of-sort-of dating a woman would go over and greet her.

"Didn't your girlfriend just walk in?" Cooper asks.

"Calista is not my girlfriend."

"Word has it you've been seen out at restaurants. At sporting events at the high school. At her apartment." He cocks his head. "You're fucking, no?"

"Just because we go out and have sex does not make her my girlfriend."

"Does *she* know that?" Tag asks.

"She does."

"A hundred bucks says she's going to want a commitment after she hears about your new status."

My eyes meet the table. Tag's right. Calista has been very patient. And I've been a jackass—stringing her along on the premise that I wasn't divorced yet. And although I've never entirely led her to believe we'd be more than what we are, it may have been implied.

"Heads up," Cooper says, nodding across the room.

Calista is walking over, her eyes as bright as I've ever seen them. "Jaxon! I just heard the news."

"I guess good news travels fast." I almost choke on the words, but they please her. And if I'm anything, I'm a people pleaser. It's one of my best qualities. Or perhaps my greatest downfall.

"Well, congratulations." She leans down and kisses my cheek. "I'm here with friends, but maybe we can get together after."

"Sure. I'll text you."

"Great. See you later then. Bye, guys."

Cooper stares me down. "You aren't going to text her later, are you?"

Lissa puts another round of drinks on the table. I toss one back. "Is it that obvious?"

Tag huffs. "Bro, you have a gorgeous woman who basically just told you she's up for a game of hide the sausage, and you're just going to go home and sulk over your failed marriage to the girl who cheated on you?"

Cooper pushes his shot in front of me. "You need this more than I do."

I drink it, knowing I'll need a lot more to numb whatever the hell feeling this is inside me.

Samantha Christy

Chapter Two

Nicky

Yesterday…

"Five minutes," my producer, Marty, says, popping his head into my small dressing room at 5:15 a.m.

"Got it."

I check my face in the mirror. After almost eight months on air, I feel I've gotten the makeup down pat, albeit far from a professional makeup job. At least I have a dressing room, even if it's not much bigger than the broom closet next to it. For all I know, this *was* a closet before WRKT hired me as their morning meteorologist. But it's a country mile from what I had before they offered me this position—which was a corner of the supply room. Let's face it, while this is basically my dream job (or at least a stepping stone toward it), WRKT is like working at a coffee cart instead of Starbucks.

When I first came to Oklahoma, I worked as a forecaster. I chased storms, researched data, and helped come up with interesting weather-related stories the 'real' meteorologists would cover. Then I caught the eye of one of the producers, who thought

I might work well on camera, so he put me in an on-camera apprentice program. It was basically an unpaid internship, and I was living in an apartment over some guy's garage surviving on tips I made waitressing at the local honky-tonk.

But I was doing what I loved. Being on camera reporting the weather was never even on my radar. Yes, I took a few TV studio classes in college taught by a former television reporter who said I should try my hand at weather broadcasting. But that's like a professor telling an acting student they should try to be in a television series. It's something a lot of meteorology students dream of but that very few will ever achieve. In reality, most meteorologists don't even work for TV or radio. They work for private companies: insurance, trucking, shipping, even the government.

I wanted to gather data, dissect the atmosphere, and make the appropriate predictions. After Marty Maxwell took an interest in me and got me the apprentice gig, I started doing small ninety-second environmental pieces about controlled burns, pollution, and deforestation. When I tested well on those segments, they moved me to weekends when Marisol Hennesee left to go to a larger station in Seattle. I was in that position for less than a month when a more prestigious position opened up right here at the station after Kyle Morrison left to go to KBLJ, a much larger New Jersey station akin to Dunkin', if we're still talking in coffee shop metaphors. It's no secret that small stations like mine are merely a pit stop until something better comes along. Turnover is common if not expected. So there I was being offered the coveted morning meteorologist slot at this small Oklahoma City affiliate of XTN, the national cable news network second only to 'the big three.'

I immediately quit moonlighting at the place where serving handsy men paid my rent and literally went from being an unknown weekend weather girl to a respected TV forecaster overnight.

Weather girl. That term grates on me like fingernails on a blackboard. It's left over from a time when they put pretty girls on TV to recite information fed to them by meteorologists. But today, almost everyone doing the weather on television has a science degree.

I look down at my chest, running a hand across my breasts, making sure my stiff nipples aren't showing. Studios are cold. It's better for the equipment, but certainly not for nipples—unless you're a horny man watching the weather who gets off on that sort of thing. Over the past year, I've gone from wearing sexy bralettes to padded, more traditional bras that cover my pointy peaks.

"On in two," Marty says as I make my way to the set.

I take my position in front of the green screen, put in my earpiece, and wait for my cue. Marty talks to me in my ear, doing a quick sound check. I nod. Marty is always in my ear. He feeds me any new and breaking information while I'm on camera. He corrects me if I say anything wrong so that I can rephrase it, and he offers encouragement when needed. He's become like a father to me. And if Marty is my father, Josh, the cameraman who always shoots me when we go out on location, is like a brother.

My broadcast starts. I never read from a script or teleprompter. Unless there is breaking weather news, my spots only last for a few minutes at a time, peppered through the morning show and the news show directly after.

Today is no different than every other day this week. August in Oklahoma is hot, humid, and mostly cloudy. Tornado season has long since passed, although we still get the occasional outbreak—a meteorologist's dream.

My spot ends and I head over to my designated workspace, grabbing a muffin and a third cup of coffee along the way. I get on the computer knowing I'll be back on air again in about thirty-five minutes. I'm always looking for something else, an edge to a story, a spin on the typical weather. Sometimes it gets boring reciting the same information seven or eight times a day.

Last month, I was sure I'd be fired when I reported about homelessness and the heat wave, getting far too political by pointing out shortcomings in how the city deals with the indigent population. Instead, Marty brought me flowers and told me to keep up the good work. A week later, I pushed the envelope again when I did a clip of my own story and why I became a meteorologist. I was hoping to inspire young women to get excited about science. The station was flooded with texts, tweets, and emails about how much they loved the human element I brought to weather segments.

A week ago, Kenny Marin, the station manager, offered me a raise. I'm now making more than my predecessor, which delights me to no end considering he was a man. I know they're afraid I'll leave. Just like everyone else leaves eventually. I've had my eye on WMBZ in New Orleans. While Oklahoma City is exciting as the tornado capital of the US, New Orleans is a hurricane magnet. And if tornadoes are the meteorologist equivalent of crack to a drug addict, hurricanes are heroin.

While I'd be happy moving to a more well-known station here in Oklahoma, I'm ready for a change after being here for two years. It doesn't quite feel like the place I'd settle down.

A hand lands on my shoulder. "Great spot," Marty says. He leans down. "Might want to get the scoop on what Scott Hayes from KMBL was reporting this morning."

Before he's even done speaking, I'm typing it in and pulling up Scott's segment. Damned if I'm going to be the last broadcast meteorologist to report on hot topics.

Someday, I'm going to be the first.

~ ~ ~

I'm home by three p.m., and that's after I've done my grocery shopping and picked up dinner. Most days, I eat my evening meal in the late afternoon. If I'm not too tired, I work out, then I'm in bed by eight, sometimes seven. That's the price I pay for having to be up at three o'clock each morning. But I wouldn't trade it for anything—I rub the pendant on the end of my chain—well, almost anything.

I put away my groceries and set my take-out sushi on the table. I open a bottle of wine and then eat as I go through my email. I've been getting more fan mail lately. It's mostly nice people telling me how much they like me, but some of it shouldn't really be categorized as *fan* mail. Hate mail is more like it. Marty warned me there will always be people like this, people who criticize my hair or say I'm too fat, too skinny, or that my clothes are hideous. People who tell me how to do my job or frankly tell me to go get another job because I suck at mine.

I try to let the negative comments roll off me, but it's hard. A lot of TV personalities have assistants to weed through their mail. Goals.

Thankfully, the last one I read is a gushing review of the reporting I did on the fires in Arizona last month.

I close my laptop on a high, putting all other thoughts aside.

I pour myself a second glass of wine and move on to my snail mail. There's a second reminder that I haven't signed a new lease for another twelve months. A credit card offer. The new *National Geographic* magazine.

Then I pause when I see it—the envelope I've been waiting for. Well, not waiting for as much as dreading. I don't need to open it to know what it says inside. It says that I'm no longer Mrs. Jaxon Calloway. Not that I ever took his name. My maiden name was always the one I was going to use for my career. Nicole Forbes has that *je ne sais quoi* that Nicky Calloway doesn't.

But this is it. It's over. Jaxon is not my husband. I'm not his wife. We're not married. It's as if the last fourteen years have been erased with this one little envelope.

Emotions I didn't anticipate bombard me. Guilt. Regret. Unbelievable sadness. I swallow them knowing there's no one to blame but myself. I shouldn't be allowed to be upset. I made this bed. It doesn't matter that I didn't leave him because I didn't love him. I *did*. I guess I just loved weather more. I know that makes me a selfish bitch, which is why I did what I did. He shouldn't have to live his life playing second fiddle to my first true love. He deserves a woman who wants the same things he does: marriage, family, Disney World vacations, and game nights. That was never going to be me, no matter how much I wanted it to be.

And according to Paige, the one friend I keep in touch with on Facebook, he's moved on with someone who may be able to give him what he wants. Just… why does it have to be Calista Hilson? My high school nemesis. The head cheerleader and class president—both junior *and* senior years. The person everyone joked Jaxon should be with, as he was not only the star quarterback but also on the student council. Me—I was too busy being in the science club, math club, physics club, and any other geeky organization I could join. I spent my weekends reading books about weather and watching TWC videos. Jaxon spent his weekends playing or watching football and organizing school events with, you guessed it, Calista.

She and I are complete opposites in every way. We couldn't look more different either. She's blonde and petite. I'm a statuesque brunette who towers over a good portion of the male population.

Opposites in every way. Maybe that's exactly why he chose her.

The doorbell rings. Thankful for the distraction, I answer it.

It's Marty. He walks in with a huge smile on his face, the kind that crinkles his eyes and shows all his teeth. "You're about to kiss me."

I take a step back. I love Marty. He's been a great friend and my biggest supporter here, but I'd never cross that line with him. Not to mention I'm not the least bit inclined to.

He laughs at my reaction. "Let me rephrase that. I've brought you an early Christmas present."

I look in his empty arms and then behind him. "What is it?"

"Get ready for your life to change."

My heartbeat speeds up incrementally. This is my producer here. He usually finds out about things before I do. "Spit it out, Marty."

"Makenna Kendall from The Weekend Show on XTN—"

"The pregnant one?"

"That's her. She went into early labor and will be out for two to three months." His smile gets even bigger, if that's possible "They want you, Nicole."

My legs almost give out from under me. I get light-headed. I'm not sure I heard him correctly. "Me?"

"Those stunts you pull—the ones you think will end up getting you fired—they actually get you noticed. People like it. You bring a human side to weather reporting that no one else does."

I pull out a barstool and sit, absorbing his words. I may as well be chasing a tornado across a grassy plain with how fast my heart is pounding. "They really asked for me?"

"They want you out there tomorrow. You'll go on air on Saturday."

"Tomorrow?" I look around my apartment. "But—"

"But nothing. This isn't the kind of offer you say no to."

"I don't even know the offer."

"Does it matter? And just so you know, it's a good one." He gets out his phone. "I've forwarded it to you. They need an answer by the end of the day."

"You'll go with me?"

He sits at the bar and absentmindedly sifts through my mail.

"That's not part of the deal. There's a reason I'm forty-three years old and still producing at a small-time station. This is where I've always been. It's where I'll always be. That's simply the way some things are."

"You sell yourself short. You should be in a larger market. I think you're comfortable here. Either way, I'll be back in two to three months, and everything will be back to normal."

"No you won't." He picks up my lease renewal papers and tears them up. "Don't sign this."

"What do you mean?"

"After being the weekend broadcast meteorologist at XTN, I promise you won't be coming back to this Podunk station. You'll have offers from all over the country, Nicole. You'll be able to write your own ticket. Don't you realize what's just happened? You've won the lottery."

I sit and stare at the still-sealed envelope that signifies the end of my marriage. My euphoria morphs into trepidation. "XTN is in New York City. It's only thirty miles from Calloway Creek."

"You're not seriously thinking about turning them down, are you?"

I hold up the envelope. "My divorce papers came today."

"Well, that's untimely. But it's no reason to give up this opportunity. You'd be a fool not to take it."

"I *am* a fool, Marty." I slap the envelope on the counter. "This proves it."

"Still. You're going to say yes, right?"

I close my eyes and breathe. Finally, the wariness loses ground to the longing, the determination, the hunger to achieve the goals I set for myself when I was a little girl.

"Nicole?"

I nod. "Yes."

"Yeehaw!"

I laugh. Only in Oklahoma do people actually say that.

He pulls a second wineglass from my cabinet and pours himself a cup. "We're celebrating."

I take a drink, and then anxiety takes hold. "They want me there *tomorrow?*"

He doesn't answer as he taps on his phone. "Done. I told them you accept. They'll send over the details of your flight directly to your email. I've taken you as far as I can. This is where I get off the train. The rest is all up to you."

"What if I can't do it? What if I'm not good enough?"

"Nicole, I knew from your very first broadcast that you were too good for WRKT."

I let it sink in. "Oh my god. XTN. It's a dream come true."

"A well-deserved dream. Now let's kill this bottle and get you packed. Josh is already on his way over to help."

"You called Josh? What if I had said no?"

"Josh and I would have strapped you to the roof of my car and driven you there against your will. Nicole, you need to realize something. You're going to be a legend. A decade from now, you'll be talked about in the same circles as Stephanie Abrams, Jim Cantore, and Al Roker."

"Shut up."

"And I'll be able to say I knew you when."

"If I'm going places, it's only because *you* took a chance on me. You saw something in me and believed in me when everyone else just thought I was a weather girl. Whatever happens to me, I owe to you."

"Remember to thank me when you write your autobiography one day."

I pull him in for a hug. Then I kiss him on the cheek.

"See?" he says. "I knew you'd want to kiss me."

Tears flood my eyes. I'm excited. I'm grateful. I'm utterly terrified.

Chapter Three

Jaxon

"Don't look at me that way," I say to Heisman as he peers at me from the end of the couch when I open another beer. "Want to trade places with me and see how *you* handle this?"

He lays his head back down but continues to stare.

I left Tag and Cooper at Donovan's. I could only take so much of us 'celebrating' my divorce. Not to mention having to endure Tag belittling Nicky. It's a ruse, my being a good man. Because a good man wouldn't let people speak badly about someone who isn't inherently bad. We've all made mistakes.

The envelope still sits unopened, only now it's on the coffee table. Why I continue to torture myself with it is beyond me. I knew it was coming. I've known for two years. Hell, I don't even talk to Nicky anymore. When she left, she cut all ties. She ghosted me on social media. We only speak through our lawyers.

The only connection I have to her is her sister, Victoria, who is a senior in my calculus class at Calloway Creek High School. And she's tight-lipped when it comes to sharing information. It's like the day Nicky walked out on me, she ceased to exist. I don't even try to Google her anymore. The last I read, she was working as a junior weather forecaster at some small-time TV station in Oklahoma City.

I take a sip and point the mouth of the beer bottle at Heisman. "You would have liked her. She loved dogs. We always said we'd get one after we had kids." I huff out a pained laugh. "Sadly, she kept pushing that off further and further until… Well, you know the rest."

He knows the story and knows it well. He gets that he was a replacement for her. Someone for me to love after the love of my life walked out on me. And fortunately, Heisman is good at keeping secrets. Even my brothers don't know that I deserved what I got. And to this day, everyone in town thinks that she's the bad guy who fucked over the 'good' Calloway brother.

Heisman jumps off the couch, tail wagging, and gazes out the front window.

"Someone here, buddy?"

He's quick to alert me of visitors, but he's a shit watchdog. Heisman's never met a person he didn't like. If Freddy Krueger himself came into my house, Heisman would probably lick Freddy as he butchered me. He may be my best friend, but he couldn't protect anyone if his life depended on it.

It's no surprise when the doorbell rings. I stumble over to see Calista standing under the porch light. I feel like a complete dick when I open the door. "I was supposed to call. Sorry. My brothers and I got kind of carried away."

"Can I come in?"

No. "I suppose. But I doubt I'll be very good company after all the drinking. I was about to head to bed and sleep it off."

"I'll be quick." She tousles Heisman's hair and walks into my house, my dog following on her heels. She turns. "There was something I wanted to ask you, though. Why didn't you call or text me when you got the papers?"

I shrug. "Wasn't that big of a deal."

"Not that big of a deal? You've been waiting on this for months."

"No. This is what *you've* been waiting on for months," I slur.

"What's that supposed to mean?"

"It means that not a day goes by where you haven't asked me if the papers have arrived."

"It's been two years, Jaxon. I mean, how long can it take?"

"I told you before, we live in different states. We don't speak to each other. It's hard to figure things out that way."

"Hard?" Her eyes sweep the room. "She cheated. She left. She gave you the house. She gave you everything. She didn't want you or anything here. What was there to argue over?"

Her words sting. Probably because she's right. Nicky didn't want anything to do with me or Calloway Creek. Neither could give her what she wanted: a career.

"You've never been married, Calista. You're not one to talk."

"No, but I have plenty of friends who have, and their divorces took six months. Even the one who had kids only took a year."

"Well, this one didn't."

She sighs heavily. "Listen, I don't want to fight. My parents will be in town tomorrow. I was hoping we could all have dinner."

"I'm not sure now is such a good time."

"Why not?"

"I don't know. I have a lot going on at school. The start of football season. The new class I'm teaching. Lots of things."

"But you have time to go out with your brothers."

"That's different."

"How is it different?"

"I don't know. Because they're not your parents."

She leans against the back of the couch. "How come we've never had dinner with your parents?"

I shrug, too much of a coward to speak the truth.

"I know them," she says. "I see them around town, and we say hello. Same as with all the other people in Calloway Creek. But you've never taken me to their house. We've never had dinner together with them as a couple." She pins me with her stare. "Are we a couple?"

I rake a hand through my hair. "I don't know."

"What am I to you, Jaxon? We've been dating for six months. We've slept together dozens of times. To me, that's the definition of being in a relationship. Are we in a relationship?"

"It's complicated."

"Would you quit saying that? I get how you said it before you got the divorce papers, but it's simple now. Do you want me or not?"

I do the worst thing possible in the history of arguments. I remain silent.

She turns and storms out the door.

"Calista," I call after her. "I told you I'm drunk. This is no time for serious conversations. If you want me to go to dinner with your parents, I will."

She stops on the porch, looking pleased. "You will?"

I nod. "Just don't make me go to some pretentious place. Donovan's okay?"

She smiles. "Donovan's would be right up their alley." She steps toward me and puts her arms around my neck. "Thank you."

My inner dickhead is screaming at me to take it back. Dinner with her parents sends the wrong message. But I have strung her along. And it's time for me to get over myself and move on with my life. Calista is kind and gorgeous and would be a fantastic wife and mother.

To someone.

But like the 'good' Calloway that I am, I pull her to me and kiss her just like everyone would expect me to.

As soon as she's gone, I run to the bathroom and throw up five beers and who knows how many shots of whiskey. Then I walk to my bedroom, Heisman at my heels. I sit, take off my shoes and throw them across the room with a loud thump. I sink into the bed, looking at the side that I never sleep on. Heisman jumps up, happy to fill the space, and stares at me.

"Stop judging me," I say, then pass out.

Chapter Four

Nicky

Earlier today…

New York City grows bigger in the small window of the airplane. The tall buildings. The busy streets. The Hudson River. They are things I never thought I'd see anytime soon, let alone before the ink was even dry on my divorce papers.

I can't believe I'm going to be this close to him. What was I thinking agreeing to stay with my parents? He'll be a half mile away. Assuming he still lives in our house. Uh, *his* house. Victoria and my parents have abided by my wishes to never speak of him, but I still know things. Things like he's dating Calista Hilson.

I have no right to be jealous. I gave up that right two years ago.

I close my eyes and lean back into the airplane seat. I should just stay in the city. It would make things easier. Except my bank account will take a hit. Two or three months in a hotel will drain my savings for sure. I know it's XTN and all, and technically I could afford it, but I should save the money. Who knows what will happen after. Marty thinks *he* does, but I can't take any chances. This could be my big break, or the nail in my coffin.

Plus, there's the fact that Tori has been begging me to come back for a visit. But I can honestly say that before the XTN deal, I had no intention of setting foot back home. In Calloway Creek, I'm a pariah. I'm the girl who cheated on her high school sweetheart and practically left him at the altar. Okay, so it was three years *after* the altar. It was a slow death. Our marriage was happy and safe at first, but when the newness wore off, it became dizzying and suffocating. I used to think we were perfect for each other. Soul mates even. Then we graduated and real life happened. Neither of us spoke of it, but we both felt the drift. The universe was pulling us in opposite directions despite our feelings for each other. And it seemed our marriage became somewhat of a ticking time bomb.

I hated confrontation. Still do. Which is why I took the coward's way out. It's so much harder to break it off with a nice guy. I knew I needed to do something drastic. Something that wouldn't have him chasing after me. Something that would make him hate *me* instead of the career I was always coveting. Something that would force him to stay in the town he's always loved.

A year into our marriage, I knew there was something wrong with me. Who wouldn't be happy with the best guy in the world? Jaxon was nice. Stable. Compassionate. An amazing lover.

I stiffen thinking about him in bed with other women. In bed with Calista.

We were each other's first.

I rub my pendant and wish away the thoughts.

I'll stay with my parents, keep my head down, and go do the job I was hired to do.

The plane taxis to the gate, and by the time I get off, I've convinced myself everything will be okay.

I collect my two large bags from the luggage carousel, having left everything else in Oklahoma. XTN will outfit me in a wardrobe of their choosing, so I only need my personal things. I'll take the train to Calloway Creek, and Mom will pick me up from the station, hopefully avoiding any onlookers that would surely make me town gossip.

I turn toward the exit of the airport when I see a man holding up a sign with my name on it. Oh, my. A sign. With *my* name on it. It's something from out of a movie.

Part of me wants to snap a picture for posterity, but I resist the urge, not wanting to seem like a silly girl when I need to be viewed as an upstanding, albeit temporary, member of one of the most popular cable news networks on television.

I approach the man in the black suit and chauffer's hat. "I'm Nicole Forbes."

"Right this way, Ms. Forbes." He takes my bags and escorts me out of the terminal and over to a waiting limousine in some VIP area I never knew existed.

VIP! I scream in my head.

"Where are we going?" I ask.

"XTN, ma'am."

"Do you know why? I wasn't aware I was needed until tomorrow."

"I'm just the driver, ma'am."

"Of course. Sorry."

On the way, I text my mother and tell her I'll be later than I thought and not to go to the train station until I contact her again.

Forty minutes later, I'm on the eighth floor of the XTN building, standing in the office of my new weather producer, Barry Remsen. *Alone.*

I glance around, keeping myself in check but knowing this is the big league. Marty's office could fit in Barry's bathroom. Floor-to-ceiling windows overlook Manhattan. Awards line one of the interior walls. Photos of news anchors, prominent politicians, and celebrities line another. I'm so in over my head.

Jenny, Barry's assistant and the woman who led me into the office, returns and hands me a bottle of water. "They'll be in momentarily."

"They?"

"Barry, wardrobe, makeup—you know, everyone."

Suddenly I'm terrified. I smile at Jenny as if I knew. She leaves and I breathe deeply. *You can do this, Nicky.*

There's a lot of activity outside the door. Someone holds it open, and people pour in. Dozens of them. They're all talking to each other—*about me*, but not *to* me.

"Uh, hello," I say quietly amongst the noise. I clear my throat and speak louder. "Hi."

"Nicole," a man says, as if I'm an afterthought. His eyes sweep me up and down, homing in on my chest. He snaps his fingers at a woman. "Clarice, you get her first. You may have your work cut out for you. She's got big boobs; you'll have to let out material to accommodate them. Bad for you, but I have a feeling weekend viewership is about to go through the roof."

I step forward. "I could sue you for sexual harassment, you know."

He appraises me like I'm a toddler. Okay, so no joking around with this asshole.

"I was only kidding," I say. "I'm actually flattered you think I'll bring in more viewers."

"Why would you sue me? I was just stating the facts. You have large breasts, and that means Clarice will have to alter your wardrobe. And, yes, men will tune in to watch."

"I hope women will too."

"That remains to be seen."

I realize this jerk just assumes I know who he is. "Where I come from, we generally introduce ourselves before making comments about each other's bodies." I extend my hand. "I'm Nicole Forbes."

He rolls his eyes and shakes. "Barry Remsen."

I turn to Clarice. "Clarice, nice to meet you." And then I ask the names of the rest of the crowd who run the gamut from assistant producers to lighting techs, makeup artists, and more wardrobe people.

"Follow me," Clarice says, guiding me toward Barry's private bathroom. Once inside, she shuts the door. "Don't mind us, we work eighteen-hour days and rarely come up for air. You'll get used to this bunch soon enough. Some of us might actually be nice people." She nods to the door. "But not all."

I don't have to ask about whom she speaks.

"I hope you don't mind getting measured," she says. "I promise not to make it awkward."

I unbutton my blouse. "Not if you don't mind that I'm wearing my comfortable airplane undergarments that look like they belong on someone three times my age."

Clarice laughs, putting me at ease for the first time today. "I think we're going to get along just fine."

After Clarice is done with me, hair and makeup get their turn.

"Keep her hair down," Barry says, butting in.

I know why he wants it that way, and it disgusts me. He's treating me like a weather girl, not a degreed meteorologist. But after earlier, I keep my mouth shut.

Henri, the makeup artist assigned to me, gets out his palette and picks my colors. "Beautifique," he says with what I'm pretty sure is a fake French accent.

"Merci," I reply, earning a wink of approval.

Two hours later, everyone has cleared the room, leaving Barry and me alone.

"Listen," he says. "Xuan Le Kim and I butted heads over this decision. I don't think it's prudent to start our relationship on bullshit. I wanted John Hansen from TTKY in Lexington. But Xuan Le's the president of the network, so I got overridden. Plus, you're only here temporarily, so it wasn't a hill I was going to die on."

I plaster on a sarcastic grin. "Tell me what you really think of me, Barry."

"Don't get me wrong, you're good. Maybe not XTN material, but Xuan Le likes your format. No scripted monologues. Off-the-cuff weather reporting. Not many weather girls can pull it off."

"Broadcast meteorologists."

"That's what I said."

"No, you said weather girl. I'm not a weather girl. I'm a broadcast meteorologist."

He leans back in his chair. "Are you always this difficult?"

"Are you always this sexist?" My mouth goes dry at my unusual confrontation. But I'm in the big leagues, so I'd better act the part.

He grunts but doesn't answer.

"Barry, I really want to get off on the right foot here. I love XTN. I'm grateful for this opportunity. I'm here to do one job—

report the weather. And I promise I'll give it my all and hit the ground running. But it would be best if we could work as a team. As my producer, you and I will work more closely than anyone. I hope we can be friends."

"Friends."

He says the word as if it's a foreign concept.

"I'm not asking you out for drinks. I just want to establish a good relationship. You know, me asking how your wife is or congratulating you on your son's graduation. You asking if I had a good day off—that sort of thing."

"I don't have a wife. I have two *ex*-wives, three kids I hardly ever see, and a cat named Chester who I, unfortunately, got by default in my last divorce. Luckily, he likes his alone time. Like *me*." He glances toward the door. "Now, we have an early day tomorrow. Be here at four. Jenny will show you to your dressing room. Go get some sleep, and be ready to work. Just because it's weekends doesn't mean it will be easy. You'll be on in the six to ten morning slot and then again at night from five to ten. The days will be long. And between weekends, you'll be expected to go out in the field. I hope you didn't come here expecting a cushy job."

"I know perfectly well what the job entails. I'm ready to work. And the less time I have to spend in Calloway Creek, which is where I'm from, the better."

Anyone else might ask why I said that. Not Barry. "Good. See you bright and early then."

I get up and hesitate in the doorway.

"Was there something else?" he asks, glancing up from his laptop.

"How are Makenna and the baby?"

He shakes his head as if I'd asked him about life on Mars. "How the hell would I know?"

"See you tomorrow, Barry."

Jenny grabs me on my way out. "Boy. Four pounds, two ounces. Four weeks early. He'll have to stay in the hospital for at least a week, they think. Makenna is doing very well."

"Thanks, Jenny."

"If you ever need someone to grab a coffee with, I'm always here." She rolls her eyes. "I'm not kidding. Always. And I love coffee."

I smile. "So do I. I may take you up on that."

"Your driver is waiting in the lobby. He'll take you wherever you need to go."

"The train station will be fine."

"He's at your disposal today, Nicole. Better enjoy it. As Barry instructed, it's the only limo service you'll get. Have the driver take you to Calloway Creek. You deserve it, with uprooting your life and getting out here in twenty-four hours."

Instantly, I know Jenny and I will be friends. And I'm grateful to have one person on the East Coast who doesn't believe I'm a back-stabbing cheater.

~ ~ ~

It's been two years since I've been home. Can I still call it that? As the limo drives through Calloway Creek, memories of the day I left bombard me. Packing my things. Leaving my house. Leaving *him*. Driving fifteen hundred miles away from a life I didn't want toward a career I was chasing.

We pull up to my parents' house. I'm grateful it's dark, or the limousine would have garnered a lot of attention. The driver takes my bags inside and leaves, seemingly happy with the hundred-dollar tip I gave him. I wish it had been more, but I haven't gotten an XTN paycheck yet.

"Nicky!" Tori yells, bounding down the stairs and into my arms.

I hug her like she's my lifeline. We haven't seen each other since March, when she and my parents flew to Oklahoma to visit me over Tori's spring break. I hold her at arm's length and take her in. She's always been a younger version of me. People have said we could be twins if we were the same age. But now, somehow turning eighteen, she's become her own person. And the highlights in her hair certainly set her apart from me and my darker locks.

"I've missed you, Tor."

"Samesies."

"Where's Mom and Dad?"

"They tried to wait for you, but they had committed to going to some charity thing with the Ashfords."

"Right. Mom mentioned it. Guess it's just you and me then."

"We can share a bottle of wine," she says. "And you can tell me all about XTN and what a superstar you're going to be."

I hold up a finger. "One. I'll let you have one glass, and only because we're home. And if you tell Mom and Dad, it'll never happen again."

"Mom and Dad let me drink all the time."

I raise a brow. "All the time?"

"Okay, once in a while. And only since I turned eighteen. And only at home."

I laugh. "You know they never let me drink until I was twenty-one."

"I know. They remind me repeatedly how lucky I am."

I point my finger at her chest, recalling what happened to Jaxon's little sister when she was the same age as Tori. "Don't ever let them regret it. Be responsible."

"Jeez, Nic, what happened to my carefree sister?"

"She's still in here somewhere. Maybe you can help me dust her off."

Victoria peruses the wine rack and pulls out a bottle of merlot. My little sister sure has grown up over the past few years. A pang of guilt twists in my gut knowing I haven't been here to see it.

We sit and drink, and yes, maybe I let her have a little more than a glass, because I sure do miss drinking with friends. I tell her all about Marty and finding out about XTN, throwing my life into two suitcases, and hopping on a plane without any real time to absorb what was happening.

The wine gets to her, and she falls asleep before ten o'clock. I'm too wound up to sleep, even though I have to be up in a little more than five hours. I take my suitcases to one of the guest rooms—the room I used to sleep in until Jaxon and I got married. Immediately, I notice a picture on the wall. My wedding picture. They never took it down. I sit on the bed and stare at it. I can't breathe. I feel like a vise is gripping my insides. I stride over, pull it off the wall, and stuff it into a drawer. Then I race downstairs and out the front door for a much-needed breath of fresh night air.

Looking left and right, my feet make a terrible decision—the worst one they could make—when they point me in the direction of my old house. Has he sold it? Is Calista living there with him, cooking in my kitchen, sleeping in my bed?

Not yours anymore.

My pace quickens as I turn the corner. I try to block out the memories of my youth, when I would sneak out of my house and run over to Jaxon's neighborhood. It was a lot farther away than the house we bought when we got married, but it was always worth the walk. He'd sneak me into his bedroom, kick out his brother Tag, and we'd talk about anything and everything. The closer I get, the more I feel like that lovesick teenager.

I stop in my tracks when I see the house. It's changed. It used to be brown. Now it's blue. I can tell, even in the dark, because of the new landscape lighting. There's a car in the driveway that I don't recognize. Maybe he did sell the house. Maybe he couldn't stand to be in the place we shared together after what I did to him.

The door opens, and a woman walks out. Or stomps out is more like it. Oh my god, it's Calista.

I hide behind a tree, hoping no neighbors catch me spying.

Jaxon walks out after her. I lose all my breath. It's the first time I've seen him since the day I walked out. His hair is longer. His chest is broader. They speak. Then she moves toward him, and he kisses her. And I watch. I watch because I know it's punishment for everything I've done.

And no matter how much I know he deserves more than I could ever give him, no matter how much sense it makes for him to be with her over me, no matter how much the universe seems right with them being together, I still feel sick to my stomach watching the only man I've ever loved fall for someone else.

I turn, go back home, and cry myself to sleep.

Chapter Five

Jaxon

I walk into Donovan's and spot Calista and her parents in a booth. I've met them before, a long time ago, but they moved away after she and her brother graduated. I never had much of an opportunity to get to know them, barring a few times I went to her house in high school.

Calista stands, walks over, and greets me, kissing me on the cheek. Then she takes my hand and pulls me to their table.

Now, some people would not find this odd. I'm not some people. For one, we've never held hands in public. Yes, we go on dates. Yes, she's taken my hand under the table or in the movie theater. This is different. It's like she's parading her boyfriend through the pub.

I'm getting some strange looks from patrons. I guess they aren't used to seeing me on the arm of someone who isn't my ex-wife.

"Dad, you remember Jaxon Calloway?" Calista asks.

He stands and shakes my hand. "Yes. Jaxon. I believe you and my daughter worked together on her campaign for student president her junior year."

I examine my fingernails. "I still might find paint under here if I look hard enough."

He laughs and pats me on the back. Oh, jeez.

"And what a senior year you had. The best quarterback this town has seen in decades. How many touchdowns that year?"

"Eighteen passing and twenty rushing, sir."

"Call me Dan."

Her mom reaches over him to shake my hand. "And I'm Tammy. Nice to see you again after all these years."

We all sit, and Lissa comes over to take our drink order. She's definitely not her usual perky self tonight. Probably because she thinks we're here planning my next wedding. Truth be told, I might rather be taking Lissa on a date right now than be stuck here with Calista's parents. I'm not sure why I give Lissa an apologetic smile. What do I have to apologize for?

"Calista tells us you're now the head coach for the varsity team at the high school," Tammy says. "Impressive."

"I do love my job."

"Well, it's a fine one," Dan says. "Stable. Teacher, coach, math club sponsor. Our daughter could do a lot worse."

I look over at Lissa, begging her with my eyes to do anything to get me out of this. She turns away, not channeling my inner thoughts. I knew this was a mistake. I had a bad feeling about tonight. I picked up the phone to cancel about a dozen times, but in the end, I couldn't think up an excuse for why I couldn't go. Everyone knows football season doesn't start until next week. If I played sick, she'd find out my lie when I showed up good as always at school on Monday. So I decided to suck it up.

I pick up the menu. "I'm starving. Anyone else?"

"Why don't we order some appetizers?" Tammy suggests. "That way we can sit around and get to know one another."

Fucking perfect.

I contemplate ordering a stiff drink, but considering I'm still nursing a hangover, it's probably not a good idea.

I continue to get looks from people in other booths. Looks like they feel sorry for me. I don't quite get it. Everyone in this town wants me to move on. People have been trying to set me up since Nicky packed up her Nissan and drove out of town. They should be happy for me. Why are they looking at me like Heisman just got run over by a dump truck?

Mrs. Gregory is giving me such a look as she waits for her take-out order at the bar. She collects her bag from Donny and swings by our booth on her way out. She greets the Hilsons and then sighs, looking at me. "How are you doing, Jaxon?"

"I'm fine, Mrs. Gregory."

She looks between Calista and me. "Glad to hear it. It's as it should be."

"Thanks, Mrs. Gregory. Have a good night."

I lean into Calista. "Is it just me, or have people in this town gone bonkers?"

"We have gotten some strange looks tonight."

Lissa brings our soft drinks, and Dan orders fried pickles and parmesan fries. Apparently, he doesn't have to eat healthy to keep up with forty football players for three hours a day five days a week. "You're good with that, right, Jaxon?"

"Of course."

Calista takes my hand under the table. She's in hog heaven. It seems my agreeing to this dinner has catapulted our relationship to another level. One I wasn't prepared for.

The three of them talk about Calista's brother. I watch the news on the television in the corner.

"Looking for scores?" Dan asks.

I chuckle. "Always."

It's painful sitting through the small talk, and I swear Donny has never taken so long preparing fried pickles in his life. When the appetizers finally arrive, I stuff my face so I don't have to talk. Thankfully, Lissa takes our dinner order shortly after.

Throughout dinner, Dan talks to me about football. Tammy and Calista talk about who's gotten divorced, who's getting married, and who's having kids. All the while my hand is prisoner to hers. My palm starts to sweat, and I feel like the booth is suffocating me. I pull my hand away. "All this soda has gone right through me. Excuse me."

Along the way to the bathroom, more looks are tossed my way from people who have been observing the whole dinner-with-the-parents night. Why did I do this? I stare in the bathroom mirror, wishing I would have stayed home and finished grading papers.

I come out of the bathroom, lean against the wall, and shore myself up to get through the rest of dinner.

When I approach the table, something isn't right. Calista's eyes are glued to the television. So are Tammy's and Dan's. In fact, the whole damn place has fallen silent, and everyone is watching TV. A bad feeling rushes through me. Are we at war? Has there been a new virus outbreak?

When I look over at the screen, it's so much worse than anything I could imagine. Nicky—my ex-wife—is reporting the weather. On TV. On *national* TV.

I stop walking and listen, my heart racing a mile a minute. Blood pulses in my ears. Knots form in my stomach. What's happening?

"Back to you, Roman," she says.

The camera goes to the news desk. Holy shit. That's Roman Bromberg. Nicky is on XTN?

Roman says, "For all you viewers who didn't watch the morning show, you've undoubtedly noticed Makenna Kendall has taken early leave to deliver her son. Mom and baby are doing well. Nicole has graciously agreed to fill in while Makenna takes some much-needed time off. We're happy to have you, Nicole."

Nicole? The camera pans back to Nicky. "Thanks, Roman. I'm happy to be here."

"Word has it you found out about the job and flew out here from Oklahoma all within twenty-four hours."

"As a meteorologist, I always have to be prepared to go anywhere on a moment's notice. In fact, I always have a suitcase packed."

He laughs. "Well, we're glad that you do. Hopefully XTN has put you up someplace nice."

"Actually, I grew up not too far from here. It'll be nice to spend time with my family."

"I'm sure they will be happy to have you for however long you're here." A picture of the president pops up behind Roman, and he moves on to other news.

I'm left standing here, feet cemented to the floor, unable to move. Unable to fucking breathe.

Someone touches my shoulder. "Jaxon," Calista says. "Are you okay?"

Glancing around the still-silent pub, I realize all eyes are on me. You could hear a goddamn pin drop. Someone coughs. I hear a few quiet whispers. Even Lissa and Donny have stopped working momentarily. Everyone is waiting to see what I'm going to do.

I swallow. My head shakes back and forth. Finally, words come. "Please thank your parents for me. And apologize."

"Apologize? For what?"

I step away from her and go out the front door.

I may not be wearing athletic shoes, but I run all the way home anyway. Then I throw up fried pickles and a turkey wrap all over my front hedge.

Heisman sees me through the front window and paws at it. I open the door and let him out. He joins me on the stoop, sitting next to me as I try to process what the fuck just happened.

Nicky is on television. In New York City. And she's staying here in Calloway Creek. In a matter of ten minutes, my life has been turned upside down.

Heisman puts his head in my lap.

"I know what you're thinking. She's not my problem anymore."

Without moving his head, his eyeballs look up at me.

"How in the hell did she end up on TV? She went to Oklahoma to chase tornadoes."

I get up. Heisman sniffs around the area where I tossed up my dinner. "Back off, buddy. Go take a pee." I get out the hose and water down the bush I yacked into, hoping the stench doesn't get too bad.

Inside, I fight the urge to turn on the television. These weather reporters usually pop in several times during a broadcast.

"Don't let me do it," I say to Heisman.

I pull out my satchel of papers to be graded, pretending to concentrate on them but never getting past the first page. My phone hasn't stopped vibrating since I left Donovan's. I can't deal with Calista right now. I know I'll have to kowtow to her for weeks to get her to forgive me.

Then I hang my head and wonder if I even want her to.

I glance at my phone. Great. It's not just her. It looks like I have texts from everyone I know and a few people I don't. *Shit. Shit. Shit.* I'm never going to hear the end of this. When I go to work Monday, everyone will know. And they'll feel sorry for me all over again. Hell, it seems like it was only yesterday when they stopped.

I go to the couch and sink into it. It makes sense now. The looks at Donovan's. Mrs. Gregory. All those people had already seen Nicky on TV earlier. And the ones who hadn't were as stunned as I was to see her during dinner.

I pick up the remote and turn on the television. I flip through the channels until I land on XTN, then feel relieved when I don't see her. Maybe I was seeing things. Dreaming. Hallucinating, even. I scroll through the forty-three unread texts on my phone.

A familiar voice echoes through the room. "If you live outside the city, be prepared for an amazing sunset. This picture was sent in by a viewer. Get out of your Barcaloungers, and go check it out. If you're in the metropolitan area, low clouds, not to mention buildings"—she snickers—"may block the view."

A graphic appears behind her, and she goes over the weather forecast. I can't pull my eyes away. She's the same, yet completely different. She was twenty-five when I last saw her. We both were. Yet she seems so much older now. Wiser. More sophisticated. Her hair isn't as long as it used to be, but it still flows beyond her shoulders. And she seems more voluptuous. Then again, they do say the camera adds ten pounds. I wish it added a hell of a lot more than that, because no matter how much I hate to admit it, she looks amazing.

A pang of… something sits heavy in my gut.

"You," I say to Heisman. "Why the fuck did you let me turn it on?"

He couch-crawls over and puts a paw on my leg. We both stare at the screen for the next twenty minutes, but she doesn't come back on. I switch off the TV and grade papers for the next two hours, my poor students becoming the victim of my... what am I even feeling—unbridled rage? Because she left me? Because she went and found the career she'd always hoped for? Because she landed a meteorologist's dream job? Because she's back in town?

Or maybe it's because she still has so much control over me.

That control is the very reason I haven't been able to commit to another woman. So, yeah—it pisses me off.

My mind wanders back to when we were in school and her hold over me began. Nicky was oblivious. She thought she was a complete science nerd; that no other guys wanted her. And I was all too happy to keep it a secret that they did. All of them. Nicky was the pretty girl next door. The shy, quiet, brainy girl who turned heads without even trying. I kept waiting for someone much smarter than me to take her away from me. I couldn't believe she was mine.

Heisman nudges my leg and lets out a soft growl, his way of telling me he needs to take a shit.

I grab my phone (only because I need a flashlight) and a poop bag. "Come on, let's go for a walk."

My voicemail and text messages continue to blow up. I put my phone on Do Not Disturb. Yeah, people, I get it—she's on TV. And she's here.

Here. At her parents' house. Around the goddamn corner from where I'm standing.

Five minutes later, I find myself at the Forbes' front door contemplating whether to knock or go home and drink a bottle of whiskey. Before I can decide, the door opens.

"Hey, Mr. Calloway."

Even though she's a student of mine, it still surprises me every time I see Victoria. Her eyes, her mannerisms, her voice—they're exactly like Nicky's. I believe it's some kind of cosmic torture, or perhaps karma, that she's been in one of my classes for the past two years.

"Victoria, I told you to call me Jaxon when we're not at school. We're fam—" *Shit.* "Well, you know."

She gets down and lets Heisman tackle her. "How are you, you big furball?"

I stand not so patiently and wait for her to finish fawning over my dog.

She looks up. "I assume you're here for Nicky?"

"Is she here?"

"No."

"Is she coming back tonight?"

She pulls out her phone. "She was on until ten, so maybe soonish. Can you believe it? XTN!"

"Yeah, that's pretty impressive. Listen, I think we'll wait out here."

"You can come in."

"Are your parents home?"

"In bed."

"I'll wait outside."

"Suit yourself. See you Monday, *Mr. Calloway.*"

"You won't be so cheerful when you see what you got on your test."

She stiffens.

"I'm kidding. You're one of my brightest students."

"Us Forbes girls excel at a lot of things."

"That you do."

"Okay, see ya." She shuts the door.

I sit on the bench by the front door. Heisman circles around and lies down at my feet. Trying to relax is a futile effort. I weed through the texts. The '*Did you see Nicky*?'s,' the '*OMG*s,' the '*Bro—your ex is on fucking TV*'s' (yeah, both my brothers said the exact same thing), the '*What are you going to do?*' from my sister, Addy.

What *am* I going to do?

Before I can answer the question, Heisman's tail thwap-thwaps against my leg, a sure sign someone is approaching. Nicky appears on the sidewalk and then comes toward the front door. She stops dead when she sees me. For a moment, the earth stands still. I don't know what day it is. What year. Hell, even my goddamn name escapes me. She's ten feet away—closer than we've been since the day she walked out sobbing, telling me what a terrible person she was. And I let her.

Heisman greets her like a long-lost relative even though they've never met. *Traitor.*

She regards him. "You got a dog?"

Her voice sounds different than it did on TV. More like the old Nicky I once knew. Is she still in there somewhere? Or did she die along with every dream I had about us living happily ever after?

I'm silent, still figuring out what to say to the only woman who could ever destroy me.

"What's your name, handsome?" She looks at his collar. "Heisman." Nervous laughter dances out of her. "You named him after a football trophy? He's gorgeous." She locks eyes with me. "Hi, Jaxon. I was wondering when we'd run into each other."

She seems so blasé about seeing me. As if her world hasn't been upended like mine has. Like it's no big deal that we're standing face to face like we had a million times before. Only now we're exes.

It occurs to me why she's not having the same reaction I am. I've done such a good job of putting her out of my mind that I hadn't even given a thought to if she had moved on. Maybe with *him*—the nameless, faceless guy who ended our marriage. Did *he* follow her to Oklahoma? A sadness I haven't felt in years runs through my soul.

I get off the bench and pace the front porch. "Why the hell didn't you tell me?"

"We haven't spoken in almost two years."

"Still, you could have warned me. I was blindsided. I was having dinner with"—I shake my head—"it doesn't matter. My point is, everyone at Donovan's saw your broadcast. And they all saw my reaction. I looked like a goddamn idiot."

"You were at dinner?"

She looks upset. Jealous, even. "Yes, dinner. Now why the hell didn't you warn me?"

"I wasn't aware we had to keep each other apprised of our career changes and whereabouts, especially after this week."

"Jesus, Nicky, the papers just came yesterday. You picked a hell of a time to show up in Calloway Creek."

She's rubbing her necklace absentmindedly like it's a nervous habit. "I'll agree it was unfortunate timing, but I have to take the opportunities as they come along."

"Of course you do. Nothing's changed there, Nicky."

She looks hurt but does a good job of hiding it. "Actually, it's Nicole now."

I huff out an exasperated sigh. "Nicole. Right. Because nothing about this place was ever good enough for you. Not your job. Not your man. Not even your goddamn name."

"Is there a point to this conversation? Because I've had a long day and have to be up again in five hours."

I duck past her and snap my fingers. "Come on, Heisman, let's go." The little fucker looks like he's considering staying with *her*. Then he must remember who gives him treats and reluctantly follows.

Part of me expects Nicky to call out to me and tell me how wrong she was to leave. Or maybe run into my arms and declare her undying love. Perhaps even beg me for forgiveness. Or at the very least, invite me in so we can settle this and figure out how to live in the same town for the next few months without killing each other. She doesn't do any of that. She doesn't even look back at me. It's like she couldn't give a shit. She just walks away. Because I guess that's what she does best.

Chapter Six

Nicky

I scan the stadium for Jaxon. He's sitting with the other students graduating from the college of education, while I'm with the ones from the college of science. He looked so handsome this morning, wearing a crisp dress shirt and tie that matches his aquamarine eyes. As the biggest sports fan I know, he's totally psyched to be graduating in Yankee Stadium, where NYU is holding our commencement this year.

He's hard to pick out. And he didn't decorate his cap like I did. Mine says "Off to chase my dream" with a graphic of a tornado I made out of glue and glitter. But at six foot two, Jaxon stands taller than most graduates, and I eventually find him. We lock eyes across the massive stadium—all else fading into the background. We made it. And I'm not just talking about school. We made it. I can't even say against all odds, because all of the odds were in our favor. Same middle school. Same high school. Same university, in which we lived in the same dorm and then the same tiny apartment. And of course we're both graduating with the same crippling debt.

We could have lived at home and commuted, but both our parents encouraged us to have the full college experience. Neither are wealthy. They helped out where they could, supplying groceries and the occasional rent payment when they could swing it.

The point is, Jaxon and I were meant to be together, and I can't wait to see where the rest of our lives take us.

After the ceremony, he finds me, sweeping me into his arms. I've never seen him so happy. And he's got a lot to be happy about. He's already secured a job as a math teacher at the high school we went to. And he's got his eye on a small house around the corner from McQuaid Circle—the heart of 'old' Calloway Creek and the place we grew up going to the park, sneaking behind the movie theater to mess around, and having ice-cream dates when we were only thirteen.

I, on the other hand, have been sending out resumes for months. The only responses I've gotten are for unpaid internships. "Something will come up," Jaxon always says. "You're going to take the world by storm one day." He always makes me feel better. He's my person. My soul mate.

Our friends circle around. Jonathan throws his cap in the air. I catch it and laugh at the decoration on his cap that reads: 4 down, 10 to go. He wants to be a surgeon, which means four years of med school followed by residency. He's one of the few men here who decorated their cap.

I hand Jonathan his cap and turn to Jaxon. "And you said real men don't decorate their caps."

"Who says I'm not a real man?" Jaxon says. His lips turn up into a smirk. "And who says I didn't decorate my cap?"

Our friends go silent, all of them staring and smiling. I glance around. "Am I missing something?"

Jaxon falls to a knee and rips the plain black cover off the mortarboard of his cap. Underneath, it reads: "Nicky, will you marry me?"

"Oh my god. Are you serious?"

He produces a sparkly ring that answers the question.

"Jaxon." I kneel before him feeling like a blubbering idiot. "Yes. Oh my god, yes."

He puts the ring on my finger then flings his cap in the air and kisses me.

"I'm going to be the best wife anyone ever had," I say.

The motion of the train jolts me awake. My face is wet from the tears I shed in my dream. It was more than a dream, though; it was a memory. And a reminder of what a failure I was as a wife.

Seeing Jaxon last night was surreal. It was bound to happen, but I wasn't prepared for it so soon. Countless things were left unsaid. My heart was screaming at me to tell him the truth, but my head kept me in check. He's moved on. He's with Calista now. Had I broken down and said everything I wanted to say, told him I've been miserable these past years without him, that I'd made a mistake, he'd have laughed in my face. He'd have said I deserved every bit of pain I was feeling. And I couldn't have blamed him. Because he'd have been right.

It's still dark out this early in the morning. On the way into the city, the landscape changes drastically from the occasional streetlight to towering buildings, fancily lit bridges, and all-night stores. Calloway Creek is a hidden treasure of a city suburb. A small town just close enough to a large city to make it commutable. A town *too* small for many.

Why did I think it was okay for me to come here? Someone left a nasty note in my parents' mailbox telling them their slutty daughter should go back to where she came from. And I've gotten more than a few similar 'suggestions' on my Facebook page.

I'll always be the girl who wronged the gem of Calloway Creek. The bitch who trampled the heart of the star quarterback who led us to the state championship. The one who cheated on the Calloway brother who volunteers in soup kitchens on holidays and organizes toy drives at Christmas.

I wish I could go back and change things. I want people to know the truth. But then they'd just call me a liar, too. I made my bed two years ago, and now I get to see what it's like to lie in it.

An hour later, hair and makeup done, Clarice is helping me into my dress. It's tight, but I don't say anything. If I had to guess, Barry told her to make it that way. I'm a guest here. No need to rock the boat.

As if privy to my very thoughts, my producer walks into my dressing room. Without knocking.

"So?" I ask.

He doesn't look up from his phone. He's actually going to make me say it.

"Barry, you're killing me here. What were the numbers? You ran focus groups, right? How did I test?"

Still not looking up, he says, "Huh? Oh, fine. Yeah, fine."

"Don't listen to him," Clarice whispers. "I heard people talking. You killed it. Everyone loved you. You shouldn't change a thing. Don't mind him. He wouldn't hand out a compliment if it came with dinner and a blow job."

"I can hear you, Clarice," Barry says.

"You were meant to."

Finally, he pockets his phone. He studies me from head to toe. "Lose the necklace. You can't wear the same jewelry two days in a row."

I cover my pendant with a hand, as if protecting it from him. "I never remove it. Not unless I'm showering or swimming."

"Pretend you're in the deep end then. Because it's definitely sink or swim around here."

"Respectfully, I'd like to keep it on."

"No."

I swallow. Am I really about to fight with the man who basically holds my career in the palm of his hands?

"Listen," I say, because apparently I *am*. "I dropped everything and flew out here with little notice, couldn't bring my cameraman or producer, and have been thrown to the wolves with zero preparation. You hired me because you saw something you liked—or Xuan Le did. This necklace is a part of that person. Think of it as a prop, something to identify me, like Jim Cantore and his baseball cap."

"You're really going to fight me over a silly piece of jewelry? Did your dead grandmother give it to you or something?"

I'm not about to tell him the significance. I continue our staredown.

"And if I tell you it's a deal-breaker?" he asks.

"Barry, there are few things I have control over in my career, but this is one of them. And this *is* the hill I'm going to die on. So, if you're dead set on winning this one, good luck replacing me in the next twenty minutes. I'm up to speed. I've spent the last forty-eight hours studying Makenna's clips. Apparently, I tested well yesterday. Firing me over this is not something you want to do."

Both Clarice and Henri stand behind me in a show of solidarity.

Barry has an internal conversation with himself, his lips forming a few four-letter words in the quiet murmuring. "Jesus Christ, fine. But if people start to complain—"

"They won't," I say.

He spins and goes for the door. "Banter with Roman. You had a rapport yesterday. People love that shit."

My jaw goes slack. "You want me to *flirt* with the news anchor?"

"In a word—yes." He comes back over. "In case you haven't noticed, I don't give two fucks about the weather. What I do care about are ratings."

He leaves, but I seem to be the only person in the room who's stunned.

"He can take some getting used to," Henri says.

There's a knock on the door. "Ms. Forbes to the studio!" someone shouts from the other side.

Clarice secures a wire underneath the back of my dress. "Good luck today."

Henri winks and blows me a kiss as they leave.

I'm alone. I take a few calming breaths and head out.

I put in my earpiece, get my clicker and test it on a few graphics, and stand on my spot. Will Jaxon be watching? Will all of Calloway Creek? Suddenly, nerves I've never felt take hold.

There's a voice in my ear. "Stop fiddling with the necklace," Barry says. "If you keep it up, either it goes or you do."

"Now to Nicole Forbes for the weather," Roman says.

I drop my hand to my side, paste on a confident smile, and do the job I'm getting paid an ungodly amount to do.

Chapter Seven

Jaxon

Everyone is staring as I stroll the halls on the way to my classroom. Funny looks, whispers, empathetic faces. Did every goddamn person in town watch XTN over the weekend?

As if I hadn't already been tabloid fodder for months after Nicky left. Poor Jaxon, the guy who was cheated on and left by his career-hungry wife. It didn't matter that I tried to defend her; it just riled them up even more, wondering how I could possibly stand up for her after what she'd done. And now it's happening all over again.

I don't stop in the teachers' lounge. I know Calista will be there, and I need to be grilled by her like I need a hole in the back of my head. It was a dick move, leaving them at the restaurant on Saturday, but damn, no way could I have sat there and pretended like everything was hunky-dory.

I avoided Calista yesterday, sitting at home in my backyard with a six-pack and Heisman. I'd throw the tennis ball; he'd get a treat (and I'd take a sip) after retrieving it. If his treats were drinks, he'd have been as drunk as I was. And drunk watching XTN is not what I should have done all night. Neither was texting Nicky and telling her that she had already ruined my life, so why did she have to come back for seconds?

She never responded. And that pissed me off even more.

There are a few more students than normal arriving early to first period.

Matt Bingham sits in his usual spot in the back corner, lazing one foot over his knee. "That's a sucker punch if I ever saw one, Coach. The ex on XTN? Whoa."

My star running back has never been a shy, or particularly eloquent, student. I sift through my weekend grading and take his paper back to him. I place it on his desk and point to the big red *D*. "If you spent less time watching TV and more time studying, you wouldn't be at risk of being benched."

"Aw, seriously, Coach?"

More students trail in. Most of them stare, whisper to their friends, then stare some more.

"Okay, listen," I say after the bell rings. "The only questions I'll be answering in this class are math questions. Got it?"

Disappointed sighs echo throughout the room. My students were hoping for a little more drama than I plan on giving them.

My next five periods are more of the same. Lunch comes and goes. I sit in my classroom, stomach grumbling. By the time seventh period rolls around, my planning period, I'm spent. If it weren't for football practice after school, I'd ditch and go home.

I head to the gym early and get changed, once again avoiding Calista, who comes by my classroom most days after school to say hello. Although maybe she wouldn't have today. I have, after all, been kind of ghosting her. Come to think of it, she hasn't exactly been beating down my door. Aside from the one text asking if I was okay… nothing. I suppose if the tables were turned, I'd be pissed at me too.

Eric Snyder, my friend, fellow teacher, and assistant coach, comes toward me shaking his head. "Fucking sucks to be you right now, Calloway."

"Don't I know it."

"It's all everyone was talking about today."

I grab some gear. "Know that too."

"What are you going to do?"

We head out to the field. "Not much I can do. Besides, as I hear it, it'll only be a few months, then she'll be gone and this whole thing will blow over."

"I'm calling bullshit. You and I have been friends for a while now. It doesn't take a genius to know you aren't over your ex."

"You're overstepping," I say. "You didn't even know her."

"Am I? You forget the drunken nights we've spent together. Alcohol tends to bring out true feelings."

"Or maybe it just makes us say shit we don't mean."

He snorts. "Whatever, man. What does Calista think about all this?"

"Don't know. Haven't talked to her about it."

"About your divorce papers or about Nicky being back?"

"Both." I throw some cones on the field as we wait for the rest of the coaching staff to join us. "Do you know what bad timing this is? She shows up in town *the day* after our divorce papers come. And Calista, she's expecting a ring or something now that I'm officially single."

He seems conflicted. Is he going to take Calista's side?

"Well, you have been together a while."

"She's not even my girlfriend. Not technically."

"And why is that? Aside from the drunk-say shit you apparently don't mean." He rolls his eyes.

"Did you not hear that my divorce *just* became finalized?"

"Two years, Jaxon. Nicky has been gone for two years. If you really wanted to make a commitment to Calista, you'd have done it by now, married or not. So maybe it's time to step back."

Players start to trickle onto the field. "Can we talk about this later? Or not at all?"

"Sure, Coach. Whatever you want."

I get what he's saying. Eric is divorced, too. He's a couple years older than me. Moved to Calloway Creek from New York City a few years ago after his wife bled him dry and took him for everything. I guess that makes him qualified to give advice. And he's right. If I really wanted to commit to Calista, I would have done it. I keep waiting to get those feelings—the ones that have your palms sweating and your heart pumping at the sight of someone you love. Why do I not get them when I see Calista? But damn it, I did Saturday night when I saw Nicky. I'm supposed to hate her. I *do* hate her. Except that I still fucking love her.

"Coach?"

My players are waiting for me to tell them what drills to run. Even the other coaches are looking at me as if I've sprouted a second head.

I point to my defensive backs. "Zone mesh." Then to my QBs and WRs, I say, "Routes on air." And to my linemen, "Barrell drills." Nobody moves much. "What's your fucking problem? Get going!"

Eric stares. I've never cussed at my players before. *Shit.*

"Sorry, guys. Coach Snyder is going to run practice today. Eric, they're all yours."

I throw my towel over my shoulder and walk to my car.

~ ~ ~

Cooper comes around back and eyes the empty bottles on the table next to me. "Do I need to look up the nearest AA meeting?" Heisman sidles up to him and gets a pat.

"Very funny."

"You've never been one to drink this much."

I raise my beer. "Have a pretty damn good reason, don't you think?"

"Which reason would that be?"

"Let's see, being the laughingstock of the town. Or maybe having it stuffed down my throat that my ex is making a name for herself, proving why she left me in the first place."

"She left you because she cheated."

I shake my head. "She cheated because it was her way out."

"She told you that?"

I gulp the rest of my beer and open another. "She didn't have to."

"Do you mean to tell me that you'd have given her a pass, knowing she cheated, if she'd wanted to stay?"

"I don't know what I'm saying," I slur. "And I shouldn't be allowed to talk about this—with *anyone*—after drinking."

He studies me. "You didn't."

"I may have."

"You contacted her?"

"Saw her Saturday. I wasn't even drunk then. But then I may have texted her last night when I was."

He pinches his brow. "Holy crap. What did you say?"

I pull out my phone and show him.

"I see she didn't respond." More scrutinizing of me. Then he laughs. "That's what has you all bent out of shape, isn't it? She isn't going to play your blame game. Dude, she's your ex. Move the fuck on."

"I *have* moved on."

"Have you?" a woman says behind us.

We both turn to see Calista standing on my back porch.

"Okay, so I'm leaving," Coop says.

"Wait. Tag said you might want to crash here."

He nods to Calista. "A conversation for another day." He passes her. "Hey, Calista, how's it going?"

"Fine. You?"

"Fine as can be. See you around."

He glances back at me with a grimace, as if he knows I'm about to be in front of the firing squad. By the look on Calista's face, he may be right.

I take a warmish beer out of the six-pack and hold it out to her. She shakes her head. "Thanks, but no." She sits on a chair next to me. Heisman trots over and puts his head in her lap. Usually, after he gets his greeting, he goes about his business chewing on a stick or chasing squirrels. But he doesn't move his head from where it sits on her thigh.

"Heisman, leave her alone."

"He's fine," she says, continuing to pet him.

"I know I was a dick leaving like that the other night. I'm sorry."

"You were shocked to see her—we all were—and then to find out she's staying here in town. I get it. I'm not even mad at you for leaving, although my dad isn't too happy that I didn't kick you to the curb on the spot."

I run a hand through my hair. "I'm sure he'd like to be the one to do it. I feel like an idiot walking out on you like that. It had nothing to do with you and everything to do with her."

"I know that. But the fact that she can still get to you—doesn't that mean something?"

"Like what?"

"Like maybe you're not over her."

"I'm over her."

Pants meet fire.

Her brows come together. "Are you sure?"

"I think I just needed time to process it. She's only going to be in town for a few months. Things will get back to normal after that."

"Jaxon, I'm not going to wait around for two more months so you can decide if being in a relationship with me is what you want. Haven't I waited long enough? Haven't I been more than patient waiting for your divorce to go through?"

I nod. Because Calista *has* been patient. And kind. And understanding. And everything most men would want in a woman. What's wrong with me that I don't?

She tries to get up. Heisman doesn't seem to want her to. He's glued to her lap. It's the strangest behavior. Does he sense that we shouldn't be together? That this could be the last time she's here? Calista moves his head off her leg and slides out of the chair. "You know how I feel about you. Take a few days, think about it. But please, if you aren't in this for the long term, let me get on with my life before it would hurt even more."

"Cal—"

She holds up a hand. "Don't say anything. Think about it, Jaxon."

Heisman and I watch her leave. Finally, he comes and lies at my feet. "That didn't go like I thought it would," I tell him. "I didn't expect to have any of my ass left." He gives me a look. "I know, I know. She's an incredible woman—the whole package, even. Stop looking at me like that."

As if he understands me, he turns away and grooms his belly. Sometimes I wish I were a dog. No worries about women, money, jobs, not to mention you can lick things on yourself that humans aren't capable of.

I grab another beer and watch him go to town on his empty ball sack.

Chapter Eight

Nicky

"How are you settling in?" someone asks over my shoulder.

I look up from the computer screen at my assigned workstation. "Hi, Jenny. I'm trying not to get too settled, if you know what I mean. I'd been gone from Calloway Creek for years. And there's my ex—lots of baggage there. It's all so confusing."

Her brows go up. "Well, I was talking about here at the station."

My head slumps and I cover my face with my hands. "Of course you were. I'm sorry."

"Don't be. Sounds like we might need to have a drink one of these days."

"I would love that. I mean it. I don't get out much. Well, I can't really. But long story."

"Those are the best kind. Saturday between shows? I know a place down the street that serves killer margaritas." She glances behind us. "I won't tell if you won't."

I knew Jenny and I would become friends. "Sounds heavenly."

"There's another reason I'm here. Barry wants you for some field reporting, some high school science experiment. He's expecting you in his office in ten."

"Thanks, Jenny."

I finish up what I was doing, which is basically trolling the other networks to see what they are reporting on. That, and searching the internet for possible weather or environmental stories is what I do on the days I'm not broadcasting.

I take the stairs up two floors to the executive offices. Jenny waves me by, and I knock on Barry's door.

"Ten minutes means ten, not fifteen," I hear from behind it.

I open it and walk through, noting the time. I may be forty-five seconds late. "Good morning, Barry. I hear you have a story you want me to cover."

Someone comes in behind me.

"This is Chris," Barry says. "He's the cameraman who's been assigned to you for field reporting."

Chris holds out his hand and we shake. "Nice to meet you," I say.

He sits on Barry's couch. "It's my pleasure."

I already miss Josh, my cameraman at WRKT. We seemed to be able to communicate without words. He'd know from a look or a gesture or a movement of my foot what angle to go to or when to cut tape. He made my job so much easier. But I fear if Chris is anything like Barry, I will have my work cut out for me.

Barry taps on his phone. "Just sent you the details. I told the school we'd have someone there today. A class is doing a weather balloon experiment. Some of the students posted questions and pictures on our Twitter page that caught the eye of one of our production assistants. Figured it'd be right up your alley since it's in your hometown."

I stiffen, trying not to seem like the breath just got knocked out of me. "You want me to go to Calloway Creek High School? *Now?*" I shake my head. "Isn't there someone else who can cover this story?"

Barry sneers at me like I'm an imbecile. "No, Nicole, there's no one else. This *is* part of the job we're paying you to do. With your education, I didn't think I'd have to sit here and hold your hand through it."

"You don't. I just…"

Can't show up at the school where my ex teaches?

Refuse to go into a place where everyone hates me?

Suddenly got a case of food poisoning?

"That'll be all," Barry says, eyeing the door.

I leave, followed by Chris, and slump against the wall.

"You okay?" he asks.

I rub my forehead, already feeling a headache coming on. "Fine."

"You don't look fine. You look ill. It's okay, Nicole. You've got this. I know this is your first field story for XTN, but I've seen your work, watched tape of you from your station in Oklahoma. This will be a piece of cake. A walk in the park. You'll be talking to teenagers. How difficult could that be? And I'll have your back."

"I appreciate that."

At least I have one thing going for me today—Chris isn't a total asshole like my producer.

I pull up the email Barry sent. "It says we need to be there for a sixth-period science class at two o'clock. It's almost eleven. With traffic and setting up, we should leave by twelve thirty to be safe."

"I'll pack the van. You go get ready. I'll meet you in the garage."

He leaves and I find the nearest chair. I'm supposed to be avoiding all public places in Calloway Creek. I swore I'd only sleep at my parents and spend the rest of my time here at XTN. Now I have to go to the high school? What could be more public than that?

It'll be fine, I tell myself. Jaxon teaches math, and if I recall, that's in a whole separate wing. I'll be in and out before school is over, and no one will be the wiser. Maybe I'll get lucky and none of the teens will even know who I am. I mean, how many teenagers watch television these days, let alone the news?

I scurry back to my desk and quickly refresh myself on weather balloons before heading to my dressing room for hair and makeup.

~ ~ ~

"You're not much of a talker, are you?" Chris asks when we're out of the city and almost to our destination.

The last thing I need to do is air my dirty laundry to everyone at XTN. "I'm just nervous, I guess. I need everything to go smoothly. I don't want to let anyone down."

"I get it. This is your big break. Happened to me four years ago when I came over from a small station upstate. You feel like you have to prove yourself. But let me tell you, the reason you're here is because you already have. XTN wouldn't have hired you, even temporarily, if they didn't think you had what it takes to be in a large market."

Chris might be as good at pep talks as Josh was. "Thank you. Would you mind telling me that again if you see me cowering in the corner?"

He laughs. "Sure thing. You'll be great, Nicole."

"You can call me Nicky. All my friends do."

"Okay, Nicky," he says as he pulls into the CCHS parking lot. "Let's go do this."

I check the time. "Not quite yet."

"But it's almost two."

"Classes will be changing right about now. If we wait a minute, we won't have to walk the halls with hundreds of students."

"You don't want your fans to accost you?"

"Fans." I huff out a snort. "Something like that."

I roll down the window and wait until I hear the bell ring. Then Chris gets our equipment, and we check in at the front office. I don't recognize the student manning the desk, but I do recognize the man coming around the corner. "Principal Thomas," I say. "Nice to see you again."

"Nicky Forbes." He smiles brightly. "When I heard you'd be coming today, I knew I had to greet you. Congratulations on your career. We'll have to add you to our Wall of Fame."

He nods to a picture next to the front desk of Peter James-Cortez, who played in the NBA for ten years. Peter is CCHS's only claim to fame apparently. That he would consider adding me makes me delighted and sick to my stomach at the same time.

"Not necessary, but I'd be honored."

"Nice of you to do this," he says. "You know, considering..."

He doesn't have to complete his sentence. We both know what he's thinking.

"It's my pleasure."

"Room forty-six. East wing. You remember the way?"

"I sure do."

And the sooner I stop talking to you and get there, the fewer people will see me.

"Perfect. I look forward to seeing the story. Please be sure to let us know when it will air."

"Will do. Thanks, Principal Thomas."

He chuckles. "I think you can call me Kurt now, Nicky."

Kurt lets us through the door to the back. I'm overcome by nostalgia as we navigate the halls. Walls of dented and scratched lockers. Handmade posters advertising school events. A glass case that I don't have to look at to know holds a four-foot-tall state championship trophy that Jaxon led the team to.

My breath catches when we come upon the bathroom Jaxon and I used to make out in between classes senior year. I'd pretend to try and get away. He'd pull me closer, his foot pressed firmly against the door to prevent anyone from entering. It was always the best part of my day.

I walk faster needing to tune out all the memories.

We pass a girl who doesn't even bother looking up from her phone. A Janitor who tips his chin.

A picture of the cheer squad hanging from the ceiling trips up my steps. Chris holds out a hand and steadies me. "Slow down, Nicky."

I focus on the sound of my heels on the old tile floors and the smell of day-old cardboard pizza as we pass the cafeteria. We turn a corner, and I look at the room numbers. Room forty-four… forty-five… forty-six. My heart stops beating. I check the number on the door again after I read the nameplate.

Mr. Calloway

I sink against the hard concrete wall.

"Nicky?" Chris asks. "What is it?"

I point to the nameplate, then close my eyes. "It's my ex."

"Boyfriend?"

"Husband. As of last week."

He laughs, then stops. "Oh, shit. Sorry. No wonder you didn't want to come. You didn't know it would be him?"

"Of course not. He teaches math, not science."

Chris peeks through the window in the door. "Well, he teaches science now. I can see the deflated weather balloon."

"I should just quit. Walk out of here and drive back to Oklahoma."

"And let him win? No way."

"There are no winners here, Chris. And *I'm* the one who left our marriage."

"Oh. Double shit. Does he hate you?"

"Yes. No. I'm not sure."

The door opens, and a student comes out. "Are you from the TV station?" she asks.

I clear my throat. "We are."

"Mr. Calloway said you can come in."

Chris leans in. "Does he know *you* are doing the report?"

My stomach tenses, churning up the sandwich I had along the way. *Does he?*

Samantha Christy

Chapter Nine

Jaxon

A built guy holding a camera walks through the door, followed by... my *wife*?

Ex-wife, my stunned brain reminds me.

"Nicky?" I remember that I'm standing in front a classroom of students, so I pick my jaw up off the ground and try not to act like a complete idiot. "Class, this is Nicky, uh, Nicole Forbes from XTN, and...?" I raise my brows at the man who's got at least an inch and twenty pounds on me.

"Chris Smithson."

My students, mostly sixteen- and seventeen-year-olds, are more interested in the camera Chris is holding than the woman standing in the doorway, sneering at me.

Chris glances around the room. "I'm going to set up over there. That way, the light coming through the windows won't glare. Would you mind having your students turn their desks?"

"You heard the man," I say to my class.

While they turn their desks, I walk over to Nicky, trying not to be distracted by her tight dress. She never dressed like this when we were together. It accentuates her cleavage, her shapely hips, and her long legs. I wonder if she wore it on purpose to rub her success in my face. My eyes settle on the necklace. I'm surprised to see it's the same one I recall being around her neck on her weekend broadcasts. The worst part is when I stand next to her, because the familiar flowery scent of her shampoo has my mind spinning back to the times she would join me in the shower. Damn it—why is my mind going there when the rest of me is filled with unbridled frustration?

"Did you plan this?" she asks quietly, looking as unhappy about being here as I am having her.

"Don't flatter yourself. My students planned this. And we were told a *reporter* from XTN would be here."

"I am a reporter, Jaxon. A *weather* reporter. You're launching a weather balloon. And since when do you teach science?"

"We were short a teacher this year. This is my only science class." I pinch the bridge of my nose. "What are the odds?" I mumble, "Jesus, this is messed up."

Nic elbows me, her wide eyes directing my gaze to twenty-one students silently watching us. "Should we get started?"

Fuck. How is this my goddamn life right now?

Nicky addresses the class. "I'm going to introduce your teacher and briefly describe why I'm here, then I will ask and take questions, after which, we'll head outside and launch the balloon. Any questions before we get started?"

Kinsey Herman raises her hand. "Are we going to be on TV?"

"Some of you will be. But not all of what Chris tapes will go on air. We'll go back to the station and edit it."

"So if any of you were planning any stunts"—I look directly at Leo Stoker—"don't bother. You'll get cut and probably asked to leave the classroom."

Some of the students grumble. I suppose the chance to be on television is more important to them than the actual science experiment we're doing.

"When will it be on?" Rhinna Dorsher asks Nicky.

"I'll be sure to let Mr. Calloway know so he can tell you. It'll probably be this weekend, but you might have to get up early to see it. I go on starting in the six-a.m. hour, but it could air anytime throughout the morning."

More grumbling.

"You can DVR it, you doofuses," Leo says, earning him a warning snarl from me.

"I don't care what time it's on," Hannah Christensen says, fluffing her long hair. "I'm watching it live. We could be famous." She turns to Nicky. "Do you think any modeling scouts will be watching?"

The room buzzes with conversation, giving me more of a headache than I already have. "Quiet down," I say.

"Any more questions before we start?" Nicky asks.

Leo doesn't bother raising his hand. He blurts, "Yeah, are you the lady my parents have been talking about?" He turns to me. "Dude, is this your ex?"

Any and all other conversations come to a halt. The room falls silent. Nicky eyes me nervously. She fumbles with her necklace and swallows.

"Any more questions about things that actually matter?" I huff. "Like what we're doing here today?"

Twenty-one pairs of eyes pinball between Nicky and me.

Chris clears his throat. "Ready to roll, Nicky?"

He called her Nicky. Not Nicole. I stare at him, wondering what he is to her if not just a cameraman. He's about our age, maybe a few years older. His arm muscles bulge when he hoists the camera up onto his shoulder. I may even hear a few distinct female sighs from the class.

I need this to be over. I stand in front of my students and put on my brooding teacher face. "Anyone who makes noise or asks inappropriate questions will be dismissed."

Nicky takes a few deep breaths and nods to Chris. He starts filming.

"I'm here at the local high school in Calloway Creek, New York, where students in Mr. Calloway's environmental science class are getting ready to release a weather balloon." She walks over to me, and the camera follows. "Mr. Calloway, I've been told your students organized this whole experiment right down to raising the funds to purchase the balloon."

"That's right. They put on a car wash to raise money."

"Ah, I remember the days of high school car wash fundraisers. Good times."

My mouth goes bone-dry. Because I remember, too. I remember Nic wearing jeans shorts and a tiny bikini top and both of us spraying each other until our hair was matted to our scalps.

We lock eyes and I swear to God she knows what I'm thinking. I spent years looking into those emerald eyes. She spent the same amount of time gazing into mine. It had gotten to the point where we became almost telepathic. We knew each other's moods. Emotions. Thoughts.

"And which one of your students contacted XTN?" she asks, seemingly unaffected by our silent exchange.

I nod to Jillian Dorsey. "Jillian."

Nicky walks over to her. "Jillian, I'm sure our viewers would want to know what you did to get XTN's attention."

Jillian's smile is a mile wide. She pushes her glasses up with a finger. "I posted some questions on your Twitter feed. Someone named Julio responded, and the more questions he answered, the more I asked, and it kind of blew up from there."

"Julio is one of our production assistants," Nic says. She turns to the other students. "Now, who can tell me what a weather balloon is and what we can expect?"

Ten hands go up, all of them eager to be on TV. Thankfully, Nicky chooses Jeremy Walker, one of my best students.

"A weather balloon floats up into the sky carrying a payload that transmits information on atmospheric pressure, temperature, humidity, and wind speed."

"That's exactly right," Nicky says. "And who knows the technical name for the payload the balloon carries?"

She calls on Linny Gundersen. "It's called a radiosonde."

"Can you tell our viewers exactly what a radiosonde is?"

"It's a battery-powered telemetry instrument attached by a string to the balloon that transmits the data and then parachutes back to the ground after the balloon bursts."

"You've done your homework," Nicky says.

"Mr. Calloway is a good teacher."

Nicky's eyes fall on me. I try to read them. I guess I'm not as good at doing it as I used to be, because I have no idea what this look is. Surprise? Unease? Tension? Or is it more along the lines of *Can we move this along before one of us does something we'll regret?*

She asks a dozen or so more questions, working the room and interacting with the students as Chris follows with the camera. Then she asks if anyone has questions before going outside.

Leo raises his hand. I expect something derogatory, sarcastic, or plain idiotic to come out of his mouth, but he surprises me.

"I read that only twenty percent of radiosondes ever get recovered. With today's tracking technology, shouldn't we be able to recover more?"

"Great question," Nicky says. "Weather balloons often get pulled into the jet stream and can drift as far as 125 miles away. Using the formula we discussed a minute ago, we can predict where the payload will land within about ten miles. But not only is ten miles a lot of ground to cover, the problem is, many of them land in bodies of water or inaccessible places, like the tops of trees. Our goal as technology improves is to be better able to pinpoint the landing sites."

"But since you already have the data, do you even need to recover them?" Leo asks.

"We'd like to. It's better for the environment, and we can also reuse and recycle them. I should note that all radiosondes come with instructions on how to return them to the National Weather Service should anyone happen upon one. Side story, that's how I fell in love with the weather."

Her entire demeanor changes. I know the story she's going to tell. I've heard it a dozen times. And for a moment, she appears incredibly happy.

"When I was nine years old, my family and I were on vacation in The Adirondacks when I found a radiosonde. I thought it was so cool." She laughs. "There's a scientific term for you. Anyway, my father and I researched them before sending it back, and through that research, I discovered my passion." Her head shakes as if the memory is overwhelming for her.

We lock eyes once more, and I see it—the passion. She still loves meteorology as much today as she did back then. Maybe more. I hate to admit it, but she's in her element.

She breaks the stare and looks away. "Well, now, should we head outside?"

The students hop up, gather our equipment, and file for the door. Chris lowers the camera.

"You weren't rolling on that last bit, were you?" Nicky asks him. "I didn't mean to get so personal."

"You're kidding, right?" he says. "Personal is exactly why they hired you. Xuan Le loves your style. This is exactly the kind of stuff that will make her drool. Good job."

He puts a hand on her lower back as they walk out. My belly clenches and my skin crawls with a new level of hatred. He's touching her, and I want to stride over and rip his Thor-like hand right off her. The need to stake my claim is powerful. The fact that it's a ridiculous thought doesn't matter to my single-minded brain. She's been with other men. Chris may be one of them. I shouldn't feel this way: possessive, covetous, jealous. But my god… I do. I do to my very core.

"You coming?" Nicky asks from the doorway.

I nod and follow, wanting this whole thing over with.

Outside, we put up the antenna, then I open my laptop, queuing up the software that will interpret the data as it gets transmitted.

The bell ending sixth period rings, but nobody moves. My students all got special permission to miss their seventh-period classes for this experiment. They are all excited about it. Me—I've never wanted class to end more than I do right now.

Once everything is set up, the two students that were picked to release the balloon hold it as I fill it with helium. "Does that seem like enough?" I ask Nicky.

"Fill it a little more," she says. She walks over and takes hold of the lever, our hands brushing, sending an unexpected bolt of lightning through my body. "There. That ought to do it."

Leo snickers behind me. I shoot him a deadly glare.

The balloon gets released to the cheers of my students. Nicky talks science stuff in front of the camera and interviews a few more students, then she spends the next twenty minutes explaining the data as it comes in. Half my students are glued to her every word. I wouldn't be surprised if a few of them even decide to go into meteorology after this. Nicky is very convincing. She makes science interesting. She makes it sexy.

Damn it. I walk away, pretending to search the sky for the balloon. But what I'm really searching for is a reason to hate her. A reason to get her out of my fucking head once and for all.

"We got some great footage," Chris says.

Nicky agrees. "Good job, everyone. Thank you for having me."

Chris comes over and holds out his hand. I'd rather have my nutsack shaved by an epileptic than shake it. If I were Tag, I might even spit on it. And Cooper, he'd probably pretend he didn't see it and walk away. But being the 'good' brother I am, I suck it up and shake.

Nicky and Chris leave, and the rest of us return to my classroom.

"Two words, Mr. Calloway," Leo says. "Sexual tension. You could have cut it with my pocketknife. If you could have seen the looks you were giving each other. I mean, it was hard to tell if you wanted to tar and feather her or bend her over a table."

I guffaw. "Leo, if you put as much effort into your weather balloon research paper as you do my personal life, you might have a chance of passing my class. And please don't tell me if you actually have a pocketknife on you, because you know that would mean a trip to Principal Thomas' office."

He holds up his hands in surrender. "Who said anything about a pocketknife?" The bell rings. "Catch you later, Mr. Calloway."

I spend the next two hours of football practice dodging questions from Eric and my players. News travels fast around here, and I guarantee Nic and I just became today's headline.

Chapter Ten

Nicky

"It was a disaster," I tell Paige, covering my face in shame. "I was a nervous wreck. I finally got what could be my huge break, and I totally screwed it up because I had to do a story with Jaxon standing five feet away glaring at me the entire time."

"I'm sure it wasn't that bad. Plus, don't you edit these things? You'll be able to come up with footage that will show you as the rock star you are."

"I am so out of my league here, Paige. I could barely keep it together. And my cameraman said he knew I was nervous because I kept fiddling with my pendant. I'll have to cut out all that footage, or Barry will have a conniption. He's my producer. He hates me."

"Calm down, Nicky. Everyone has to pay their dues when taking a new job."

"Temporary," I tell her. *"Temporary* job."

"Either way, things will get easier over time."

I refill our wineglasses. "Thanks for hanging out with me on a Wednesday evening. I know you have an early day tomorrow."

"Not as early as *your* days start on the weekends. How do you even do it?"

"I go to bed by ten, get five hours of sleep on Friday and Saturday, and catch up the rest of the week."

Mom walks through the kitchen and gives me a sad look. I know she's happy to have me home, but she gets how awkward and uncomfortable it is for me. "Can I get you girls anything?"

"We're twenty-seven, Mom. We're hardly girls."

"I don't care how old you get. To me, you'll always be the little girls I used to take to get ice cream every Saturday. Remember that?" She touches Paige's shoulder. Paige and I had been joined at the hip since preschool, and she's the only friend from Calloway Creek who I still talk to (or who talks to *me*.) "I sure have missed having you around. How are your parents?"

"They're doing well."

"Glad to hear it." She gets a bottle of water from the fridge. "I'm off to watch that show your father likes so much."

"*Yellowstone*?" I ask.

She peeks in the other room. "Don't tell your father I secretly love it. That Kevin Costner has aged as well as a fine wine. Who knew cowboys could be so sexy?"

Paige and I giggle as she leaves.

I trace the rim of my glass, deep in thought.

"You know what your problem is?" Paige asks.

"There are just so many."

"Funny. Your problem is you're keeping yourself trapped here in your parents' house. You need to get out."

"I could use a night out. Want to go to the city with me tomorrow?"

"You need a night out *here*."

My head shakes vehemently. "Nuh-uh."

"Come on, Nic. Friday is our tenth reunion. Come with me."

I tense up. "Oh my gosh, I completely forgot. But you are out of your mind if you think I'm showing up at our reunion. Besides the fact that I wasn't even invited—"

"Because nobody knew your address."

"Besides that." I give her a stern glare. "I'm the leper of Calloway Creek. Everyone hates me. To them, all I am is the girl who cheated on the town golden boy."

"They need to get over it. You aren't the only person who has ever cheated on a spouse. If you remember, my mom cheated on my dad. They are both happily married to other people now, attend the same church, and nobody is leaving flaming bags of poop on her doorstep. Plus, you're a rock star. You can shove that in all their faces if they snub you."

"*If* they snub me? Paige, there was a ticker-tape parade when I left town."

"You are so exaggerating. There was not. It was only a small celebration at Donovan's—a few dozen people."

My jaw slackens.

"I'm kidding. Honey, you have to show people they can't decide who you are. And if anyone says something mean, kill them with kindness."

"Kill them with kindness?" I sip my drink.

Paige smiles. "You're considering it, aren't you?"

"It's ridiculous. And, I have to be up at three in the morning the next day."

"So pop in, stay an hour, show them they can't drive you out of town, then leave."

"I can't even imagine the things that will be said about me after."

"If you're Suzy Sunshine, they won't *have* anything to say."

"You really want me to be your third wheel?"

"Sam can't go. He couldn't get the time off work."

"If you show up with me, you'll be a pariah too."

"No I won't. People love me."

It's true. Paige is everyone's friend, the quintessential girl next door. Sadness washes over me knowing I was too, once upon a time. "Lucky bitch."

She stands, fisting her wineglass. "Let's go pick your outfit. Hey, maybe they'll let you borrow one of the dresses from the show—those are hot."

I roll my eyes. "My producer likes them that way."

"I can't blame him. I'll bet male viewership is up since you started."

"Don't even get me started on Barry. He and I rub each other the wrong way."

"And the cameraman?"

"Chris is great. He reminds me a lot of Josh. I hope I get him on every assignment."

"Is he hot?"

I wiggle my brows. "Very."

"I can see it now—cameraman falls for weather girl. I know you hate that term, but it would look amazing on the front page of the news."

"He's not going to fall for me. Nobody is. I'm focused on my career. Relationships aren't an option right now. Maybe not ever."

"That's silly. You have to date. Tell me about the last guy you dated."

"There hasn't been anyone since I moved. I told you my career is my number one priority."

"Wait. No one? As in you've been celibate for two years?"

"That's what I'm saying."

She eyes me skeptically. "Did you swear off men out of guilt?"

"No."

More scrutinizing stares. "Oh my god. You're still in love with your ex. That's why you think you flubbed it today. That's why you won't go anywhere in town. I'm right, aren't I?"

"I'm not in love with him." I finger my pendant.

"Then why are you fiddling with that thing like you're as nervous as a long-tailed cat?" She takes it in her hands. "In fact, you seem to do it every time Jaxon's name comes up. What is this, anyway? It's beautiful."

"Just something that keeps me grounded is all." I grab my wine. "Come on, let's go find me a killer dress."

"Nicky, you could show up in a burlap sack, and you'd still turn heads. I hate that about you, you know."

"Says the girl crowned Miss Calloway Creek High 2012."

We laugh, then lock elbows and go up to my room.

Chapter Eleven

Jaxon

Pulling up to my house, I see Addy's car in the driveway. Great. As if my friends, students, and brothers aren't giving me enough shit, I have to deal with my baby sister, too.

I love Addison, and we've only grown closer since her accident three years ago, but she tends to be blunt. An in-your-face kind of girl, even though it's bottled up in a sweet girl-next-door exterior.

I find her in the backyard with Heisman. She throws him a tennis ball. "He needs more exercise," she says. "He's getting fat."

Heisman trots over to greet me. "He is not getting fat. He's growing up."

"You give him too many treats, and all he does is lie around all day when you're at work."

"I do pay a dog walker to come every day, Addy. Twice a day during football season. It's not like he's cooped up in the house for ten hours."

"Dog walker," she says pensively. "How much do they make?"

I toss the ball at her. "You're not going to college so you can walk dogs for a living."

"Seems a lot less stressful than being a physical therapist."

"You're not happy in your exercise science program at CCU?"

She shrugs. "I love school and all. And yeah, I am interested in helping people like Lionel helped me. I'm just not sure I'm meant to go to school for three more years after graduation."

"It'll be worth it."

"I'd have to move away. Calloway Creek University doesn't have a DPT program. Not to mention my grades aren't exactly stellar. With a three-point-three, I'll be lucky to get into *any* program, let alone one in New York."

"Three-point-three is a good GPA."

"Not good enough for most doctoral programs."

"Well, you'll never know unless you apply, will you? You could always become an athletic trainer. You could make really good money if you work at the college or professional level. And it only requires a master's degree, one you could get at CCU."

She shrugs. "I don't know. I'd rather work with little kids. Adults can be dicks."

I don't have to ask what she means. She's gotten some pretty douchey comments about her leg over the years. Yet she has no problem traipsing around in short shorts or a bikini—which I love about her.

I turn on the grill. "I was going to throw on a burger. Want one or are you still doing the vegetarian thing? Or was it gluten-free?"

"It was lacto-ovo. And no, I'm not doing it anymore. I missed meat." She follows me into the house, Heisman behind her. "I'll stay if you make fries."

I dig in the freezer and pull out a bag before throwing it at her. "*You* make the fries." The bag misses its target, and she falls reaching to get it. I run over to help. "Shit. Sorry, Addy. Sometimes I forget—"

"That I'm missing a leg?" She laughs. "Yeah, sometimes I do, too. It's a bitch when I get up to pee in the middle of the night and forget my prosthetic isn't on and face-plant the floor."

"Oh, jeez. That sucks."

She spreads frozen fries on a cookie sheet. "I heard about Nicky showing up in your class today."

I stop what I'm doing. "Seriously? It was like three hours ago. Don't people in this town have anything better to do?"

"Karly's sister Linny is in your class."

"Right."

She leans against the counter, eyeing me strangely.

"What is it, Addison?"

"Not to start a pity party or anything, but what do you think is worse, losing a limb or losing your soul mate?"

"Fuck, Addy, really?"

"I'm serious. You've never lost a leg. I've never lost the love of my life, so how do we know how it compares? Like if you asked a hundred people, which do you think they'd rather suffer?"

"As if it's even a question. You lost a leg. Even with prosthetics, it's not something you can ever get back. People can go on to love other people. Huge difference."

"Hmm," she says, putting the fries into the oven.

I grab a beer and the burgers and head out back. Addy and Heisman trail behind. Heisman puts his paws up on a lounge chair, mouths his tennis ball, and brings it over. I throw it across the yard then put the meat on the grill.

"So you think Mom would rather lose Dad than a limb?" she asks.

I scrub a hand across the scruff of my jaw. "I don't know. I mean, I guess not."

"So my point is proven. Your life is shittier than mine."

"One: it's not a contest. And two: obviously Nicky wasn't my soul mate or we'd still be together."

"If you really thought that, you'd quit feeling sorry for yourself and move on."

I toss her an annoyed glare. "I do not feel sorry for myself."

"Then why haven't you moved on?"

"I have."

"I don't see you bringing Calista to family dinners. In fact, I've never even heard you call her your girlfriend. Why is that?"

"Because I was married until last week."

"You were separated. And lots of separated men have girlfriends. Heck, lots of married ones do."

"Addy, you're young. You don't get it."

"I'm twenty-one, Jaxon. And I get it more than you know. And believe me, I'm the queen of self-pity. Don't you remember how I was for six months after my accident?"

"Not really. We were all still numb because of Chaz."

"Well, I was wallowing in it. It wasn't until I got my head out of my ass and accepted my fate that I could start to make the best of it."

"You're saying I need to get my head out of my ass?"

"What is it Dad says, shit or get off the pot? Nicky isn't your wife anymore. She hasn't been for years. Calista is right there. She really likes you. She's amazing. And she can give you everything Nicky couldn't. But here's the thing, big brother. You're stuck in this rut. You need to—"

"Take a massive shit and ask her to be with me, or get off the pot and break up with her."

"Now you're seeing the bigger picture."

I flip the burgers.

"Want my advice?" she asks.

"Why do I get the feeling you're going to give it to me anyway?"

"Take the shit, Jaxon. Nicky is gone. She may be here temporarily, but look at what's happening to her. Her career is only beginning to take off. If you have any crazy ideas about getting her back and settling down, you're kidding yourself. She's working at XTN. What's next, *The Today Show*? She's on her way up. I know you still have feelings for her, but just like how I loved the leg I no longer have, I needed to say goodbye and learn how to love my life without it. And so do you. Once and for all."

Everything she says hits me square in the chest. She's right. I sit. "Shit, Addy. When did you become smarter than me?"

She wraps me in her arms from behind. "I love you, Jax. I want you to be happy."

"You think I should go all in with Calista?"

"I think you should try."

I nod. "Friday at our ten-year reunion. Maybe I'll make it official then."

"That's a great idea. Make it romantic. Like during a slow dance or something."

"Have you ever thought about going into social work or psychology?"

"Ha! Maybe." She points. "The burgers are burning."

I hop up and look at the charred beef, somehow feeling it's a metaphor for my life.

Chapter Twelve

Nicky

We pull up behind Donovan's Pub in Paige's car. The parking lot is packed. It's a public lot, so people who are going to the movie theater, bowling alley, or anywhere on McQuaid Circle, also park here. Even so, it's far more crowded than I remember.

"How many people will be here?" I ask.

"According to the Facebook page, 120 said yes, 29 said maybe, 60 declined, and 19 failed to respond."

I snort. "Or weren't invited."

She lovingly pats my leg.

Paige parks. I don't move to get out. I let my head fall back onto the headrest. "So there could be 150 people here."

"Relax, Nic. Think of it this way: the more people that are here, the better chance of you blending into the crowd."

I run my hands down my short black skirt, wondering why I even agreed to this.

"You look amazing," Paige says. "And I promise I'll have your back. Just give it an hour, okay?"

"One hour."

"Two if they don't lambaste you."

"One."

"Okay, one. Come on, let's go."

As soon as I open the car door, I hear music coming from the patio of the pub. With the front of Donovan's along McQuaid Circle, the patio off the parking lot is the most popular point of entry. Hung above the patio door is a banner: **Welcome Cavaliers Class of 2012**.

"Do you think this is some kind of bad karma?" I ask. "Technically, this reunion should have happened over the summer. It's almost September. What are the odds it would get scheduled right when I come back to town?"

"Maybe it's *good* karma. And it was scheduled long before anyone knew you'd be here."

"Good karma doesn't tend to follow me."

"What do you call the job at XTN?"

"I call it temporary."

Paige stops walking and punishes me with her stare. "Nicky, one mistake doesn't make you a bad person. I honestly think you are the only one who holds it over your head."

I nod to the pub. "Guess we're about to find out." After two more steps, I see a familiar car. There's no mistaking whose it is. Nobody else in this town drives a Honda with a bumper sticker that reads: *WHEN IN DOUBT, PUNT*.

My stomach becomes tied in knots. *He's here*. I knew he would be, probably with Calista on his arm. Hell, she probably planned the whole thing, being she was our class president and all. Thoughts of last Friday night and him kissing her in front of his house play on a continuous reel in my head. Will he kiss her here? In front of me? The knots become tighter. Karma has definitely come for me, and she wants her pound of flesh.

"Nicky Forbes," a low, sensual voice says from behind.

Unfinished **EX**

I turn to see Hunter McQuaid stride up to us. "Hunt—oof!" I barely get his name out when he pulls me into a crushing hug. Paige and I lock eyes, wondering what's going on.

Once finished with the hug that lasts far longer than your typical haven't-seen-you-in-a-while hug, he stands back and scans me from head to toe. He lets out a low whistle. "Damn, girl. Whatever they've been feeding you in Wyoming sure seems to be working."

"Oklahoma," I say.

"Yeah, that's what I said. Saw you on TV last weekend. I have to say, you're even hotter in person. The last few years have been really kind to you."

"And you."

Hunter McQuaid is the middle of the three McQuaid brothers. Like their enemies, the Calloways, they were all blessed with good looks, impeccable hair, and somewhat misplaced charm. His older brother, Hawk, helps run their family's many car dealerships. His younger brother, Hudson, went to medical school. For the life of me, I can't remember what Hunter does. Maybe he just sits back and counts his money.

He smirks. "Like what you see?"

I roll my eyes. "Still the same cocky guy I remember from high school."

"But things are different now," he says, draping an arm over my shoulder. "We're both single."

"Haven't you always been single, Hunter?"

"Okay, so *you're* single. Do you even know how many of us waited in the wings for you and Calloway to break up?"

I narrow my eyes, knowing he's exaggerating.

"Seriously," he says. "We may have even formed a club."

"Shut up." My cheeks heat at his egregious proclamation.

He starts for the door, me still under his arm. Paige clears her throat and Hunter holds out his other arm. "You can come too."

"Gee, thanks," she says.

The three of us walk onto the back patio just as Jaxon and Calista come out from inside. We stop. *Time* stops. All of us look at each other in silence. Conversations around the patio have ceased, and the only sound comes from the speakers. It doesn't escape me that the song blaring through them is "Jack and Diane." I swallow. Jaxon does too. He was my Jack. I was his Diane. It was us against the world—teenage lovers in a rural town. It was always supposed to be us.

"Well, this could be awkward," Hunter says, his eyes bouncing between Jaxon and me as he chuckles.

Jaxon isn't looking at me. He's glaring at Hunter's arm around me. Calista pastes on a smile, laces her elbow around his arm, and whispers something in his ear. As they walk by, Jaxon ignores me. But Calista doesn't.

"Hi, Nicky. Nice to see you again," she says in a cheerful greeting.

I'm speechless. I can't get myself to respond so I smile awkwardly and let Hunter pull me inside.

"Ladies," he says, "let's get a drink. I'm buying."

"The drinks are paid for, Hunter," Paige says.

"Who do you think donated the money for this soiree?" He squeezes my shoulder. "Although, with your up-and-coming status as a national celebrity, you may be the one sponsoring future events."

"I'm not a celebrity."

He nods to our surroundings. Dozens of people inside stop talking and watch as we make our way to the bar. "By the looks of things, you are. Around here anyway."

"Infamous is more like it," I say, trying not to let the blatant stares get to me. "They aren't staring at me because I'm on TV."

"You're right, they're not. The men are staring because they want to fuck you. And the women are staring because they *know* the men want to fuck you." My jaw drops as he pounds a fist on the bar and shouts, "Three tequilas!"

Donny, the owner and current bartender, shoots Hunter a nasty glance, then lays eyes on me and comes over. "Nicky, how are you? Caught you on TV last weekend. Good for you, darling. This town should be proud."

Should be. Isn't.

"Thanks, Donny. It's really nice to see you. Hey, how's Serenity?"

His smile falls when I ask about his daughter. Serenity was engaged to Jaxon's brother Chaz when he died. She took off and hasn't been seen in Calloway Creek since his funeral.

"Working in Sitka, Alaska."

My eyes go wide. "Alaska?"

"Got herself a manager position at a bar up there."

"But... Alaska? That's about as far away as you can get from here."

He pours our shots, looking sad. "I think that was the point."

I put my hand on top of his. "I'm sorry, Donny. I know you must miss her."

Everyone knows the story of Donny and Serenity. Donny's wife died during childbirth. Serenity almost died right along with her. He raised her alone. She grew up in this pub, learning the business from top to bottom. I know he wanted to pass it down to her one day.

"Like I'd miss my right arm," he says. "But you're back, so maybe there's hope she will be too someday."

"I'm not back, Donny. I'm only here for a few months."

"Enjoy 'em," he says. "And be sure to spend time with your folks. Believe me when I say I know how much they've missed you."

"I will."

Hunter passes out our shots and raises his glass. "To ten years and us just gettin' better."

We drink.

Lindsey Schumer crosses the room. Lindsey and I were almost as good of friends as Paige and I were. Then she dropped me like I was on fire when the town heard the news about my infidelity. She approaches with arms wide open. "Nic!" She hugs me, squishing our boobs between us. "It's been forever. I've missed you."

Clearly, considering you haven't bothered to call, text, or even message me over the past two years. "I've missed you too. What are you up to these days?"

"I'm an RN over at the hospital. I work in the ICU."

"Impressive. Congratulations."

"Not as impressive as you. XTN? You've really made something of yourself."

"You save lives, Lindsey—there's no comparison."

"Hunter," she says with a cringe.

Like a lot of girls I went to high school with, she dated him for a while. Well, dated is a stretch. She slept with him until he tired of her. It's the MO of Hunter and his brothers.

"Buy you a shot?" he asks.

"I'm not sleeping with you," she says.

"That ship sailed eight years ago, Lindsey. It's just a fucking drink, not a marriage proposal."

"I'm good. My friends are waiting."

I peek over her shoulder. Erikka Cage, Jen Wilson, and Johnna O'Donnell are all watching us. I'm pretty sure they were all part of the parade that escorted me out of town.

"Okay, maybe we can talk more later."

"I'd like that."

Paige sidles up to me. "Told you not everyone would loathe you."

"Two," I say. "Lindsey and Hunter. Everyone else is treating me like I have the plague."

"Nicky!" someone calls. "Over here!"

Tate Emler and Andrew Tyner are waving me over.

"I'll be right back," I say to Paige. "Thanks for the shot, Hunter. See you later."

He moves down the bar to Rebecca Jordan. "Buy you a shot?"

I shake my head as I cross the room, wondering if it's Hunter's goal to get as many of us drunk as possible. We all know he's a toad, so getting us drunk would increase his chances. But toad or not, he's being nice to me, and for that, I'm grateful.

Tate and Andrew were both on the football team with Jaxon. I'm fully prepared for them to spew words of disgust my way. But isn't that what I signed up for when I agreed to come here?

"Damn, Nicky," Tate says. "You look incredible."

"The camera really does add ten pounds," Andrew says. "But in your case, in all the right places."

"Uh… thanks?"

Tate holds out his pool cue. "How about a game?"

I eye it, more memories flooding back. I haven't played pool since Jaxon and I played on our second anniversary—right before things started to take a turn in our marriage.

Because of me.

Playing pool with Jaxon right outside isn't exactly topping my list of fun activities. "That's okay. I'm just making the rounds."

"Rumor has it you're only in town for a few months," Andrew says.

"The rumors are correct."

"How about you go to dinner with me while you're here? Next week?"

I narrow my eyes. *Isn't he still friends with Jaxon?* "I don't think that's a good idea."

He motions to the door. When I glance over, Jaxon and Calista are walking through. "He won't mind. He's with Calista now."

I have no intention of going on a date with Andrew, or anyone else, but I search my mind for a good excuse. "Still, isn't there some kind of bro code that prevents you from dating a friend's ex?"

"If you don't want him to know, we won't tell him."

Because I need more *secrets in my life.* "I'm flattered, Andrew, but my job is pretty demanding. I don't have the energy for anything else."

He sets the balls in the triangle. "If you change your mind, you know where to find me."

Shane Frommel joins us, scooting around me before leaning against the pool table. "Well, if it isn't Nicky Forbes."

I'm quite sure I've never heard my full name spoken more times than I have in the last ten minutes. "Hi, Shane."

"Congrats on the weather girl thing."

"I prefer broadcast meteorologist, if it's all the same. Weather forecaster, weather reporter, or even just meteorologist will do."

"It *is* the same, isn't it?"

"Sure, Shane."

"Hey, you want to catch a movie or something?"

"Uh, no, but thanks. It's been nice seeing you guys. Paige is waiting for me."

I head back toward the bar.

"Nicky Forbes," a man says.

For Pete's sake, what now? I look over. Tony Truman is approaching. He pulls me into his arms and starts dancing to the music, swaying me back and forth.

"Hey, Tony. Sure, I'll dance with you."

He laughs. "I heard you were in town. Didn't think you'd show your face here, however. You've got some lady balls."

"It hasn't been that bad so far."

"You mean you haven't been attacked by the sharks in the corner?" He nods to the large booth under a television. In it sits a half dozen girls, all from the cheer squad, if I recall. All Calista's friends. And they're staring at me like I just told them Botox lost FDA approval.

"Haven't had the pleasure."

"Not to mention your ex staring a hole in the back of your head."

Anxiety crawls up my spine. "Jaxon is watching us?" Tony swings me around. I search over his shoulder until I see Jaxon. The venom spewing from his eyes could kill a rhino. "Oh, jeez. He really does hate me."

"I'm pretty sure it's *me* he hates. For dancing with you. If the man had a gun, I fear I'd be bleeding out on the floor right now."

"I'm sure that's not true. But I'd better get back to Paige. She made me come, and now I'm ignoring her."

He pulls me close. "Not until you agree to go out with me."

Is there something in the water? Or the tequila more likely. "I'm really trying to focus more on my job right now, Tony. But thank you."

"Just as well. I do kind of value my balls, and that ex of yours looks like he wants them on a platter. Talk to you later, Nicky."

"Thank you for the dance."

Paige is all smiles when I return. "I told you."

She pushes a fresh shot of something in my direction. I down it. "I've been hit on three times in the last five minutes. And that doesn't count Hunter."

"That's got to be some kind of Calloway Creek record. If you think about it, it makes sense. You and Jaxon were together since middle school. Nobody else ever had a chance with you. Maybe they're trying to make up for lost time." She laughs. "Or maybe there really was a club." She takes my elbow. "Come on, those guys finished their game. Let's shoot some pool."

"I don't want to."

"You need something to keep your mind off everything." She motions to Donny. "A few beers at the pool table?"

"You got it."

It's pointless to make an argument not to play. The last thing I want to do at this point is start a conversation about Jaxon. So I stand here studying the pool cues as if it matters which one I choose. But it keeps my eyes from wandering. I only need to make it another half hour.

Male hands appear from behind, holding a cue. "This one," a man says.

I crane my neck. "Oh, hey, Carlos. Long time no see." I turn to Paige in surprise. She mouths, "Wow."

Carlos Wilkerson was a bigger science geek than I was, complete with coke bottle glasses and a pocket protector. He moved away after high school. The years have been generous to him. Talk about an ugly duckling turning into a swan. The glasses are gone, replaced with contacts presumably, showing off his striking brown eyes. And by the looks of it, he exchanged his library card for a gym membership.

"Mind if I play with you?" he asks.

Unlike every other guy here, I actually believe he's not talking in innuendos.

Paige puts down her cue stick. "You two play. I'm going to talk to Lauren and Missy at the bar." She winks at me. I roll my eyes. I know what she's doing and it's not going to work. I have no intention of dating, hooking up with, or even flirting with anyone in this room.

Donny puts two beers on the edge of the table. I offer one to Carlos.

"Saw you on XTN," Carlos says after taking a sip. "I knew you were into meteorology, but I wasn't aware you wanted to be in broadcasting."

"I wasn't either. I took a few classes in it at NYU, but it wasn't until a producer back in Oklahoma took a chance on me that it started to become a reality. What have you been up to?"

"I work for NASA, actually."

"Oh my god. That's amazing. *You* should be on the CCHS Wall of Fame, not me."

He laughs. "I didn't even know such a wall existed. Anyway, I'm not an astronaut. I got an internship with them my junior year in aerospace engineering at the University of Florida, and they hired me after graduation. Even helped me get my PhD."

"You're a doctor?"

Carlos chalks his cue and leans over to break. "Looks like we both achieved our dream jobs."

Behind Carlos, back against the far wall, Jaxon is watching me. He's talking to Calista and a few others, but his attention is all on me. And Calista doesn't fail to notice. She pulls him onto the dance floor and tries to keep him as far away from me as possible. Does she think I'm back here for *him*?

"Nicky?" I look up. Carlos is waiting on me. "You're solids."

"Great. Thanks." I lean over and position myself behind the cue ball, but I can't focus because all I see in the distance is *him*. Watching. Staring. Judging.

Is he remembering all the times we played on this very table? How it was like foreplay the way he helped me with my shots, his arms around me, positioning the cue stick.

I shoot and completely miss. My stick doesn't even make contact with the cue ball.

Carlos comes up behind me. "Here, let me show you." I stiffen as he bends me into position and adjusts the stick in my hands.

He doesn't make it sexual like a lot of guys would. I think he's genuinely trying to help my game. But Jaxon doesn't know that based on the deadly look on his face. He's still on the dance floor, hands around *her*. No other couples are between them and me. It's as if karma is forcing me to watch. I take a breath, close my eyes, and shoot.

"Hey, look at that," Carlos says. "You got one."

I turn away from the dance floor. "Apparently you're a good teacher."

We play the rest of the game the same way, him showing me the best angles and shots, and me trying to ignore my ex's hands on the head cheerleader. Once, when I glance over, I swear I picture her wearing the short little blue-and-white skirt and carrying pom-poms.

I hand Carlos my stick. "Thanks for the game."

"Anytime."

He goes back to his friends. I go back to mine. My one. My singular friend in this whole town.

Lauren and Missy whisper to each other. "It wasn't enough you broke that man's heart," Missy slurs. "Now you have to come back and ruin his new relationship? Why don't you go back to Ohio already?"

"Oklahoma," I say.

"Whatever." The two of them leave Paige and me standing at the bar.

"Ignore her," Paige says. "She's drunk."

"I don't blame her. I'd hate me too. She's right, you know. I shouldn't be here. I've made everyone uncomfortable." I scan the room for Jaxon and Calista, seeing them standing with a few of his old teammates. Calista's smile seems forced. Jaxon looks indifferent. They're both watching me, and everyone else seems to be looking between the three of us as if we're tonight's main attraction. "I'm the one who left Calloway Creek. This reunion belongs to them more than it does me."

Hunter sidles up to me again. "What are you ladies talking about?"

"How I shouldn't be here," I say. "It's not fair to Jaxon."

"Fuck him." He leans close. "You know what would really piss him off? Dance with me."

"Do you have a death wish?"

He laughs. "First of all, Jaxon Calloway could not kick my ass. And secondly, he has no hold over you anymore. You can do whatever the hell you want, including dancing with a McQuaid."

"It's not going to happen, Hunter."

He leans over me and snatches another drink off the bar. "Anytime you want to see that man blow his top, I'm here to help." He kisses my cheek before leaving.

I sneak a peek at Jaxon. Of course he was watching. I just can't tell if it's me he wants to kill or Hunter.

"Do you think those two families will ever settle their differences?" Paige asks.

I spin around, refusing to continue torturing myself by watching him. Because every time I do, I question why I left. I think about our first touch. Our first kiss. The day he took my virginity under the stars. Our wedding. I clear the lump in my throat. "I don't think they even remember why they're fighting. I think they just do it for fun."

"Oh, look," Paige says. "Calista has finally extricated herself from him. I thought she was going to remain surgically attached all night to show you he's taken."

In my periphery, I see her walk toward the bathroom.

"Aren't you popular?" a familiar voice spews behind me.

I stiffen, then turn. "Jaxon." I spin back and motion for Donny to give me another refill.

My hair gets moved aside, and strong fingers come around the side of my throat. For a second, I think he might strangle me. Then his grip relaxes, and his thumb brushes against the hollow of my neck. Sensations, tingles, zaps of… something… shoot through my body. It's the first time I've felt his touch in two years. Paige's eyebrows reach her hairline.

"As if being all over television isn't enough, you have to come here and rub it in my face? I mean, what the hell, Nic? Is there any guy here you *haven't* come on to?"

"Give me a tiny break." I shrug his hand off me and huff. "It's my reunion too, Jaxon. And if you don't want to see me on

TV, change the damn channel. Anyway, don't you have a *girlfriend* you should be dancing with?"

The disdain in our voices is surprising. We never spoke like this to each other when we were married. And I'm not sure why I'm speaking to him this way now. He doesn't deserve it. But seeing him on the arm of another woman all night has been… devastating, to say the least. And my defenses are up.

He takes my arm, pulls me behind him, and leads me out to the dance floor.

I know I should resist, but I don't. Not much anyway. "What are you doing?"

"Talking with my ex. And showing everyone here that we can be civil."

I glance around the pub. Everyone is staring. And guffawing. And videoing. I suppose they either think I'm going to punch him or fuck him.

"*Can* we be civil?" I ask. "Because based on the two times we've seen each other, we're either glaring at or ignoring one another."

"I think we should try to be. How else are we going to survive two months of you being here?"

"Avoidance," I say, consciously trying to ignore the warmth of his hands. The solidness of his body. The familiarity of his scent that is permeating my every pore. The roughness of his voice that still speaks to me in my dreams.

Every synapse in my brain is firing, telling me to pull away. But my heart strings—apparently they think we're still tethered together, and I find myself swaying to the music.

He moves with me. "How's that working for you? Apparently not well since you decided to show up at the one place you knew I'd be. Not to mention all my friends."

"Oh, *your* friends."

"Yeah, *my* friends. You left them too. Or have you forgotten?"

"I remember perfectly well. More than you could ever know." I break away from him because being in his arms is suffocating. "I have to go. I need to be up early."

"Then why did you even come?"

I shake my head. *Why did I?* "It was obviously a mistake." I go back to the bar and Paige, who is holding up another shot. I've never needed one more. "Thanks. And now I'm leaving."

She checks the time. "Well, you almost made it an hour. Truth be told, that's longer than I thought you'd last." She glances behind me. "Oh shit."

I turn to see Calista standing in the back hallway, the sadness of her stare burning through my skin from twenty feet away. She saw us dancing.

Not bothering to say goodbye to anyone, I wave to Carlos and Donny and hightail it to the back door. I'm barely to the back gate when I hear, "Why can't you leave well enough alone?"

Slowly, I rotate around and face Calista. She walks toward me in what seems like slow motion. Is she going to call me names? Pull my hair? Tackle me to the ground? Behind her, people pour out from inside.

"Calista, now is not the place or time. We've both been drinking."

"You think I'm going to cause a scene?"

"No, because I'm walking away." I get another thirty feet when I hear her heels on the pavement behind me. Oh my god, she's really doing this.

She runs ahead of me and stops my progress. Not with her fists or her body, but with her eyes. Her sorrowful, poignant stare that makes me feel even more guilty over being here.

"Calista, I have to be up in six hours. I don't have time for this." I start walking.

"You left him. You cheated. You chose your career over him. You were selfish, uncaring, and insensitive. Not to mention you broke him. Do you know how long it took him to even ask someone out?" She laughs sadly. "Come to think of it, he never did. *I* asked *him*."

"Cal—"

"No. You don't get to speak. It's *my* turn. You had your turn. You had your chance with him. You don't get to waltz back into town and pretend like everything is normal when *you're* the reason he can't be. You ruined him. He was just starting to heal. And tonight, I had a feeling he might even commit to this relationship. Then you show up, and all anyone can do is look at you and look at him to see if he's looking at you and look at me to see if I'm bothered by any of it. Why are you here? You made your choice. You don't even want him, so why don't you stay away and give him room to breathe? Please, Nicky. I'm begging you."

I'm stunned by the lack of anger in her confrontation. But I shouldn't be. Even when we butted heads back in high school, she was still nice about it. She didn't get to be head cheerleader, class president, and prom queen by intimidation. She did it because she was delightful, caring, and perky. The kind of person who's perfect for Jaxon.

Jaxon comes out of the pub, and a few of his buddies hold him back when he tries to head our way.

Calista turns and then glances between us. "Unless you still want him." Her eyes become glassy. "Do you?"

"I…" I clutch my pendant. "I have to go."

I run through the parking lot. Then I run down the street. Then I take my shoes off and run barefoot until I get inside the house and up to my room. Then I collapse on my bed, knowing everything she said was one hundred percent true.

Especially the part about me wanting him. Because I was lying to myself. Being in his arms wasn't suffocating. It was like going home.

Chapter Thirteen

Jaxon

As if on autopilot, my car ends up in front of Calista's apartment. I don't turn the engine off. I'm still reeling from tonight's events.

Calista has been staring at me the whole ride home. Ever since she confronted Nicky she's been staring at me, like she's trying to see inside my soul. I reach over and give her hand a reassuring pat. Reassuring her for what, I can't say, because honestly I don't know my ass from my head right now. I can't even blame the fuzziness in my brain on alcohol as I cut myself off hours ago.

We're silent, the only noise coming from the engine and the muted conversation of some passersby.

She sighs heavily. Then she leans over and kisses my cheek. "I think this is goodbye."

"Okay." I rub my brows. "See you tomorrow?"

"No. I mean this is goodbye, Jaxon."

"Seriously?"

Her shoulders slump. "Will you even be sad after I get out of the car?"

"Yeah, sure. So *why* are you doing this?"

"You'll be sad, but not devastated."

"I'm not sure what you want me to say. I'm trying here."

"That's the difference between us. I will be devastated. I *am* devastated. And I deserve someone who would be, too. Someone who feels like when I'm not with them a piece of them is missing. But I get it now. You could never feel that way about me when it's how you still feel about *her*."

I scrub a hand across my jaw. Because how do I defend her accusation when it's entirely fucking true? "Calista, I—"

"Don't say anything, Jaxon. There's nothing you *could* say. This is my fault as much as anyone's. I don't blame you for my getting too attached. I kept coming back even though the signs were there. I stupidly thought things might get better. And then earlier tonight, before Nicky showed up, I even felt something might have changed between us. For a while there, it was different—*you* were different. Then she walked in, and you completely pulled away. Emotionally. Physically. And I knew for sure nothing would ever change."

"Then why did you let me bring you home?"

"To say goodbye, I guess." She puts a hand on the door handle, then turns back. "For months now, I thought I was in love with you. But I think I was in love with the idea of having what you had with her. I'm not mad at you, Jaxon. I hope we can still be friends."

She gets out of the car and doesn't look back. I sit in the darkness, feeling guilty as hell when a wave of relief floods through me.

~ ~ ~

A hairy paw rests over my face as sunlight shines through the window. "Stay on your side." I shove Heisman away, which is no easy feat considering he weighs sixty-eight pounds. He regards me for a minute, then drifts back to sleep.

Light crawls down the wall as I lie awake wondering about last night. What was Nicky thinking showing up at the reunion? Nobody wanted her there. Except the dozen or so guys who wanted in her pants. Hunter fucking McQuaid would have loved to rub that one in my face.

What was *I* thinking pulling her on the dance floor? Heisman rolls over and gives me the stink-eye as if he's privy to my thoughts. "Yeah, okay, so I screwed everything up. What's new?" I hop out of bed and hit the bathroom. Then I walk out the bedroom door. When Heisman doesn't follow, I peek my head back in. "Get your lazy ass off the bed. We're going for a walk."

An hour later, after our usual Saturday morning stroll through the park, we're standing on Tag's doorstep. His fiancée, Maddie, opens the door. *Fiancée*—my brother is engaged. I still can't believe it. Apparently pigs do fly.

"Sorry to show up unannounced," I say.

"You're welcome anytime," Maddie says. "Tag made pancakes. Come in and pull up a chair."

"My brother cooks?"

She laughs. "I wouldn't call adding water to a mix and pouring it on a griddle cooking."

A puppy runs over and almost collides with Heisman. He lowers his head to sniff things.

"Sissy!" Maddie's five-year-old daughter calls out, coming around the corner.

I bend down and pet the little furball. "Sissy? I thought you were going to call her Princess, Gigi."

"Mommy said it would be too confusing for her since Tag calls *me* princess."

"It's good you brought Heisman," Maddie says. "We need to socialize Sissy with other animals."

"Take her to the park. There are plenty of dogs there."

"Can't until she's had all her shots. She could pick up something."

I ruffle Heisman's fur. "I took him every day when he was a puppy, and he never got sick."

"You were lucky then."

"I think you're being a little overprotective."

Tag appears. "What's this about my fiancée being overprotective? Surely you jest."

Maddie swats the back of his head on her way to the table. "Come on, Jaxon, let's get you those pancakes."

"You have somewhere else to be?" Tag asks as we eat. "You keep checking the time."

"The piece on the weather balloon is supposed to air soon."

"How exciting," Maddie says, going over to turn on the TV.

After breakfast, the three of us move to the living room, keeping an eye on the television as we watch Gigi play with Heisman and Sissy.

"Heard there was some excitement at Donovan's last night," Tag says.

Maddie elbows him. "You said you weren't going to say anything."

"That was before he crashed our breakfast. Actually, someone said there was a cat fight between your girlfriend and your ex."

"There wasn't any fight. They had a conversation is all. And she's not my girlfriend. She broke it off late last night."

"Because you danced with Nicky?"

"Christ, did you have spies there or something?"

"There's this thing called Facebook," Tag says quietly. "Maybe you've heard of it. It's where people post photos and make comments and shit. Well, the posts about your little reunion about broke the fucking internet."

"You and Calista broke up?" Maddie asks.

"If that's what you want to call it. We were never officially a thing."

"If dating someone for six months doesn't officially make you a thing, I don't know what does."

"So I've been told."

Maddie's face lights up. "Oh, it's on. Tag, turn it up."

Nicky looks amazing. I wonder if that Chris guy is behind the camera ogling her. She talks about the weather and then leads in to the experiment at the school. The three of us are glued to the TV.

"Ten pounds, my ass," Tag says when I appear on screen. "If you plan on being on TV again, brother, you might think about going off the carbs."

"Fuck you," I whisper.

All in all, they edited the clip to under two minutes. Surprising because they spent over an hour and a half with us.

"She really must hate you," Tag says. "She didn't give you much screen time."

"It wasn't about me, you idiot. It was about my students."

"Still. Ouch."

"I thought he was great," Maddie says, patting my shoulder before going off to play with Gigi and the dogs.

The front door opens. Cooper comes in. "Don't you knock?" Tag says. "It's not just me here anymore."

"It's okay," Maddie says. "He's family."

"What if we were, you know"—he glances at Gigi—"indisposed?"

Cooper walks over to Gigi and covers her ears. "You mean fucking? Dude, you have a kid now. I highly doubt you're bumping uglies in the middle of your kitchen."

Maddie smirks. "How do you know what we do when she's away at school and we sneak home for lunch?"

"Well, damn." Cooper offers Tag a high-five, which he turns down. "I stand corrected. I'll knock from now on."

"You just missed this clown on TV," Tag says.

"I'm sure you DVR'd it. I'll watch it later. Right now, I want to go hike the trails. You up for it?"

Tag looks at Maddie.

"Oh, sorry." Coop turns to Maddie. "Maddie, can Tag come out and play?"

Tag punches our little brother in the arm, then he hops off the couch. "Give me a minute to change."

I snap my fingers. "Heisman, want to go for a walk?"

He trots over to the door and waits.

Twenty minutes later, we're entering one of Calloway Creek's many hiking trails that starts behind the park on McQuaid Circle. Heisman runs ahead, greeting every person he encounters. My brothers and I often hike these trails when Cooper comes to town.

We hike for about five miles, past Joe Henson's one-room cabin in the middle of nowhere.

"That old bastard still lives there?" Cooper asks.

"Probably till the day he dies," Tag says.

"How do you know he hasn't?"

I glance back at the old cabin. "Should we check it out?"

"He's still alive," Tag says. "Maddie's friend Ava delivers coffee beans to him every week."

"Ava Criss delivers? Since when?" Cooper asks.

"What don't you get about the man being a recluse? I don't even know what the hell he did before online grocery delivery became a thing."

I find a good throwing stick and toss it ahead for Heisman. "How long will you be hanging around?" I ask Coop.

"Not long. Been here for too long as it is. Boredom has set in."

"So you don't need a place to crash?"

"I have a place to crash."

"Your van cannot be comfortable for long periods of time. Isn't that why you stayed at Tag's for a month?"

"No, man. I stayed with him during renovations to make the van even more livable. You should see it now."

I shake my head. "I don't get how you can live in something so small. It's like being in a box. Don't you get claustrophobic?"

He runs ahead and balances on the fallen tree that hangs out over the creek. He stands in the middle and raises his arms to the heavens. "You call this being claustrophobic?" Then he loses his footing and disappears into the creek fifteen feet below.

"Shit," Tag says, looking as horrified as I feel.

We quickly slide down the bank and scan the creek. It's deep here, maybe ten feet, and murky. I'm ripping off my shirt to dive in when Cooper surfaces laughing.

Tag and I sit on a large rock and stare at each other. I know exactly what we were each thinking for those ten seconds. We were thinking it was Chaz all over again. We're both breathing heavily, waiting for our blood pressure to come down.

"Goddamn daredevil motherfucker!" Tag shouts.

Cooper swims to the edge, pulls himself out, and strips down to wring out his clothes.

I glance around. "You're just going to do that right here?"

"Dude, I shit in the woods on a regular basis. This is nothing."

Two women runners approach, conspicuously slowing before they pass.

"Ladies." Cooper salutes in all his nakedness.

They both giggle as they jog away.

I stand and roll my eyes. "You're such a fucking bonehead."

Tag motions to the fallen tree. "And you need to quit doing shit like that."

"We all did shit like that when we were kids, Tag."

"That was before. We didn't know any better."

"I'm not stupid. I'm not going to get myself killed."

I bend at the waist and belt out an incredulous laugh. "Coop, you jump off buildings and bridges and out of planes. I'd say the chances of you getting yourself killed are about as good as they get."

He pulls on his shorts. "I'm always safe about it."

"Like you and Chaz were safe on that mountain?" I regret the words the instant they leave my mouth.

He throws his shirt down and pins me to the nearest tree. "Don't fucking talk to me about him. You think I don't go over that day in my head every goddamn day? You think I don't retrace our steps looking for what the hell I could have done to prevent it? You think he doesn't haunt my motherfucking dreams every night?"

"Hey now." Tag nudges us apart. "Jaxon didn't mean anything by it. He's just worried about you. We all are."

"Well, don't be." He picks up his shirt and heads up the embankment.

Tag throws me a venomous stare.

"What? Like you weren't thinking it."

"Yeah, but dude... not cool."

"I know it was a dick thing to say, but I'm tired of worrying about him every time he goes off on another excursion. I'm sick of seeing Mom get crippling anxiety waiting for a phone call that he's injured or dead."

"We all are, Jax, but he's a grown man. We can't tell him what to do. If we try, we may make it worse."

"Shit." I rub my temples. "I know. I'm sorry."

He pats my back. "Come on, let's go find your dog before he makes friends with Old Man Henson."

~ ~ ~

I sit at the table with my steak.

Heisman's eyes follow me as I retrieve the TV remote from the couch. "What?" I say. "I'm just catching the end of the Bama game." He doesn't look away. He thinks I'm lying. To prove a point, I sit and eat and actually watch the game for two hours before flipping through the channels.

He stares at me again. He knows I'm going to do it. *I* know I'm going to do it. I tap my foot against the hardwood floor. I bite the inside of my cheek. I roll and re-roll the magazine on the coffee table. Then I turn on XTN.

I glance at Heisman. "Shut up."

She's not on. I pull out some papers to grade, then go to the kitchen to find a new Sharpie. I hear Nicky's voice and race back out before leaning against the doorway to watch her. Her spots never last very long—a few minutes maybe. I don't even pretend to stop myself when I grab the remote and queue up the show I recorded this morning. Then I view it four times.

"Goddamn it!" I throw the remote. "Get out of my fucking head."

But instead of getting drunk and going to bed like any sane man would do, I sit alone in the dark on the front porch and wait. I wait because my house is in between the train station and her parents' place. And I know she's going to walk by around eleven o'clock.

And apparently, I'm a masochist.

Chapter Fourteen

Nicky

Two little girls play on the floor of the train as their parents try to control them. It's late. I'd be misbehaving too if I were three or four and it was this far past bedtime. Finally, their mother calms them down by reading them a book.

I rest my head against the window and let the rocking of the train lull me into a trance.

"Morning, wife." Jaxon is smiling from ear to ear as he brushes a clump of hair out of my eyes.

I lean over to kiss him. "Good morning, husband."

"Do you think that will ever get old?"

I gaze at my finger that has two rings on it now. "Never."

"Did you have fun last night?"

"Well, I don't know," I tease. "Which part are we talking about? The wedding part, or the part that came after?"

He pins me to the bed and hovers over me. "The whole part."

I seductively bite my lower lip. "Best night of my life. If I was in that movie, Groundhog Day, and had to live one day over and over again forever, that would be the day."

"I fucking love you." He leans down and kisses me. *"I even love your morning breath."*

I laugh, giving him a big dose of it.

My phone alarm goes off, alerting me it's time to take my birth control pill. Jaxon moves off me, grabs my phone, and silences it. "Maybe you should skip it. Maybe you should skip all of them."

My jaw drops. "Jaxon Calloway, I know you're not suggesting we do something reckless like get pregnant the day after we got married."

"How would that be reckless? We're twenty-two. We're married. We've been together for nine years. Hell, with as much as we have sex, pill or not, I'm surprised it hasn't happened yet."

I giggle. "We are kind of like rabbits."

He puts a hand on my stomach. "Do you know how gorgeous you'll be when you're carrying my baby?"

The sheet comes with me when I sit. "Okay, I kind of thought you were joking, but now you're scaring me. We said we'd wait until we were both established in our jobs. I know you have one, but it could be a while before I get a decent offer within a good commuting distance."

"What if we do family first, job next?"

"We both have a mountain of student loans. Not to mention we already agreed we'd wait. And we're only twenty-two. We have plenty of time to have a baby."

"Babies. Two. I'm thinking girls. Close together so they can be best friends."

I shake my head. "You really do have this all planned out, don't you?"

"Nicky, I've known you were going to be the mother of my kids since we were fifteen."

My eyes narrow. "But we've been together since we were thirteen."

"Yeah, but it took you two years to touch my dick. That's when I knew."

Lowering my head to rest on his chest, I laugh. "Babe, you'd have thought anyone who touched your penis at age fifteen would be a good catch."

"You may have a point." *He wiggles his butt.* "Listen, all this talk about my man meat has it wanting some attention."

I lift the sheet and stare at his growing erection. "Well, hello there." *I lick my lips.*

"Wait." *Jaxon cups my head in his hands.* "I just wanted you to know that while you give head better than a porn star on a donkey's dick, that's not why I married you."

"Uh... thank you?"

"All I'm saying is you're it for me, Nicky Calloway." *I give him a look.* "Yeah, I know technically you're still a Forbes. You can be Princess Nicky Consuela Bananahammock for all I care, as long as we're together until the day we die."

My eyes become glassy.

"Promise me," *he says.* "Promise me that whatever we do in life, we'll die together, in bed, eighty years from now."

"I promise."

Then I kiss down his chest, past his abs, and right to his throbbing penis, and I seal the promise like a porn star.

"I apologize," a woman says, waking me.

I shake away the memory and look at my shoe, which is wet.

"She spilled her juice," she says, pulling a wad of tissues from her bag and wiping it up.

"It's fine."

"We kept them up way too late. They're slaphappy or something. Tell the nice lady you're sorry, Amanda."

The little girl's lip juts out in a pout. "I'm sorry."

"It's okay, sweetie," I say. I take the tissues from her mother. "Really, no need. These are my commuting shoes. No big deal."

"Do I know you?" she asks, studying my face.

"I'm not sure."

Please don't let her be someone from Calloway Creek who is now going to praise her daughter for ruining my Nikes.

"I feel like I've seen you before," she says.

The train comes to a stop. *My* stop. I gather my things and stand. "I get that a lot. I hope you have a nice night."

"You too. And again, very sorry."

I hurry off the train. Ordinarily, I'd love to be recognized, but for the right reasons. Considering where we are, the likelihood of that isn't great.

As I make my way back home, it starts sprinkling. I do my best not to look over toward Jaxon's house as I approach it. He was there last night. On his front porch. In the dark. Was he taking his dog out, or did he know I'd be heading home?

The rain picks up a bit as I pass his house.

"A good weather girl would have an umbrella with her!" I hear shouted.

I stop, the rain starting to seep through my top. He knows more than anyone how I hate being called a weather girl. "Are you stalking me?"

He laughs. "Wow, you really think you're something, don't you? This is *my* front porch. I have every right to sit on it."

"And I have every right to walk down a street and not be harassed."

His porch light comes on. I can see him clearly now, albeit through the thickening sheet of rain. *Why are you standing here in the rain? Go. Move.* He's wearing jeans and a T-shirt. A blue shirt that I know matches his eyes. His feet are bare, not to mention dry. And he's looking at me like I'm the devil reincarnate. "Indeed you do. I was simply pointing out that you must not be a very good forecaster if you didn't know rain was coming." He pulls out his phone and snaps a picture of me, soaking wet. "I'm sure your groupies would be interested in knowing you suck at predicting the weather."

And with that, he goes inside, shuts the door, and turns off the light.

Don't do it. Keep walking.

I open the gate.

Or do that.

I step through, go up the sidewalk, climb the three stairs to the porch (noting they've been painted), and pound on the door.

"Nobody's home!" I hear.

I pound more. "Jaxon! Answer the damn door."

It opens. He clutches his chest like a surprised superfan. "Oh my god, *Nicole* Forbes." Then his hand drops to his side and his demeanor changes. "Sorry, I get my weather reports from someone who actually knows what they're doing."

"Shut up, Jaxon." His dog appears. I lean down and pet him. "Hey there, Heisman."

"Heisman, go to bed."

The gorgeous golden doesn't move.

"Heisman," he says sternly. But Heisman ignores him and starts licking my shoe. "Damn it." Jaxon cracks his neck from side to side in obvious frustration.

"It's the juice on my shoe. A little girl spilled it on me on the train."

"Thanks for the play-by-play. Now, want to tell me what you're doing at my house?"

Behind me, the heavens open up and sheets of rain come down. Streams of water roll off his roof. I can't even see the streetlight in front of the Simperson's house anymore.

"I don't know. You said what you said, and I got mad. I should have kept walking." I glance behind me. "And now this. Can I just sit on your porch until it passes?"

His lips scrunch together and move from left to right. "Hmm. Maybe we should call a meteorologist and find out when that might be."

"I did predict a twenty percent chance of storms."

"Way to beat the odds," he says sarcastically.

"I didn't blow the forecast, you know. The atmosphere is extremely complex. Even supercomputer models that run logarithmic equations can't accurately resolve atmospheric dynamics. It's not a CYA percentage. Twenty percent means the atmosphere is generally stable, but there's just enough moisture or heat to squeeze out a shower in a limited area. That limited area is here."

He examines his fingernails, pretending to be bored. "Are we done with the science lesson? Maybe you forgot, but *I'm* the teacher here."

Thunder crackles behind me, shaking the house and scaring Heisman. He runs toward the living room.

Jaxon rolls his eyes and opens the door further. "Your father would have my head on a goddamn platter if he knew I let you walk home in this. You can stay until it passes."

My eyebrows shoot up. "Inside?"

"No, Nicky, in the doghouse out back. Of course inside. Don't drip all over the hardwood."

I crane my head around the corner and peek into the living room. "You put in hardwood floors?"

"Always said I wanted to." He gestures to the kitchen. "Wait in there. I'll get you a towel."

Entering the house that used to be mine is surreal. And overwhelmingly emotional. Aside from the hardwood in the living room, nothing much has changed. I peek down the hallway at the 'picture wall'—well, except that. It's completely bare. Not even nails remain on the wall that was once lined with pictures of us: our wedding, our graduation, our engagement, our home purchase. Our *everything*. And it dawns on me that Jaxon may not have a single photo of his past that doesn't include me.

It's not lost on me, however, that not a solitary picture of Calista is anywhere in sight.

"I said stay in the kitchen," he says, handing me a towel.

I glance at my feet, which are technically on the kitchen floor, but I don't argue the point. Then I sit at the table that I once had coffee at every morning. The table Jaxon and I made love on after I got offered my first internship at a small station in the city.

He stares at it, too. Then turns his back on me. "Coffee?"

"That would be nice. Thanks."

My heart races. My mind is all over the place. I'm sitting in a house I once owned, staring at a man who was once mine, touching a table that we once christened. It's torture to the extreme.

This is a very bad idea.

So why, then, am I'm not making any attempt to leave?

Chapter Fifteen

Jaxon

Another clap of thunder echoes. The lights flicker. Nicky's hand covers her mouth in amusement. "Oh my gosh, I forgot how we used to lose power every time it stormed."

Then her face goes white. Because, apparently, she just remembered what we used to do during the blackouts. As if fate is playing a twisted joke on me, the lights go out.

"Well, shit," I say, feeling my way to the cabinet that contains the flashlights.

"I got them," she says. "You still keep them in the one by the fridge?"

To the very bottom of my soul, I wish I had moved them. Why does her knowing everything about this house sit with me like a wad of undigested gum in my gut?

We bump into each other. Her hand lingers on my arm. I don't like it there. Or I do. *Fuck*, my head is all over the place. I pull away. "Sit. We can't have Calloway Creek's newest celebrity stubbing a toe, now can we?" I say bitterly.

"Very funny."

Three rumbles of thunder drum in quick succession.

"This night just keeps getting better," I say.

"I can have my dad pick me up."

I reach the cabinet and turn on a flashlight. "Nobody should be driving in this."

"It's a half mile. I think he can handle it."

"I said don't worry about it, *Nicole*. Jesus, can you for two seconds quit being the one who has to control everything?"

"Me?"

I don't have to shine the light on her to know her jaw is hanging open. I can *hear* that it is. "Yes, you."

"I don't have to control everything."

I laugh and lean against the counter. "Seriously? Let's see. Who picked the college we went to? The dorm we lived in? Which one of us decided the date we got married and where we went on the honeymoon? Even this house—"

"Stop right there. That's not fair. *You* picked the house."

"Yeah, but you made us tour ten more before we made an offer."

"Because that's just good sense. And for your information, I picked NYU because I knew *you* wanted to go there. I picked February eighth because it was after football season. And I picked Gatlinburg because I knew how much you love the mountains, and I didn't want us going further in debt. Every decision was made with you in mind."

I search my thoughts for a comeback, an argument. There's only one I land on. "*Every* decision? How about the one where you dropped me like a piece of hot coal and hightailed out of town before they could even spell out the details of your job offer?"

She gets up angrily and almost rips the cabinet door off the hinges retrieving another flashlight. She shines it in my eyes. "And how about the one where you *let* me." She lowers the light, puts it on the table, and lets her head slump into her hands.

My stomach turns. For two years, ever since she walked out that door, I've wondered if things would have been different if I had followed her to Oklahoma. "You wanted me to come after you?"

"Yes. No. I don't know. Probably not. Even if you had, it wouldn't have worked out, but I kind of expected you to yell at me. Maybe I even needed you to."

"Yell at you?"

"You've never yelled at me. Not once. Not the night you came home and found my bags packed. Not even after I told you I had cheated on you. Jaxon, I deserved to be yelled at. Why didn't you yell at me? What I said was horrible. Unforgivable. Why aren't you yelling at me now?"

I let out a long slow breath and walk into the living room. Heisman is curled up in a ball under the coffee table—his hiding spot during storms. "It's okay, buddy." I sit, feeling like the two-faced liar nobody knows I am.

Nicky follows me in and sits on the floor next to Heisman. He plops his head in her lap, enjoying the company, even in his anxiety.

I reach over and turn off her flashlight. Then I turn off mine, leaving us drenched in blackness.

"Jaxon?"

I don't want her looking at me when I tell her what I have to tell her. When I tell her what I've never told another soul except the dog with his head on her leg. The secret I've kept for two years so I could keep being the 'good' one. "I never yelled at you because I had no right. I never came after you because I was no better than you were. You thought it was all your fault, and I let you believe it. Hell, I let everyone believe it."

"I don't understand."

"I cheated on you, Nic. I cheated too. Only I did it first."

I hear her sigh. I feel her breath displace the hairs on my arm. I sense her emotions. The silence in the room is even more deafening in the dark. And it seems to last an eternity. I see things. I sense things. I anticipate things. But the one thing I fail to predict, the thing that throws me for a fucking loop, is what she says next. "I lied, Jaxon. I didn't cheat on you."

I turn on the flashlight. *"What?"*

Her eyes close. "I didn't cheat on you."

I stand and pace. And then finally, after all these years, I yell at her. "What the fuck, Nicky?"

"Jaxon. Sit down. Please."

"Don't tell me what to do. Who the hell lies about cheating when they didn't cheat? That makes zero sense whatsoever. You expect me to believe that?"

"I'm not sure it matters anymore, but it's the truth."

"Why? Why would you do that?"

She doesn't answer. She pets my dog instead.

I pace some more. Then it dawns on me, and I kick a hole in the living room wall—square through the Sheetrock.

She startles. Heisman runs over and leans into me protectively. "Fuck." I hold my foot and hobble to the couch. Trying to ignore the pain shooting up my leg, I shine the light away so she can't see me. "This whole time I thought you left because you couldn't live with what you'd done. I mean, I get that you wanted the job. But you could have asked me to go with you. I would have gone with you. But you didn't want me to. Goddamn you, Nicky."

"I wasn't going to be the reason you hated your life. You love Calloway Creek. You love your job. If you'd followed me to Oklahoma, you would have left everything behind. Don't you ever think that maybe we got married too soon? Sure, we were together for a long time, but people change after college. When they discover who they are and where they fit in the world. We wanted different things. We always wanted different things. We just didn't know it until it was too late."

"Well, you got one thing right. *You* are the reason I hate my life."

"Jaxon." She sighs loudly. "What about your job? Your family? Calista?" The last word exits her mouth like it tastes bitter.

"What *about* Calista? She dumped me, or haven't you heard?"

A hand covers her mouth. "Oh no. Because of me? The reunion?"

I shake my head. "It was a long time coming. It was never going to work out."

"Why not? She seemed… kind of perfect for you."

"Yeah? Well, it looks like I have a terrible knack for being able to pick which girls are perfect for me."

"I'm sorry."

"*You're* sorry."

"Yes."

My flashlight starts to dim. I go to the dining room and light some candles. "Shouldn't *you* be the one yelling at *me* now?"

"What would be the point?"

"The point is, *I'm* the bad guy here. I'm the one who cheated. I'm the one everyone should hate, not you. Nobody is going to blame you for going after your dream career."

She rubs that thing on the end of her necklace like a genie might come out of it, and it occurs to me that I haven't ever seen her without it. Not in person. Not even on the air.

She sniffs. "Can I ask why you did it?"

I feel like the scum of the earth when I hear her voice crack. I know she's holding back tears.

Returning to the couch, I sit, crossing my foot over my knee to rub my sore ankle. "Truth? I was jealous."

"Jealous of whom?"

"Not who—what. Your aspirations. Your drive. I'm a high school teacher. I love my job, but really, if I'm being honest, it's not like I set the bar for career aspirations. But you—you had passion. You wanted to make a difference."

"You're a teacher. You make a difference, Jaxon. Way more than I ever could."

"I appreciate that. But I'll never change the world. Not in the way that you want to with your goals of earlier warning systems and better forecasting. I had my job. I was comfortable in my life. I was ready to concentrate on us and starting a family. I was way ahead of where you were, and we became distant. I missed the closeness we had in college and the first year after. I missed you. You worked long hours at your internship, and I just…" I scrub a hand across my jaw. "I became some bitter version of myself."

She gets off the floor and sits on the opposite end of the couch, picking at the fabric like she always did when we fought—which was hardly ever. "Who was she? Do I know her?" Her hands steeple over her mouth. "Oh my gosh, was she at the reunion?"

"It's no one."

"You don't want to tell me. I get it. I probably don't deserve to know after everything."

I look away, not wanting to see how hurt she is. Because I know what she's feeling. I felt it myself two years ago when she dropped the very same bomb on me. Except her bomb wasn't real. Mine still haunts me to this very day. What I don't understand is why she seems to care so much after all this time. "Her name was Monica. She was at a bar in the city my brothers and I used to go to after Nighthawks games."

"Tag and Cooper knew?"

I shake my head. "Nobody did. Not a single, solitary soul. I could barely live with myself. So I pulled away. Don't you see? *I* drove the wedge between us, not you. Not your job. It was my fault."

"Did you see her again?"

"No. It was just the one time. And it was only a kiss, I didn't let it—"

"Wait, *kiss?*" she says in surprise. "You didn't sleep with her?"

"No. I didn't. But kissing is still cheating, Nic. And that makes me a goddamn bastard."

"Can you tell me about it?"

"You really want to hear the play-by-play of me ruining our marriage?"

She swallows hard. "You didn't ruin it, Jaxon. Believe me, it was a mutual effort. And, yes, I need to hear it. I need to hear it all."

I blow out a long breath, the memory of that night still fresh in my head. "She was there alone. On business or something. She was talking to all three of us. It was just fun conversation and innocent banter. Or so I thought. I swear I wasn't there to..." I close my eyes. "Tag and Cooper got up to play darts in the other room. The two of us sat at the bar alone. I guess I liked the attention. You were working mostly nights at your internship in the city, and with me teaching, it seemed we barely crossed paths. You had just turned down two jobs. Jobs I knew you wanted. And I knew you turned them down for me. And I knew I was an asshole to let you. There was unspoken tension between us. And we let it fester. While at the bar, I got a text from you saying you'd be late. It was the third time that week. I was sitting there thinking of how different we'd become, and she was right in front of me being all attentive and available. And then she kissed me. There was no warning. She just did it. And damn it, I let her. Before I could really comprehend what was happening, I was kissing her back. Because in that moment, I felt alive for the first time in a long time. But it didn't take long for my brain to take over and remind me of everything I was putting on the line with that one horrible mistake. So I ran out of the bar, took a cab all the way home, and got in the shower, scrubbing every part of myself raw as if that would somehow absolve me of what I'd done."

"It was shortly after my birthday, wasn't it?"

I nod in shame, still feeling as if it was just last night, not two years ago.

"I knew something had changed," she says. "But it was football season, and you had a lot going on with school and the team and the playoffs."

"It wasn't any of that. It was my guilt. It was eating away at me."

"And that's why you let me go." I watch a lone tear travel down her cheek. There was a time when I would reach over and wipe it. And although the urge is strong, I don't. "Oh, Jaxon."

Suddenly, swarms of what-ifs swirl through my head. What if I hadn't kissed that woman? What if she had never lied? What if I went after her? What if we were still together?

"I'll tell everyone," I say. "I see how women treat you around here—at the reunion. I hear them talking. Poor Jaxon being dumped by that selfish slut. I felt bad enough letting them think it even when I thought you'd cheated on me, but now…" My head falls back onto the couch pillow. "It's even more unfair letting people believe it was your fault."

"Don't bother. The damage is done. Besides, I'm still a liar. I'm still the person who left you."

"Nobody will see it that way once they know the truth, that I'm the one who broke our vows."

"You don't get it." She rubs her necklace thing again. "I'm still the bad guy, Jaxon."

"No, you aren't, and I can't have people—"

"I was pregnant."

Her words are like a punch to my gut. A knife to my very soul. "You were *what?*" I try to process what she said. "But you just told me you didn't cheat."

"I didn't."

The words bounce around in my head, blazing a fiery path all the way through my body. I catapult myself off the couch and circle the room. I stop when realization dawns. I lean over, hands on my knees, trying not to throw up. I peer over at her, hatred I've never known spewing from me. "You aborted my baby?"

"Please sit down, Jaxon."

"It's a simple yes or no answer, Nicky. Did you kill my fucking child?"

"I need to tell you the whole story."

My hands grip the hair on either side of my head, almost ripping it from my scalp, mainly to keep myself from launching an attack on her. "There's a story? Oh, well, if there's a story behind why you aborted my baby without my knowledge, please do tell.

I'm sure I'll understand how it was best for *you*." I walk to my bar cart and open a bottle of whiskey, not even bothering to pour it into a glass.

The backyard momentarily illuminates with flashes of lightening. Heisman jumps onto the couch and presses into Nicky. *Goddamn traitor.*

"Jaxon."

I hold up a finger to shut her up. I'm not nearly drunk enough to hear what she has to say. I take two more large swallows, then take the bottle over and sit in the chair opposite the couch—which is way nearer than I want to be to her right now. "Fine. Tell me—did you take pills to kill our kid or use a fucking coat hanger?"

Tears that mean nothing to me stream down her face. The urge to wipe them, to kiss them away, are gone forever with the words she uttered moments ago. Over the past few years, I tried to hate her. I never could. But now, in this moment, I understand hatred. I thought I hated the McQuaids, but that's nothing compared to how I feel about her. It's an all-consuming rage that I feel in every cell of my body. I didn't even know it was possible to feel this way about another human being. And the only reason she's still sitting on my couch instead of being pushed out my front door is that I need to hear her tell me. I need her to feel every fucking ounce of my pain so that it will stay with her for the rest of her miserable life.

Chapter Sixteen

Nicky

I know the next few minutes are going to be brutal. It's never something I was going to tell him. But tonight has become the night we purge all our secrets. And he deserves to know.

I rub my pendant with one hand and his dog with the other.

"Heisman, come here," Jaxon demands.

He lifts his head, looks over, then settles back against me.

"Heisman. Come *now*."

This time, his furry friend doesn't move at all.

"As if you haven't done enough," Jaxon spouts, "you have to break my goddamn dog, too?"

The lump in my throat is so large that I wonder if I'm even going to be able to speak. "Could I…" I clear my throat. "Could I have a glass of water, please?"

He laughs maniacally. "Oh, sure. Is there anything else I can get you? A cane to whip me with? A gun to put a bullet through my brain?"

I swallow over and over, my throat and eyes burning.

He huffs, gets out of his chair, and goes to the kitchen, coming back with a glass of lukewarm water. I drink, the water hurting as a bolus of it makes its way to my stomach. I put the glass down and blow out a long breath. "I didn't know I was pregnant until after I got to Oklahoma."

"And that makes everything—"

"Jaxon, you have to let me tell this. If you keep interrupting, I'll never get through it."

I watch as the bottle of whiskey meets his lips.

"I thought it was the stress of leaving you, lying to you, and starting a new job. I knew I hadn't felt right in many months, but it made sense to me. I'd spent weeks contemplating the job offer before I decided to leave. I felt sick over it. I lost a lot of sleep. So it came as no surprise when I missed a period or two and then had some spotting. Stress can do that to a woman's cycle. Being pregnant was never on my radar. I was on the pill and took it religiously."

"Your trusty phone alarm never failed to alert you," he says malevolently.

"Do you want to hear this or not? Because despite what you might think, this is hard for me, too."

Even in the dim light, I can see his eyes roll and his head shake from side to side.

"When I finally went to see a doctor, I was informed I was twelve weeks pregnant."

The whiskey drops to the floor when he bolts from the chair. "Twelve weeks?" He studies the mess and picks up the bottle. "Shit." He disappears and comes back with a rag.

I'm glad he's cleaning the floor. It keeps him from glaring at me.

"You have to understand that I was the new girl in a strange city. I was just starting out at WRKT. I thought if I was pregnant, I'd be sidelined. And then there was the whole single mom thing."

He looks up from the floor, daggers coming from his eyes. "Single mo—"

"Jaxon, please."

He throws up his hands in frustration, sits back in the chair, and takes another swig from the almost-empty bottle.

"I'd gotten all the brochures, set up an appointment. I even drove to the clinic. But I couldn't go through with it."

His eyes lock with mine. "Jesus, Nicky. Do I have a kid?"

My gaze meets the floor.

"Nic, tell me what the fuck is going on here."

"No, we don't have a kid."

"Then what the hell happened?"

"I tried to go back. I made two more appointments that week, but I never made it past the front door. I don't know if it was the thought of knowing what I'd done or the guilt I knew I'd feel over taking away the one thing I knew you wanted in life, but I couldn't do it. So I decided to have the baby."

"You're confusing the shit out of me, Nic."

"I was going to take a few days off and fly back here and tell you so we could figure things out. We lived across the country from each other—how would it work? Would he spend summers with you? Half the year with each of us? Would a baby somehow bring us back together?"

"Wait... *he*?" he says, his voice cracking.

I nod, tears in a free flow. I wipe my nose on the back of my hand. "I had a miscarriage at fifteen weeks."

He turns away, but I can hear the painful sob.

"I knew it was my punishment. For leaving you. For lying. For even considering ending the pregnancy. It didn't matter that over the course of the two weeks before I miscarried I fell in love with him. It didn't matter that I'd vowed to be the best mother I could and try to make things work. None of that mattered after the damage I'd done."

I'm ugly crying now, and Heisman practically climbs into my lap. "It was a Thursday. I'd just gotten home from work when I started bleeding. It wasn't a lot of blood, but enough to send me to the doctor. They did an ultrasound and couldn't find a heartbeat. I told them that was impossible; that the day before, I'd felt the baby move for the very first time. I'll never forget that feeling. It was the moment I felt like a mother. But they said he was gone, and they gave me three choices: go home and wait for labor to start within a few days, have them induce labor, or have a D and C. I chose the induction."

His eyes glisten with tears. "Oh my god."

"It wasn't without pain, but I refused any medication. I knew I had to feel every contraction. It was my penance. And when the baby came out, I was stunned. Jaxon, he was fully formed but so incredibly tiny. They let me hold him. He fit in the palm of my hand. That's when I discovered he was a boy."

Both of us are sobbing, our faces wet with agony and despair. He comes over and sits next to me, pushing Heisman onto the floor. He pulls me into his arms, and we cry. We cry for the life lost. The memories we'll never have.

We part and gaze sadly at each other. "Don't cry," he says, his thumbs brushing under my eyes to wipe my tears. When they continue to fall, he kisses them. Then he kisses *me*. And I let him. It's unlike any kiss we've ever shared. It's full of hurt and desperation. But it's exactly what I need in this moment. Being in his arms again is like finding myself after I'd been lost. I pull him closer, needing him more than I've ever needed anything. It's a visceral reaction. He's the oxygen in my lungs. The blood pumping through my veins.

Before either of us can fully comprehend it, we're removing each other's clothes. I tug off his shirt. He unbuttons my blouse. We toe off our shoes. We're naked in a matter of seconds. His hands are like fire when they touch my breasts. Sensations I haven't felt in years, or maybe ever, shoot through me.

His lips are strong and demanding, taking everything I'm willing to give. When his tongue tangles with mine, it's both a memory and a promise. A promise of what, I don't know. My fingers weave through his hair, keeping him pressed against me. Surely one of us will come to our senses and put an end to this. But not yet. The years of pain, they fade into the background. His hands on me, his lips, are somehow healing.

We break apart, breathing heavily, and stare into each other's eyes by candlelight, both of us wondering if this is really going to happen, perhaps marveling at the fact that it is. And before either of us has a chance to change our mind, I reach out and take his penis into my hand. He gasps but doesn't tear his eyes from mine. He's hard and throbbing, the tip of him wet, letting me know he needs this as much as I do. His fingers find my folds, tantalizing me, teasing me, maybe even challenging me. I arch into him, needing more. Needing this. Needing him. Then, without so much as a word between us, he kneels on the floor in front of me, pulls me to the edge of the couch, and sinks himself inside me.

Both of us cry out at the sensation. The sound is guttural. Tormented. Our eyes glisten as he moves oh so slowly. I rack my memories to find a single time when making love to him was this emotional. It was always sweet. Fun. Never filled with a feral need for each other. Never wrought with as much happiness as pain. Never feeling torturous and exhilarating at the same time.

He grunts and comes quickly, but I don't mind. This isn't about me. It's about us. Our connection. Our loss. Our devastation.

He collapses onto me when it's over. We embrace for a moment, then the lights come on and the moment is over. The spell is broken. The feeling has passed.

It's quiet outside. The storm is over. I don't know what to do. Do I dress and leave? Do we pretend this never happened?

He pulls away and studies my face, leaving me wondering what he's thinking. I'm sure I'm a sight. Makeup must be streaked down my cheeks. I wipe under my eyes. He removes my hand. "Don't. You're beautiful." He touches the pendant on my necklace, the only thing I'm still wearing.

"That's him," I say.

His eyes capture mine. He swallows hard.

"I had him cremated. He was so tiny. And someone at the hospital told me that people in my situation sometimes put ashes in jewelry."

He holds the pendant and rubs it between his fingers as more tears flow.

"Jaxon."

"Can we just… not talk for a minute? I need to process this."

We dress quietly, enormous questions lingering in the air around us. I busy myself. I go to the dining room and blow out the candles. I freshen myself up in the bathroom. I get sanitizing wipes and make sure the whiskey is all cleaned up. Then I assess what's left of the bottle, deciding I need a drink more than I've ever needed one. So I take one.

I break the deafening silence. "I'm sorry I never told you. As much as it affected me, I knew the pain I was feeling was nothing compared to what you would feel, and I wanted to spare you that."

"I need to believe you're telling me the truth, Nic. Were you really going to go through with having him? Were you going to tell me?"

"My bags were already packed. I was supposed to fly out the following day. I was grateful, you know. Not for the miscarriage, but for having it before you knew."

"You could have told me anyway. Maybe things would have been different."

"Or maybe we would have ended up in the very same place."

"I'm sorry you had to go through it alone," he says.

"It was of my own doing."

"You didn't cause the miscarriage. It wasn't a punishment, Nic. Those things happen."

I nod and pretend I agree. "Do you want to see a picture of him?"

He sits and puts his forearms on his knees. "You have a picture?"

"I do." I pull out my phone and page through to the one photo I have. The photo the nurse said I needed even though I tried to refuse. I hold my phone out to him.

He doesn't take it. He hesitates, breathing as heavily as he was when he was inside me.

"I didn't want a picture," I tell him. "But the nurse told me I should have one anyway. She said I didn't even need to look at it right then, but someday, when the pain wasn't so bad, I'd want it to remember him by. And she was right. I did. And now, you do too. It's okay, Jaxon. You can look. You need to look."

Finally, he takes my phone. Tears roll down his cheeks as he stares at the tiny baby in my hand. I'm holding him close to my heart, the blanket covering him removed so we could see his entire body. His perfectly formed body that never had a chance to grow.

Jaxon zooms in and traces the baby with a finger. "My god." He reaches over and grabs my hand. "Did you name him?"

I can't speak. I simply shake my head.

"Do you think we should?"

I bellow out a sob and nod. "Okay." I sniff and touch the pendant. "Billy?"

He squeezes my hand. Jaxon's middle name is William. I knew it's the name he'd want to give a son. He nods over and over as his tears soak the front of his shirt.

"Billy," he repeats, putting down the phone and pulling me into his arms.

Chapter Seventeen

Jaxon

Dawn breaks through the living room window. I'm on the couch. Nicky's head is in my lap. We cried each other to sleep. Then I woke up sometime around three a.m. and have been staring at her ever since. Last night was an absolute mindfuck. She never cheated. She was pregnant. The picture of our tiny baby. I run a finger along the edge of her pendant. What I wouldn't give to have been there. I want to be mad at her, but I find it nearly impossible after hearing what she went through. She was going to fly back here and tell me. We could have worked things out. Maybe it's not too late. I check the time and nudge her gently. "Hey."

Her eyes open and she smiles sadly.

"Don't you have to be at work?" I ask.

"I get Mondays and Tuesdays off."

I push a wisp of hair off her forehead. "What now?"

She sits up and tucks her legs beneath her. "I don't know. I mean, last night was…"

"Heavy."

"To say the least."

Heisman walks over and plops his head on the sliver of couch between us. "Come on, bud." I let him out the back door and leave it open. Then I fill his water and food bowls. "You want breakfast?" I ask Nicky, not knowing exactly where we stand.

"I..." She hesitates. "I should probably go."

Her words sting, but I don't try to stop her. "Yeah, sure."

She gathers her things and heads for the door. What's going to happen if she walks out? Last night was more than just devastating. It was the culmination of two years of regret, hopelessness, and sorrow. It was as amazing as it was agonizing. Suddenly, my heart pounds. I see a future without her, and it looks exactly like the last two years. *Empty*.

"Nicky, wait." I run up behind her. Somehow, I feel if she walks out the door it will be like last night never happened. I need to know it did. I need to feel her lips on my skin, her hands on my body. I need it like I need air. "I know we did what we did last night because we were overcome by emotion. But that doesn't change the fact that I'm glad it happened. I'm not expecting anything. And I know we both have baggage now. But... fuck... I don't want you to walk out that door."

She turns, gazes at me, then drops her purse and satchel on the floor. We come together and kiss, my tongue sweeping into her mouth, needing everything she'll give me, wanting everything she won't. I expect her to pull away. She doesn't. I pick her up, and she latches her legs around me.

I whisper in her ear. "I want to do everything to you that we didn't do last night."

One word escapes her. "Yes."

My room is dim. The sun isn't fully up, and my shades are drawn. I put her down on the bed. She glances around. "Nothing's changed much."

Unfinished EX

"That's not true." I nod to the bathroom. "I got a new toilet seat."

She laughs as I remove her clothes for the second time. I inhale the familiar scent of her skin, letting it permeate through me. She moans when I lick the supple cord of her throat. Christ, I'd almost forgotten what her moans do to me. She goes for the button of my jeans, but I brush her hand away, remembering how quickly I came last night. "Not yet. I owe you one first."

Her teeth draw the edge of her lower lip into her mouth in a sexy way that has my dick throbbing. She licks her lips. I trap them with mine, needing her to feel what the last two years without her has done to me. And unlike last night, I take my time with her. Tasting her. Savoring every kiss. Chronicling every touch. Because part of me knows this may be all she's willing to give.

My mouth works its way down, stopping to give ample attention to each nipple before traveling south. When my lips dust across her stomach, I think of the baby that was once inside. She holds me against her, and I know she's thinking of him too.

Going lower, I test her first with my fingers, dipping them inside to find her tight and wet. It's a place I never thought I'd go again, let alone twice in one day. It doesn't take long to find the spot I know drives her wild. It took me years to find it and another few months to perfect my manipulation of it. We made it a game to see how fast I could get her off with just my fingers inside her. It made me feel like fucking Tarzan to make her come that way, without even touching her clit.

I know when I've found it. She arches into me and makes 'the noise.' *Fuck*. I'm about to jizz inside my jeans at the sound. I think about Heisman taking his morning deuce. I think about my lesson plans for today. I think about anything other than how much I still fucking love the woman who's falling apart beneath me. Because if I think about that, I'll completely lose my shit.

"Jaxon… oh… god…"

I rub diligently, needing her to come harder than she has before. Needing her to need this as much as I do.

She grips my hair and shouts as her body convulses. I lower my head and press my tongue on her, extending her orgasm. Five seconds go by. Ten. Then she goes limp next to me, pulling her sensitive clit away from my continuous assault.

"Fucking hell, Nicky."

She smiles, her eyes half-lidded. "You can say that again."

I rid myself of every scrap of clothing and sidle next to her. She reaches for my cock and holds it in her palm. I remove it because I'm about to blow my load like a thirteen-year-old watching his first porn movie.

She sits up. "You said everything, Jax."

Her head lowers, and she takes me into her mouth. *Ho-ly shit*. I've been with two women since Nicky, mostly to try and fuck her out of my head, and I'm confident in saying nobody knows how to give a blow job like my ex.

My ex.

I almost deflate on the spot when I remember what we are to each other. But she doubles down on me and massages my balls, making me forget my own goddamn name. I'm coming in her mouth before I can even lie back and enjoy it.

A second later, she's jumping out of bed.

"Something wrong?"

She cringes. "I need water. I'd forgotten how much I hate the taste."

The bathroom sink turns on. I rise up on an elbow. "If you hate the taste so much, why swallow?"

She gargles, spits, then returns, walking naked through the room. "Because you always loved it."

"Sure, I love it, but not because you swallow. You can always finish with your hand." Something occurs to me. "What do you mean by you forgot how much you hate the taste? How long has it been?"

She shrugs. "A while."

I pull her down and pin her beneath me, needing the answer but afraid to hope what it will be. "Define a while."

"Two years, give or take."

Searching her eyes, I ask, "Which is it, give or take?"

"Fine. It's been over two years."

"Since you gave head or since you've fucked anyone?"

"Since I gave head. It's been a lot less since I've been with a man."

"How much less?"

She smirks. "About six hours."

"Nic. How long has it been?"

"You're the last one I slept with." Her eyes capture mine, and I know it to be true. "You're the only man I've ever been with, Jaxon. You're the only man I've ever done *anything* with."

I roll off her and rub my forehead, feeling guilty as hell. "Jesus Christ, Nicky." My heart soars and stings at the same time.

Heisman jumps on the bed and crowds her. I chuckle. "You're in his place."

"Or maybe he's in mine."

More shit is happening inside my heart. "Nic, what's going on here? Should we even be doing this?"

"I have no idea. All I know is that I never stopped thinking of you. And right or wrong, this feels good."

I pull her to me and kick Heisman off the bed. I rub my burgeoning hard-on against her. "Before we decide anything, how about we finish what we started?"

She smiles and climbs on top of me.

~ ~ ~

Thirty minutes and a few orgasms later, we're surrounded by sticky sheets and the heavy scent of sex. "I need a shower," I say. "And Heisman needs a walk."

She checks the time. "When is your first class? Nine fifteen?"

"I usually get there by eight thirty. But I'll make an exception today. I have an hour. Time for a quick walk and a shower. Join us?"

"I don't have any other clothes."

"Come here." I hold out my hand. She lets me pull her out of bed. It's a gesture that comes naturally. One that's been missing from my life. I guide her to the third bedroom.

Still naked, she runs her hands over the boxes in the corner. "You kept them?"

"You never sent for them."

"I thought you would have burned them or something. Why did you keep them?"

I shrug. "Didn't have any use for the room really." She stares me down. "What do you want me to say, Nic? Maybe I still wanted a small piece of you."

So many words go unspoken as she opens a box, sifts through it, and comes out with a pair of shorts and a shirt. "This will do."

We go back to my room and change, collect Heisman, and head out the front door.

Nicky stops short of the sidewalk. "Do you think this is a good idea? People might see us."

"So let them."

"They'll talk. You know how the rumor mill goes around here."

"Who gives a fuck what anyone says?"

"I guess I thought you did, Jaxon. You're the one who will have to deal with this. I'm out of here in a few months."

And reality sets in.

"Sorry," she says, looking sad. "Did I just ruin this?"

"You didn't ruin anything. We're adults. We can do whatever we want. I don't care what anyone thinks." I walk ahead. "You coming?"

As Nicky anticipated, we get looks from almost everyone we come across. People whisper to each other. Gawk at us. Sneer at her.

"Yeah, so you're going to have to do damage control," she says, after someone murmurs a nasty comment in the park.

I pull the tennis ball out of my pocket and throw it. Heisman dashes across the lawn to retrieve it. "Are we going to talk about the elephant in the room?"

"You mean about the fact that our divorce was finalized less than two weeks ago and we just slept together?"

I hold up four fingers. "Several times."

Heisman brings back the ball. *To her.* She throws it for him. "Okay, so let's talk."

"What do we do now?"

"I don't know. And, honestly, nothing has changed, right? I'm there, you're here."

"Is what happened last night and this morning going to happen again while you're here?"

"Do you want it to?"

"Stupid question, Nicky."

She smiles. "Okay then. Me too."

"So we're going to have sex and tell everyone to mind their own business and just see where it takes us?"

"I suppose. But Jaxon, my contract is up in two months. I have no idea what's going to happen after that. Marty thinks I might end up with multiple offers, which means I might not be going back to Oklahoma, but I'll probably end up somewhere else. And no matter what happens, I won't let you give up everything you have here to follow me."

"Marty?"

"My producer at WRKT."

"Should I be jealous?"

"I haven't ever slept with anyone but you, Jax. What do *you* think?"

I think I want to pound on my chest, pick her up and toss her over my shoulder, and hide her away so no other man can ever have her. *Hypocrite.* "I think I want to skip school and spend the day with you."

She shakes her head. "We both have jobs we need to do. Jobs that are important to us."

"Dinner, then?"

She smiles and runs over to Heisman before getting down on the grass to play with him. "I'll bring the wine."

Chapter Eighteen

Nicky

Mom is drinking coffee at the kitchen table when I walk in.

One time in high school when I'd snuck out to meet Jaxon, she was sitting in this same seat, sipping from the same cup, giving me the same over-the-rim expression that guaranteed I was going to be grounded for a month.

I roll my eyes. "I am twenty-seven now."

"A call or text wouldn't have killed you."

"I did text."

"At five thirty this morning."

I pour myself a cup. "I'm sorry. Things got crazy last night."

"At work? Because of the storm?"

"Not exactly."

"What are you wearing?" Her eyebrows shoot up. "You told me you lost that shirt years ago."

I plop down into the chair next to her and blow on my coffee in silence. Where do I even begin?

"Nicole Janine Forbes, what did you do?"

Victoria bounds down the stairs with her backpack. She takes in our stark expressions. "What did I miss?"

I pull out the chair next to me. "Sit." Then I take a deep breath, pull on my proverbial big-girl panties, and scoop my necklace out from under my shirt. "I have so much to tell you two."

~ ~ ~

I don't have to look out the window to know who is ringing the doorbell. Paige has been blowing up my phone with texts all day. *What's this I hear about you and Jaxon being seen together in the park this morning? … OMG, I just found out Jaxon and Calista broke up. Did you have something to do with this? … Girl, the rumor mill is churning up some serious shit. Will you please text me back?*

I did finally text her back. Not with details, but with an invitation to stop by after work. I laugh as I note the time before opening the door. "Did you *run* over here? Didn't class end ten minutes ago?"

She plows past me and drops her bag, breathing heavily. "Talk."

"Well, hello to you too."

"Hello, yeah, whatever," she says, pulling me into the living room. "Come on, you know I'm dying here. Your sister was a closed book today, even though I cornered her at lunch. I know she knows something. What did you do? Oh, my god, you slept with him." She squeals. "Please tell me you did the deed with your ex. Are you getting back together? Are you moving here? Oh shit, is he going to Oklahoma? What will you tell everyone? Like, can you undo the divorce?"

"Paige, slow down. You're getting way ahead of yourself. Do you want coffee?"

"Coffee?" She gives me crazy eyes. "This conversation calls for wine."

"Can't," I say. "I'm going out later, and I don't want to drink too much before."

"Going out? With *him?*" She claps. "Is this really happening?"

"First of all, yes, I'm going out with Jaxon. Not out, out. To his house for dinner."

Her eyebrows waggle. "Dinner? Is that code for getting naked and making up for lost time?"

I can't help my smile. "We already made up for lost time." I hold up four fingers.

"Four times!" More squeals. "You're killing me. Tell me everything."

By the time I finish regurgitating the whole story (again), Paige's eyes are red. *My* eyes are red.

"So that's it," I say. "That's everything."

Her head shakes in wonderment. "Nic, someone should write a book about this. Wait! Isn't Tag's friend Amber Thompson related to that famous author, Baylor Mitchell? You should definitely contact her. This is like the greatest love story of all time."

"Hold on now, you've got it all wrong. Jaxon and I aren't a love story. I don't know *what* we are."

"Nope. Not hearing it. You guys will get back together. I know it. Everyone knows you belong together."

"*Everyone* thinks I cheated."

"Tell them you didn't."

"Then they'll just say I'm a liar. Listen, this isn't about me trying to absolve myself. I've still done things I'm not proud of."

She puts her hand on mine. "I wish you would have called. I could have been there for you."

I nod. "I should have done a lot of things differently."

"What are you going to do?"

"I'm going to have dinner with him. Then I'm going to throw myself into my job. What else can I do? It's way too early to make plans or commitments. It's even too early to make assumptions."

"But you want him."

"I never stopped."

"And he wants you."

I shrug. "I mean, I think so."

"So what is there to plan?"

"Last night was a culmination of everything that happened two years ago. It was emotional. We were both hurting and had things that needed to be said. Maybe instead of it being a new start, it was closure."

"I'm calling bullshit on that."

My sister comes around the corner. "I'm calling bullshit too."

"Way to eavesdrop, Tor."

She drops her backpack behind the couch and plops down next to me. "I was in his class, Nicky. I seriously don't think I've ever seen the guy so happy."

My heart does a backflip. "He was happy?"

"That might be a slight understatement. I swear to God I saw him skip down the hallway. Who the hell skips? It totally gave me secondhand embarrassment."

It's painfully hard to try to contain my smile.

"See?" Paige says. "You have your answer. It definitely wasn't closure."

"Even if it wasn't, we're still right back where we were. My job here is temporary. His is permanent. He loves it here, and I would never ask him to leave. Even if he volunteered to, I wouldn't let him. He'd never be happy anywhere else." I get up and pace the carpet. "I should cancel dinner. I don't want to lead him on."

"Don't you think it's a little late for that?" Victoria asks. "Erm, *four* times?"

"Jeez, Tori, how long were you listening?"

"You should move back here," she says. "It's the only solution."

Paige huffs. "But then *she* would be unhappy. Why is it the woman who always has to give something up?"

"Either way, one of us would be unhappy." I sigh. "That's why this will never work."

"You're killing this before you even give it a chance?" Paige asks. "Forbes, you aren't half as smart as I thought you were."

"It's better to do it now than drag it out and end up in the very same place we were two years ago."

Paige stands and puts her hands on my shoulders. "Or perhaps you'll end up getting everything you've ever wanted. Nic, give it a chance. Don't go back to Oklahoma with even more regrets."

I rub my eyes, knowing she's right. "I have to go get ready, and there's an errand I need to run."

"What are you going to tell him?" Tori asks.

"Honestly? I have no idea."

~ ~ ~

Hands—shaking.
Heart—racing.
Mouth—dry.
Why am I so nervous?

Jaxon opens the door before I get a chance to knock. Heisman greets me first, rounding my feet and then sitting, begging for a pat. I kneel. "Hey, bud." I reach into my bag and pull something out. "I brought you this." I look up at Jaxon. "I hope it's okay."

"A sleeve of tennis balls? I think you just became his new favorite person."

A heavenly smell wafts out the front door. I stand. "Is that…?"

He holds the door open. "It is."

"Since when do you cook?"

"There are a lot of things you don't know about me." He laughs. "Okay, one. There's *one* thing you don't know about me."

"But lasagna? I tried to teach you a dozen times. You could never get the noodles quite right."

"Maybe I never wanted to."

I cock my head.

"Watching you cook was one of my favorite things to do."

He leads us into the kitchen, where I hand over the bottle of wine. "Good thing I got red. It'll pair well."

A low whistle escapes him when he examines it. "Nice bottle. Were you expecting the Pope?"

"Did I overstep? And I definitely didn't intend to—"

"Parade your very fat bank account in front of the guy who teaches high schoolers?"

Guilt consumes me.

"It's okay, Nic. I'm kidding. Anytime you want to bring over a bottle of Caymus, be my guest. I'll cook."

"What do you make besides lasagna?"

"Take your pick. I make a killer pot roast. My tacos are to die for. And I've perfected grilling steaks. Did you know the secret is to sear them for a minute on both sides? It locks in the flavor."

"I didn't know that. Looks like bachelorhood suits you." I regret the comment as soon as it leaves my mouth. "I mean… God, I didn't intend to be so awkward."

He retrieves two wineglasses, then leans against the counter, a smirk crawling up his jaw. "Are you nervous, Nicky?"

I let out a sigh. "Yes. Is that strange?"

He opens the wine and sets it on the counter to breathe. "I changed three times before you came over."

My eyes wander over him. He's wearing a blue button-up, sleeves casually rolled to the elbows. It matches his eyes. I always told him I loved him in blue. His black jeans fit snugly in all the right places. His slightly long and roguish hair surely makes him the product of all his female students' fantasies. How is he even more gorgeous today than he was a few years ago?

I nod to the bottle. "I guess I was trying to impress you. It was stupid."

"If you want to impress me, keep doing what you did last night." He winks. "And again this morning."

My face heats up. It surprises me. I don't think I've blushed in front of him since I was sixteen.

He opens the pack of tennis balls. "We have a couple of minutes. Want to toss him a few?"

Heisman waits patiently in the kitchen doorway, tail wagging when he sees the ball. I take it from Jaxon. "Let's go play fetch, Heisman."

He turns in a circle and beats us to the door.

"So about last night and this morning," Jaxon says with an air of hesitation. "We were kind of reckless. I should have asked if you wanted me to use a condom. Or are you still on the pill? And so you know, I've never gone without a condom except with you."

I throw the tennis ball across the backyard, not wanting Jaxon to see my face. It's hard for me not to picture him making love to Calista and kissing some faceless woman from the city, who in my mind looks like Marilyn Monroe. How many others has he dated?

"Three."

My eyes narrow. "Excuse me?"

"You forget how well I know you, Nic. You were wondering how many women I've… done things with since you."

"You don't have to tell me."

"There was the girl I kissed." He pinches the bridge of his nose and blows out a frustrated huff. "You have no idea how fucking sorry I am for that. If I could take it back…"

I shake my head. "Like we said this morning, we both did things we regret."

"My mom introduced me to Brittany, her friend's daughter from White Plains. We saw each other for a month or so last year. And that brings us to Calista."

By my count he's slept with two other women. A small number by most people's standards. Still, jealousy grips my insides at the thought of him with anyone but me. I try to push the emotion away. I have no right to feel it. I throw the ball, harder this time. "You've really expanded your repertoire." I sit, perch my head on my hands, and close my eyes. "Sorry, that was completely uncalled for."

"You don't think I've thought about you with other men a million times? You don't think I've tied them up and dismembered them in my dreams? Do you know how long I went around town suspecting everyone with a cock?" He takes the seat next to me. "Makes me a goddamn hypocrite."

"Can we agree to never again talk about who we did or didn't sleep with?"

"Hallelujah to that." His phone timer goes off. "I need to take the lasagna out. Want to help me make the salad?"

"Sure. Come on, Heisman, let's go inside." He trots over dutifully, and I ruffle his tuft. "You've trained him well. It's almost like he can understand us."

"You have no idea. I swear that dog is half human."

It feels eerily familiar when I open the refrigerator and get out the salad ingredients. Everything is where it always was, right down to the salad dressing in the lower right bin. It's as if time stood still.

"Holler if you need help finding anything," he says. Then he winks. He knows I don't.

I busy myself tearing lettuce. I figure now is as good a time as any to tell him my other news. "Back to our previous conversation. I'm not on the pill." I peek over. He's surprised, but almost in a way that makes him look pleased. For a second, my heart sinks. "Don't worry about it, though. I won't end up pregnant."

"Do I seem worried? And why not? You keep track of your cycle?"

I will not cry. I will not cry.

"After my miscarriage, I needed a D and C because some of the placenta remained attached."

He takes off the oven mitts and leans against the counter. "I feel an *and* coming."

"And nothing happened at first. It was a normal recovery. But as time went on, my periods became out of whack. I even missed some completely, which was never normal for me."

"Fuck, Nicky. Is this something we should have a glass of wine for?"

I shrug. "I have something called Asherman's Syndrome. It's a condition that can happen when scar tissue develops after a D and C. There are treatment options that can remove the scar tissue, but since I wasn't having any pain, and I wasn't planning a family, my gynecologist said doing nothing was the best option."

"But..." He runs a hand across his jaw.

"But it means it's highly unlikely that I can get pregnant." I pick up a tomato and paste on a smile. "Which is good, right? Since we didn't use protection."

He pours me a glass of wine. "Damn it, Nicky. I'm sorry."

I take a sip and swallow the tears burning my throat along with the wine. "I knew I was still being punished for what I'd done."

"Come here." He pulls me in for a hug. Being in his arms feels safe. It feels right. "None of this is your fault. I've had all day to think about this. You didn't cause the miscarriage, and you certainly couldn't have caused the complication. You're punishing yourself by even thinking it."

I pull away and nod to the baking pan. "We should eat before it gets cold."

He pours himself some wine. A very large glass of it. I can tell the news is eating away at him. This complicates things further. If he did want us to get back together, we may never be able to have children. I could have surgery to remove the scarring, but nothing is guaranteed. I may still have lifelong fertility issues. Will this change things? Do I want it to?

We dish out dinner and sit. "Can you tell me more about when it happened? Was anyone with you? How long did you get to hold him?"

Memories flood me as if it was yesterday. "I was alone. I didn't have good enough friends yet to confide in, and I hadn't told anyone here, not even my family. Not until today."

"I can't imagine you having to go through it by yourself."

"The nurses were incredible. Do you know when you have a miscarriage or a stillborn baby in the hospital they put angel wings on your door so nobody assumes it's a happy occasion? After he was delivered, they took him away, but then one asked if I wanted to see him. I was terrified. What would he look like? Would any parts of him be missing?"

"Jesus." His eyes fill with tears.

"I can stop."

"No. I want to hear all of it."

"I didn't want to see him, but they talked me into it and said I had better do it soon because his coloring would continue to change. They said it would offer me closure and allow me to start the healing process." My throat thickens. "They were right. It was the best decision I ever made. I was able to say hello and goodbye to him. I was immersed in the moment, hanging on to the seconds as if they were years. And though I only held him for a few short minutes, they were the best and worst of my life, if that makes any sense. For just a moment, I was a mother—something I never thought I wanted to be. It was surreal. They took the picture. I hugged him. And that was that. They took him away and sent him to be cremated, and I left the hospital with a hollow belly, empty arms, and a memory box."

"Memory box?"

"It was something the nurses put together. It has his handprints and footprints, a symbolic birth certificate, and the rest of his ashes in it. Sometime later, I added my wedding rings to it."

"I'd like to see it one day. And"—his voice cracks—"if it's okay, can I have the rest of the ashes?"

"It's at my parents' house."

He pushes his plate away. "Let's go."

"Now?"

"I'm not hungry anymore."

He strides to the front door with sheer determination. I quickly cover the meal and put it into the fridge. Then we collect Heisman and walk to my house.

Chapter Nineteen

Jaxon

This past week has been incredible. It's like Nicky and I are teenagers again. We've done a lot of sneaking around, mainly because the gossip mill is in full force, and we don't want to feed it.

Neither one of us has talked about what happens at the end of her contract. We're either in denial or trying to live in the moment. Maybe it's a bit of both.

She even showed up at the football game on Friday. She wore a ball cap and stood off to the side so nobody would see her, but I couldn't have been happier.

"Get your lazy ass off the bed," I tell Heisman, wondering if he's ever going to have to find another place to sleep. Nicky hasn't slept over again, not since we fell asleep on the couch. But that doesn't mean we haven't done a lot of bedtime-type things. *A lot.*

I almost trip over a package on the welcome mat when we go out for our morning walk. "Oh shit," I say to Heisman, who's sniffing it. "Is this…?"

Nicky said I could have the rest of the ashes, but she asked if she could do something with them for me. Who was I to deny her? After all, she knows me better than anyone.

"Should I open it now?" I ask my walking partner. He sits. "I'll take that as a yes."

We go back inside. It's a small FedEx package. I have no idea how long it's been out there. Must have been delivered early this morning. I set it on the coffee table and study it. **Saintly Treasures** it reads. And it was delivered to Nicky's parents' address. *She* must have dropped it off.

I open it. It's a box within a box within a box. When I get to the final one, it's got angel wings on the outside. *Angel wings*—like the ones Nicky said were on the door of her hospital room. I draw in a deep breath and lift the lid. Inside is a ring. A large, chunky men's ring. The center of the ring is the same blueish color as Nicky's pendant. It's slightly translucent, so you can tell ashes are inside but it's not obvious. For all anyone knows it could be sand. I remove it from its velvet home and examine the sides. The date she delivered him is on one side. On the other, one word: *Billy*.

I slip it onto the ring finger of my right hand. It fits me to a T. If I had to pick something out myself, it wouldn't have even come close to being this amazing. I stare at it knowing she must have pulled some serious strings to get this done so quickly.

"I fucking love that woman," I tell Heisman. "But don't go telling her that. I shouldn't play all my cards just yet."

I text her.

> **Me: Got the ring. I couldn't have picked anything more perfect. Thank you.**

Heisman nudges me, growls softly, and goes to the door. "Okay, okay, I'm coming."

Outside, I see a *For Sale* sign going up in my neighbor's yard. I stop in front of the house and shout to where Mr. Papadakis is watching the realtor from the front porch.

"You're moving?" I ask.

He descends the front steps and walks over, coffee in hand. "Been here for decades. Raised our kids here. But it's too much yard for me to handle."

"I'd be happy to mow it for you."

"You do too much as it is. Painting the fence. Fixing my mailbox. Pressure washing my driveway. It's time Mirna and I retire to someplace smaller. We plan to spend the proceeds on trips to see the grandkids, and maybe one to Paris. Mirna always wanted to see France."

"Well, it sure has been a pleasure having you as my neighbor."

"I'm happy to say I feel the same way, Jaxon." He pats Heisman. "You enjoy your morning walk."

~ ~ ~

While this week's football game will most likely be a walk in the park, two weeks from Friday we play our primary rival. We need to gear up for it *now*. I practice my guys hard. Run all the routes. Do all the drills. They're a good team, and I get immense satisfaction being their coach.

"Don't worry." Eric smacks my shoulder. "We're going to kick the shit out of the Bruins."

I thought he might be mad at me. He's been avoiding me all practice and giving me strange looks. Not that strange looks are, well… strange these days. Everyone is talking, whispering, and gossiping about Nic and me. But this is Eric. We've been friends for two years.

"I hope you're right. We've lost to them three years in a row. We're due." I turn and shout, "Pack it in, guys!"

Eric stays close, giving me more unusual stares as our players put the equipment back where it belongs and head to the locker room.

"What is it with the skittish glances all afternoon, man?" I finally ask him. "You got something to say, spit it out."

"Listen, so I know you and Nicky are back—"

I glance down at the ring. "We're not back together." *I'm not sure* what *we are*. "We're just having fun while she's in town."

"Whatever it is, I think it's great. And you seem to be completely over Calista."

"Yeah, so?" I narrow my eyes. "What's this about?"

He squares his shoulders. "I was wondering—hoping really—if you wouldn't mind if I… took her out."

I bend over laughing. "That's what this whole dog and pony show was about? You wanting to get with Calista?"

"I know there's a code between friends. Exes are off-limits. And six months ago, I swear you beat me to her by about two minutes. I was going to ask her out, but then I saw you together in the park walking your dog."

"Damn. Wish you would have. Would have saved me a lot of drama."

"So you don't mind?"

"Nah. She's great. Just not great for me."

"Good. Because we've already been out." He steps back. "Twice."

"Dude, I'm not going to deck you. I think it's a good idea. But I appreciate the ask." I chuckle. "What would you have said if I told you I wasn't cool with it?"

"It's you, Jaxon. You're the most agreeable guy on the planet."

"Maybe that's not such a good thing. It's what had me getting with Calista in the first place when I knew it wasn't a good idea."

"She doesn't hate you, you know."

"I know. She actually smiled at me in the hallway yesterday." Realization dawns. "Wait, she smiled at me. You're fucking." Snickers from a few players strolling by remind me I shouldn't be talking so loudly. "You're fucking?" I say again, quietly this time.

"You're not jealous, are you?"

"Jealous, no. Surprised maybe. She seemed pretty into me."

"Well, now she's into *me*."

I pat his back, and we start for the locker room. "Congratulations, man. I'm happy for you."

"Thanks. I get the idea Calista is a *love the one you're with* kind of girl. But I guess I'm cool with that as long as *I'm* the one she's with."

My phone vibrates in my pocket.

> **Nicky:** I'm glad you like it. Sorry I didn't get back to you sooner. It's been a heck of a day. And I've got some good news.

> **Me:** I've got some interesting news myself.

> **Nicky:** You first.

> **Me:** Eric, my assistant football coach, is dating Calista. And apparently they're already pretty tight. Guess I'm an easy guy to get over.

Nicky: Believe me. You're not.

Hope, or something like it, dances in my gut. Is it possible she wants more than what we have?

Nicky: Now me. Makenna Kendall wants two more months of maternity leave, so they extended my contract through the end of the year.

Me: No shit? That's great.

Eric nudges me. "What's up? You win the lottery or something?"

I look up and raise a brow.

"You're smiling from ear to ear, man."

"It's Nicky. She found out she's going to be staying in town longer."

"I guess that's good. But you know that'll make it even harder when she leaves."

I stop walking. He doesn't. His words sink in. *Fuck*. He's right. But I don't care. I want her for as long as I can have her.

Nicky: I'm glad you think so. See you tonight?

Me: Thought we'd try the whole lasagna thing again.

Nicky: Yum! You certainly know the way to a woman's heart. Later.

I reread the text. Was that just a saying, or is there a deeper meaning?

Chapter Twenty

Nicky

In the break room, I stare at a picture on my phone, one I took a few days ago. He's wearing the ring. As far as I know, he hasn't taken it off since he got it. Some days I still can't believe all this is happening, that we've spent the past month acting like teenagers falling in love.

But love is not a word either of us has said. Because maybe we both know once that happens, things get more complicated. Right now, life is good. Fulfilling. Easy. It's like the old days before we were married. Before we had to become grown-ups and figure out adulting.

Brenton walks by with his lunch. "Handsome guy."

"He's my ex."

He nods. "Have a few of those myself."

"Except, I think he's my boyfriend."

"Well, now, that makes things a bit more complicated."

I shake my head. "You have no idea."

Brenton Carmichael appears on the five p.m., six p.m., and eleven p.m. weekday newscasts. He's our chief meteorologist and XTN's longest-standing weather forecaster. And it shows. The lines creasing his forehead and face speak of decades of long hours, storm chasing, and endless reporting. And his short mane of fully gray hair gives him that air of wisdom and grace. As I take him in, though, it dawns on me that if I ever make it to a position like his, I'm sure Barry would make me dye my hair, get Botox, and have lipo.

So unfair.

"You're doing exceptionally well," Brenton says. "I've watched many of your clips. I see good things for you ahead."

I feel like I should jump up and down, high-five someone, or do a fist pump. But this is Brenton Carmichael. Doing any of those in front of him would make me look like a complete idiot, not to mention undermine the professionalism he just complimented me on. So while I'm about to burst at the seams, I control my enthusiasm and thank him kindly. "That's some kudos coming from you."

"You earned it, young lady. Keep up the good work."

"Will do. I hear you're on your way to California?"

"That's why I'm here." He slaps a paperback book against his palm. "Left my book here. Needed it for the long flight."

"Those poor firefighters. I did some field reporting on some during the wildfires in Arizona."

"We'll hold down the fort," Tom Killian says, sweeping in behind us.

Tom is a weather anchor and senior meteorologist; not to be confused with chief meteorologist. He's second only to Brenton and appears on the weekday morning show, sometimes co-anchoring the third hour. Tom will be on standby to cover Brenton's spots, and I'll be on standby to cover Tom's. Basically, that means I'll be on call for the rest of the week. But it also means

I could get weekday airtime—*on XTN*—which would be amazing. Something else I have to contain my excitement over.

"Hey, Tom."

He takes the seat next to me. "You two see the low-pressure system off Bermuda yet?"

"Doesn't concern me," Brenton says.

I was going to say I was watching it like a hawk, but now I feel it would make me seem stupid in front of two men who are considerably smarter than me. "Yeah, same," I say, then mentally kick myself. I should be able to speak my mind. But I'm a visitor in their house.

Brenton leaves, Tom eats in silence, and I pack up my trash, vowing to actually have a damn opinion next time.

~ ~ ~

Truman's Grocery is right next to the train station. Jaxon and I hadn't made plans for tonight, but with my schedule this week up in the air, who knows when I'll get another chance to make him dinner. So I'm surprising him with a meal—all assuming the key hidden under the rock next to the third porch railing hasn't been moved.

I'm inside the store perusing the packages of chicken when I see Regan Lucas and Ava Criss, both small-business owners on McQuaid Circle. They whisper to each other before approaching me. Here we go.

"I heard a rumor," Regan says.

"Surprise, surprise," I say in a far too bitchy tone for someone visiting *their* stomping ground. "Sorry. It's just sometimes all the gossip can be overwhelming."

Ava cocks her head. "Rumors aren't necessarily true, but gossip usually is. So the story about you not cheating on Jaxon. Rumor or gossip?"

My eyebrows shoot up.

"Regan heard from Amber, who heard from Quinn, who said Tag told him you never cheated on his brother."

I'm going to have words with Jaxon's brother later. "I didn't. But that makes me a liar." I pick up a package of chicken, pretending to inspect it.

"Why'd you say it then?" Regan asks. "Surely you knew this town would brand a scarlet letter on your forehead."

I shrug. "In hindsight, it was a mistake, but at the time, I didn't see any other way."

"So you did it to be a martyr?" Ava asks, hand to her chest.

I motion to Regan. "Perhaps you should look up the definition of a martyr in her bookstore, because that's the last thing I am." I pinch my brows. "God, that was so mean of me to say. I should quit talking."

"We get it," Regan says. "You're tired of being talked about. And believe me, you're talked about a lot. Like really a lot."

Oh joy.

"And I for one think it was kind of a badass move putting your job above all else," Regan continues. "Who says only men are allowed to do that?"

"I should have figured out a way to have the job *and* the man."

"Well, you have them both now," Ava says. "Rumor has it you've been spending a lot of time together."

I flash a smile. "You mean *gossip?*"

Ava claps. "Oh, I love a good ending to a love story."

I cough. "Wait, no. We're spending time together, end of story." My heart twists because it wants a lot more of this story to be written.

"Guess we'll see," Regan says with a grin. "Hey, what are you doing next Tuesday evening?"

Searching my mental calendar, I come up blank. "I try to stay to myself, so not much."

"You know Maddie Foster from the flower shop?"

"Sure, Tag's fiancée. Well, I don't *know her* know her, but we've crossed paths."

"The three of us meet for coffee behind the ice cream shop every Tuesday evening. Want to join us?"

Friends. What I wouldn't give for them. Paige is great, but she's got her own circle. I need more. "Thank you, that would be amazing."

"Seven o'clock," Ava says. Then they walk away, elbows entwined.

I pull out my phone and start a text to Paige.

Me: You'll never guess who invited me to hang—

Someone walks in front of me, and I stiffen. Calista Hilson. I pretend not to see her and finish my text.

—OMG, Calista is here.

Paige: Calista Hilson invited you to hang out?

Me: No, Regan and Ava did. Calista just walked up to the meat department at Truman's.

Paige: I'm glad to see you finally showing yourself in public again. I was worried you never would after what went down at the reunion. We still having drinks Thursday?

Me: Absolutely. Hey, she's staring at me but trying to make it seem like she's not. I have to go.

Paige: I want details later.

Me: Always.

I look up and smile, trying to seem casual. "Hey, Calista."
"Hi."
Short. Sweet. To the point.
"How are you?"
"Fine. Good. Great." She picks up a pack of steaks. "You?"
"Yeah, same."
"Good. Well, bye."
If that wasn't the most awkward conversation I've ever had.
Fifteen minutes later, I'm dropping my bags on Jaxon's front porch. I run my fingers along the spindles of the railing. One, two, three. I crouch down and pick up the rock below. Underneath is a slim tin can. In the can is the key.
I smile.

Unfinished EX

When I look up, a woman is standing on the sidewalk, two dogs on leashes at her side. Her eyebrows are raised.

"Uh, hi," I say with the confidence of a novice burglar. "You must be Mr. Calloway's dog walker."

"Actually, I'm Heisman's dog walker. Mr. Calloway can walk himself."

I laugh nervously and hold up the key. "I was just"—I point to my bags—"coming over to make dinner."

"Mr. Calloway didn't leave you a key?" she asks suspiciously.

I don't recognize this woman, and I have no idea if she knows my relationship to him. "He didn't have to since I already knew where to find one."

She appraises me. "Should we give him a call?" She pulls out her phone.

I step forward. "Oh, no. He's expecting me. He's still at football practice. I was…" *Wow, I'm a bad liar.* "Okay, yeah, he has no idea I'm here. I was going to surprise him with dinner. I'll walk Heisman. I won't tell him you didn't, so you'll still get paid. It's no trouble."

Her head cocks. "You're that new weather lady on the news. I used to watch Makenna what's-her-name."

I offer my on-air smile as well as my hand. "Nicole Forbes. So nice to meet you, Ms…"

She shakes and one of the dogs sniffs my leg. "It's just Denise."

The expression on her face tells me my status might be more important than her suspicions. "So we're all good?" I ask, still smiling.

"Pretty necklace," she says. Then she turns and goes back down the walk.

Greeting me at the door is a happy dog. "Hello, Heisman." I leave the key on the foyer table and pull a toy from the bag, snapping the tag off it. "Here you go." I throw it across the hardwood floor, and he chases after it. "Let me mix up this casserole, and then we'll go for a walk."

I guess he recognized the word *walk,* because he drops the toy, sits in the doorway to the kitchen, and watches my every move, tail thwapping the hardwood.

"That ought to do it." I set the oven timer for thirty minutes and take Heisman out the front door, pulling it closed behind me. "Shit!" I say, failing to stop it before it latches. I jiggle the handle. Yup—locked. I totally forgot the inside handle sometimes did that. We always swore we were going to have it replaced. I can't believe he hasn't after all this time. It's the reason the key is under the rock. Shortly after buying the house, we got locked out one night after a run. We were on a shoestring budget because I had an unpaid internship, and after-hours locksmiths were expensive. So we went around back and fell asleep on the lawn furniture. It started to rain in the middle of the night. We didn't run for cover. We made love right there in the backyard in the rain. It's one of my favorite memories.

I peer down at Heisman. "Nothing we can do about it now. I just hope your dad is home within thirty minutes."

Dad.

My heart lurches. I've never said the word out loud. I grab onto my pendant as we walk. Jaxon always wanted kids. *Two girls,* he'd say. *None of that boy shit. I grew up with a bunch of cocky brothers.*

I wonder what kind of father he would have been.

The best kind.

Twenty minutes later, Heisman and I wait on the front porch. I check my watch every few minutes. Finally, after another thirty-five, the familiar Honda pulls up.

"Hurry!" I say when Jaxon gets out.

"Where's the fire?"

"Maybe in your house."

He runs up the walk. "Seriously? And... what are you doing with my dog?"

"Long story. Just open the door, please." He lets me in, and I race to the oven. Smoke plumes out when I open it. The smoke detector blares. Heisman barks. I throw the charred casserole into the sink and grab a dishrag, waving it in circles over my head to dissipate the smoke. When I look over at Jaxon, he's bent over laughing. "You think this is funny?"

"It's hilarious."

I throw the dish towel at him. "You're taller. You do it."

After opening some windows and airing the place out, the piercing sound abates and Heisman calms.

Arms come around me and secure my back to his front. "You getting romantic on me, sneaking in and making dinner?"

I stare at the inedible remains of the casserole in the sink. "Looks like it was all for nothing."

He squeezes me tighter. "Not for nothing." My hair gets brushed aside, and his lips touch behind my ear. "I wasn't really hungry. For dinner, anyway."

Tingling sensations travel through me at the feel of his breath on my neck. "So you're not mad?"

"Mad?"

"That I broke into your house."

"Let's see, you went to an actual public place, bought food, made dinner, and walked my dog. No, Nicky, I'm not mad."

The erection pressed into my backside tells me he's being truthful. "*Burned* dinner is more like it."

"We'll order takeout." He spins me around. "But first…"

I'm lifted onto the counter. Nimble fingers unbutton my blouse. The two halves gape open. He teases the exposed skin with his thumb, running it from my chin to the waistband of my pants, causing my skin to pebble.

"I love that I can do that to you." His tongue follows the same line. "I love that I can do a lot of things to you."

My pants get unbuttoned as his heated stare makes promises of what's to come. I lift my butt off the counter, and he slips the clothes off my lower half, dropping them and my shoes onto the floor. Heisman comes over, sniffs them, then takes off with my panties. Jaxon runs after him, retrieving the undergarment before exiling his dog to the backyard. Poor Heisman.

"Way to ruin the moment," Jaxon gruffs before coming back into the room. Then he realizes I've added more clothes to the pile and am sitting completely naked on his counter, legs open just enough to be a tease.

"Fuck dinner," he says. "Do *this*"—he strides over—"every day. Break in and do this." He falls to his knees, still fully clothed, and puts his mouth on me.

The sensation of his tongue is overwhelming. He's done this a dozen times since I've been back. And hundreds, if not thousands, of times in the past. Yet he never fails to make it seem like the first time. Like it's an unexpected gift he cherishes. Like he's grateful somehow. Grateful for me—even after everything I did.

He drapes my legs over his shoulders. I lean back and brace myself against the counter, careful not to bang my head on the cabinets. Not that I'd feel it. Not that I'd feel anything over the sensation of him completely ruining me. It's a welcome devastation. One I missed out on for so long.

My clit becomes stiff and tender, each lick, suck, and swirl sending me higher. His hands grasp my ass, securing me against him when he feels me coming. He has no intention of pulling away until he's extracted every quiver. His name echoes through the room. His hair gets trapped in my fingers. His head gets squeezed between my thighs.

Finally, he retreats, sitting back on his haunches, his shimmering mouth in a full-on smile. "I think I like this dessert before dinner thing."

I giggle and slip off the counter. Naked, I retrieve my phone, pull up a food delivery app, and order his favorite.

His eyebrow raises. "Checking your email?"

My phone goes back into my purse. "Ordering food. It'll be here in forty minutes." I wiggle my bare ass as I walk toward the bedroom. "I wonder what we could do in forty minutes."

Laughter follows me. Then I'm swept into his arms.

~ ~ ~

It's still completely dark outside when Heisman worms his way between us.

"Get off," Jaxon murmurs, nudging him with his foot.

"Let him stay," I say sleepily. "He was here first."

"Yeah, but I want *you* to be here last."

Suddenly, despite the pre-dawn hour, I'm not tired anymore. It's been a month, and neither of us has said anything remotely indicating a future. I've thought it. Every day, I've thought it. Surely he has too, but things have been going so well that I surmise neither of us wanted to jinx it.

I can't see him in the dark, but I'm sure his eyes are open, and he's staring in my direction.

"Nicky?"

"Yeah."

"Did I scare you?"

"Yeah."

He searches for my hand, holding it tenderly upon finding it. "I want to do this." I stiffen. He notices. Now he *does* kick Heisman out of the way. He pulls me to him. "Do you want to be with me?"

"Of course I do. But Jaxon, we're right back where we were before."

"We're not. We're older now. Wiser. We both know what we want. Who says we can't have a bicoastal relationship?"

"We'd never see each other."

"Have you heard of this amazing new thing called the internet? It lets you connect with people anywhere in the world. It would be like we were right there with each other."

I wiggle into him. "Well, not *just* like it."

"It could work, Nic. I'll fly to Oklahoma. I get two weeks off over the holidays, a week for spring break, and another few weeks in June before the start of summer football workouts. And when it's not football season, I could even come for the occasional weekend. You get vacation time, too. You could come back here. We probably wouldn't have to go more than a month without seeing each other. And what if Makenna decides not to come back to XTN and they offer you the job permanently?"

"Okay, whoa. Let's not get ahead of ourselves. That probably won't happen."

"Even if it doesn't, I'm willing to do the traveling thing. I want this to work. Don't you?"

My phone rings. I know I have to answer it. Nobody calls at four a.m. unless it's an emergency. I push myself out of his arms and grab it. It's Barry. "What is it?" I ask, trying to pretend like I was asleep and not having what could amount to be one of the most important conversations of my adult life.

"We need you in North Carolina."

My heart races. I bolt up and flip on the light. "Invest 48-L?"

"So you've been doing your homework."

I put him on speaker and pull on my clothes. "What do I need to do?"

"It's blown up overnight. It's now a tropical depression, and our models have it quickly turning into Tropical Storm Louisa as early as this afternoon. Chris and your crew are already on their way to your house. ETA twenty minutes. You won't be able to make it to Wilmington, where we think it'll make landfall, but if Chris can drive like a bat out of hell, you might make it out to Nags Head in time to catch some outer bands coming in. Throw some shit in a bag and be ready."

The line goes dead. I look at Jaxon, stunned. "What are you waiting for?" He pulls on jeans. "Let's get you the hell home."

"You're not mad?"

"Nicky, this is what you live for. Go chase the storm or whatever." He comes around the side of the bed. "Just be careful."

I glance at the bed, knowing we've left so much unresolved. "What about…"

"I'm not going anywhere, babe. But Louisa is."

It's not until after he races me home, I quickly pack, and am on the road heading south that I have time to think about things. Three years ago if I was asked to stay late at work, got called away from dinner, or, God forbid, woken in the middle of the night, Jaxon would resent it. And now he's… *supportive?*

Hours later, I'm jolted awake by motion of the van. I rub my eyes and study the GPS. "Do you think we'll make it?"

Jessie, one of the other crew members making the trip, hands me my laptop. "Better get on this thing. The storm has shifted. Not only will we make it, we might end up in the fucking eye."

Cheers erupt from all four of us.

My adrenaline spikes.

I've waited my whole life for this.

Chapter Twenty-one

Jaxon

I check the weather app during my planning period and almost drop my phone. The storm has shifted, and it's headed right for... *Nags Head?*

Me: Uh, Nicky? Have you seen the radar?

I don't get a single paper graded or lesson planned. Is it horrible of me to hope traffic was so bad they couldn't make it? What am I thinking? Everyone will be leaving Nags Head, not driving toward it. Only crazy people do that. Unless they do that traffic flow reversal where they use both sides of a freeway to evacuate. Surely they won't be able to go out to an island everyone is trying to get off of.

In the absence of her reply, I stalk The Weather Channel. Louisa is a full-on tropical storm now. It's not expected to become a hurricane by the time it makes landfall, so I guess there's that.

The final bell rings. I head to the cafeteria for the team meal.

Drake, my defensive coordinator, doesn't fail to notice my unusual pre-game silence. "Everything okay?"

I nod and barely look up from my phone.

"Damn," my strength and conditioning coach says, looking over my shoulder. "Hell of a storm."

"I'm quite aware." I slap my phone on the table and choke down some barbeque.

"Why do you care about a storm down in North Carolina?" the athletic trainer asks. "It won't affect the weather up here."

Eric and I share a look. He's the only one of my guys who knows about Nicky and me.

"I guess I shouldn't care, then."

After our meal, the players and coaches head off to the offensive and defensive meetings, then the players get taped and dressed. The whole time, I'm trying to keep my thoughts off Nicky. After all, this is the biggest game of the year. The last thing I need is for my mind to be four hundred miles away.

Just before warm-ups, I get a text.

Nicky: I have. It's amazing.

Me: Where are you?

Nicky: Nags Head.

Me: Shit, really?

Nicky: Don't worry about me. I've got a cameraman and two crew members who will be spotting for me the entire time. We're one of the few teams that got here before they initiated the contraflow lane reversal. Do you know what that means? Other stations may

even carry my feed. NBC, ABC, CBS. Jaxon!!!!!

Me: I'm... excited for you. Damn, it was hard to even type that. Be careful, Nic.

Nicky: I have to go. Please don't worry. Bands are coming in stronger, and the power has been going in and out. If you can't contact me, don't panic. Cell towers may either go out or be overwhelmed.

Me: You're making this so much better.

Nicky: Sorry. Just trying to prepare you. Hey, good luck tonight. Go Cavs!!!

Me: Somehow I feel I'm the one who should be wishing you luck.

Nicky: Not necessary. Bye.

Not necessary my ass. TWC is saying this may only be a tropical storm, but it's a strong one, and it's moving slowly. That could mean more rainfall, higher storm surge, and possibly higher wind gusts.
I think.
Fuck.
The urge to call her and beg her to get somewhere safe is strong. But I'm not going to be the boyfriend who keeps her on a short leash. Hell, I'm not even sure I'm her boyfriend. We never

finished our conversation. At this point, the only thing I know for sure that I am to her is her ex.

A hand grips my shoulder. "She's a big girl, Jaxon," Eric says. "This is what she does for a living."

"Is it?" I shake my head. "I don't even know if she's done this before. Yeah, she chased tornadoes and shit, but those come and go quickly, and you don't actually put yourself in the direct path. This is different. She's on an island with no way out, and it's coming for her."

"I watch that Cantore guy all the time. He's usually the one in the direct path. As far as I know, he never has problems."

"He's a lot older and has decades more experience."

"I'm sure her team isn't going to let her do anything dangerous."

I laugh. "Simply by being there, they're doing something dangerous."

"You know what I mean." He picks up a football and twirls it on the tip of a finger. "So, hey, is this going to fuck up your head? We do have kind of a big game tonight."

"No. I'm good." I look at my phone and check my messages. "But listen, you may have to hold on to this for me, or I might check it obsessively."

He takes it. "Good idea. Nothing you can do about it anyway. But what you can do is coach our guys to a win. You up for it?"

"Hell yes, I am."

"Then let's get through warms-ups, and then you go give them the best damn pep talk of your life and lead them out on the field like you mean it."

~ ~ ~

Unfinished EX

Halftime rolls around, and I'm impressed with myself. I haven't once asked to see my phone. We're only down by a field goal. We have a real chance this year. People cheer as we trot off the field. Someone yells from the stands, "Dope video of your ex. She still alive?"

I glance up, but no one claims the shout.

"Eric." I hold out my hand.

"You said not to give it to you."

"I don't care if you have twenty pounds on me. I will fucking tackle you to the ground and show our defensive backs how it's done if you don't hand me my goddamn phone right now."

He reluctantly retrieves it and hands it over. "Guess Drake and I will rally the troops," he says while I type in Nicky's name.

"Fuck!" I shout at the first hit I get.

He reads the headline over my shoulder: **XTN meteorologist struck by debris**.

"Deal with them," I say, nodding to the team. "Say something inspirational."

He looks worried. "I hope she's okay, man."

I run into the athletic office and shut and lock the door behind me. If I'm about to find out she's hurt—or worse—I don't need some punk-ass teenager walking in on it.

With my back pressed to the door, I hit play. Nicky is reporting. She's wrapped in an all-weather jacket that is cinched over the top of a baseball cap on her head. She's barely able to keep her feet in place. Behind her, water runs in sheets across the road that looks more like a raging river. Every few seconds, she has to shore up her stance and wipe off her face.

"Thanks, Lester. We're back again from Nags Head on Bodie Island, one of the Outer Banks barrier islands here in North Carolina. As you can probably see, the winds have picked up quite a bit since our last feed. You can see here"—they zoom in on the device she's holding—"I've measured the sustained wind speed on my handheld anemometer at forty-five miles per hour, that's up from thirty miles per hour just a half hour ago. I'm sorry to say that means they will have closed all bridges to the Outer Banks by now. If you're local and watching this, take cover in a sturdy building above the ground floor, as storm surge could be high with slow-moving Louisa."

She holds up her handheld device for a moment. "The gusts are measuring close to sixty-five. When we talk about gusts, that means a sudden burst of wind speed that typically lasts less than twenty seconds, whereas sustained wind is the average wind speed over two minutes." She stops talking to steady herself. "That was a strong one." She checks her device. "Sixty-eight." She points. "If we can show these buildings right over there, you'll see we're actually quite protected where we are." The camera pans right, showing two buildings with about twenty feet of space between them. "The winds are coming from the northeast, directly behind these buildings that are offering us shelter. But let me show you something."

The camera follows as she walks slowly, struggling to get to the edge of one of the buildings. "The air is rushing between these buildings, creating a wind tunnel. I'm going to try and hold my anemometer out to show you." Her arm gets whipped back as soon as she puts it out. "Whew! Almost lost it there. Let me try again." She does it successfully this time and then pulls it back. "Can we get a close-up on this, Chris? Eighty miles per hour, folks. And I suspect that's sustained. If I took two steps to my left, I'd be in hurricane force winds. Attempting to walk in sixty to seventy-mile-per-hour winds is dangerous. There is a high risk of being blown over and sustaining injuries. This is why it's very important to evacuate. Even a car driving by a wind tunnel such as this could be affected. Possibly even overturned. If you've been unable to get out of the path, stay put in an upper interior room. And remember, if you are in the path, don't go outside as soon as the weather clears. You may be in the eye. Hundreds of people get injured or killed every year thinking they are in the clear. This is no—"

"Nicole!" someone yells, right before tackling her to the ground when a large piece of debris comes out of nowhere.

The video ends.

I stare at my phone. "Holy shit! What the fuck happened?"

I call her. It goes right to voicemail. I search the internet again and see many more videos. They all stop at the same time. Finally, one keeps going, but it cuts back to the news anchor in New York, who looks more than a little concerned when he says he'd give an update as soon as they know anything.

I call her father. It goes to voicemail. I call Victoria.

"Did you see it?" she asks immediately.

"Is she hurt? Is she…" My entire body shakes. "…dead?"

"We don't know anything. Dad has a call in to XTN. But my sister is a badass."

"Call me as soon as you know anything, okay?"

"Will do, but Dad said it could be a while. They weren't even in the worst of it. The eye wall won't reach them for another ninety minutes. How's the game going?"

"Who the fuck cares about the game?"

"Well, you should, for one. Don't you get it? She's out doing what she loves, Jaxon. Don't be stupid and bail on what you love just to sulk until you hear that she's most likely okay anyway. You know she'd hate that, right?"

I slide down the door until my ass hits the floor. "You're right. Since when did the student become the teacher?"

"She's going to be fine. This is Nicky we're talking about. She's the strongest person I know. If you want to worry about someone, worry about the dude who threw himself on her. Now there's someone I want to meet. I wonder how old he is."

How she manages to get even a tiny snicker out of me at a time like this is beyond me. "Thanks, Victoria. And call me. I don't care if I'm still at the game."

"Will do, Coach. Now go slaughter those Brauns."

"Bruins," I correct.

"Whatever."

I get up, dust my ass off, and storm out to the locker room. I jump up on a bench. "Listen up, guys. The woman I love is literally in the middle of a goddamn hurricane right now with no one to help, no way to contact me, and no way out. So if I can get over my shit and coach you, you can get your own heads out of your asses and win this fucking game. Now are we gonna let those pansy-asses score one more point?"

"No, sir!"

"Are we going to go out there and roll over them like we own the place?"

"Yes, sir!"

"Bring it in!"

They huddle around, and the team captain, Trevor Hornsby, leads a chant and gets them fired up before we go back on the field. On the way, I hand Eric my phone, because Victoria is right, there's nothing I can do right now but my job. "If Victoria, her dad, or Nic call me, answer it. If it's bad, tell me. If I don't hear a word from you about anything other than football, I'll consider it good news."

"Got it."

I coach the rest of the game, but not well. I can't help looking at Eric the whole goddamn time to see if he's on my phone. Good thing my guys come through for me. They hold the Bruins the entire second half and get a last-minute touchdown to win the game by four.

The players are celebrating out on the field. I pull Eric aside. "Nothing?"

He hands me my phone. "Voicemail."

"From her?"

"No. It said unknown number."

"And you didn't answer it? What if it's a hospital or something?"

"You said only to answer if it was Richard, Victoria, or Nicky."

"Damn it, Eric." I run, ignoring all the people trying to congratulate me, until I find a quieter place to listen.

When I hear her voice, I collapse onto the pavement, relief rushing through me like oxygen. "Jaxon, it's Nicky. I hope you can hear me. The connection isn't great. I was able to borrow a satellite phone from another crew. I don't know if you saw the broadcast, but I'm okay. I'm fine. Well, I have a hell of a bump on my head, but it's nothing."

As I listen, I realize more and more just how much I love her. I love everything about her. Even her drive to do crazy shit like go onto an island when everyone else is hightailing out of there. How could I have been so stupid, not fully supporting her career aspirations? I was selfish. A goddamn bastard. She's amazing. Always has been. So full of life, especially when she's clearly doing what she loves.

"Oh my god, Jaxon, I was on NBC! This is the most fun. It's like a dream come true." Laughter dances through the phone.

"Does that make me crazy? Anyway, I have to let these other guys call home. And then we have to prepare for the second half of Louisa to come through." My heart stops beating. She's calling me from the eye of the storm. "I hope you won or are winning. I'll be in touch later when we have service. Bye."

Someone tries to talk to me. I wave them away with a sharp flick of my arm and pull up my weather app. Holy mother of God. The second eye wall is pounding the Outer Banks. And Louisa is now a category one hurricane. My stomach heaves, but I haven't eaten, so there's nothing to throw up. I don't go back to the locker room. I don't even go to my car—the traffic to leave the game is already bumper-to-bumper. So I run. I run all the way home and sit in front of the TV, phone in hand, hoping for something. Anything.

Everyone in my family has called, texted, and offered to come over. But I want to be alone. I haven't seen her. But she's all over TV. Every station is playing endless reels of her and the guy, Jessie, who jumped on her getting hit by what they say was the hard plastic top of a dumpster. And while they are reporting that both survived with minor injuries, she hasn't been back on the air.

Because the storm is pounding her.

What if her 'minor' injuries are more than minor? What if the bump on her head results in bleeding in her brain? There would be no way to get help. She could die.

I pace around the room, thinking about my dead brother. Then I think about the men with Nicky—are they helpless, watching her die like Cooper had to watch Chaz? Losing him was unimaginable. And Nicky was there to support me through it. I'm not sure I'd have survived if she wasn't. Would I survive this? Losing her? I know to the core of my soul that I wouldn't. Together or not, she's always been my other half. And I promise myself if she makes it through this I'll fight for her come hell or high water.

Then she's there. On my television. Live. Thank fucking god. I collapse onto the couch and turn up the volume.

"And we're back in Nags Head, North Carolina. Many of you have seen the footage by now, and you can rest easy. My team and I are okay." She pulls her hood aside, revealing a bandage on the right side of her head. There's also an abrasion covering the entire right side of her face. Yet she's still on TV. "Just a few bumps and bruises. Louisa's second eye wall has passed, and we're in the outer bands." She holds up her anemometer. "Still over thirty miles per hour but going down steadily as it moves inland. Louisa threw us for a loop, becoming a hurricane for a brief period of time before making landfall. And while back to a tropical storm, that doesn't mean she didn't cause a lot of damage. Chris, let's pan around and show—"

My doorbell rings. Heisman wonders why I'm not moving off the couch. But I ignore it until her feed ends and the XTN anchor starts talking.

She's amazing. I get it now. What she did back then. Why she left. Even though she went about it the wrong way, I understand it. And I'm not without blame. I was always telling her there were so many places around New York City where she could work. I scoured the internet, pointing out jobs. I sent her emails with links to openings at small stations in towns not much larger than Calloway Creek. I laughed when she brought up dreams of chasing tornadoes. I was a damn fool.

I also understand this time will be different. Because I'm giving her the chance to do what she loves and still be with the man that... *Fuck, does she love me?*

The doorbell rings again. I'm sure it's Tag, Coop, or my parents. I race to the door and open it, not wanting to miss if Nicky comes back on. But I'm surprised to see who it is.

"Hey, Jaxon," Calista says with a sad smile.

"Calista." I pause to listen to a voice on the TV. "Hey, uh, did you and Eric break up or something? He didn't say anything. Listen, I can't really chat, there's a storm."

"I heard. So Nicky's covering it?"

"Yeah. I don't mean to be rude, but…" I leave the door open and walk to the end of the hall where I can see the television.

"Can we talk for a minute?" she calls after me.

"Can't it wait? The woman I love is risking her life here."

The second the words leave my mouth, I realize what a dick that makes me sound like. After all, Calista and I were sort of a thing a month ago. But she's with Eric now. And if his new demeanor is any indication, they are the happiest of couples.

She comes in and shuts the door. "The woman you *love*?"

"Yes. I never stopped. I'm sorry."

"Yeah, well, the woman you screwed trying to get over the woman you love is pregnant."

Suddenly, my attention is no longer on the television. "Come again?"

She sits. "I'm pregnant."

"Is it mine or Eric's?" *Okay, stupid question since she's standing in my living room.*

Heisman immediately snuggles next to her as if he could possibly understand the situation.

"It has to be yours. I should have gotten my period weeks ago but didn't think about it until I ran into a nurse friend of mine after school. One conversation led to another, and I realized how late I was. I took like twenty tests a few hours ago. I'm still trying to wrap my head around it."

I resisted all night, but now I go for my bottle of whiskey. I toss back a shot when something dawns on me. "You haven't told Eric."

She shakes her head. "I needed to be sure first. He and I… It's great, but it's still new. I'm just not sure what I want. And I thought you should know first since you're the father."

I look at my ring. *Father.*

I shake my head, wondering how this became such a clusterfuck of a day.

My phone pings with a text. It's only one word.

Nicky: Yes.

My brain isn't even functioning right now after the bomb that was just dropped.

Me: ??

Nicky: Yes to everything. Bicoastal relationship. Me spending vacations and whatever weekends I can in New York. You coming to Oklahoma on your time off. Yes, Jaxon. I want it all.

I drop my phone. Because… *fuck.*

Chapter Twenty-two

Nicky

"Great job," Chris says. "Some of us are heading out for drinks. You've definitely earned one. I hear they gave us the day off tomorrow."

"Well, we did work for almost forty-eight straight hours." I smile at the thought of having a Sunday off.

"Complaining about the working conditions?" someone says behind me.

I curse inwardly when I see Barry. "Me? No. I, uh—"

"Kidding, Forbes." He tosses out a charming grin on his way by.

I turn to Chris. "Did he just *smile* at me?"

Chris seems as surprised as I am. "That's as good of an endorsement as I've seen him give anyone. Take the win."

We walk to the elevator. "Thanks for the invite, but I think I have to pass. I have a bit of a headache." I gently touch the right side of my face. Henri did a great job covering it for my spots on the nightly news, but now, with the makeup off, it's red and angry and still a little swollen. And I might also be using it as an excuse to get home.

"All right, take care of yourself. See you Tuesday."

"Tuesday? But—"

"You didn't think Barry would actually give us an *extra* day off, do you? He only shifted them this week."

I chortle. "Of course not. See you then." In the lobby, I sling my duffle over my shoulder and head for the subway.

Once I'm on the train to Calloway Creek, it's hard to contain my excitement. I can't wait to see Jaxon. It's strange, though, how he's been holding back. He's probably upset about the video. An assistant producer told me the one on YouTube had over four million views. I know if the tables were turned, I'd have been terrified for Jaxon. Still, I expected more than the smiley face response to the text I sent agreeing to a long-distance relationship. And the one-word text he sent earlier when I said I'd be coming by tonight.

Okay.

I said I was coming over and had the whole day off tomorrow to do whatever he wanted. He said *okay*. Is he having second thoughts about us after seeing the demands of my job?

Or…

Maybe he's going to surprise me with candles and roses and melted chocolate, and he was trying to throw me off.

I'm going with scenario number two. Because that has me getting all kinds of naked with him.

The rest of the ride home, I study the calendar. I know his schedule well. I'll be back in Oklahoma right after New Year's. A warm feeling rushes through me knowing we'll be together for the holidays. The past two years without him have been empty.

I genuinely thought the emptiness was because I hadn't achieved my career goals. I felt like my cup was half-full. And although Louisa was the hairiest situation I've ever been in as a meteorologist, it's not like I haven't been in similar predicaments. Tornado season in Oklahoma is like months of Christmases to those of us who love weather. I've had to outrun an F3 on the back of a motorcycle after our van broke down thinking I'd be decapitated the entire time by flying debris. I've been airlifted off the top of a car during a flash flood. Once, I was stranded for thirty-six hours with my crew in three feet of snow, with two bottles of water and a granola bar between us. But through all that, even with all the adrenaline, I never felt one hundred percent fulfilled. Until last night. Hunkering down inside that building, nursing my injuries as the eye wall passed through, I knew my cup would never truly be full and my life never complete without him. I touch the bump on my head under my hairline. Either that or the dumpster lid knocked some sense into me.

"You're the lady from the video," a teenager says. He taps on his phone and shows something to his friend. "You are. Man, that was sick. Hey, can I get your autograph?"

"You want my autograph?"

Attention has been drawn now, and multiple people are showing interest.

A woman holds up a newspaper. There's a picture of me just below the fold. "This is *you*?" she asks.

"Can I have that?" the kid asks. She hands it to him, and he holds it out to me. "Do you have a pen?"

"Yeah, sure." I reach into my bag and retrieve one. Then I try to sign my very first autograph without shaking. By the time we get to my stop, I've signed five more and regaled them with the story.

I practically skip all the way to Jaxon's. I can't wait to tell him what happened on the train.

"Knock, knock!" I say, walking through his front door. Heisman runs around the corner, almost sliding into the wall in his enthusiasm to get to me. "Hey, buddy. Did you miss me?" I drop my bags in the foyer and crouch down to receive his wet kisses. I turn my head so he only licks the left side of my face.

When I look up, Jaxon is leaning casually against the wall wearing a pensive expression.

I offer him a sultry smile. "Hey, you."

His eyes home in on my face, and he strides forward. "Damn, Nic. It didn't look that bad on TV."

"My makeup artist is amazing. Hurt like hell to remove it, though."

He brushes my hair aside, further examining it. "Are you okay?"

"I'm fine. It looks worse than it is. I'll be as good as new in a few days." I throw my arms around him. "I kind of expected to jump into your arms and be whisked away to the bedroom." I jut out my lower lip in a pout.

He doesn't whisk. He doesn't laugh. He doesn't even smile.

A nervous sigh escapes me. "What is it, Jaxon?"

"We need to talk."

Anxiety grips me. "Okay. But in my experience, no good conversations have ever begun with those four words. Like, *ever*."

"Come on."

He leads me to the living room couch, where Heisman settles at our feet.

He's silent for far too long.

I swallow. "You're scaring me."

He takes my hand. "I just don't know where to begin."

Oh, my god. Is he going to ask me to marry him again? Is that what this is? Him being nervous? My heart thunders. *Would I? It's too soon. It is too soon, right?*

When he drops my hand and hops off the couch, pacing the floor, I know it's not that. No man has ever paced the floor while proposing. My stomach tightens into a knot. *Is he ending this?* Two seconds ago I thought he might ask me to marry him, and now I'm terrified that he won't. I could be losing him all over again. I get up, stand in front of him, and put my hands on his chest. "Jaxon?"

He closes his eyes for a beat. I can feel his heart race. He huffs out a breath, then rubs his brow. "Calista is pregnant."

My whole world implodes with those three words. Calista. His ex. Nice, stable, available Calista. My hands fall from his chest. And now I'm the one pacing. He touches my shoulder tentatively as if he thinks I'll turn and deck him.

"I swear we used protection every time. You have to believe me."

"I believe you," I say, my voice cracking.

"I'm still processing this myself. She only told me late last night. I don't really know what to say."

Emotion clogs my throat. I motion to the bathroom. "Give me a minute." Once behind closed doors, I let the waterworks flow, turning on the faucet to cover my sobs. Tears burn as they roll across the scrapes on my cheek. I close the lid to the toilet and sit, rubbing my pendant. How could this even happen? Everything was going so well. We were happy. And it was going to work this time.

It's your own fault.

I wad up some toilet paper and blot my eyes.

"Nicky?"

"Be right out!"

I splash water on my face, hoping to reduce the redness under my eyes. I stare in the mirror knowing karma is a bitter pill to swallow.

When I return to the living room, he's on the couch. He immediately stands. I head for the door.

He follows. "You're leaving?"

"You should be with her." I pause, because saying those words were *almost* the hardest words I've ever said to him.

"No."

"Jaxon, she obviously loves you. I knew it at the reunion. And she's carrying your child, and she's here. You're both teachers. It makes sense. She can give you everything you ever wanted."

Now *he's* the one holding back tears. "Don't you get it, Nic? *You're* everything I've ever wanted."

Hearing those words breaks me, and I slump against the wall, my back sliding down until my butt hits the floor. My hands cover my face.

He sits next to me and forces me to lace my fingers with his. "My feelings haven't changed. I still want you. I want us. However I can have us. This just... complicates things."

"She hates me. This will only make it worse. And surely she wants you to marry her."

"She doesn't. She's dating Eric, remember?"

I lift my head and lock eyes with him. "And he's okay with this?"

"She hadn't exactly told him about the baby yet, so I don't know."

"Jaxon, there are very few men who will want a woman who's pregnant with someone else's child. If he breaks up with her, she'll want you back. Maybe even if he *doesn't* break up with her."

"That's not going to happen. Even if he breaks things off, it won't change the fact that I don't want to be with her. Even if you weren't here, if the last month hadn't happened, I still wouldn't want to be with her."

"But you're going to be there for the baby. You wouldn't have it any other way."

He nods.

"How far along is she?"

"She's not sure. She took the test yesterday. Hasn't been to the doctor yet."

"But she's sure it's yours and not the other guy's?"

"They've only been sleeping together a few weeks. So, yeah, it has to be mine." He grips my hand tighter. "We haven't talked logistics. I'm still wrapping my head around it. I have no idea what she wants or expects. But I know what *I* want. I want to be involved in my kid's life. I want to support him or her and be there when it matters. But Nic, I can do that *and* have you. These past few days have shown me that nothing could be worse than not being with you. Don't run away again. Give us the chance we deserve. We can do this, babe." He puts a finger under my chin and lifts it, making me look at him. "Can't we?"

Holding my pendant, a sadness I've never known washes over me. He's going to get the child he always wanted. *With her.* Jealously courses through my veins as my past decisions come back to haunt me. But I've no one to blame but myself. Not him. Not Calista. Only me.

I put my head on his shoulder and nod.

Samantha Christy

Chapter Twenty-three

Jaxon

"Thanks for agreeing to stop here before hitting the doctor's office."

Heisman bolts around the front door when I open it, sidestepping me to get to Calista.

"This will only take a few minutes," I say. "My dog walker had a conflict this afternoon, and I didn't want to leave him inside for too long considering I have to go back to practice after your appointment."

She walks into the living room. "It's no problem."

"Get a soda or a glass of water while I take him out back."

"I'm fine here," she says, sitting on the couch.

It's strange having Calista in my house again. And although there's a good reason, I still feel like it's also a betrayal of sorts. Would Nicky have an issue with it? We haven't talked about it. Any of it. We decided that until we had more information, we wouldn't make assumptions or plans. We wouldn't talk about the future that we'd just recently promised. We stayed in our pajamas all day Sunday and binge-watched an old Netflix series. We tiptoed around each other, each not knowing what to say or how to act.

And we didn't have sex.

Not one time.

She went home Sunday night and spent all day yesterday with her mother. I spent all day with my head anywhere but on my students. Same as I did today. Counting down the hours until Calista and I were going to her OB to confirm the news that will alter the rest of our lives.

"Okay, bud. Two more times," I tell Heisman. "Then I have to go."

"Woof!" he answers, chasing after the tennis ball.

Back inside, Calista has fallen asleep on my couch. *How long was I gone?* Heisman pads over and lays his head near her stomach. He stares. It's goddamn creepy. I swear my dog was a clairvoyant human in a past life. I check the time and gently wake her.

"Sorry," she says. "I'm so tired lately that I can barely keep my eyes open. I've taken to napping instead of grading during my planning period this week."

Other than her text yesterday asking if I'd like to accompany her to the doctor, it's the first we've even remotely spoken about the situation since she told me Friday. "Is that normal?"

"According to the book I bought, yes."

My brow shoots up. "You bought a book?"

"It's not like I know anything about being pregnant, Jaxon. A few of my friends have kids, but this is a whole new world for me. Sore boobs. Upset stomach. Exhaustion."

"Already? How can that happen so soon?"

"The book says it can happen very early."

"Guess I'll have to pick one up myself."

She looks pleased. "You plan on being involved?"

I throw a treat to Heisman on our way out the door. "What kind of question is that? I'm not going to bail on my kid."

"I thought maybe you were coming with me to make sure I wasn't scamming you or something."

"Why would you scam me?"

"I wouldn't. And I didn't get pregnant on purpose. I hope you know that."

"Yeah. Jeez. Of course I do." I hold the passenger door open for her, then run to the other side. "So Eric?"

"Haven't told him yet."

"I figured as much when he didn't say anything at practice yesterday."

"Whatever I decide to do, I'm not forcing you into anything, you know. You can be as involved as you want. I know you didn't sign up for this."

At a stoplight, I turn and study her. "You seem to be okay with this. Aren't you freaking out even a little?"

"Believe me, I had multiple freak-out sessions over the weekend. But I've come to terms with it. I'm twenty-seven years old. There's no reason I can't do this. The school district has a great maternity leave policy. And if you decided not to help, there's nothing wrong with being a single mother. I can do this."

"I'm sure you can. But I'm going to help. Both monetarily and physically. I want to be involved, Calista."

She smiles. "I want that, too."

I realize there is one thing I need to settle right now, before things go any further. "You should know something," I say, turning into the parking lot of the doctor's office. "This won't change things between you and me. Nicky and I, we're back together. Even after she leaves, we're going to be together. I don't know what that means for"—I glance at her belly—"*this*. But I need you to know she'll be a part of my life."

She gazes out the window. "You mean to say she'll be a part of this baby's life."

"I guess so, yes. Will you have a problem with that?"

"Do I have a choice?"

"You are the mother."

"I am. Just so long as she realizes that and doesn't try to undermine me."

I park and we get out. "She would never do that."

"She's bound to have some jealousy over this." She holds a hand firmly against her flat belly. "Until you've had a baby growing inside you, another person you're fully responsible for, you can't understand. *She* can't understand."

"She *can*."

Calista narrows her eyes in question.

"She lost a baby. *We* lost a baby. Nicky miscarried at fifteen weeks." I show her the ring. "Some of his ashes are in here."

A hand flies to her mouth. "I had no idea." She studies the ring. "You've never worn this before."

"I didn't know about it until recently. And as a result of the miscarriage, her fertility was compromised. So if she seems jealous, cut her a break."

"I promise to try."

I hold the office door open for her. She checks in and we're seated. Thank God the waiting room is empty. I didn't even think until right now how it would look if anyone saw us here together.

"Calista Hilson," a nurse calls.

"Should I…?"

"It's okay to come with me," Calista says.

We're escorted to the back. A nurse takes me to an exam room while they take Calista down the hall for a few minutes. When they enter, the nurse asks Calista to remove everything below the waist. We look at each other funny. The nurse doesn't fail to notice. She points to a curtain attached to the wall. "You can use this for privacy and drape this sheet over your lower half. The doctor will be in shortly."

The nurse leaves, and Calista pulls the curtain. "They had me pee in a cup and stuff. Confirmed the test was positive."

"Now what?" I ask, sitting in the far corner next to a bunch of equipment.

"They want to do an ultrasound to see how far along I am."

My heart rate increases. "As in, we're going to *see* it?"

She pushes the curtain away, her lower half draped in a paper sheet. "Guess so. Isn't it exciting?"

Exciting would be if I were in this room with Nicky. Exciting would be if the woman I love got pregnant by accident. I'd hardly call what's happening here exciting. More like stressful. Frustrating. Utterly derailing.

There's one knock on the door, and it cracks. "Ready?"

Calista sits on the exam table. "Yes."

The nurse comes back in, followed by a doctor. My stomach turns. Not just any doctor. Hudson fucking McQuaid. I stand. "Oh, hell no."

Everyone looks at me. Then Hudson realizes what's going on, and his body shakes in silent laughter. He holds out a hand, trying to look all professional. "Jaxon Calloway, nice to see you."

"Nice? I don't want you anywhere near my kid. Are you even a real doctor?"

"I'm an OB resident. So, yeah, I'm a real doctor."

"I want someone else."

"That's not your choice, now is it?"

"He works with Dr. Peterman," Calista says. "Do you know how fortunate I was to get Dr. Peterman as my OB? He's in high demand."

"Then why isn't Dr. Peterman here?"

"We switch off," Hudson says. "One visit you'll have me, and the next you'll see him. That way we'll both be familiar with Calista's pregnancy if the other isn't available for delivery."

"You are not delivering my kid."

"Jaxon, hush," Calista says. "Dr. Peterman will do the delivery. Hudson, er, Dr. McQuaid, is just a backup."

Dr. McQuaid. It's hard to even think this man is compassionate enough to help others. Not to mention that with all his family money, he chose to go into the medical profession. Then I think of what branch of the profession he's in, and it makes sense. Pussies. He's in it for pussies.

"It's okay, you can call me Hudson," he tells her. Then he turns to me. "Not you."

The nurse tries not to smile when I flip him my middle finger.

"Can we get this over with?" I say.

Calista lies back on the table, and Hudson grabs some dildo-wand thingy and goes for her crotch. He holds it up, speaking very professionally. "Early ultrasounds are transvaginal."

Shit. I swear to God if it were Nicky lying on the table, Hudson would be flat on his back with my fist up his nose.

"Don't ultrasound techs normally do these?" Calista asks.

"In some practices, yes," Hudson says. "We like to do our own here."

He and the nurse say some stuff, but all I can think of is how Hudson McQuaid is a damn doctor. I knew he went away to college and med school, and I've seen him around town, albeit far less than his brothers, but he's still one hundred percent

McQuaid—which means one hundred percent douchebag. And he'll probably be on the phone to his brothers the minute he leaves the room. Everyone knows Calista and I aren't together anymore. And he's the first to know this juicy little tidbit.

"There we go," he says, pointing at the monitor. "We got lucky. I can see a heartbeat."

"Oh gosh, really?" Calista asks excitedly.

"Give me a minute, and I'll have an estimated fetal age." He punches keys on the laptop. "Based on your last menstrual period and these measurements, it appears you're approximately eight and half weeks along."

"Two months?" I ask. "How come you didn't know sooner?"

"I…" Calista looks at the other two in the room and then back at me. "We had just broken up," she whispers. "I wasn't exactly thinking about getting my period. Then Eric and I got together, and things happened so fast."

Eric. Damn. Why can't *he* be the one sitting here? This kid should be his, not mine.

I shake my head, feeling guilty. Because I'd never want any child of mine to feel unwanted, no matter how they came into the world.

"Your due day is May eighth," Hudson says.

Calista smiles. "Perfect. Close to the end of the school year. I'll be able to enjoy all summer with the baby."

"Is it a boy or a girl?" I ask.

Hudson shakes his head. "Too soon to tell."

"I don't want to know," Calista says.

"Why not?" I ask.

"This whole thing started as a surprise. I want it to end that way, too."

"I'll make a note in your file," the nurse says.

Calista studies the screen. "How big is it?"

"Not very," Hudson says. "A little over a half inch. You can't see it here, but the arms and legs are already well formed. Soon, the fingers and toes will grow longer and more distinct. And at your next appointment, we should be able to hear the heartbeat."

Calista seems considerably happier about this than I am. She grabs my hand. "We're going to be parents." She sees my dull reaction and pulls away. "Sorry. I know we're not… I guess I'm just overly emotional. I mean, there is a tiny human growing inside me. I didn't even know this was something I wanted."

I try not to think about the fact that it's something *I've* always wanted. Just not the way it's happening now. "Do you know how much longer this will take?" I ask, trying to hide my displeasure that the woman on the exam table isn't Nicky. "I have to go run football practice."

"You can get dressed," Hudson tells Calista. "Janice will print out an ultrasound picture for you, and I'll meet you in my office to go over some things."

"I'll wait outside. Anything I need to know, Calista can fill me in on." I pull Hudson aside. "And I'm pretty sure there are laws against you telling anyone about this. That includes your asshole brothers. Nobody knows about this yet, and I'll be damned if everyone is going to find out from you."

"I'm a physician, Calloway, not a gossip monger."

I thumb to the door. "I'll see you out front, Calista."

The nurse follows me. "I printed one for you as well," she says, handing me a small black-and-white photo. "Considering it doesn't seem like you're…"

"We're not." I take it. "Thank you."

I go outside the building, sit on a bench, and study the photo, wondering how my life became so fucking complicated.

Chapter Twenty-four

Nicky

I've prayed for a story. A stray tornado. A waterspout on the Hudson River. A volcanic eruption. Something. Anything. But today has to be the most boring weather day in the history of the world.

It's after four p.m. I know where he is. Is he staring at a picture of his child on the ultrasound screen this very moment? Is he holding Calista's hand dreaming up names as they see the tiny blob? Is he tearing up because becoming a father is everything he ever wanted?

To make myself feel better (and kill more time), I page through comments on XTN's website and Twitter feed about my reporting on Louisa. Still—what should have been the best weekend of my career has now been marred by personal undertones.

My phone alerts me of a text.

Jaxon: Can you come over after work? Say 7:00?

I check the time. It's later than I thought. If I leave now, I might just make it. I was supposed to meet Regan, Ava, and Maddie behind the ice cream shop, something I've done for a few weeks now in an attempt to integrate myself back into the town I grew up in. Jaxon knows this, so whatever he wants me there for must be important.

Me: Leaving XTN now. See you then.

No reply as I make my way to the train. Not even a thumbs-up. What does that mean?

Jaxon never got to see our baby. He wasn't at the ultrasound that changed my whole view of life. He didn't get to say goodbye to Billy. And it scares me to death that he's going to overcompensate and try to make up for that loss by doing everything he can for Calista and this baby. I feel guilty even thinking it, because he *should* do things for them. Realistically, I know this. But practically, I know the jealousy I'll feel—*I'm already feeling*—could turn out to be an issue.

Off the train now, my feet move slowly, in no hurry to find out how happy he is after today's ultrasound. Will he want me to share in his excitement? A wave of nausea rolls through me thinking he may want me in the hospital with him. How hard will it be to see him and Calista so happy about their perfect new arrival?

I turn the corner and see an unfamiliar car parked in Jaxon's driveway. I also see Jaxon and Heisman waiting for me on the front porch. Heisman sees me first, prancing over to do his usual happy dance around me before I pet him.

Jaxon approaches, looking guilty. "Don't get mad. This was Calista's idea."

I swallow. "She's inside?"

"She wanted to come up with a plan."

"Don't you have like seven or eight months to do that?"

"A plan for now. What we tell people and when."

"I suppose that's not an entirely bad idea." No matter how much I want it to be. "But why do you need me here?"

He reaches out and tentatively takes my hand as if he thinks I'll pull away. "Because we're together, Nic. I want us to be a team."

I snort. "I'll bet Calista will have something to say about that."

"Just come."

"Wait. Did you see the baby on the ultrasound?"

He nods.

"Did they give you a picture?"

He nods again.

"I don't want to see it." I grab my pendant. "This whole thing is going to be vastly different for you than it will be for me. You'll be inside of it. I'm a spectator. Please understand that my absence of enthusiasm doesn't indicate a lack of desire to be with you."

"Noted." He leans in and brushes my hair behind my ear. "Now how about we get this over with so we can do what we didn't do all weekend?"

I'm a bit surprised he's ready to be with me like that again so soon.

"What?" His brows lift. "Do you know how hard it was to keep my hands off you after I thought I'd lost you in that storm? Nicky, all I dream about is being with you. Kissing you. Touching you. Making love to you. Getting you to scream my name. That hasn't and will never change. But I get that we both needed a minute to absorb this."

It's a silver lining on the cloud surrounding me. "I dream about being with you too."

"Good." He whistles and Heisman trots over from the spot he'd plopped down on under a tree.

Inside, Calista is on the couch. Heisman goes over and puts his head in her lap. *Et tu?*

"Can I get you a drink, Nic?" Jaxon asks. "Water? Tea? Double shot of whiskey?"

Neither Calista nor I laugh.

"No, thank you." *No need to prolong this.*

I don't think it's lost on anyone that Calista and I don't greet each other like long-lost friends.

"Okay, then," Jaxon says, motioning for me to sit in the chair across from Calista and then standing by my side. "We've got ourselves quite a pickle. Anyone want to go first?"

"I'll go," Calista says. "I know you're a couple now or whatever, but I'm not sure why she's even here. She has nothing to do with this and won't be involved in any decisions."

"You can talk directly to me," I say.

"Fine. Jaxon tells me you had a miscarriage. I know that must have been devastating, but it could also lead to you having negative feelings about this." She touches her stomach protectively. "I mean, even more negative than another woman having Jaxon's baby. I just don't want you getting territorial or anything."

"Territorial?" I bite.

"I need you to understand that while I get Jaxon is yours, this baby is *mine*. Even when Jaxon has it for weekends or whatever, he or she is still mine, and what I say goes."

"You mean what *we* say," Jaxon says, "as it's mine too. And to be perfectly transparent, I'll be asking for more than weekends."

"Do we really have to argue over that now?"

"We don't have to argue over it at all as long as you get that this kid is mine, and I'll want equal time with it."

"Assume you do get equal time," Calista says. "Nicky may want to mother him or her, and that's not something I'm okay with."

Jaxon puts a hand on my shoulder in a show of support. "Calista, I'm not sure you have much of a say in who I let see our kid when it's with me. Everyone will be clear about whose kid it is. You don't have to worry."

"Won't I?" she cocks her head and stares directly at me.

"While I intend to be supportive of Jaxon, you can rest assured that I won't be trying to replace you as the mother."

"You say that now, but you can't tell me you aren't jealous."

"Jealous? If you think I'm at a time in my life where I can even consider being a mom, you're crazy. Did you see what I was doing this past weekend?"

I almost sound convincing. I'm just not sure who I'm trying to convince, her or me.

"What about you?" Jaxon says to Calista. "Say you and Eric end up together, or you meet someone else next month or in two years. That guy might try to take my place. We both have a lot at stake here."

Her arms fold over her middle. "Okay, fine. But Nicky doesn't need to go to any appointments. And she won't be at the birth. Or the hospital."

"Appointments, fine," he says. "Birth, understandable. But if I want her at the hospital to support me, you can be damn well sure she'll be welcome there. Calista, you'd better learn the art of compromise before the baby comes, or we're going to have a big problem."

His hand is still firmly on my shoulder. I'm grateful. Although he's defending his baby, he's showing her where his loyalties lie.

I'm starting to believe what he said the other night about being able to do that and have a relationship with me.

"About making an announcement," Calista says. "It's probably best to wait a month, until we're past the first trimester."

I want to tell her that guarantees nothing, but I don't want to start another argument.

"Will Eric keep his mouth shut?" I ask.

"Eric doesn't know."

I'm stunned. "You haven't told him?"

"I broke things off."

"Mind telling me when?" Jaxon asks. "He was happy a few hours ago at practice."

"Did it on the way over. He shouldn't be saddled with another man's baby."

"Don't you think that should be *his* decision?"

"No. It's mine. I know you're his friend, but I expect you to abide by my wishes and not tell him."

"I think you're making a mistake," Jaxon says. "Anyway, it wasn't Eric I was worried about. Shit, Nicky, you won't believe who her doctor is."

"He's *not* my doctor," Calista says.

"Whatever. The resident who works with her doctor, and the one who saw her today, is Hudson McQuaid."

My jaw drops, and I cup my mouth to stifle a laugh.

"You find this funny?" he asks.

I try not to smile. "Kinda, yeah."

"You realize if he blabs before we get the chance to tell everyone, this will get blown way out of proportion. Plus, I'd really like people to know you and I are solidly back together before the rumor mill gets going."

"Oh, yes, by all means let's do what makes this easier on *you* two," Calista bites.

The sweetheart class president of Calloway Creek High has left the building; bitchy momzilla seems to have taken her place. But I don't say anything, because, yikes.

"I'll take care of Hudson," Jaxon says. "Do the three of us agree we'll wait a month, and we'll talk about it before we share the news?"

"My friend Megan knows," Calista says.

"Damn, that's right. Do you think she's told anyone?"

"She's a nurse, so probably not. I'll call her and tell her not to. And I told my parents last night, but they don't live in town, so you don't have to worry."

Jaxon looks ill and sits on the chair next to mine. "And now your father hates me more than he already did."

"Why does your father hate him?"

"Because he ran out on dinner with my parents the second he saw you on TV."

I shift in my chair and try to pretend I don't feel like I just won. Then I'm knocked down a peg when I remember why we're here in the first place.

"So we're all in agreement?" Jaxon says. "We won't tell anyone else, and we'll make sure anybody who knows won't blab until we're ready to make an announcement."

"Exactly how do we plan on doing that?" Calista asks.

Jaxon laughs. "In the most tactful way possible. But, hey, we have a month to figure it out."

It's now that I realize Heisman hasn't once come over to me since we came inside the house. He's glued to Calista's lap. Is this some kind of indication of how it's going to be with Jaxon? Will she call him with every ache and question? Summon him late at night for her culinary cravings? Will she expect him to be at her beck and call?

Jaxon stands. "I guess we're done here. Walk you out?" he asks. "Heisman, get off her lap, buddy." Reluctantly, Heisman pulls away and lets Calista leave.

On her way out, she turns to me. "Nicky, I'm sorry if I came off like a raging bitch. Maybe it's the pregnancy hormones. I want this to work out for everyone, I really do."

I nod and offer a smile.

The front door shuts, and Jaxon comes back in the room. "Shit, that was…"

"Stranger than any conversation I thought I'd ever have." I go to his bar. "I think I'll take that double whiskey now."

He grabs the bottle and pulls me toward the bedroom. "The glasses," I say.

"Don't need 'em. I plan on sucking it out of your belly button. You game?"

I giggle. It's a drinking game we used to play in college. A game where everyone who plays is a winner.

I smile and run ahead.

Chapter Twenty-five

Jaxon

Avoiding Eric is impossible. He is, after all, my assistant coach and offensive coordinator. Today at school, it was easy enough. I simply went straight to my classroom and avoided the teachers' lounge at lunch. I guess I'm good at keeping secrets; I did keep mine for over two years. This is different. He's one of my best friends. My co-worker. A fellow coach. And then there's the possibility that he'll hate me when it all comes out. Even if we kept it a secret longer than a month, Calista would start to show sooner or later. I scrub a hand across my face on the way to the field. This wouldn't be Calloway Creek without some sort of scandal arising every so often. I just wish Nicky and I weren't going to be the center of one—*again*.

Eric beats the other coaches to the field. He sees me and runs over. "Where have you been hiding all day?"

"Got backed up on grading. Worked through lunch."

Our players trickle out and get started on their warms ups as we set up for practice. We push the blocking sled into place and then get out the cones for drills. Eric drapes his arm over the back of the sled, looking glum. "Calista broke it off with me."

I know. "Ah, really? I'm sorry, man."

"The thing is, everything was going so well. I was sure she was into me. I don't mind telling you we fucked like bunnies. But something changed after the Bruins game. I had to go upstate for my cousin's wedding, so we didn't talk all weekend. Monday, she made excuses as to why she couldn't see me, then Tuesday, she came over to my place after practice and ended things."

I busy myself pushing cones around. "She say why?"

"Something about not being ready for another relationship. But I think she's holding something back. I could tell that wasn't it." He glares at me. "You don't think she's still hung up on you, do you?"

I shake my head. "I think that ship sailed when you started dating her."

"I thought it had, too. Maybe she doesn't believe you and Nicky are back together. Nobody has seen you out except for walking your dog. Maybe Calista believes she still has a chance."

"Eric, she doesn't want me. And even if that were the case, would you really want to be with someone who still has feelings for someone else?"

"I shouldn't. But damn it, I do." He punches the pad of the blocking sled. "She was the first woman I've really wanted since my divorce. Guess I'm a sucker, huh?"

Fuck. I feel like a traitor. And a real shitty friend. "You're not a sucker. And, hey, you never know—she could change her mind."

Drake and my other coaches come up behind us, and the players are ready for direction. I clap a hand on Eric's shoulder. "Come on, let's go work it out on the field."

~ ~ ~

Unfinished EX

I slip into a booth next to Addy at Donovan's. Tag and Cooper are on the other side. I kiss my sister's cheek. "Why the sibling meeting?"

Lissa places drinks down. She doesn't gaze at me longingly. "Huh," I say when she leaves. "That was different."

"She's fucking Lucas Montana," Tag says, earning him a kick in the shin under the table.

"Damn, Addy," he says. "I don't think you realize how hard that bionic leg of yours is."

"I'm glad she found someone," I say.

Tag chortles. "Fucking and found are two different things. Ouch! Addy, keep your goddamn leg to yourself."

"I thought Lucas was seeing Angela Pearson," Cooper says. "Or was it Angie Beckham?"

"Yes and yes," I say. "Our cousin gets around."

"Still? I thought he got married."

Addy sips her wine. "If you'd stay in town long enough to know things, you'd know he called off the wedding at the last minute. It's actually the second time he did it. With two different women. He's the runaway groom of Calloway Creek."

I set my beer down. "I assume we're not here to talk about Lissa or Lucas. What's up? Everything okay with Mom and Dad?"

Tag thumbs at Cooper. "He's leaving. This is his goodbye party."

Addy reaches across the table and takes Coop's hand.

"I don't know why you're surprised," I say. "He is a nomad. Where are you off to now?"

Cooper's face lights up. I haven't seen him act this excited the whole time he's been here. "Parahawking in Nepal."

Addy drops his hand. "Sounds dangerous. What exactly is parahawking?"

"It's paragliding with birds—mostly vultures, eagles, or black kites. I was promised an Egyptian vulture."

"And you have to go all the way to Nepal to do it?" she asks. "Isn't it hard to get there?"

He pulls up an app on his phone. "Let's see, I go from JFK to Qatar to Kathmandu. Then on to Nepal, where I'll run off the foothills of the Himalayas."

Tag drains his glass. "It's unbelievable that people pay you to do that shit."

"It's a hell of a life," he says, almost looking happy but not quite.

"How do they get the birds to land on you?" I ask.

"Buffalo meat."

"Please be careful," Addy says.

Cooper laughs. "The flights to and from Nepal will be more dangerous than the jump, believe me. Hell, taking a cab in the city probably carries more risk."

Donny comes out from the kitchen and puts a huge plate of nachos on the table. He stares at Cooper. Cooper wipes his mouth. "Is something on my face?"

Donny shakes his head. "Sorry, son. I just can't get used to seeing you. Every time I do, it reminds me of your brother and my daughter." He nods to a booth in the corner. "Chaz used to come in almost every shift Serenity worked. On her break, they'd sit at that table, holding hands and sharing a plate of fries."

"I remember," Cooper says. "I did work here on the weekends, Donny."

We're all silent for a beat. Because all of us know Donny lost two workers when Chaz died. One is hiding away in Alaska; the other is hiding from his true self. Both are hiding from the pain.

"Right," Donny says. "You know if you ever need some extra cash, I'm always looking for good help."

"I'll keep that in mind," Coop says, the four of us knowing bartending is the farthest thing from his mind.

Donny blinks twice, still focused on the corner. "I swear my old eyes play tricks on me, and I can still see them there sometimes." He puts a hand on Cooper's shoulder. "I sure do miss that boy, as I know you all do. And I miss the hell out of my daughter."

"You haven't seen her?" Addy asks.

Sadness deepens the wrinkles on his forehead. He pulls his phone from his pocket. "Only on this thing. We talk on that face app every once in a while, but it's not the same. When your brother died, a part of her died right along with him."

He slumps and walks away, leaving the four of us thinking of Chaz.

"It's so sad she hasn't been back here," Tag says. "She always said she never wanted to leave. I wonder why she's stayed away so long."

"Isn't it obvious?" Addy says, looking at Cooper. "Think about it. If Maddie died and she had an identical twin sister who you'd run into everywhere in town, would you really stick around?"

"You think she left because of him?" I say. "Cooper isn't even here most of the time. Everyone knows that."

Cooper picks at the table. "If she's staying away, it's because she doesn't want to be around the person who's responsible for his death."

Addy sighs sadly. "Would you stop saying that? You are the only person who thinks it."

Cooper looks over at the bar where a picture of Serenity and Donny is proudly displayed on the wall next to the large bar mirror. "No. I'm not the only one."

We all drink in silence, our normally chatty foursome at a loss for words.

Finally, my sister turns to me. "So, what's new with you?"

Suddenly, I feel like I'm on stage, and a spotlight is pointed directly at me. I can't tell them.

"A lot, if the rumors are true," Coop says.

I swear to God I'll rip Hudson McQuaid's throat out if he said anything. "Rumors?"

"About you and Nicky getting back together. I knew you were sleeping with her, but Ava Criss told Amber Thompson that it's more serious than that."

"It is more serious than that. In fact, we're going to try this thing long distance when she goes back to Oklahoma."

Addy bounces in her seat, clapping. "I'm so happy for you. I knew you belonged together. And now that I know she never cheated on you, I love her again. I'm still mad at her a little for leaving you, but I can't blame her for going after a career. Do you think you'll get married again? Oh, please get remarried. What a story that would be for your kids."

Kids. Aaand fuck, the elephant sitting on my chest just got a lot heavier.

"One, it's way too early to be thinking about marriage. And two, don't be mad at her, Addy. It was my fault, too. We both had a hand in things going wrong."

"How did *you* have a hand in it?" Tag asks.

I look down at the table, guilt consuming me as I finally reveal my secret. "I'm the one who cheated, not Nicky."

I don't need to look up to know that three pairs of stunned eyes are watching me. Their silence tells me all I need to know. "You slept around on her?" Tag looks at me with more disappointment than I've ever seen. "What the fuck, Jaxon?"

"I didn't sleep with anyone, but I could have. I stopped it before it went any further than a kiss." I run a hand through my hair. "I know I messed up big time. Believe me, I've apologized to her. There are a lot of things we both apologized for."

"A kiss?" Cooper says, laughing. "You're all getting your panties in a twist over a kiss?"

Addy leans over and swats his arm. "A kiss is still cheating, you idiot."

"Barely. And why the hell would you even tell her about it?"

I shake my head. "Addy's right. It *is* cheating. And I told her because the guilt has been eating away at me for years. No matter what was happening in our marriage and how distant I felt we'd become, it was reprehensible. There was no excuse. And I've been a fool for letting people around here think she's the one who did wrong."

Addy sits back and crosses her arms. "Of all my brothers, you're the last one I would have expected this from."

Fuck. I feel about two inches tall. I know I've let down more than just Nicky.

Tag drinks slowly, still brooding. I get it. He was devastated when he found out about Mom cheating on Dad. I find it a bit ironic, however, that the former Casanova of Calloway Creek is the most upset by my revelation.

"Listen," I say. "Mind if we talk about something else? Like if Tag and Maddie have set a date yet?"

"She wants a spring wedding," he says. "May probably. Or June. She's checking out places for the reception."

"Places?" Cooper laughs. "Isn't there like one place here—that hall over on 8th Avenue?" He glances around. "Or here. Plenty of people have receptions here."

"Dude, I'm not having my wedding reception in a neighborhood bar and grill."

Cooper shrugs. "I don't see why not. Hey, Donny! You'd throw my brother here a hell of a wedding party, right?"

He holds up the glass of whatever he's pouring. "Sure would. But bachelor parties are a hella more fun."

"Fuck yeah," Cooper says. "Now your bachelor party is something I'd come back for."

Tag pins him with his stare. "But not the wedding?"

"Fine. The wedding too. It is kind of a momentous occasion, the playboy of Cal Creek getting hitched and all."

"Says the other playboy of Cal Creek."

"Nah, man. Not anymore. Women are far more trouble than they're worth." He turns to me. "Case in point."

"Hey," Addy says, faking being overly offended. "I am a woman, you know."

"Yeah, and you're a pain in the ass," he says with a smile that could charm the spots off a leopard. He lifts a glass. "To parahawking, bachelor parties, and ex sex." He tosses back his drink and turns to Addy. "Sorry, sis. We'll toast to you too when you do something worth toasting."

I can tell he moves his legs before he can get kicked under the table.

"I'm graduating next spring," she says. "You'll come back for that, won't you?"

Cooper points between our two siblings. "Tell you what, how about you coordinate the bachelor party, wedding, and graduation all within a week or so, and it's a deal."

"We'll have to get back to you on that," Tag says. "I'm not about to dictate to my fiancée when we have to get married. She's a florist. She lives for this shit."

"Whatever. All I'm saying is you could drive it that direction."

"I'll see what I can do."

Addy elbows me and motions to the counter. "Speaking of exes."

My eyes follow hers to where Calista is waiting on a food order. She looks over and waves. I wave back awkwardly.

"You on speaking terms?" Addy asks.

Damn, I'm tired of lying to people today. "I guess so."

"I heard she was dating Eric Snyder," Tag says. "Is it strange having your assistant coach ball your ex?"

"They broke up. And no, it's not strange. I was never that into her."

"Ouch," Addy says.

"Mind if we not rehash that shit again?" I finish my drink and get Lissa's attention for another round.

"Rehash what shit?" Cooper asks.

"Addy coming to my house and reading me the riot act about shitting or getting off the pot with Calista."

Tag laughs. "Way to go, little sister."

"Did you know she actually equated her losing her leg to my breakup with Nicky?"

"You shush." Addy covers my mouth. "Which is worse— losing a limb or the love of your life?"

"Limb," Cooper says. "No fucking comparison."

"Says the guy who's never loved anyone." Tag shakes his head. "I'd gladly give up a leg to keep Maddie."

Addy removes her hand. "See, told ya. Love trumps limb."

"Wait," Coop says. "*You're* the one who said you'd rather lose a limb?"

"I still have a leg," she says, knocking her prosthetic against the base of the table. "You can never get back a lost love."

"This is one fucked up conversation," Tag says.

Addy leans across the center of the table. "Come on, guys, bring it in. Sibling hug."

The three of us laugh, then do what she asks, because damn if any of us could ever deny our little sister.

Chapter Twenty-six

Nicky

Jaxon has been laying it on thick the past few nights. Yesterday, he paraded me around McQuaid Circle on his arm, stopping in almost every establishment: Ava Criss' coffeehouse, Regan Lucas' bookstore, Maddie Foster's flower shop. He even found an excuse to pop into the bowling alley, the hardware store, and the market. Then to top it all off, we got ice cream and sat on the bench by the statue of Lloyd McQuaid—smack dab in the middle of the circle's roundabout, where every driver was sure to see us.

I'm just not sure what he's doing will make the situation less scandalous, or more.

Tonight, we're eating at Donovan's Pub. Everyone hangs out at Donovan's on Friday nights. The last time I was here was a month ago, the night of the reunion. I'm hoping this time proves to be a better experience.

"Ignore them," Jaxon says of the dozens of eyes staring at me. "They're only curious about what such a big star is doing in a local joint."

I about spit my Diet Coke out. "You aren't a very good liar. Nobody here sees me as a television personality, and we both know it."

"Well, let them be surprised. They're going to have to get used to it."

Lissa places our dinner on the table. She eyes our clasped hands. "You two getting hitched again?"

"Uh, no," I spew, maybe a bit too quickly for Jaxon's liking.

"We're dating," he says.

"Oh, that's nice."

He scoots closer. "Yes, it is. How's Lucas?"

Lissa's eyes go wide.

"You should know by now that nothing's a secret in Calloway Creek."

"I guess I should. He's fine. Enjoy your dinner."

I roll my eyes.

"What?" he asks. "If she's going to dig into my private life, she should be prepared for me to ask about hers."

Boisterous laughter rolls through the front doors, along with Jaxon's archenemies. He stiffens when Hudson McQuaid spots us.

"Have you had a chance to talk with him yet?" I ask.

"Not yet. He is bound by law. I could sue him if he says anything to anyone."

"Good luck proving it, though. His family is so rich they probably have five lawyers on standby."

They pass our table, then stop and turn. *Uh oh.*

"Well, if it isn't the happy couple," Hawk, the eldest McQuaid brother, says. "Guess her being a TV star trumps all the cheating she did on you. Kinda makes you a shallow fucker, don't it?"

Jaxon tries to stand, but I coax him down. "Don't let them get to you."

"She didn't cheat on me. It was a misunderstanding."

"As in some dude's cock mistakenly wound up between her legs?" Hunter laughs. "And I'll bet she has some land in Siberia to sell you too."

Hudson looks between Jaxon and me. "So you two are... together?"

Jaxon puts his arm around my shoulder. "We are." Hudson laughs as they walk away. Jaxon scoots out of the booth. "Be right back."

"Jaxon, don't goad them."

"I just need to talk to Hudson. I'll be quick." He taps him on the shoulder. "A word."

They step out of earshot of Hudson's brothers.

"I know what you're going to say," Hudson says. "Yeah, I hate your guts, but that doesn't mean I can spill your secrets. But damn..." He glances over at me. "I can't wait for this to come out. Does she even know yet?" He's speaking in hushed tones, but I'm pretty sure he meant for me to hear every word. He really is a douchebag.

"Fuck you, McQuaid." Jaxon walks away.

"You and what dick? Only a pussy would take back a lying cheater."

Jaxon flips him the bird without turning around.

"I see that went well," I say.

"About as expected. He won't say anything. But I'm pretty sure he thinks I haven't told you."

"I heard. He must be salivating over this." I put my sandwich down and turn up my nose. "You know the whole town will be. I don't even know what to expect. Will they hate me again because you're with me instead of her? She would be the obvious choice considering everything."

"They won't hate you. If it comes down to it, I'll tell everyone I was the cheater. I'll print out flyers and post them on every corner."

"You will not. There's no need to perpetuate more gossip."

"But I hate that most people still think you're the one who did wrong."

"Jaxon, I left you. I *am* the one who did wrong."

He pushes his food away, looking guilty. "I did wrong *more*."

"It's not a competition. And we agreed we'd put it all behind us and start fresh."

"I'll never stop being sorry."

My hand rests on his thigh. "Me either."

He notices my food has gone mostly uneaten. "Something wrong with your dinner?"

"I'm not hungry."

"Because of them?" He nods to the McQuaids over at the pool table.

"No."

"Because of me?"

I shrug. "It's been a tough week. A lot to wrap our heads around, you know?"

"It's going to be okay, Nic. There may be some bumps in the road, but we're going to do all right. The whole thing with Calista is separate from us. The way I feel about you has nothing to do with her or the way I feel about the baby. I want you any way I can have you. As unbelievable as you may think it sounds, if you'd had a baby with another man, or were pregnant with one, I'd still want you back."

I gaze at him longingly. "You would?"

"I would. And you know what? I'd bet the bungalow that Eric feels the same way. I know they were only dating for a short time, but I see him watching her. The man is head over heels." He elbows me. "Kind of like I was for you when I was a horny teenager."

"Was?" I ask playfully. "You're still a horny teenager if you ask me."

He kisses my neck. "Only around you, Nic."

"Maybe they'll get back together once she goes public. But it's not Eric I'm worried about. It's me. What if *I* can't handle her pregnancy? There was a woman at WRKT who got pregnant last year. I couldn't stand to be in the same room with her."

"I doubt that will be much of a problem. Looks like the two of you don't want anything to do with each other."

"What if I can't be around the baby?"

He pulls me close. "We have plenty of time to get used to the idea. And more than likely, you'll be in Oklahoma most of the time. When you're here, I'll make sure the baby is with Calista."

"What about Christmas breaks and summers? The times you said you'd come to me. You're going to want to be with your child on Christmas, Jaxon. And what if I can't be around him or her? It'll be like you're living two separate lives."

"That's not going to happen."

"How do you know?"

"Because you love me. And when you love someone, you accept every part of them. The baby will be a part of me."

My heart races. Neither of us has said the words. "I *love* you?"

He pops a fry into his mouth and smiles while he chews. "You may not have said it out loud, but I know you do." He washes his food down with a drink. "And I may not have said it either. Doesn't mean it's not true."

My entire body tingles from head to toe. Did we somehow just declare that we're in love?

Chapter Twenty-seven

Jaxon

I adore watching Nicky sleep. I think I've missed it most of all over the past two years. My eyes follow the edge of the sheet until it meets the top of her breast. Okay, maybe second most.

She starts stirring. I push a chunk of hair off her forehead and kiss her. "Morning."

Sleepy eyes gaze at me. The edges of her mouth curve into a slow smile. These first moments when she wakes are the best. She's happy. Carefree. These are the moments I cherish. The small sliver of time between her dreams and our reality. Before she wakes and remembers I'm going to be a father to someone else's baby.

Because it happens. Every time she's slept over in the past two weeks, I see it. I watch the realization cross her face.

And it breaks me.

"Morning." She snuggles into me. She quickly drifts off to sleep as I rub her back.

"Nic, you'll be late."

Waking again, she pouts. "Why can't I have the day off, too?"

"The perks of being a teacher," I say. "A four-day weekend for Fall break. We'll get to spend the whole day together on Monday."

When she doesn't respond, I chuckle and nudge her. "Babe, wake up."

"I'm up, I'm up," she says sleepily.

Heisman jumps up on the bed and lies behind her, his head propped up on her hip—something he used to do to *me* every morning. The more Nicky stays over, the more attached he's become to her. He stares at me and whines. "All right, bud, let's take you outside." I pull on my sweatpants, then lean over and plant a kiss on Nicky's lips—the lips that did all kinds of amazing things to me last night. "Nicole, get up. Seriously."

While Heisman is out back doing his stuff, I make coffee. I fill two mugs and take one to the bathroom for Nic. But she's not in the bathroom. She's still in bed. And she's staring at my phone.

She looks green. "She texts you with updates on the baby?"

I set down the mug and scoot in next to her. I read the text that just came through.

Calista: Baby is the size of a lime! Can you believe it? It's 1.6 inches long, almost 3x what it was at the ultrasound. Fingers and toes will no longer be webbed. Nipples on the chest will be visible. OMG, Jaxon, only one more week and we'll be in the second trimester!

Tears coat Nic's lashes. "Your phone vibrated so I looked. When I saw the text was from her, I couldn't help myself. And then… well, you never changed your code. I read all of them. She texts you every week?"

I put down the phone and pull her against me. "Nicky, I can't help what she does. You saw my responses, right? All I do is tell her that's great."

She nods, fingering the pendant. Tears fall. It kills me that this is killing her. I'd give anything to be going through this with Nic instead of Calista. It would be like a dream come true.

"I don't want to go to work today," she says.

"Now that's something I've never heard come out of your mouth before." I lift her chin. "You can't let her texts bother you. We've been good, haven't we? These pasts weeks when we've been out together. The nights you've slept over. It's been amazing."

"It kind of has."

Heisman's bark reaches all the way to the bedroom. "Hit the shower. I'll make breakfast." I grab my phone, kiss Nicky's head, and run out to let him in.

Making breakfast, I talk to my dog. Sometimes I wonder if other people talk to their pets as much as I do. But when you're a bachelor living alone, it seems perfectly normal. "Do you like having Nicky here?"

He momentarily glances up from the bowl of kibble he's devouring.

I stir the eggs. "I like it. You know you'd permanently lose your sleeping spot if—"

"Who are you talking to?" Nic says, rounding the corner.

"Heisman and I have deep, intimate conversations. Didn't you know?"

"What do you talk about?"

"Mostly sports."

She giggles.

I split the eggs between two plates, throw on some bacon, and set them on the table. "And you. We talk about you sometimes."

As if Heisman knows we're talking about him, he trots over and puts his head in Nic's lap. "What do you tell Jaxon about me?" she asks him. "You promised you wouldn't say anything about the piece of steak I slipped you the other night."

"You better not turn my dog into a beggar," I say, pointing my fork playfully.

"I thought you liked it when people beg."

My dick stirs. I pull her chair closer. "People—no. Dogs—no. You—hell yes and back for more."

Vibration comes from my phone. Nicky looks at it wearily. I check the text.

"It's my mother confirming lunch today."

She pushes away her plate. I've never known her not to finish breakfast. She's really upset about Calista's texts. I can't blame her. If the tables were turned… Fuck, I can't even imagine if the tables were turned. I try to put myself in her shoes. Every text from Calista is a reminder of someone I slept with. Every time she sees her is a devastating reminder of her own loss. I don't even want to think about what will happen when Calista is visibly showing. No wonder she's lost her appetite. I've sure as hell lost mine.

I throw the rest of our breakfast in the sink and wrap my arms around her as she checks messages on her phone. "Come right back here after work. It's our bye week. We have all night together."

"It's Friday," she says. "I have to be in bed early."

Spinning her chair around, I trap her to it with my arms and lean close, letting my breath flow over her ear. "Oh, I plan to have you in bed early. I plan to have you all kinds of ways."

"Then I'd better get going. If I play my cards right, I can be out of there by four and into your bed by five."

My dick likes her answer. It stresses my boxer briefs.

~ ~ ~

Drying off after my shower, I hear what can only be an eighteen-wheeler pulling up outside. I peek through the slats in my blinds. The Papadakis' moving truck is here. I have hours before I need to meet Mom. I throw on a T-shirt and jeans and go out to see if I can help.

"Morning, Mr. Papadakis," I say, finding him on the front sidewalk. "Moving day, huh? Is there anything I can do to help?"

"I appreciate the offer, but four men bigger than your linebackers just went inside. Looks like they have it covered."

"It's going to be strange not having you around. I'll never know when it's Saturday if I don't smell your brisket."

He appraises the yard he's spent decades mowing. "It's been a great twenty-five years livin' here. But it's time to move on."

"Do you know when the new family will move in?"

His head shakes back and forth. "That deal fell through. Something about the financing. Poor things. I know they really loved it here."

"I'm sorry to hear that. Back to the drawing board?"

He studies me strangely. "I thought for sure you'd heard. We sold it to that pretty little thing who comes around your house sometimes."

A smile splits my face in two. "Nicole Forbes bought your house?"

"Not her. The other one. Technically, she hasn't bought it yet. The deal was only signed a few days ago. She'll be renting until the sale goes through 'bout a month from now. Moving in tomorrow actually."

My stomach turns as my future flashes in front of me. "You're selling to Calista Hilson?"

"That's the one. Cash sale, too. I think her daddy helped her. Should happen quickly."

Standing here pretending my world isn't tumbling out of control is very hard to do. "Okay, then. I hope you enjoy your new condo. You've been great neighbors."

He shakes my hand. "You too, son. Good luck with that football team of yours."

"Thank you."

I walk casually back to my house, get Heisman and my running shoes, and then hit the pavement, not stopping until I'm banging down the door to Calista's apartment.

It opens and I plow through. "What the hell are you pulling here by buying the Papadakis' house?"

She bends over and pats Heisman. "Well, good morning to you too," she sings happily.

Glancing around her place, all I see are boxes, packing paper, and rolls of tape. "I mean, what the fuck, Calista?"

"It makes sense, doesn't it? Think about it, Jaxon. When you told me you were going to want shared custody, all I could see was us carting the baby back and forth, shuttling him between our places. This way, we're both right there. We'll be thirty feet away. We can literally walk our child through the grass to each other's house. I was even thinking of removing the fence between our yards. Wouldn't it be great? We can put in a huge swing set. Maybe even a pool when the baby is older."

The more excited she gets, the more pissed I become. She's played it cool the past three weeks. The texts have been the only real communication we've had about the baby. At school, we pass in the hallway and say hello. We talk cordially in the teachers' lounge. It's been better than I thought it would be. Now I know why. "Have you been planning this all along? Is this a stunt to get me back?"

"Stunt? This isn't about you, Jaxon. Believe me, I don't want you back. I deserve a man who loves me unconditionally. This is about the baby, plain and simple. When a realtor friend of mine told me about the deal that fell through on the house last week, it all started to make sense. I believe it was fate. Don't you think so?"

"Fate?" I glance at her still-flat stomach. "You think fate had you getting knocked up just when my wife came back in the picture?"

"*Ex*-wife."

"Fuck! Whatever."

"Listen, what's done is done. I'm moving in tomorrow in case you're interested."

I peek in one of the boxes. It's loaded with books. "You have help?"

She leans against the back of her couch, smiling. "You offering?"

"You shouldn't be lifting heavy boxes, especially down from the second floor. And, no, I'm not offering to do it myself, but I'll help pay for someone so you don't get hurt."

"Look at you being all protective of me."

"Calista, I don't have any other choice. Protecting you is the only way to protect my baby."

"While the chivalry is appreciated, my dad paid for the movers."

I stare her down. "Like he paid for the house?"

She sits. "So he wants to be a doting granddad. Can you blame him for wanting his grandchild to grow up having a backyard, with a park and an ice cream shop nearby?"

I huff and back away, needing distance. "You need to understand something right now. I'm not sure if you have ulterior motives here, but you need to know that whether you live two miles away or two feet away, you and I will never be getting back together. So if this really is all part of some grand scheme to make that happen, I'd tell your father to kill the deal right fucking now."

She rolls her eyes dramatically. "Get over yourself. I'm perfectly capable of being a single mother. And you have to admit living next door will make things easier. What if I go into labor in the middle of the night? What if after the baby comes he or she gets sick. You'll be right there. What if he's with you and needs his mother? You can practically yell over and get me. And surely you agree it'll be what's best for our child—us being there for him or her, together, even though we're not."

I lean against a pile of boxes, wanting to argue but knowing what she says is true. Just a few weeks ago, I was telling her I had every intention of being in the baby's life as much as I could. But damn… this is a hefty dose of *be careful what you wish for*.

Nicky will be so upset.

"Guess you've thought of everything then." I go for the door but hesitate. "Except Eric. He really misses you, you know."

"He wouldn't if he knew about the baby."

"I don't think you give the guy enough credit. Accidents happen, Calista. Women get pregnant when they have sex. It's a fact of life. It was before you and he got together. Eric is a very understanding guy. He might surprise you."

She stares at the wall. "I've had one too many heartbreaks this year. I don't think I'm up for another."

"But you didn't even give him the chance to walk away. He's one of my best friends. I hate to see him go through this."

"Go through what?"

"Losing the woman he loves. You said it yourself, you want someone who loves you unconditionally. Well, I'm pretty sure you had him."

"Loves? We weren't even together a month. How can you say that?"

"So now love has a timeline?" I open the door, then remember Heisman is here. "Come on, buddy." He doesn't move. I go over to see him doing that thing again. He's on the couch, his head glued to her as if… *does he know she's pregnant?* Can he smell it or something? Or maybe it's just the change in her demeanor. But I know that's ridiculous. He wasn't around her enough to notice a change. "Heisman," I say sharply. "Come."

Reluctantly, he follows. We walk the two miles home, him chasing every squirrel we come across, me wondering how I'm going to break the news to Nicky.

Chapter Twenty-eight

Nicky

Jaxon rolls off me again after another marathon session. He's really trying to make me forget who moved in next door a few days ago. Calista, on the other hand, seems intent on not letting that happen. Every time I'm here, she has some emergency. Saturday night it was her air conditioner. Last night it was a leaky faucet. Funny how these 'emergencies' only seem to happen when *I'm* here. It occurs to me that maybe Jaxon doesn't tell me about any others.

I visit the bathroom, then put on panties and one of his funny teacher T-shirts that makes a joke about *their, there, and they're*. Although I'm taller than a lot of women, I still drown in the shirt, but it just barely covers my butt cheeks. Jaxon rubs one when I climb back in next to him.

"You're handling this better than I thought you would," he says.

I don't dare tell him I've done nothing but cry since I found out about it. I don't tell him I've been crying for weeks. I cry in the bathroom at work. On the train ride home. Even at his house in the shower. Just thinking about it now has me feeling ill. But I'm not about to be the needy girlfriend who demands all of his attention. This is Jaxon. After everything that's happened in the past, I know he'll be loyal to me at all costs. I also know he'll do anything for his kid. Balancing the two is a line he's treading very carefully.

"I don't have a choice. The sooner I accept it, the easier this will be on all of us."

He traces a finger down my jaw. "You're amazing."

Heisman stands at the end of the bed, his head on the sheets, whining to come up. The poor dog has been displaced. I pat the covers next to me. "Come on up, Heisman."

He gives a happy 'woof' and jumps up, wiggling his way between us. The more I stay here, the more Heisman has warmed up to me. Not that he ever disliked me. He likes everyone. But I almost get the feeling he knows who I am, like maybe he even wants me here. Like now, his head is on my stomach, and he's staring at me intently.

"Your dog is strange," I say. "Don't get me wrong, I love him. But lately he's been different. Almost protective somehow."

Jaxon bolts up in bed.

"What is it?" I ask.

"Nic, is there any chance you could be pregnant?"

I cough. "Hardly. Why would you ask such a thing?"

"Because I swear Heisman is acting the same way around you as he started acting when he was near Calista right around the time we found out she was pregnant."

I ruffle Heisman's tuft, not wanting to hold it against him that he likes *her* too. "I told you my doctor said it was unlikely."

"Unlikely but not impossible?"

"I suppose, but Jax—"

"When was your last period? I can't even remember you having one."

"They've been unpredictable due to the Asherman's."

He's out of bed now, pacing the room. "Has there been anything? Cravings? Anything at all?"

I laugh at the ridiculousness of it. Then I stiffen.

He freezes. "Tell me."

"It's nothing, I'm sure. Just me dealing with our situation."

"What is it?"

"I guess I've been off. Not wanting to eat as much. And I suppose I'm more emotional."

"Have you felt sick at all?"

I think back over the past week or so and look up, my expression tense.

"Oh, shit, you have."

"Jaxon, there's no way."

"But you said yourself, it's not impossible. And we've had sex like fifty times since you've been back. *Without protection.*"

"Still…"

He pulls on clothes in record time. "I'm going to get you a test."

"You're being ridiculous. I'm sure it's nothing."

"Heisman says otherwise. I'm going. Be back in twenty."

I spend the next twenty minutes throwing up.

~ ~ ~

Jaxon sets his phone timer for three minutes.

Tears run down my face.

He cups my chin. "Hey, it's okay."

"It's not. You don't understand. Even if I'm pregnant, it could be risky. Scar tissue can complicate things."

"You're pregnant. I don't have to see the test. Your boobs have changed." He smirks. "I thought I was imagining it."

"Jaxon, how can you joke about this? Even if I was and everything was okay, do you realize what that means? You'd have two babies within, what, a month or two? It would be crazy."

He kisses the side of my head. "It would be perfect." He checks the timer. One minute left. "Move in with me."

"Aren't you being a little premature?"

"I was going to ask you on Friday, but I didn't want it to seem like I was only asking because Calista was moving in next door."

"Yeah, but now you're asking because of this."

"Nic, I don't care if you're pregnant or not. I mean, I do care. I want you to be." He laughs. "It's crazy, but I want it so badly. But either way, I want you to live here. Even after you go back to Oklahoma, I want this to be the place you call home when you're in town."

"If you're serious—"

"As serious as the heart attack I might have if I'm having two babies."

His phone timer goes off, and I get off the bed. He pulls me back down. "Can I get an answer?"

"You need an answer *now*?" I motion to the bathroom.

"Yes. Move in with me, Nic. I love you. I've always loved you. And no matter what that test says, or what happens in the future, nothing will change that. You and me, we're unfinished. We have so much more left."

Tears cloud my vision. "How can a girl say no to that?"

He pulls me into his arms. "It's going to be great. Trust me. Now let's go see if I'm about to have a coronary."

Unfinished **EX**

I race ahead of him and look at the stick. My heart flips. I'm terrified and ecstatic at the same time. "Well, then, we'd better call 911."

Chapter Twenty-nine

Jaxon

I don't think I've ever been so nervous. The past eight hours have been stressful. I'm tied in knots researching this condition she has: Asherman's syndrome. The scarring in her uterus may have made it harder for her to get pregnant, but that's not the only obstacle. It could also cause a miscarriage, hemorrhage, placenta previa, and other things I can't even think about.

As soon as she told the doctor her condition, they were able to squeeze her in as the last appointment of the day. We pull up to the same medical building as Calista's doctor, and I get a sick feeling. "Nicky, if you tell me Hudson McQuaid is your doctor, I'm going to throw an actual fit right here."

"God no. I know better than that. I spent all morning on the phone finding the best doctor for high-risk pregnancies."

High risk. My gut twists.

"It's the same building."

"Jaxon, there are only five obstetricians in Calloway Creek, and they're all in this building."

I glance around the parking lot. "I don't even want to see that prick."

"You won't. Park around back."

"In the back? Why?"

"I asked them to keep this discreet, given my—"

I grin. "Celebrity status?"

"I wouldn't say that, but I am a public persona. And I don't want XTN finding out about this."

"They can't fire you."

"I know. But on the remote chance Makenna doesn't come back, they could decide not to hire me as her permanent replacement."

"Right. So we keep this on the down low."

"As if we aren't already doing that with Calista." She covers her face. "Jaxon, do you know how messed up this could get?"

I squeeze her thigh. "We can think about that later. Right now, I just want to see if you and the baby are okay. That is the only thing that matters."

She pulls out her phone and sends a text.

Five minutes later, someone opens a back door.

Nicky exhales a long, slow, anxious breath. It kills me that we can't even be excited about this. I open the car door. "Babe, we got this. Whatever happens, we're in this together."

Like with Calista, a nurse takes Nicky to a different area, and then they meet me in an exam room with the same ultrasound machine. In fact, it could be the same room, but I can't swear it since we came in a different way.

"Everything off from the waist down," the nurse says. "Then lie on the table. The doctor will be in momentarily."

It's like déjà vu. Nicky is right, this is going to be a fucking mess. What will we tell people? The gossip will rise to colossal levels. What will the people at school say? What if XTN finds out? Our only hope of her staying might be if Makenna doesn't come back. Suddenly, a million questions loom heavily. Will she still go back to Oklahoma? And if so, I'll not only be a bicoastal boyfriend—I'll be a bicoastal dad.

The door opens and an older doctor comes in, bringing me a wave of relief. Thank the Lord for small favors. He walks to Nicky and extends his hand. "Ms. Forbes, I'm Dr. Peterman. Nice to meet you."

I stand so quickly, my chair falls back. "Wait, Dr. *Peterman*? No." There's another knock on the door, and my archenemy walks through.

Fuck. Fuck. Fuck.

Hudson tries to keep a straight face but isn't doing a very good job.

"No goddamn way," I say, standing between Hudson and Nicky. "Excuse my language, Dr. Peterman, but no way is this asshole getting anywhere near my wife."

"You mean *ex*," Hudson says. "She is still your ex, no?"

"Slip of the tongue," I say. "I want you out."

"What's the issue here?" Dr. Peterman says.

"Their families don't like each other very much," Nicky explains.

"I want another doctor."

"Jaxon, Dr. Peterman specializes in high-risk pregnancies."

"Then how come he's also Calista's doctor?"

"We handle all kinds of pregnancies," Hudson says.

"You." I point. "Shut it." I turn to the elder doctor. "If you're the best, we want you. But he doesn't get near her. Not her head, not her stomach, and sure as hell not her pus—uh, vagina."

Dr. Peterman gives McQuaid a flick of his head, and Hudson leaves. My blood pressure is through the roof.

"Ms. Forbes," Dr. Peterman says. "Do you concur with your partner?"

Nicky locks eyes with me. She knows I won't stand for it. "If I do, can you still be my doctor?"

"Of course. You're the patient. Dr. McQuaid is a resident. Although important that he learn from cases like yours, if you don't want him involved, he won't be. I have another colleague you can meet at the next appointment who can be my backup."

"Thank you," Nicole says.

I eye the door. "Can you wait two minutes, please? I don't want to miss this, but there's something I have to do."

"Jaxon, really?" Nicky says, rising on her elbows.

"Two minutes." I beg Dr. Peterman with my eyes, hoping he gets me man to man. "Please."

He checks his watch and motions to the door. "Go. I'll get her history."

I run out the door and glance right, then left. "Where's Hudson?" I ask a lady in scrubs. "Er, Dr. McQuaid?" *God—it tasted bad to say that.*

"Just left." She nods to the back door.

I race over, open it, and see him getting into his sleek red Maserati. "McQuaid!"

He shakes his head and stands at the door, smirking.

"Not a fucking word. I will hunt you down and kill you. Nobody, and I mean no one else, knows about this. Not even family. If word gets out, I'll know it's you, and I will do whatever it takes to ruin your career. I'll go to the medical board. I'll even go on TV. I've got connections at a pretty damn good network. Breathe a word to anyone. Make a joke. Even look at us funny, and I'll nail you to the wall."

"I know the goddamn laws, Calloway, so you can fuck off with your threats." He gets into his car, laughing as he pulls away.

Goddamn it.

I head back inside. "My apologies," I say, entering the exam room.

Dr. Peterman looks up from his chart. "My resident still alive?"

"For now."

"We understand the need to keep this private, Mr. Calloway. You have my word it will remain that way." He puts down the file and picks up the wand thing. "Shall we get started?"

I right the chair and sit down, taking Nicky's hand. We're both scared. The ultrasound takes far longer than Calista's did. This can't be good. Nicky squeezes the blood from my fingers. I gently caress her forehead to help her relax, the whole time sending up a prayer that this will turn out all right. I dig deep, searching for that gut feeling I get sometimes. It's not there. And I find myself at a crossroads between hope and desperation.

Nicky finally speaks up. "Dr. Peterman?"

He turns away from the screen. "Sorry. I'm trying to be as thorough as possible." He points back. "This right here is the fetus. It's measuring at eight, eight-and-a-half weeks. Since you can't pinpoint your last menstrual period, we'll go strictly by the measurement and put your estimated due date at May twenty-ninth."

May? I don't even have time to process that yet. My heart thunders. "There's a due date? So everything is okay?"

The nurse prints out a picture and hands it to Nicky.

"I can't say either way," Dr. Peterman says. "There are some things we just can't see this early. Like the extent of these bands of scarring. I can see scar tissue here by one of the fallopian tubes, which should have made it increasingly hard for you to conceive. Pregnancy requires a normal uterine cavity. Scarring can cause complications. The major area of concern with Asherman's is the placenta attaching over areas damaged from your D and C. This would be called an invasive placenta, where it digs deeper into the uterine wall. And if the fetus were to be carried to term with an invasive placenta, a C-section with hysterectomy would be indicated."

Nicky gasps. "Hysterectomy?"

"If the placenta is too deep, the whole uterus will have to be removed, or we risk life-threatening bleeding."

Nicky begins shaking. Dr. Peterman puts a hand on her arm. "But let's not get ahead of ourselves. That's a worst-case scenario."

She shakes her head and grips her pendant. "No. The worst thing that could happen would be losing the baby."

"We'll know more around the eighteen- to twenty-week mark, when you'll have an anatomy ultrasound. We'll also get a consult by MFM—maternal fetal medicine. They specialize in high-risk cases. They'll see you at least once. More if necessary, but we'll play that by ear. In the meantime, I'd like to get the records from your doctor in Oklahoma. Once we have all that information, we'll have a better idea of the level of risk."

"Eighteen to twenty weeks?" Nicky's voice cracks. "We have to wait *ten* more weeks to know anything?"

"Can't you do it earlier?" I ask. "She may be back in Oklahoma by then. And with her previous miscarriage, I'm not sure we could stand the wait. There must be something you can do. Look at how freaked she is. I'm begging you."

He studies the screen. "I'd be willing to do another one at fourteen weeks, but no sooner. And there are no guarantees we'll be able to get concrete information from that one. You'll still need the other ultrasound."

"Good. Thank you. That's all we can ask."

"Still. Six weeks," Nicky says. "This will be torture."

There is a gigantic knot in my throat that cuts like shards of glass when I swallow. "Doctor, if Nicky was your daughter, what would you tell her? How would you honestly feel about this? We already lost one baby. We didn't think this was a possibility. I want to be excited about this, but all that stuff you said has me terrified."

"It's okay to get excited. Every pregnancy comes with a risk of complications and miscarriage." He motions back to the screen. "Right now, I see a healthy fetus with a strong heartbeat. So let's not worry until we know for sure there's something to worry about. It's possible you could have a normal full-term pregnancy; let's focus on that for the time being."

Nicky runs a finger across the picture. "Is it really okay to be excited?"

"Yes, of course." He smiles, offering us a modicum of relief. "You already beat the odds by conceiving. Thinking positively and taking care of yourself are the best things you can do at this point."

He and the nurse leave the room. I bend over the table and pull her into my arms. "You heard him. You beat the odds. You could have a normal pregnancy. We're going to be okay, Nic. This baby is meant to be. I know it."

She looks at me through balls of tears. "You think so?"

I put a hand on her belly. "We're going to be a family, in whatever fucked-up way that might happen."

She laughs. "I want this, Jaxon. I want this so much."

"I want you. I want this baby. I want all of it—any goddamn way I can have it."

Chapter Thirty

Nicky

Jaxon and Heisman vie for position on my stomach. I don't mind at all. Heisman's intrusiveness lets me know I'm still pregnant, which offers me reassurance.

"Do you think we should rent him out?" I ask when Jaxon nudges Heisman away to get more room. "You know, as a pregnancy test?"

He chuckles and kisses my stomach, something he's done daily since the day I peed on the stick two weeks ago. "Hell no, he's our own baby barometer. Is it strange that I want him to keep doing it? Like if he doesn't, something might be wrong?"

I run my fingers through his hair. "I was thinking the exact same thing."

My phone chimes with an email. When I see who it's from, I stiffen.

"What is it?" Jaxon asks. He scoots up next to me and reads it over my shoulder. "Who's Harold Lynchburg?"

As I get further into the email, my heart races steadily. "He's a producer at WYTV in Detroit. They're an NBC affiliate." I put the phone down and squeal. "*NBC*, Jaxon. And Detroit is a huge market. They want me to fly out there next Monday."

"They're offering you a job?"

"Not technically. But an invite like this implies they will be."

He sighs and leans back. "They want to grab you before the networks start fighting over you."

"No one is going to fight over me."

"Nicky, you've shown me the ratings and the fan mail. *Everyone* is going to want you."

I run a hand along my belly. "It's hard to even think about that right now."

"Will you go?"

"Would you be mad if I did?"

"I swore I wouldn't be upset when the time came. I knew you being here was temporary. And even though the stakes have changed, like, big time, I'd be a fool to stand in your way. We aren't going to end up like we did two years ago. I'll quit coaching if I have to so I can fly to you every weekend. It'll be hard as hell to be away from you and the baby for a day, let alone a week, but I told you we're going to make this happen. No matter what."

"You're not going to quit coaching. You love it. And you quitting would put a strain on us someday. We'll just have to figure out a way to achieve our career goals *and* our family ones."

He climbs on top of me and gives me a kiss. "We'll do whatever it takes."

It's been weeks since we found out about the baby. I half expected him to propose. Then again, maybe he's waiting to see what happens. Will our relationship survive if this baby doesn't?

We haven't talked about the baby much. There's been no planning. No online shopping. No dreaming up names. We're both scared. Maybe talking about it would make us become more attached. But I'm already attached. And losing this baby would be even more devastating this time because I've wanted it since the second I took the test.

Heisman jumps up next to us and licks my arm. "Someone needs to go out," I say.

Jaxon springs out of bed. "I'll do it. Then I'll make breakfast while you shower."

Fifteen minutes later, while wrapped in a towel, I go out in search of my one cup of morning coffee. Because some things you just can't give up. I hesitate when I hear Calista's voice. I round the corner, not caring what I'm wearing, and stop cold when I see her shirt up, flaunting her small bump.

Jaxon sees me and takes two steps away from her. Guilt crosses his face even though he was doing nothing wrong. "She thought she felt the baby move."

"It's too early," I say.

Calista narrows her eyes. "How would you know?"

"Seriously, Calista," Jaxon says, stepping to my side. "Do you have to be so goddamn insensitive?"

She at least has the decency to look guilty. "Right. Sorry. I forgot you had a miscarriage. But I really did think I felt a kick. It could happen any day now."

I try not to let jealousy consume me. She gets to enjoy her pregnancy, and I have to sit here and take it all in like a kid eating her most hated vegetables. We can't even tell her I'm pregnant. We can't tell anyone—not yet and not for a long time.

Calista gets out a glass and pours herself a cup of milk like this is her kitchen and not mine. It *is* mine. I've been living here for two weeks now.

Jaxon looks at me and rolls his eyes. He doesn't want her here either. I get it. He doesn't want her, that I'm sure of, but he's going to be nice to her for the sake of the baby. The last thing he needs is to end up in a custody battle. I wouldn't wish that on anyone. So I bottle up my feelings and pretend to go along with it.

"I'm going to get dressed," I say.

"Lucky," Calista murmurs just loud enough for me to hear. "Most of my clothes are getting way too tight."

I touch my stomach, praying I'll be able to say the same thing in a few weeks' time.

When I return to the kitchen, Jaxon doesn't seem happy. But at least Calista is gone. "She wants to start telling people soon."

I plop down into the chair next to him. "She's in the second trimester. It makes sense."

"I would rather she wait until we can announce our own news."

"That won't happen for a long time, Jaxon. I can't risk my job, or future job. I'm going to need a month or two to figure out where I'm going to end up. And we for sure have to wait until after the fourteen-week ultrasound."

"No way will she wait that long." He takes his cup to the sink and practically throws it in. "She's going to steal our thunder, Nic."

"Somehow I get the idea there will be a hell of a lot more of it when people find out about *this* one."

"People will say you got pregnant because she did."

"Let them. What do we care?"

"I *do* care. People already have a negative attitude toward you, despite our recent show of solidarity."

"You can't help what people will think, Jaxon." I look to the floor. "Besides, it might not even be an issue if—"

He races over. "If nothing. This baby is going to be okay. I know it and Heisman knows it. And Dr. Peterman is going to confirm it in four more weeks."

"I hope you're right." I put my arms around his neck. "I really need you to be right."

He kisses my forehead. "Yeah, me too."

Chapter Thirty-one

Jaxon

I can't begin to count the number of hours I've watched her sleep over the past weeks. Somehow pregnancy has made her even more beautiful. And damn sexy. Her skin is luminous. Her breasts fuller. My morning erection is straining against my boxer briefs.

Her eyes flutter open. "You're staring again."

I brush hair off her face. "Can't help it. You're gorgeous."

"I'll bet you say that to all the women pregnant with your babies."

My jaw slackens. It's the first time she's ever joked about our... situation. "Why, Ms. Forbes, you *do* have a sense of humor."

"Want to know what else I have?" She seductively bites her lower lip.

I shimmy against her. "I hope you're going to say my dick in your hands in two seconds."

She laughs. "I was going to say a raging libido, but that'll do." She reaches under the waistband of my skivvies, and I moan.

It's been weeks since we've been together. Between her feeling sick and both of us being stressed, the timing just hasn't been right. Obviously, something has changed this morning. It occurs to me what as she's rubbing my cock. "You'll be in the second trimester soon. I've read some women get really horny then."

"I'm surprised our neighbor hasn't asked you to help her out with *that* considering the fact that she's asked for help with everything else."

"Babe, talking about her is about the only thing you could do to deflate my hard-on."

"Sorry." She strokes harder as I run a finger along the edge of her panties and slip it beneath to find her already wet.

"I think I'm going to like the second trimester very much." My foot connects with Heisman's backside, and I nudge him off the bed. He thumps onto the floor, letting out a disappointed groan.

"I'm not even twelve weeks," she says. "We still have a bit."

"Yeah, but you've always been very advanced."

She giggles. "I don't think pregnancy works that wa—uuuugh."

Her back arches when I plunge a finger inside her. I push up her shirt and latch onto her breast, teasing her nipple with my tongue. Her entire body shivers. I double my efforts knowing her nipples have become ultrasensitive. With only one finger inside her and another flick of my tongue, she's falling apart beneath me.

"Wow," I say after her walls stop pulsating. "That was fast."

"Shut up and make love to me."

"Gladly."

In a matter of seconds, we're both naked and my cock is sliding in. I hesitate when I remember just where it is. Nic grabs my ass and holds me against her. "You're not going to hurt the baby, Jaxon."

I hover above her. "I know that. But—"

Her eyes roll. "It's not going to see your penis."

"What if—"

"It's not going to reach out and grab it either."

It's a ridiculous thing to think. So why am I even thinking it?

"Jaxon? Do I have to get out my vibrator?"

Suddenly I'm jealous of a piece of plastic. I start moving. "Nothing is going to make you come except for my cock."

I move slowly within her. She thinks it's because of the baby. But really, I just want to watch her build. She undulates beneath me, needing more. I pull out of her for a second, then push back in, her breath catching when I'm fully seated. I inhale her scent—flowery shampoo mixed with pheromones—and devise it's my favorite smell. The sensation of her fingers running up and down my backside drives me wild, but I hold back.

"Jaxon…" My name comes off her lips like a prayer. One I hope to hear over and over again.

Her mouth opens slightly; her eyes are half-lidded; her legs wrap around me and grip me tightly. *Not yet.* I pull out again, and she groans her displeasure. That is, until I quickly work my tongue down her body and give a few strong licks on her clit. Then I brace myself above her and sink my dick into her, pumping twice. Repeating this cycle over and over, tongue, cock, tongue, cock, she spirals up and out of control. When she starts to scream my name, I pump inside her, needing to feel her walls grip my dick and milk me dry. Holding off as long as I can to watch her come, I finally let go, spurting inside her as I grunt exaltations into her shoulder.

I collapse onto her, sweaty and satiated. "Holy shit, Nic."

She giggles, bouncing me on top of her. "You can say that again."

Moving to her side, I lie next to her and caress her flat stomach. "Are you sure you're up for flying to Detroit today?"

"After two orgasms, I'm more relaxed than I've been in weeks. I'll probably sleep the whole way."

"You're not nervous?"

"About the meeting? No." She puts a hand over mine, and they rest over her belly button. "All my worry is tied up in this one. I don't think I have the capacity to be anxious about anything else."

The urge to ask her not to go is strong. For weeks, we've danced around the subject of her job. Her leaving. The baby. Hell, we've danced around *every* subject. It's obvious neither of us can think about the future. We still have almost three weeks to go before her next ultrasound. And even then, Dr. Peterman said we might not know anything concrete.

I prop up on an elbow. "You love me, don't you?"

She touches me on my chest, right over my heart. "I never stopped."

"Why haven't you said it?"

"I didn't know we were there yet."

"But I said I love you."

"Yeah, the day we found out I was pregnant. I didn't know if you only said it bec—"

I pull her close. "Nicky, I've loved you since I was thirteen. I loved you even when I thought you cheated on me." Guilt squeezes me like a vise. "I loved you when I cheated on *you*. I loved you the second I saw you on television and every moment since. And I'm going to love you until the day I fucking die, just like I promised on our wedding day."

Her tears wet the pillow. "I'm going to love you until the day I die, too."

~ ~ ~

It's hard not to think of Nic all day. How is her meeting going? Would she take the job without discussing it with me? What if they make her an offer she can't refuse?

At lunch, Eric bursts through the door of the teachers' lounge. "Is it true?"

Fuck. Looks like it's time to pay the piper. I get up and move out of earshot of everyone and into the small kitchenette. He follows.

"You don't know how bad I feel about this. I swear to God it happened before Nicky came back. Before you guys got together."

"I get that. But you should have given me a heads-up, man. We're friends for Christ's sake."

"Have you talked to her?"

"No. I overheard some kids talking after third period." He shakes his head, clearly frustrated. "Fucking students knew before I did."

I narrow my eyes. "You haven't even talked to her? Why aren't you questioning if the baby is yours?"

"Because I know it's not. I'm infertile. It's why my ex divorced me."

"Ah, man. I'm really sorry." *And apparently I'm the most fertile fucking guy on the planet.*

"Why didn't you tell me, Jaxon?"

I back against the wall. "Because this is going to be a real shit show."

"She's not the only woman to accidentally get knocked up around here."

"You don't know the half of it, man."

"What's that supposed to mean?"

"Nothing. I just wish the two of you were together. It would make things easier."

"I wish we were too."

I raise a brow, happy that he's confirmed my suspicions. "You'd still be with her? Even now?"

"Maybe especially now. Wait, exactly when did you find out she was pregnant?"

"Shortly before she broke up with you." I put a hand on his shoulder. "I'm sorry I couldn't say anything. We wanted to keep it quiet for obvious reasons, but she also begged me not to."

"Is she trying to get back with you? Or did she think I wouldn't want her anymore?"

"I'm fairly sure it's the latter. She even said something the other day about not wanting to go through another heartbreak. I honestly think her breaking up with you was a preemptive strike."

"But that doesn't make sense. I heard she bought the house next door to you."

"For convenience. I don't want her. She doesn't want me. But living next door will be what's best for the kid even if the downside is that it's easier for Calista to disrupt my life by asking for me to fix every little thing that goes wrong in her house."

He grips my shoulder. "I've been telling you all along what a good man you are."

I shrug him off. Because I know I'm not. But I am working on it.

"Damn, I get what you mean about the shit show. People are going to salivate over this. What does Nicky have to say? She's got to be torn up."

You have no idea. "She is. We both are. But there's nothing we can do to change it. I'm going to support the baby, and I hope Calista and I can remain friends, but that'll be the extent of our relationship."

The door to the lounge opens, and Calista walks in. All eyes turn to her. I guess Eric and I weren't as quiet as I'd hoped. Or news traveled faster than expected. A group of women swarms her. She looks over at us, and I wonder what she's thinking. Is she happy being the center of attention? Is she surprised Eric and I are talking and not fighting?

"Now that everything is out in the open," I say to Eric, "you should try to get her back."

"You mean you want her off *your* back."

I laugh. "I suppose that would be the silver lining. Hey, you up for a little game of bait and switch?"

"Not if it means you're going to lead her on."

"Nah, nothing like that. But how about the next time she summons me to fix a leaky faucet or reach something on the top shelf…"

"You giving me your sloppy seconds—again?"

"Eric, she was never as happy with me as she was with you. Her constant cravings and demands are probably more about annoying Nic than anything else."

"Are you saying pregnant women can be unreasonable?"

"Fuck, man—you said it, not me. I'm not about to get my balls roasted by saying something like that. No matter how true it might be."

I leave him laughing and beeline for the door. I don't plan on hanging around to be grilled, judged, or sneered at by two dozen other teachers.

"Mr. Calloway," Matt Bingham says, running up to me from down the hallway. "You dog, you."

"Matt, I don't know what you heard, but I'm going to say this once. Whatever it was is none of your damn business."

Back in my classroom, I pull out my phone and ask Tag and Addy to meet me at Mom and Dad's right after practice.

~ ~ ~

The room falls silent. Four pairs of eyes stare in disbelief—five if you count Cooper's, who has joined us via FaceTime.

Addy is the first to speak. "So much makes sense now. Her breaking up with Eric and buying the house next door. I thought she was stalking you."

"How does Nicky feel about this?" Mom asks.

"How do you think she feels? She hates it."

My mother is the only one in my family who knows about Nic's miscarriage, and it kills me that I can't tell her she's pregnant too. But Nic and I agreed to say nothing, even to family, until we get more news.

"What do you think is going to happen after she goes back to Oklahoma?" Tag asks.

"She might not be. She's actually on her way back from an interview in Detroit. A lot of stations are going to want her. I'm just hoping some of them will be closer."

Dad grips my shoulder. "My son is going to be a father. You may not have planned it this way, but that doesn't mean you can't love this child with everything you have."

"I know, Dad. I plan to. I plan to love all my kids equally, no matter what."

Mom raises a brow but keeps quiet. Perhaps she's the only one who picked up on my faux pas.

"Listen, there's bound to be a ton of gossip about this. The company line is Nic and I are solid and plan to stay that way. And while I'm going to be there for the baby, there is no chance Calista and I will get back together."

"You should tell everyone to mind their own fucking business," Cooper says.

"Well, *I'm* excited," Addy says. "I'm going to be an auntie!" She turns to Tag. "No offense, I love Gigi with my whole heart, but she was already five when she became a part of the family. I can't wait to hold a little baby. I love babies."

"Feel free to babysit anytime," I say. "Believe me, I'll need the help."

Mom gives me another strange look. I get up before I say too much. "Nic will be home soon. I want to go see how her interview went. I'll catch you guys later."

Chatter echoes as I head out the front door. Apparently my family loves a good scandal as much as anyone.

Samantha Christy

Chapter Thirty-two

Nicky

This day has been a wake-up call and an indicator of how the next twenty-eight weeks are going to be. I'm exhausted. Even after getting a nap on the plane, I feel like I've been up for forty-eight hours, not fourteen. The nap, however, came with a nightmare of epic proportions. Seems I dream about the baby a lot these days. Or more accurately—I dream about everything that could go wrong with the baby.

I gaze out the window on the train and wonder how much of a strain it's going to be if I move. Even just working another job will stress our relationship. Being the weekend meteorologist at XTN is the best job I could have. I rarely have to travel, and my weekday hours are more traditional. Jobs like the one in Detroit, while mainly Monday through Friday, would require me to be up at three a.m. five days a week, not two. And while most of my weekends would be free, let's face it, I'd be making up for lost sleep and possibly commuting back to New York. *With* a baby. My only hope is if Makenna doesn't come back to work. But honestly, in today's world, that rarely happens. Would she give up a prestigious job at one of the top cable news networks?

I look down at my stomach. *Would I?*

A call comes in. It's my old producer, Marty. I forwarded him the email from Harold Lynchburg earlier today.

"Marty, what's up?"

He chuckles. "What's up is that I'm giving you a huge *told you so*, Nicole Forbes."

"They didn't exactly offer me the job."

"Yet. Tell me about it."

The events of the day whiz through my head. I still can't believe it myself. "Harold picked me up in a limousine."

"Good start."

"Oh, that's not even the good part. He took me on a tour of the WYTV studio. The dressing room they showed me is as big as Brenton Carmichael's. Everyone greeted me by name like they were all in on some elaborate scheme."

"They're courting you hard."

"We watched the noon newscast. Marty, they had a chair with my name on it. And after, Harold and two of the news anchors took me to lunch at a place where the hamburgers were made from Wagyu steak and cost more than I spend on my weekly groceries."

"How did you leave things?"

"At the airport, Harold asked me to give him a number."

His low belly laugh sounds like Santa Claus. "I hope you didn't lowball it, Nicole."

"I didn't give him a number at all. I told him I wasn't ready to make any decisions yet."

"Playing hard to get. That'll get you more money any day of the week and twice on Sunday."

"I'm not playing hard to get. I have some stuff going on personally that I have to figure out."

"Right. You're back together with your ex."

I sigh. If that were the only issue, this would be so much easier. "It's complicated. And part of me thinks maybe Makenna Kendall won't come back. She's already extended her leave. I know it probably won't happen but..."

"But all things being equal, you'd rather stay in New York."

"Yes."

"Detroit is not the only market that will want you. There will be other offers."

"I hope so." I stare at lights in the distance. The train is almost home. *Home*—it's the first time in a long time that I've thought of Calloway Creek as home. "I miss you, Marty. Barry Remsen might just be the death of me. I don't think I really appreciated you until I didn't have you anymore." I sit up straight when something dawns on me. "Hey, do you think I'd have any leverage with Detroit or whoever about bringing in my own producer?"

"I think you could ask for a lot of things, Nicole. And they'd be fools to deny you. You are on your way up, and everyone who watches you knows it."

"You watch me?"

"Every chance I get. The pride I feel—like a teacher watching a former student. And you should have heard the buzz at the studio after Louisa. You're a celebrity around here."

"You *were* my teacher, Marty. Or maybe my biggest cheerleader. Everything happening to me is because you took a chance on me."

"Everything happening to you is because you are incredible."

"How about you just accept the compliment."

"Right back at you."

"I'm at my stop. Thanks for the call. I'll let you know what happens with Detroit."

"Don't sweat it, Nicole. Big things are going to happen whether or not it's in Michigan."

"Nicky."

"Pardon me?"

"My friends call me Nicky. Nicole is my on-air name."

"Now that might take some getting used to. Nicky. It *does* suit you. I hope I'm not overstepping when I say that despite all these issues you've brought up, you seem happier now. Anyway, I'll talk to you soon, Nicky."

"Bye, Marty."

Twenty minutes later, I'm collapsing on the couch. Heisman immediately snuggles next to me, offering me the comfort I so desired after my long day.

Jaxon comes in the room, fresh from a shower. He leans over the back of the couch and kisses me. "I'm glad you're home."

We don't need to talk about my day. I already told him how it went on a phone call from the Detroit airport. "Me too." I pat Heisman, who is hovering protectively. "I really needed this." I don't have to explain myself. Jaxon knows that I wake up every day worried that Heisman won't jump on the bed and settle his head over my tummy. "I had a bad dream."

Jaxon sits next to me and pulls my feet into his lap. "Want to talk about it?"

I swallow. "Billy was there. Except he was older, like our age, but I knew it was him. And he was holding a baby."

He rubs my arches. "Jeez, Nic, that's deep. But you know it's only your subconscious playing on your worst fears."

"I know." I sniff back tears. "It was just so real. And the baby… it was a boy."

Jaxon twists his ring before going back to my feet. "Do you think it's a boy?"

"The truth? I try not to think about it."

Try, but fail.

"We should be able to find out at the next ultrasound, right?"

I shake my head fervently. "I don't want to know."

"You don't? I figured you'd want to know everything you could."

"Yeah, about the health of the baby. Not the gender." I sigh and sink further into the couch, ashamed. "Am I a horrible person for wanting a girl? I think I might even be sad if it's a boy, like he'd be here to try to replace Billy. So I want to wait, because boy or girl, if things go well, I know as soon as I see that little face I'll be in love."

"In six months, I'm going to have two kids, neither of which I'm going to know the sex of." He laughs.

"I *hope* you'll have two kids in six months."

"I already do, Nic." He leans over and takes hold of my necklace. "In fact, I have three."

I trap his hand beneath mine. Does he have any idea how much I love him? He's far from perfect. But he's the kindest, most optimistic man I've ever known. And nobody on earth could ever be a better father.

"Tell me about school today. Was it bad? Was Calista gloating?"

"It was like she'd gotten elected class president all over again. She was the talk of the school, and she was basking in the attention." He pinches the bridge of his nose. "By fifth period, the news was all over. I put a note on my whiteboard that anyone making comments about my personal life would get into trouble."

I shake in silent laughter. "How many kids did you send to detention?"

"Only one. Leo Stoker. Oh, and I called a family meeting at my parents' house and told them."

My eyes open wide. "Told them?"

"About Calista. But damn, Nic, it was torture not being able to tell them about you."

"If you really want to, you can. It's not fair of me to make you keep this from them."

"Waiting is the right call. I love Addy to death, but no way would she be able to keep this a secret, especially with everyone talking about Calista. I'm not about to jeopardize your job over this."

"About that. I've been wondering why not. Logically, the easiest way to get me to stay here is to let the world know I'm pregnant. Nobody would want to hire me, and you might be stuck with me."

He laughs. "First of all, I'm quite sure everyone would still want you. Pregnancy isn't an affliction that you have for life, Nic. It's temporary. And you're amazing at what you do."

"And second?"

"That's the selfish part. Because if you turned out to be right and didn't get any offers, you'd go back to your old job fifteen hundred miles away."

"You're anything but selfish, Jax."

He looks away. "That's not true, and we both know it. There's nothing more selfish than what I did to you."

"Stop it. None of that matters anymore."

Jaxon slides onto the floor and kneels by my side. "I promise I'll never cheat on you again. I was a fool. You were and are the love of my life. And even if you end up back in Oklahoma City, I swear to you I'll be faithful."

I drink in his gorgeous blue eyes knowing every word of it is true. "And I promise never to lie to you."

"It's you and me against the world. Always."

Tears fill our eyes. If he asked me to marry him right now, I'd say yes. I'd say yes and book a flight to Vegas for next Monday. *Why isn't he asking me?*

"What's wrong?" he asks.

"Nothing. Everything is right." I close my eyes and press a hand to my stomach. "Well, almost everything."

Jaxon's phone illuminates with a call. It's Calista. He offers an apologetic grimace before answering. He puts her on speaker. "Hey, Calista."

"I'm sure you've heard we're the talk of the town."

"I assumed we would be."

"Everyone is speculating. You know there's even talk of us being a threesome?"

Jaxon guffaws. "Really?" More guilty glances. "Fabulous. Was there something in particular you needed?"

"The baby has a craving, and I was hoping you could help a friend out."

I roll my eyes. Jaxon asks, "What is it this time?"

"Macaroni and cheese from Goodwin's. With extra bacon."

"Sure, Calista. I can make that happen."

I pin him with a punishing stare. Why is he giving in to her every whim? She's taking advantage of him, and he seems okay with it. In fact, he almost looks happy about it. I try to get up, but Jaxon holds me in place.

"Perfect. Than—"

He hangs up. I go to speak, but he shushes me and makes a call. "Eric, hey. Feel up to running a quick errand?"

Chapter Thirty-three

Jaxon

It's the call I've dreaded since the moment we found out Nicky was pregnant.

"They want me in Miami," Nicky says.

My stomach turns. And I find myself doing what I promised myself I wouldn't—putting my foot down. "Nic, no way. I've tried to be understanding about your job, but you have to draw the line at putting yourself in danger, at least right now. Anyway, isn't hurricane season over?"

"Hurricane season runs through the end of November in the Atlantic. But this isn't a hurricane. It's an environmental story. No danger involved. I promise."

Still not wanting her to go but knowing there isn't a damn thing I can do about it, I ask, "When do you leave?"

"I'm on the way to the airport right now."

"Now? Don't you need things?"

"I learned a long time ago to keep an emergency suitcase in the office."

"How long?"

"A day. Two at the most."

"But you'll be back by Tuesday, won't you? It's kind of a big day."

"I'm not sure even a late-season hurricane could keep me from the… appointment."

Appointment, not ultrasound. She must not be alone.

"I know how important your job is, Nicky, but this is our child. If it comes down to it, you'd tell them, wouldn't you? You know, before they send you into the eye of the storm again?"

"If it came to that, yes. I'd never do anything to jeopardize this."

"I love you, Nic. Stay safe."

"Same. Bye."

"Come on, Heisman. Let's go." I put on a coat and walk to Donovan's for drinks with Tag. After all, what else do I have to do on a Saturday when my girl is working? We sit outside under the heaters on the patio and watch football. Donny brings Heisman a bowl of water and us some drinks. He looks to be in pain when he hobbles away. "Hey, Donny," I call. "You okay?"

"It's my darned hip. Thing has bothered me for ages, but even more so now that the cold weather has set in."

"I'm sorry to hear that. Anything I can do?"

"Yeah, run this place for three months while I convalesce after a hip replacement."

I cringe. "Yikes. That's hard core. You'd have to stay off your feet for sure."

"Why do you think I keep puttin' it off? Ain't nobody I trust to keep things running around here." He removes something from his pocket and pops some pills into his mouth. "I'm living on ibuprofen. Hell, my stomach might give out before the old hip does."

"Go easy, Donny. No need to come out here. I'll come in and get the next round."

He nods. "You're one of the good ones, Jaxon Calloway."

"Thank you, sir."

One of the good ones. I know what he means by that. One of the good Calloway brothers. The other one being Chaz, his daughter's dead fiancé.

"You think I'll *ever* get rid of my bad fucking rep?" Tag asks after Donny walks away.

"Not so long as you talk with the mouth of a sailor in a whorehouse."

"As if you don't swear like a trucker."

"Around you, sure. Not around Donny. Or random strangers, for that matter."

"Whatever." He nods to my phone. "You see Coop's latest video? He posted it today."

I don't like the look on his face. I grab my phone and pull up Cooper's YouTube channel. "Iceboat racing? Seriously? As if jumping off shit isn't scary enough, now he's risking falling through the ice. Have Mom and Dad seen it?"

"Doubt it." He shakes his head in frustration. "Mom would have shit bricks. We'd have heard about it. Where the hell is Lake Minnetonka anyway?"

"Minnesota."

"Just wait," he says, watching the video over my shoulder. "He flips the fucking boat."

My eyes snap up. "I'm assuming he's okay?"

"I read him the riot act a few hours ago, so don't bother. Said he's bruised along his left side and has a mild concussion."

"What's that, his third one?"

"You know he lives his life with one foot in the grave."

"And he keeps digging it deeper. One of these times, he won't be so lucky."

Tags eyes blaze. "If he puts us through it again—puts *Mom* through it—I will kill him a second time just to make sure he's fucking dead."

I put a hand on his shoulder. "Let's hope he grows out of it soon."

"Drink up, bro," he says, looking in the direction of the parking lot. "Because this day is about to get shittier."

Hawk, Hunter, and Hudson McQuaid get out of Hunter's sleek black Mercedes Maybach, which puts Tag's Range Rover to shame. My eyes zero in on the dickhead doctor. If my venomous glare could kill, he'd be vulture meat.

"Well, if it isn't the infamous daddy-to-be," Hawk says, knocking my chair on his way by.

Heisman growls. I stiffen and watch Hudson closely. His expression gives nothing away—except for his disdain toward me, but nothing new there.

"Calista Hilson?" Hunter says with a low whistle. "She's pretty fine. You could do way worse as far as baby mamas go. I'm surprised your tiny pencil dick could even knock someone up."

As riled up as he's trying to get me, I still feel a sense of relief. Everyone in Calloway Creek has found out about Calista over the past few weeks. But Hudson obviously kept his mouth shut about Nicky. I'll bet it's killing him right about now.

"Fuck off, guys," Tag says.

"Kiss my ass, Calloway," Hawk spews at my brother. He turns to me. "Bet your lady is having a fit over this. Or maybe she's all into that threesome shit. Ah, man, I'm picturing her right now in one of those tiny dresses they put her in that fits like a glove on a donkey's dong."

I stand up so fast that Hawk jumps back. Then he chortles. He knows I won't take a punch. I haven't since high school, when Tag and I used to go out by the football field and rough it up with Hawk and Hunter. Hudson and our younger brothers were still in middle school at the time, or they'd have been there too. It was practically a Friday night date between the four of us to see who could fuck up whom the most. It was usually a draw. Which is why I quit fighting once Tag graduated. It was pointless. We still fight, but with words—insults, belittlements, and the occasional nasty rumor.

I expected them to rile me up over the Calista debacle. When they go after Nic, however, all sense goes out the window, and I might just have to find my fighting gloves. But for now, I sit and give a death stare to the young *Doctor* McQuaid.

Hawk looks between me and Hudson. "Oh, man, you're Hilson's doctor, aren't you, Hud?" When Hudson doesn't say anything, Hawk and Hunter break out in laughter. "Shit, you are. You see that pussy yet? I saw it in high school once. Sucks she had to go and wreck a good thing by letting this asshole's cock inside her."

"Damn it, Hawk," I bite. "Mind your own business and go find someone else's night to ruin."

"Come on," Hudson says, putting a hand on each of his brothers. "I'm thirsty."

Hawk and Hunter mumble more disparaging remarks as they walk away.

"What the hell was wrong with Hudson?" Tag asks.

"What do you mean?"

"He didn't have anything to say. Don't you find that unusual?" His eyes go wide. "Dude, is he really Calista's doctor?"

"Kind of. He's a resident. He works under this other guy, Dr. Peterman. But yeah, he was there when Calista and I first went in."

Tag looks more than a little surprised. "And he kept it from his brothers all that time? Damn. They must not be as good of friends as we are. We never keep shit from one another." He gives me a pointed look. "Except when you cheated on your wife. You kept that from me. Any other deep dark secrets you need to confess?"

Only that my ex-wife is pregnant and due only three weeks after my ex-girlfriend. And Hudson knows that too, and as soon as everyone else does, Nic's job could be in jeopardy, not to mention the tabloid fodder that will follow.

I stand. "You ready for another drink?"

Chapter Thirty-four

Nicky

"See you tomorrow?" Chris asks as our car pulls up to XTN.

"I'm coming in too," I say, getting out. "I know it's my day off, but Clarice wanted me to stop by for a few fittings."

"Some day off. First our flight gets pushed to this morning, now this. Looks like you won't get *any* days off this week."

I shrug. "All part of what we signed up for." Up on the sixth floor, I try to appear less exhausted than I feel.

Clarice catches up to me in my dressing room, dragging a rack of clothes behind her. "Thank you for stopping by. I'll do this as quickly as possible."

"It's not a problem as long as I'm out of here by one."

Nervousness overwhelms me. I hadn't thought about the ultrasound in at least a few hours. These past six weeks have been the longest of my life.

She browses through a few pieces of clothing, chewing on her lip in thought.

"I was surprised you even wanted to do this, considering I'll be gone in less than a month."

"That's a few weeks too long if you want to keep this under wraps." She nods to my stomach. I take a step back, stunned. "Who do you think told Makenna to take a pregnancy test?" She laughs. "Wardrobe is always the first to know."

"I, uh…"

"Sweetie, it's not my place to go blabbing your business. But there's only so much I can accomplish with a well-placed pleat or ruffled hem." She studies my midsection. "I'd say we have about two weeks before people start noticing. And by people, I mean Barry. He's going to wonder why we've taken you out of your signature dresses."

Thumping down on my couch, I cover my face. "This is not how I wanted to do this."

"Women get pregnant all the time, Nicole. It's nothing you need to hide."

"It's more complicated than that."

She holds out her hand, helping me up. "Let's get on with this so you can go home and rest."

"Thank you for being discreet, Clarice. I really appreciate it."

~ ~ ~

"What if it's bad news?" I ask Jaxon while we wait in the car behind Dr. Peterman's office.

"It won't be."

"What if—"

"Nic." He cups my face. "Don't you think I've gone over every horrible scenario in my head, too? But I'm not sure that's any different than any other guy who's about to be a dad."

I protectively cover my belly. "I'm fourteen and a half weeks along, Jaxon. I was fifteen weeks when I lost Billy."

"Damn it, Nic. Why haven't you said anything? I didn't even think about that. This week must be so hard for you. I want to be here for you. For all of it—the good and the bad."

"We haven't talked about the baby much. I get it." I gesture to the building. "We've been waiting for this. Personally, I just haven't wanted to jinx it."

"How could you jinx it?"

"By being excited. By making plans. By dreaming of a future. Come on, Jaxon, you can't say you don't feel the same way. We're both afraid of what we could find out today."

He turns away and stares out his window. "Okay, yeah, I'm scared. Is that what you want to hear? That I'm terrified something will happen to this baby, and then you'll be put through hell by having to watch me and Calista have ours? You don't think I spend every day wondering what will happen to us if this baby doesn't make it? Because as much as I want our baby, I want you more, Nicky."

The back door of the office opens. I wipe my tears and get out of the car.

Jaxon runs over and takes my hand, holding it all the way into the office until they ask him to step aside so they can take my vitals. And as soon as they're done, he grabs it again, offering as much assurance as anyone can at a time like this.

Dr. Peterman comes in the room. He sees the looks on our faces. Empathy crosses his. He takes the stool next to the exam table. "There are no guarantees here. You'll need another scan in four to six weeks."

"We understand," Jaxon says.

"Let's get started, then."

I raise my shirt and lower my pants. He tucks a paper thingy over the waistband and squirts gel on my lower tummy.

"This could take a minute. Please try to be patient."

I'm glad he told us that before starting because it does take a while. He's being extremely thorough. And his expression gives nothing away. Jaxon and I look at each other, both of us out of our minds with worry.

Finally, he puts the probe down. "I'm pleased with what I'm seeing."

My heart thunders. Jaxon's grip tightens. "Pleased?" Jaxon asks, his voice laced with hope.

"While we have limited views of the anatomy and placenta due to the early gestational age, from what I can see, the placenta doesn't seem to have attached over any synechiae."

I give him a blank stare.

"Scar bands," he clarifies. "As I said, you'll need an anatomy scan in a month, and that will give us a better picture of the placenta. As the placenta continues to grow, these scar bands can potentially interfere, but at present, I'm not seeing signs of placenta accreta. That's not to say it won't or can't happen." He studies the screen again. "But I'm cautiously optimistic."

"You are?" I feel my racing heartbeat in my ears. "That's good, right?"

He smiles. *Smiles!* "As good as can be expected at this early stage, and better than I anticipated. The reason being, you seem to be a little further along than we thought. Based on my measurements and the lack of information about your last menstrual period, I've recalculated your estimated due date to be May twenty-first."

Jaxon laughs. He leans down and plants a kiss on my forehead. "Two weeks," he says. "My kids will be born less than two weeks from each other."

I'm crying. In this moment, I don't even care that he will have another baby a few weeks before this one. All I care about are the words Dr. Peterman said. *Pleased. Cautiously optimistic.* I feel I've won the lottery.

"Jaxon, that means I'm over fifteen weeks," I say through my relieved tears.

We kiss again, both knowing what a milestone it is.

"Would you like to know the gender?" Dr. Peterman asks.

I swallow. "You know?"

"I do."

"We don't want to know," Jaxon says. He looks into my eyes. "We don't care if it's a boy or a girl. We already love it more than we can say."

I squeeze his hand. "Jaxon, I think I want to know."

"You do?"

I nod. "I love him or her so much. I'm tired of being scared. I want to make plans. I want to talk about tea parties or T-ball. Pink or blue. I want to be able to do everything we couldn't do last time."

"All right, doc," Jaxon says. "Let's have it."

Dr. Peterman smiles. "Tea parties it is."

My hands cover my face as I blubber the ugliest happy cry anyone has ever heard. Jaxon collapses onto me. "It's a girl, babe. It's a girl."

~ ~ ~

Hours later in bed, we're still reeling. And Jaxon has taken to talking to the baby.

"Do you know how lucky you are to have the mom that you do?"

"I'm the lucky one," I tell him. "But we still have to be careful. You heard what the doctor said."

"Yes, I did. He said you're farther along than we thought. Over fifteen weeks, Nic. Did you know anatomy scans can be done as early as sixteen weeks? That means what he did was basically one of those."

"For regular pregnancies," I remind him. "They wanted me closer to twenty weeks because of the Asherman's. They need a more detailed view of the placenta."

"Nicky, can we please take this win? She's going to be fine. And we're going to be an amazing family."

"Clarice—she's the one who does my wardrobe—already knows. She's going to try to get me through the next few weeks, but Jaxon, we'll have to tell people sooner rather than later." I run a hand across my tiny bump. "Especially now that I'm even further along than we thought."

Something occurs to me, and I reach for my phone. I search for a due date calculator because there is something I need to know. I snuggle back into his shoulder. "Guess what?"

"What?"

"We got pregnant the first time we did it."

"Nicky, the first time we did it you were fifteen and we were in the back of my brother's pickup truck in the parking lot behind the high school."

I giggle.

He slings himself on top of me, careful not to squish me. "It was meant to be. It was always meant to be."

He runs a hand along the side of my jaw, down the cord of my neck, under the *V* of my shirt. And then he gives me two of the best orgasms I've ever had.

Chapter Thirty-five

Jaxon

Nicky pulls my duffle bag from the closet. "You are not canceling. We promised we wouldn't change our lives for each other and fall back into old habits. Plus, you already found a sub for today and tomorrow."

"It's a weekend camping trip with my brothers, Nic. Not a meeting with the Pope. I think they'll understand."

"First it's a canceled trip, then we're bending over backwards to fit our careers into each other's lives. Then before you know it, we'll be back to resenting the situation. Jaxon, I'm fine. You need to go."

"We only have a few more weeks together as it is."

"A few more weeks and our whole lives. Yes, it looks like I'll be leaving to go… somewhere. We knew that was a probability."

"Oklahoma," I say bitterly. "Nicky, you could be so much closer. You've turned down a half dozen offers."

She sits and runs a hand across her burgeoning bump. "Oklahoma is what's best for now. I'm established there. The pay isn't as good, but the hours aren't nearly as long as the jobs I've been offered. And Marty is willing to go to bat for me."

"*Marty* knows? I thought we weren't telling anyone yet."

"I had to find out my options. If I go back there, he's sure they'll give me four months of maternity leave. Think about it, Jaxon. I'll return to WRKT after the holidays, work through the end of April, then I'll come back here until August."

"Through the end of April. During tornado season."

"I'm not stupid. And they aren't going to put me in the field when I'm nine months preg—" She stops talking suddenly, and her whole demeanor changes. Both hands cradle her belly.

I race to her, worried. "Nic?"

"Jaxon, she's moving." Her words come in a whisper as if she doesn't want them to jinx it.

I drop the clothes in my hands, fall to my knees, and put a hand near hers, desperately needing to feel my daughter inside her. "What does it feel like?"

"Like gas bubbles dancing in my stomach. Small flutters." She grabs my hand and repositions it. "Here."

I close my eyes and concentrate on feeling something. I don't. But when my eyes open, I know it doesn't matter, because *she* can. And the look on her face is everything. In all my life, I've never seen her look so breathtaking. So completely wonderstruck. So utterly at peace with herself. And I can tell when she feels another kick. She inhales and I swear it's like she's seeing God at the gates of heaven.

"Did you feel it?"

"No. I'm sure I will soon. And then you'll have to live with my hand affixed to your belly for the next twenty-four weeks."

"Jaxon, I've never been so excited, yet terrified at the same time." She rubs her pendant. "I want this. I want her so badly. I want *you*. A few months ago, if anyone had told me I'd feel this

EX

way, I'd have called them crazy. How has my life completely changed so quickly in ways I didn't even know I wanted?"

I pull her to me. "All of this—every bit of it—is like a dream come true. I was a shell of a man, going through the motions of living my life, trying to find moments of happiness here and there. You were always what was missing." I touch her belly again. "This was what was missing. We're going to be a family, Nic, in whatever way we can be. And I've never been happier."

The doorbell rings.

I stand. "Excuse me while I go thump whoever just ruined one hell of a moment." Like I even need to look to see who's there. Only one person would come over at seven in the morning. I open the door. "What is it now, Calista?"

"Good morning to you, too," she says, plowing past me with a bag of food. "The baby is craving eggs and my stovetop isn't working."

"Sure it isn't." Part of me wants to kick her out. I'm tired of her invading my personal space all the time. She has all the control here. If I push her too far, she could hold my baby prisoner from me. If I keep her too close, it could jeopardize my relationship with Nicky. It's a damned if you do, damned if you don't situation that keeps me up more nights than I care to admit.

Calista turns and glares at me. "Do you really think I'm so desperate as to fake a stove emergency just to see you?" She laughs. "I'm hungry. Coming here is quicker than going to Goodwin's. End of story."

Nicky comes around the corner and quickly grabs a blanket off the couch, wrapping it around her to conceal her small baby bump. She raises her brows at me. I know she's asking me what the hell Calista is doing in our kitchen.

"Oh, hey, Nicky," Calista says. She holds up the egg carton. "Sorry, I only have enough for two."

"I don't need any," I say. "Nicky can eat."

Calista giggles and rubs her belly. "I was talking about me and the baby. But if you have more eggs, I can cook for all of us if you want."

"That's okay. You go ahead. Nic and I will be in the bedroom." I pull Nicky along with me before Calista can get in another word. Not bothering to close the bedroom door, I lead Nicky to the bed, push her down, and climb on top of her.

She glances at the open door. "What are you doing?"

I kiss her neck. "Something about kissing you when you're half-naked with her in the kitchen is so satisfying. Maybe it'll teach her a bit of a lesson."

"I have to say, that's kind of twisted, Jaxon. Except she has no idea what we're doing."

I tickle her ribs, something that always makes her squeal. Heisman trots in to see what the noise is about.

Nicky scoots out from under me. "You're terrible." She gets off the bed and riffles through my drawers. "Now, where are your heavy socks? It's going to be freezing. Why can't you guys go camping in June like other sane people?"

"Cooper planned this. He's anything but sane."

"At least you won't be getting the weather that's coming here. I checked and it's going to be unseasonably warm in Vermont this weekend."

I put down the socks. "There's a storm coming?"

"I shouldn't have said anything. Not a storm. A weather system. Less than a few inches of precipitation."

Concern grips my insides. "Nicky."

Unfinished **EX**

"Oh my god, Jaxon." She pushes me toward the bathroom. "Quit worrying about me. Everything is going to be fine."

~ ~ ~

Thirty-six hours later, her words echo through my head as I stare at the radar on my phone. "Fine, my ass." I start packing my shit.

"Where do you think you're going?" Cooper asks, frying up trout for dinner.

"Home. The *weather system*"—I air quote—"has turned into a goddamn ice storm."

"If that's true, no way will we make it back. The roads will be closed."

Tag holds out his phone. "Dad just texted me. A lot of the power is out."

I tap out a text.

> **Me: Weather system my ass. Nic, from what I can see Calloway Creek is under a few inches of ice.**

> **Nicky: I know. It's beautiful! Heisman doesn't like it very much, though. He can't find his footing outside.**

She's at home. I breathe a small sigh of relief before remembering she'll have to go to work before the crack of dawn.

> **Me: What about tomorrow?**

Nicky: Tom Killian lives in the city. He'll cover me if I can't get out.

Me: You shouldn't even be out walking in this. What if you fall?

Nicky: I'm one step ahead of you. My dad put chains on his truck. He'll drive me to the train station.

Me: And once you get to the city? XTN is three blocks away.

Nicky: Stop worrying. I promise I won't go in if it's too dangerous. And just so you know, we lost power thirty minutes ago. Heisman and I are enjoying a snuggle by the fireplace. I'll probably sleep on the couch. See—it's kind of like we're camping, too.

Me: Call me if you need anything. ANYTHING. And if you do go to work, let me know. In fact, can you turn on your phone tracking and give me access?

I can feel her rolling her eyes, but I don't give a shit. This is the woman I love and my goddamn baby.

I get a notification on my phone that I've been given access.

Nicky: Happy now?

Me: I'm not going to be happy until you're snuggling *me* by the fireplace.

Nicky: I think that can be arranged as soon as you get back.

Me: If I weren't here with my brothers, I would FaceTime you right now and tell you exactly what I plan to do during our snuggle.

Nicky: Phone sex? Why, Jaxon Calloway, who knew you were a little smutty?

Me: We better start practicing. I plan on having a hell of a lot of phone sex after you go.

Nicky: I'll admit, I'm a little turned on right now. You think Heisman would mind if I got out my vibrator?

Me: Save it until I get home Sunday night. I promise to make it worth your while.

Nicky: You're not jealous of a vibrator are you?

Me: Hell yes I am.

Nicky: OMG, Jaxon. You'll never believe what I heard today. We're not the only ones being gossiped about anymore. Shannon Greer and Hawk McQuaid hooked up, and now she's pregnant.

Me: No shit?

Message unable to deliver.
I hit resend.
Message unable to deliver.
Shit.

I shove my things into my duffle. "Get me somewhere with a TV."

"Don't you think you're overreacting just a tad?" Tag says.

"Give me your fucking keys, or I'll take them from you."

"Calm down," Cooper says. "She is a meteorologist. If anyone can handle themself around weather, it's her."

I turn back to Tag. "Don't make me tackle you."

"Christ," he says. "Way to ruin the trip. Might as well leave our shit here. We'll still need a place to sleep later." He stands. "Let's go if it will shut up your whiny ass."

Coop asks Tag, "When did you become such a damn softie?"

I lean over and put my hands on my knees, wanting to protect my family but knowing there's not a damn thing I can do from this far away. "Nicky's pregnant."

My brothers' jaws hit the dirt simultaneously. Tag bends over laughing, the asshole he is. "Holy shit, bro. You have to be fucking kidding."

"Do I look like I'm kidding?"

"How in the hell did you get yourself into this?" Cooper says.

"It's not like I planned it. Both were accidents. We didn't even think Nic could get pregnant. We already lost one baby. I'm not about to lose another."

Tag's head whips in my direction. "What do you mean you lost a baby?"

I twist the ring around my finger. "I never knew she was pregnant. It's a long story. The gist of it is she was pregnant when she moved to Oklahoma. Neither of us knew about it. She had a miscarriage, which left her with scarring in her uterus."

"So much for not keeping secrets from your brothers," Tag says.

We get into his SUV. "I couldn't say anything. If XTN finds out, it could jeopardize her job. Not to mention she's considered high risk. And then there's the fact that I'm having two kids with two different women, so the longer we can keep this under wraps, the better."

When we get to the paved highway, Cooper points right. "I saw some backwoods dive bar on the way here. About five miles out."

I keep trying to text Nicky the whole way. None of my texts are delivered. I can't get a hold of my parents either. Or anyone back in Calloway Creek.

"What are you going to do?" Tag asks.

"Maybe we can find some chains and make it back home?"

"Not about that, about your situation. Two babies? Shit, Jaxon."

"That's not the half of it." I scrub my hands down my face. "They are both due in May, within two weeks of each other."

Tag laughs again, and I hit him from the back seat. "How about we be adults for two seconds here."

"Sorry, bro. But you have to admit this is all kinds of fucked up."

"I'm plenty aware what this is."

"No one else knows?" Cooper asks.

"A few people Nic works with is all. Oh, and Hudson McQuaid."

Two pairs of eyes snap back at me, and we almost run off the road. "Hudson knows?" Cooper asks.

"He works with Nicky's doctor. But he's sworn to secrecy by law. Luckily, he's kept his mouth shut."

"Wow," Tag says. "I did not see that coming. So that time we ran into them at Donovan's?"

I nod. "He knew."

"I gotta say, I almost have to respect the guy." He shakes his head. "Okay, that tasted like shit coming out of my mouth."

"Speaking of the McQuaids," I say, remembering what Nicky told me. "Apparently Hawk had a one-night-stand with Shannon Greer, and now *she's* knocked up."

"Is there something in the goddamn water around Cal Creek?" He chuckles. "After all the shit he gave you, dude's going to get some major payback the next time I come across him."

"He probably won't even support the kid despite being a millionaire," Coop says. "Ten bucks says his daddy finds him a way out of it." He turns to me. "Speaking of which… *Two* kids on a teacher's salary? Ouch."

"You'd probably keel over if I told you the offers that have been rolling in for Nicky. I doubt money is going to be a problem."

"Any of the jobs local?" Tag asks.

I shake my head.

"So how's that going to work?"

"A lot of time on airplanes, man."

Unfinished **EX**

"Sounds horrible."

"Yeah, but you do what you have to do for the woman you love."

Suddenly it's as if Tag understands. We lock eyes in the rearview. And he gets it.

"There," Cooper says, pointing ahead.

A few old pickup trucks are parked outside of an old shack that has a sign hanging off the hinges. It reads: **Billy's**.

I swear if it were any other day, I'd make Tag keep driving. But I have to get to a television.

The OPEN sign flashes sporadically as if it's got a short. A few beer signs are illuminated in the window. Inside, heads turn when the three of us walk in. I guess they only get locals in here.

The bartender calls us over. "What can I get fer you? Name's Bill."

I point over his head to the television currently tuned to a station with some guys playing corn hole. "Can you change the channel? There's a storm in New York, and we have family there."

Three coasters are placed in front of us. "Long as you keep drinkin', you can watch SpongeBob SquarePants for all I care."

"Three whiskeys." I get out my wallet and throw two twenties on the bar. "Mind if I have the remote?"

He slides the remote across the bar. "You boys let me know when you need a refill. I'll be playin' pool with my lady."

I page through the channels until I find XTN. Then I sip my drink and watch as Brenton Carmichael salivates over the ice storm. He talks about things like road closures, power lines, and the weight of the ice causing problems. The longer he talks, the more concerned I become.

"Don't even think about trying to talk us into leaving right now," Coop says. "Even if we could find chains, the roads will be closed. We'd be stranded. You have two kids to think about. And she's home safe."

"He said the storm will blow through by midnight." I look at Tag. "Go pack up the stuff. We'll stay here until we're kicked out, and then we'll drive as far as we can."

Tag calls out to the owner. "Bill—you got any idea where we could get a set of chains for my tires?"

"Whatcha planning on payin'?" a man with a mullet asks.

Tag pulls a few hundred-dollar bills out of his wallet. I drain mine, adding two fifties. He holds up the money.

The guy slaps his leg. "Well, all right then. I live down the road. Be back in a jiffy."

Tag looks around me to Cooper. "You good with that? I do have family I'd like to get home to if it's really as bad as they say."

"Who knew you guys were as crazy as me." He laughs. "Yeah, I guess I'm good with that."

Chapter Thirty-six

Nicky

I wrap myself tightly in my sweater as I stand under the roof on the back porch waiting for Heisman to do his thing. "Hurry up, buddy. It's freezing out here."

There's a cracking noise out in the yard. I know that sound. I turn on my phone's flashlight in time to see a branch fall by the fence. "Heisman!"

He runs up next to me, and I take a breath. I get down and hug him. "That's the last time you go out. I hope you can hold it until morning." I shine my light on the branch. It's not a huge one, but it's coated with ice. It could have hurt him, for sure. I trace the base of the tree up, looking out at the branches that are heavy with inches of ice. No wonder we lost power. If it's like this everywhere, the whole town is probably without it. We go back inside, I kick off my boots, and I check to see if my phone has service. It doesn't. Not since it stopped mid-conversation with Jaxon two hours ago.

There are a lot of things that can affect the transmission of electromagnetic waves—which cell service relies on—including snow, wind, and ice. It's strange how isolated I feel without the use of my phone. I plop down on the chair next to the fireplace and listen to my battery-operated weather radio. All roads within fifty miles have been closed. Jaxon must be beside himself. I can just see it now, him forcing his brothers to cut their weekend short so he can check on me. But they'd be fools to try and drive through this. They're likely to end up in a ditch. I hope one of them has the good sense to wait until the storm passes and the roads have been cleared.

From outside, I hear more cracking. Actually, splintering is more like it. And popping. Like the branch sounded earlier only a hundred times louder. Oh, god. It sounds like a tree. Quickly determining we're way too close to the windows, I call Heisman and we run for cover in the front hallway. I keep him tucked protectively next to me so he won't scamper away. I can sense his tension. Or he can sense mine. "It's okay, bud."

Even from this far, I can still hear the cracking. I know that once ice accretions reach a certain thickness, it causes large branches to breach. And fast-growing trees, like the elms out back, have softer wood, which makes them more susceptible to the extra weight. There's a loud snap followed by a quick succession of what sounds like a whoosh of a rain shower, then it stops as soon as it started. I can only imagine a branch coming loose and shards of ice falling and spearing the ground below. Part of me wishes I could be out there watching. But ice is dangerous. Even a single icicle dislodged from a rooftop or tree branch can spear you. There must be a million icicles hanging off the trees out back.

Suddenly, what sounds like gunshots echo throughout the house. I know these sounds, and I pray whatever is falling misses the house. Then the ground shakes, and a thunderous bomb-like noise reverberates throughout my entire body. I pull Heisman close and brace for the impact that never comes. There's no splintering of wood. No glass breaking. No roof trusses splitting. Thank God.

When the noise completely subsides, I get one of the high-powered flashlights from the kitchen and shine it through the back sliding door. Relief courses through me when I see that the large elm at the edge of the property line narrowly missed the house. I can see the dark roots unearthed, like a tornado had toppled it over. As I shine the light further along the fallen trunk, I see the fence has been taken out—and although disappointing, it's by far the lesser of two evils.

But then I realize I can't see the rest of the tree. I can't see it because it's lying inside Calista's house. "Oh, God!"

I get out my phone to call 911 before I remember it doesn't work. I pull on my boots. "Heisman, stay." I race through the back door. Other than potentially falling on my ass, I should be safe, the largest tree having already fallen.

As I step over part of the downed fence, I gasp, shining the light into her house. The entire side of her house is caved in, right where the living room meets the kitchen. "Calista!" I call, approaching. Maybe she went to a friend's house to ride out the storm. I stand near the patio, wondering how I can even get inside. I stick my head between some branches. "Calista! Are you here?"

"Help!"

It's one word. And it's muffled. But it has my heart stopping and my stomach turning. Her sliding doors are intact. I'm sure she wouldn't mind if I used something to break them. Fortunately, when I try to open them first, they're unlocked. I step through into a war zone. With limited light, I try to make heads or tails of what I'm seeing. Branches are everywhere. Shards of ice are scattered across the floor. Or perhaps it's glass from broken windows; it's hard to tell. I shine the light overhead, trying to determine if we're in danger of the roof collapsing, but part of it already has. "Calista!"

"Here. I'm here."

At least she's talking. "Where? I can't see you."

"Kitchen... I think."

Good. I can get to the kitchen. I make my way around the mess and into the hallway, coming in from the other side. This isn't so bad. I shine the light around, then scream when I see her lying on the ground, flattened by the kitchen table and a portion of the wall. The top of the tree pierces through what was the ceiling. "Calista!"

I find a place to set the flashlight so I can assess the situation. When I see blood pooling around the side of her that's exposed, I try to hold it together. She's on her back. What if the weight of the table and the wall hurt the baby? "I'm going to try and pull you out."

I put my hands under her arms and tug. She doesn't budge. "It's my leg," she says. "It's caught on something." She brings a hand up to her face to wipe off wetness dripping from the branches above her. Blood smears across her face. She stares at her hand in horror. "I'm bleeding! The baby? Oh, please no."

But I notice the blood is concentrated on her arm. "Lie still. Let me see." I take her arm and examine it with the flashlight. It almost looks like a bullet went through just below her elbow. An icicle must have speared her. "It's your arm. It's bleeding badly."

"Have you called 911?" she cries.

I sit, put her arm in my lap, and try to stop the bleeding. "Calista, I can't. Phones are out. Everything is out."

Blood trickles in a stream from her arm down my leg. I have to stop the bleeding. I take off my sweater, leaving me in my thin tank top, but I don't feel the cold. Adrenaline is keeping me warm.

I wrap the sweater around her arm like a tourniquet. "Does anything else hurt?"

"I... I don't know. The baby. How's the baby?"

"I can't tell. And the only way to get you out is for me to leave and get help."

"Don't leave!"

I gently put her arm down and get up. "I have to. I'm sorry. I can't get you out of here, and you need medical attention."

"Can't you call 911?"

I close my eyes. Jeez. She could have a head injury, too. "I can't, the phones are out. I'll go over to Mr. Hamm's house. He has a truck. Maybe he can go for help."

"You have to come back."

"I will. I promise. I'm leaving you the flashlight. I can use the one on my phone. I'll be back as soon as I can."

I run to the front door, then I carefully cross the yard, knowing if I slip, we'll never get help. I bang on Mr. Hamm's door. No answer. I move along to the next house.

Mrs. Simperson answers and looks me up and down. "Dear? What's wrong?"

"Calista Hilson is hurt. A tree came down into her house. Is your husband home?"

"I'm afraid he got stuck in Boston due to all incoming flights being rerouted."

"Can you go over to Mr. Gregory's house? He has a truck. Tell him to bring fire rescue and an ambulance. She's bleeding pretty badly, and she's pregnant. I have to get back to her."

She gets her coat. "Yes, of course."

"Please be careful, Mrs. Simperson. It's very icy out there."

"I will. Now you go back and wait for help. I promise we'll send it."

I avoid all trees on the way back. It's not hard, most of the larger trees are in the backs of houses. What I wouldn't give for Jaxon to be home right now.

"Calista, I'm back," I say, coming through her front door. She's crying. I sink down beside her. "It's going to be okay."

"The baby isn't moving. What if—"

"He's probably sleeping. The baby is well protected. You can't think the worst. You need to keep up your strength."

"Is help coming? My arm hurts. My leg."

"Yes. Help is on the way, but it might be a while. The roads are covered with ice. Let's take some deep breaths together, okay? Here we go. Breathe in. Hold it. Breathe out." We do it a few more times. "Better?"

"Why are you being so nice to me? You hate me."

"I don't hate you, Calista. Do I love the idea of my boyfriend's ex-girlfriend having his baby? No. But it is what it is, and we all need to make the best of it."

"But I've been such a bitch to you. You'd think you would leave me here to die."

I shine the light on myself so she can clearly see me. "I would never do that. You're still a person. And believe me, I know it wasn't your fault that you got pregnant. Accidents happen."

Her eyes suddenly become clearer. She studies my face, then her gaze travels south. She gasps. I look down and realize that when I gave her my sweater, my baby bump, even as small as it is, is clearly visible, especially to someone who has their own baby bump. "You're *pregnant?*"

I lean against what's left of the wall. "Surprise."

"You're… Wait, am I hallucinating? Am I dead? Is this a joke?"

"You're not hallucinating."

"How, uh, why? Nicky, why aren't you telling people? Why haven't you told *me?*" Her eyes close and she sighs. "I've been so terrible to you. Flaunting my pregnancy in front of you. And this whole time, you've been in the same boat."

"My pregnancy was a surprise, too. Because of the miscarriage and some scarring from a D and C, I didn't think I could get pregnant. And due to the scarring, I'm high risk. We didn't want to tell anyone until we were fairly certain the baby would be okay. And also because of my job."

"And will it be okay?"

I run a hand over my bump. "We hope so. Dr. Peterman let us do an ultrasound earlier this week. He's optimistic that she'll be okay."

"She?"

I nod. "It's a girl." I take her hand. "You know what this means. Your baby will have a half-sibling."

She sniffs back tears. "I always wanted a sister. I'm glad my baby will have one." Her eyes go wide. "I just felt the baby kick!"

"Thank God."

"Nicky, can you ever forgive me?"

"That depends. Can you stop being so needy around my boyfriend?"

Tiny spurts of nose laughter tell me she must not be hurt too badly. Or maybe she just hasn't succumbed to her injuries yet. *Where are emergency services?*

"You want to hear something crazy?" she asks.

"Calista, you aren't dying." *I don't think.* "So don't go confessing your deep, dark secrets to me."

"I don't even want Jaxon. Not in the least. I think all of this was about *you.* I guess I was just jealous."

My brows hit my hairline. "Of *me*? If you aren't after Jaxon, why would you be jealous of me?"

"I told you it was crazy, but it's been a hard pill to swallow knowing my baby was going to be spending time with you and that the three of you would be this happy family."

"I had no idea. I thought you just wanted Jaxon back."

"I know. Like I said, I'm a bitch. I wasn't always one. I think it's the pregnancy. But it's like I had to win, if that makes sense. I know it sounds ridiculous."

"Coming from the head cheerleader, class president, and prom queen, not so much."

"I'm also going for teacher of the year. It comes with a new car."

I laugh. "And this whole time, *I've* been jealous of *you*. Even being pregnant myself, I'm still well aware of the lifetime connection your baby will forge between you and Jaxon."

"What's even crazier is that the man I really want is available and wants me, and I'm too darn stubborn to admit I made a mistake."

"Eric?"

"I think he might even love me. Can you imagine? Loving someone who's carrying another man's child? I've been so stupid. He may never take me back."

"When this is over, it looks like we all have some decisions to make."

"Can you ever forgive me?" she asks. "Our kids will be related. We owe it to them to get along."

I push a bead of water off her forehead. "I already have."

"When are you due?"

"Well, that's *my* crazy news. Two weeks after you are."

"Oh my god. How is Jaxon dealing with this?"

I shrug. "Denial. Camping. Whiskey."

She laughs and then moans in pain.

"Don't move," I say. "They'll be here soon." There's pounding on the front door. "See, what did I tell you?"

"Wait!"

"What is it?"

She points. "There's a sweater on a hook by the pantry. Nobody is going to learn your secret under my watch."

I smile and cross the room, wondering if my nemesis and I just became friends.

Ten minutes later, the scene is secured and Patrick Kelsey, along with a few other firefighters I remember from before, are lifting Calista onto a gurney. As EMS wheels her out the door, she calls out to me. "Nicky, come with me?"

"Me?"

"Please. I'm scared. They'll do an ultrasound. Nobody else could understand if—"

I run up beside her. "Everything is going to be okay. And yes, I'll go with you. After all, one day, I plan on being your kid's stepmom."

"Thank you. And Nicky? When phone service comes back, can you call someone for me?"

"I'm sure Jaxon will be here as quickly as he can."

"I know he will be. But I was talking about Eric."

Chapter Thirty-seven

Jaxon

Tag weaves through downed trees on the way into town. It took us twice as long as it should have to get home, but we're finally pulling up to the hospital a few minutes before noon. My nerves are still shot. When Nicky finally got through to me at eight o'clock this morning and told me to meet her at the hospital, my world imploded. When she quickly added that she was fine and wasn't the patient, and everyone was okay short of Calista's arm injury and bruised ankle, I found myself overcome with relief.

Tag drops me at the entrance. Nicky is right inside, and we wrap each other in a hug. Neither of us has words. We just hold on.

"I was so fucking scared," I tell her after swallowing the knot in my throat. "Thank God you and the baby are okay, and both of them are as well."

"Jaxon, it was awful. Her house is ruined. Do you know how lucky she is? Had she been five feet closer to where the tree fell, we'd be going to the morgue."

"Jesus." I put my hands on her shoulders. "And you saved her?"

"Hardly. I couldn't get her out. I had to run to a few neighbors' houses until I found someone who could go for help."

"You saved her, Nic."

"She'd have done the same for me."

I cackle out a laugh. "I sincerely doubt that."

"Come on." She takes my hand and leads me to the elevator.

"Where are we going?"

"To see Calista."

"She's okay, though? They said the baby is all right?"

"Everyone is fine."

We go to the second floor, right to Calista's room, as if Nicky had been here all night. Something's different. When we enter, Calista smiles. *At Nicky.* And Eric is at her bedside holding her hand. I turn to Nic. "What the hell happened during that ice storm?"

She giggles. "Okay to come in?"

"Sure, yes." Calista rubs her belly. "The baby is fine."

"Nicky told me. Uh, hi, Eric. What's up?" The three of them look at each other and laugh. "What am I missing?"

Nic shuts the door behind us. The four of us are alone. "Let's see," Calista says. "I almost died. Your girlfriend saved me. Eric and I got back together." She grins at Nic. "*She's* pregnant. Oh, and Nicky and I are friends."

"You… friends… Eric… *what?*" So much is going through my head right now, I can't even figure out where to begin. I turn to Nic. "You told them?"

"She didn't have to," Calista says. "When she took off her sweater to stop my arm from bleeding out, I saw her bump."

My gaze bounces between her and Eric. "And you two?"

"I was being stupid and selfish and adolescent," Calista says. "I guess being pregnant isn't attractive on me, because it made me into someone I never wanted to be."

"I think pregnancy is *very* attractive on you," Eric says, leaning down to kiss the back of her hand.

"And you?" I turn to Nic and motion toward Calista.

"What can I say?" Nic says. "We're two women about to have a hell of a lot in common, and we'll be tied together by you and the babies for a long, long time. I guess it took a tree falling to make me realize I was being jealous."

"And for me to realize who I'm really in love with." Calista gazes up at Eric.

"Which is a good thing," Eric says. "Because you'll need a place to stay for a month or so while your house gets fixed."

"And you're really okay with all this?" I ask him.

"I told you I can't have kids, man. I never expected to be a part of anything like this. I'm just happy to be along for the ride."

"Okay, then. Looks like everything worked out. Calista, can I get you anything?"

She chuckles. "For once, no." She latches onto Eric's arm. "I have everything I need."

"She's going to be released later this afternoon," Eric says. "I'll get her settled at my place and then head to her house to pack her things and assess the damage."

"Let me know if you need help. I guess I'll get Nicky home. And please, can you both not say anything? I know this is unbelievable, but until she announces it, let's keep it under wraps."

"You got it," Calista says. "That's what friends do for each other."

I shake my head as we leave. "I feel like I was gone for months. How did everything change so quickly?"

"Near-death experiences can do that," Nic says.

"Is that why you said yes to giving us another go? Because of what happened to you during Louisa?"

"Well, that and I never stopped loving you."

I pull her to me. I don't care that we're standing in a hospital hallway. I run a finger down the bridge of her nose, across the tip, and to her lips, where she kisses it. "You'll never know how scared I was. What if it was you under that tree?"

"I heard it coming down. Heisman and I took cover in the hallway."

"My smart girlfriend."

"I'm not sure I'll ever get used to that again," she says. "You calling me your girlfriend."

"You're sure as hell no longer my ex. And legally, I can't call you my wife." I pin her to the wall with my stare. "Unless…"

"There you are," Cooper calls from the elevator. "Would it be too much effort for you to answer your goddamn phone? We're double parked, and Tag wants to get home to his people."

I forgot I turned my phone on silent when we pulled up. "Sorry. Ready to go home?" I ask Nicky.

"I need to get cleaned up for work."

"Work? But most of the roads are impassable."

"The train is running. I told them I'd be in before the five o'clock show."

"Fuck, Nic. After the night you had?"

"*Especially* after the night I had. Jaxon, what happened to me is news. In fact, I'm going over to Calista's to take pictures. This is great stuff. I mean, now that we know she's okay."

It's hard not to laugh at the absurdness of it. "You're always looking for a story, aren't you?"

"Are you mad?"

I let her in the back seat of Tag's SUV. "No. I'm not. In some twisted way, your crazy job makes me want you even more. But babe, I'm going with you. There's still a lot of ice everywhere. If you insist on going in, I won't stop you, but I'll damn sure make it so you get there in one piece." I tap Tag on the shoulder. "Can I borrow the Range later to get us to the train station?"

"How about I take you?" Cooper says. "I'll take you home and then Tag, then I was thinking about helping out around town since we've got the chains and all. Just call me when you need a ride."

"It's settled, then."

Nicky puts her palm on my thigh. "I suppose if I must have a babysitter, there are worse people I could think of."

Three hours later, after forcing Nicky to take a nap while I took pictures of the tree, we're stepping off the elevator onto the sixth floor of XTN.

"Nice of you to make it to work," some guy says when he sees Nicky.

I can't tell if he's being sarcastic or not, and it makes me want to thump him.

"Did you get my pictures, Barry?" Nicky asks.

Barry. The asshole producer.

"Production is working on the slides right now."

"Great. Oh, and I'm okay, by the way. Thanks for asking."

He dismisses her with a wave of his hand.

"What a prick," I say, watching him walk away.

"That was him being nice."

"Is it always like that around here?"

"I like pretty much everyone else." She leads me down the hall. "Here's my dressing room. You can hang out with me here while I get ready, then you can either stay here or come into the studio when I do my clips."

"Are you kidding? I came all the way here. I want to watch you work."

She smiles as if that pleases her.

Over the next forty-five minutes, I meet several of her co-workers. Her makeup artist, Henri. Clarice, who brings her an outfit and also gives me a suave look like I'm Don Juan or something. *Right—she's the one who knows about the baby.* Then there's Jenny, her dickhead producer's assistant, who Nicky often goes to lunch with.

There are also two or three other people who hand her papers while she's getting ready. When all is said and done, *I'm* the one who's exhausted just watching what she goes through before her shows. How she's managing to keep up this pace while pregnant is beyond my scope of imagination.

But that's not what amazes me the most. When I'm escorted to a chair that I'm instructed to sit in while she goes on the air—that's when I fully get it. That's when I understand what she does, why she does it, and how she's gotten a half dozen job offers over this past month.

She effortlessly reports on last night's storm as if she practiced her monologue a hundred times. The pictures of Calista's house and the uprooted tree come up behind her, along with others of downed power lines, ice-lined branches, and icicles that look like spears hanging from the edges of bridges and buildings. As she tells of her personal ordeal, giving it a human spin that few others can, I can see it—the drive. The passion. Nicole Forbes is exactly where she's meant to be.

And I finally realize that no matter how much I dislike the situations this job may put her in, all of it—the good and the bad—

makes her the person she is today. The person who has single-handedly increased viewership of the weekend news by ten percent. The person who laughs on screen when most meteorologists are stoic, delivering the weather as if reading an obituary. The person who banters well with the news anchors, causing the viewers to become more interested.

And the person who I love more than I ever thought I could love another human being.

Chapter Thirty-eight

Nicky

I close my laptop and get ready to leave for the day. Now that football season is over at CCHS, Jaxon and I get to spend more time together after work. I try to leave by five on weekdays. Hitting the bathroom one more time (because this little ballerina likes to dance on my bladder), I find it difficult to zip my pants. I study myself sideways in the mirror. There will be no hiding it soon. We have to tell everyone. But not before I tell my parents and Victoria, which Jaxon and I agreed would happen at dinner on Friday. They need to be prepared for the barrage of gossip that will encircle the three of us. As if there isn't enough already.

Leaving the bathroom, I bump into Jenny. "I was just looking for you," she says. "I thought you might have left."

"I'm on my way out."

"Xuan Le and Barry would like to see you in Xuan Le's office."

I'm being called to the president's office. This is big. I keep myself from touching my stomach. I fear that's the reason they want to see me. Clarice warned me Barry would be onto my wardrobe changes before anyone else.

"Thanks, Jenny. See you tomorrow."

Shuffling my feet on the way to the eighth floor, I contemplate everything I'm going to tell them. I pass Makenna's dressing room and notice activity inside. My breath catches. Are they cleaning it out? She's due to be back in two and a half weeks. Oh my gosh. Is she leaving? Are they going to offer me her job? Suddenly my feet are no longer dragging as I practically skip the rest of the way. This would be the answer to my prayers. Two full days off every week. Home by six Wednesday through Friday. And Jaxon would be home on the weekends. We'd only need three days of childcare.

I knock and Xuan Le calls me in. I haven't been in her office since I first started here. It's huge. It takes up an entire corner of the eighth floor, with floor-to-ceiling windows overlooking the city. There's a wet bar on one side, a conference table on the other, a seating area larger than my living room, and four big-screen televisions embedded in the wall behind her desk.

"You're in a chipper mood for a Wednesday," Barry says in his normal clipped manner.

"It's hard not to be when you love your job."

A little sucking up never hurt anyone.

"Sit," Xuan Le says, motioning to the chair beside Barry, whose face looks to be in a permanent scowl.

Making sure my bump isn't showing when I sit, I try not to seem too excited.

"We wanted to talk to you before word got around and rumors started flying."

I pull my sweater tightly around me. "Okay."

"As you know, Makenna Kendall is set to return the first of the year."

"Yes, of course."

But she's not? I try not to bounce in my chair.

"In fact, you may have seen them outfitting her office with baby shit," Barry says. "She actually wants her nanny to bring the kid here for feedings. This is a place of business, not a damn wet nursery."

"Barry, must you be so anti-feminist?" Xuan Le says. "I might remind you we are well into the twenty-first century now."

Wait, wait, wait. I had this all wrong. This is them telling me I've been a great team player and how grateful they are to have had me here and good luck in my future endeavors.

I paste on a smile, even though I want to cry. "Yes, I saw them working. You must be thrilled to be getting her back."

"We are," Xuan Le says. "But there's been a new development."

"Oh?"

"Brenton Carmichael turned in his resignation two weeks ago."

"Brenton? The chief meteorologist?" I want to slap my hand against my forehead, because obviously they know he's the chief meteorologist. I'm stunned, and breathless as I wait to hear what they say next. Because what I think they are going to say is that Tom Killian will take over the nightly news, and Makenna will move to the daytime slot, leaving weekends for me. It's perfect. This is going to work out just as I'd hoped.

"I'm not going to get into his personal details, but he has cited health reasons for the decision."

"I'm sorry to hear that."

And while I truly am, part of me feels like a traitorous opportunist, salivating over what they're about to offer me. The baby flutters. She must feel my excitement.

"Here's how this has played out," Xuan Le says. "Tom is being promoted to chief meteorologist, leaving the weekday morning weather anchor slot open."

"Makenna will be perfect for that," I say.

Xuan Le and Barry share a look. "That's not really the direction we were going."

I stiffen. "What?"

"We want you to be XTN's new weekday weather anchor."

I put a finger to my chest, stunned. "Me?"

"Don't look so surprised," Xuan Le says. "You've done a spectacular job. And don't worry about any bad blood between you and Makenna. When she heard about Brenton leaving, she came to us preemptively. As a new mother, she didn't want the added hours or pressure of morning weather anchor. As a mother, I get it. It's a huge commitment. But between the three of us, the job was never going to be hers. We love Makenna, and she's a valuable part of the XTN family, but she doesn't quite have what it takes to be an anchor. We believe you do."

Barry rolls his eyes. He's reluctantly going along with this. Over the past months, I've come to realize he views all female meteorologists as weather girls, preferring humans with testicles to be in such positions.

Xuan Le pushes a packet across the desk. "Here's our offer."

While paging through, my excitement wanes when I realize what will be expected of me. In addition to the early morning hours five days a week, it specifically cites things like traveling to the Olympics, embarking on a state-by-state weather broadcast marathon, and co-hosting the third morning hour on a more regular basis than my predecessor had.

I close the packet. "This is... overwhelming."

Unfinished EX

"Congratulations, Nicole," Xuan Le says. "You've managed to do what few women have done, especially at your age. You've been given the brass ring."

"Thank you so much for the offer. Everyone here has been so welcoming and accommodating, and I've enjoyed every second." I place the folder on her desk. "But I'm afraid I'm going to have to pass."

Chapter Thirty-nine

Jaxon

There's a van in my driveway when Heisman and I return from our after-school walk. A large white van. And I wonder if Cooper traded up and is back in town. When someone who isn't my brother emerges, Heisman runs over and sniffs his shoes.

"Delivery for Nicole Forbes," the man says.

I stand at the back of the van. "I can take it."

"It's big. I'll carry it inside."

"I'll go unlock the door. Come on, Heisman, leave the guy alone."

The man pats Heisman's head and opens the back of his van. When he follows me inside, he has to turn sideways and carefully work his way through my front door. He wasn't kidding. This has got to be the largest flower arrangement I've ever seen. "Where do you want it?" he asks through the dense bouquet.

"Kitchen table. These aren't from Gigi's Flower Shop, are they? I thought I knew all of their delivery guys."

"I drove in from the city."

My eyes widen. "You drove all the way from the city to deliver these?" I pull out my wallet, embarrassed that all I have is fifteen dollars. I hold it out. "I wish it could be more."

He refuses the cash. "It's been taken care of. XTN tips very well."

Excitement courses through me. If XTN sent these, I know it's good news. "Thank you."

The guy leaves Heisman and me staring at the huge bouquet that takes up half our kitchen table. Heisman likes the smell. He circles the table, tail wagging. I circle it myself, searching for a note buried within the flowers. I find it sticking out the back side. I shouldn't read it, but I can't help myself. This could be everything we've dreamed about these past months.

I open the envelope carefully, intending to put the note back and act surprised when Nicky tells me the news. But what I read turns out to be the opposite of what I'd hoped for.

Nicole,

Please reconsider our offer. You breathe light into XTN. These few months with you have shown us what's missing. You would be a welcome permanent addition to our family.

All my best,

Xuan Le Kim

Xuan Le? As in the president of XTN? The president sent her a note and a basket of flowers that probably cost more than a year's worth of dog food, begging her to reconsider.

Unfinished EX

The front door opens. Heisman rushes to greet Nicky. I pull out a chair and sit next to the monstrous arrangement. She turns the corner and sees the flowers. "Wow, those are—"

"From XTN."

"I don't leave for another few weeks, but that was still nice of them."

I shake my head, anger crawling up my spine like rungs of a ladder. "We promised we'd never lie to each other again, Nic."

"Lie?"

I hold out the note. "You got a job offer and turned it down? What the hell were you thinking? This is everything we've hoped for."

She reads the note and sits heavily on the chair next to me. "It's not what you think."

"Then enlighten me, because unless the job they offered was overnight janitor, you have some goddamn explaining to do."

"Brenton Carmichael resigned."

"The nighttime guy?"

"Yes. Tom Killian was moved into his position of chief meteorologist. I was sure they'd want Makenna for Tom's position, but they wanted me."

"You? As weekday weather anchor? Oh my god, Nicky. That's incredible. Isn't that a senior position?"

"A senior position that demands a great deal of hours and huge responsibility." She rubs her small baby bump. "A lot has happened this past week. I still have a high-risk pregnancy, not to mention how much time I'd have to spend away from you and the baby."

"But it's everything you've ever dreamed of."

She swallows and looks away. I can tell this is tearing her apart inside. "My priorities have changed."

345

I get up and lean against the counter. "What does that mean? That you'd rather work fifteen hundred miles away at some cushy job in Oklahoma City than bust your ass for the one you've worked so hard to get right here in New York? You'd rather us spend weekends on planes for, what, thirty-six hours with each other? You'd rather our kid only get to spend a few weeks here and there with me? *Those* are your priorities?"

"I don't think you fully understand this. I'd have to be up at three a.m. Monday through Friday. That means I'd need to go to bed by eight p.m."

"We'd have weekends."

"In a perfect world. But do you know how often I run into Tom at the station on weekends? The weather doesn't stop at five p.m. on Friday night, Jaxon. I'd basically be on call all the time. Weekday anchors put in a lot more time. I'd be expected to do more traveling. We'd hardly see each other."

"But if you go back to Oklahoma, or Detroit, or Indianapolis, or wherever, we'd never see each other then either. At least with this job, you'd be living here. We'd be together in the same house. In the same bed."

"You misunderstand, Jaxon. It's not just that I'm turning down the XTN job. I'm not taking *any* job. I'm going to stay right here with you, and we'll see each other all the time."

I pace, confused. "You're quitting?"

"For now."

"You're kidding me."

"I'll go back to work someday. When she's older."

"Someday." It comes out like a curse word. "Nicky, you have momentum now. In a few years, nobody will remember the woman who filled in at XTN for a few months. You'll have to start over at someplace like WRKT. And who knows if you'll ever be given a

Unfinished **EX**

break like this again. This choice may determine the rest of your career."

"It's done. I've already decided." She pulls one of the flowers out of the arrangement and studies it, then looks up at me. "I thought you'd be happy about this. This is everything you wanted—me, a child, and us here together."

"If that's what you really think, then you don't know me very well. And you sure as hell aren't the woman I fell in love with all those years ago. The one who not only chases storms but her dreams. I'm not saying staying home with kids isn't a noble calling—it is. But you and I both know it's not *your* calling. If you give this up, what kind of message are you sending to your daughter—to all the daughters of the world?"

"It's what's best for us."

"What's best for us is that both of us be in fulfilling careers that make us happy. The rest will work itself out."

"Like I said, it's been done."

"You can't see the forest through the trees, can you? This is so screwed up. Don't you understand what this will do to us? I know you, Nicky. Weather is your life. You'll never be happy without it. Imagine yourself sitting on this couch watching Tom and Makenna day in and day out. You can't honestly sit there and tell me you won't long for it. And that longing will turn to resentment. Toward me. Maybe even toward our little girl. You can't do that to her. To us." I motion to the flowers. "You can still take the job. They still want you."

"I've made my decision, Jaxon."

I cross the room and whistle for Heisman. "And I've made mine."

"Meaning?"

"Meaning I refuse to be the person you come to resent. We did that once. Heisman and I are going for a walk. I'd like for you not to be here when we get back."

"You want me to leave?"

"Yes, Nicky. I want you to leave. Doesn't feel so good to be blindsided, does it?"

I grab my coat and am out the door before she can reply.

"Don't look at me like that," I tell Heisman. "What she's doing is wrong, and you know it."

We head back to the park, even though we were there twenty minutes ago. I find a stick, then sit on a bench and throw it to him. The irony of the situation is not lost on me. Two years ago, she left because I couldn't deal with her job aspirations. And now I'm asking her to leave because *she* can't. The crazy thing is, I know she wants it. I get that with the baby and all, it complicates things. But if she doesn't do this, she will regret it. I'm one hundred percent certain.

"Hey, Jaxon."

Eric and Calista wander up. Heisman trots over and showers attention on her.

"You look like a steamroller hit you," Eric says. "Only one thing that could mean. Trouble in paradise?"

I throw the stick. Heisman doesn't chase it. He tucks his head into Calista's lap when she sits on the bench opposite mine. "Nice to see you up and around," I say, ignoring Eric's spot-on observation. "How's my kid? You keeping him or her warm?"

"Nice and toasty," she says, rubbing her stomach. Her coat falls off her shoulder when she partially raises her arm in the sling. "At least they expect a full recovery. With some physical therapy, I'll be able to cradle this little one in both arms come May."

Unfinished **EX**

May. Every time I think of it, it hits me how much my life will change. Two babies. By two women. Sometimes I can't even wrap my mind around it. It seems absurd, yet somehow, I've noticed myself becoming excited about it. All of it. Or I was until an hour ago. "I'm glad to hear it. I saw them working at your house today. The tree is out. When will the work be done?"

"After the holidays." She gazes at Eric. "I don't mind. It's been nice staying at his place and having someone at my beck and call."

"Why not make it permanent then? Your house is plenty big enough."

Eric gives me a brooding stare. "Way to steal my thunder and beat me to the punch, man."

"What punch?" Calista asks.

"I was going to wait until Christmas Eve to ask, but since Dudley Do-Right here spoiled it, I was thinking maybe we should move in together. I know it's only been a few days, but it feels right."

She throws her good arm around him. "It feels right to me, too. But are you sure? In five months, you'll have to share me with a crying, pooping tiny human."

He chokes up. "I've never been more sure of anything." He pulls her up. "Come on, let's go give notice on my apartment before you change your mind." As they walk away, he tosses me a look over his shoulder. "Good luck with the steamroller. Whatever it is, it'll work itself out."

What he doesn't know is that it won't. It can't. XTN will hire someone else, and we'll be right back where we started as soon as she gets that itch again. Why can't she understand that?

"Wow," I say to my dog. "So in a matter of an hour, I've kicked out my soul mate and Eric has moved in with his."

I text my brother.

> **Me: Meet me at Donovan's?**
>
> **Tag: On a Wednesday? What did you do?**
>
> **Me: It's not what I did. More like what Nic didn't.**
>
> **Tag: Give me thirty.**

I spend the next half hour wondering how I can fix this. But I'm not sure it can be fixed, or at least that *I* can be the one to fix it. This is something Nic needs to figure out on her own. If she can't, maybe she's not the woman I thought she was.

Chapter Forty

Nicky

The past few days have been torture. I thought he'd come around. I figured he'd show up at my parents' house with a dozen roses and thank me for the sacrifice I'm making for our family.

But nothing. And tonight was the night we were supposed to tell our families about the baby.

I pick up the phone and call Makenna Kendall.

"Nicole Forbes," she answers happily. "I was hoping I'd hear from you. But I have to say I'm a little surprised to find out you won't be the new weekday weather anchor. Better offer? Did NBC pick you up or something?"

"Makenna, why did you decide to come back to work?"

She sighs. "I see. You were hoping for *my* job."

"No. It's not that. I mean, maybe it's that. But that's not why I'm asking. I'm um… pregnant."

"Oh, wow. I did not see that coming."

"Neither did I. And nobody knows yet. Not even my family."

"Is that why you turned down the job?"

"Yes. So can you answer the question?"

"Ryan is a wonderful baby. Everything I ever wanted in a son. Two months with him wasn't enough, but four… I love him more than anything, but I'm not the kind of person who can be fulfilled by being a wife and mother. I know a lot of women are, and in many ways, I envy them, but personally—"

"You need more."

"I need more. I'm guessing you do too, and that's why you called."

I lean back in bed and put her on speaker. "Have I made a huge mistake?"

"Not one that can't be undone. Word around town is you've had a lot of offers."

"But none that will give me everything I want."

"Which is what?"

"I suppose to eat my cake and have it too. To have a family *and* my dream job. But also the time to give to each. To have a man who won't let me make stupid decisions because I'm a raging ball of hormones." I sink into my pillow knowing I already have that one. Or *had*. "I've ruined everything."

"As someone who knows where you're coming from, I can tell you it's best to make decisions with your head, not your hormones."

A baby cries in the background. My heart lurches. "You'd better go and enjoy him while you can."

"Haven't you seen my dressing room, Nicole? I plan to enjoy him even when I'm at work. You know, so I can eat my cake and have it too. Bye now."

~ ~ ~

Unfinished EX

A second crash of thunder has Jaxon removing his lips from mine, grabbing the blanket, and tugging me toward the dugout.

"What's the rush?" I ask. "It's not even raining yet."

"Haven't you ever heard that lightning can strike from seven miles away?"

"It's not that close."

"How do you know?"

"Because I can count."

"Oh, right. What is it, like a second for every mile?"

I shake my head, still resisting as he's urging me away from our adolescent make-out spot in the outfield of Calloway Creek High School's baseball field. "Not exactly. If you count the seconds between the flash of lightning and the thunder, and then divide by five, you'll get the distance in miles. Five seconds equals one mile. Fifteen seconds equals three miles."

"I didn't know that. Did you learn it in Mr. Henderson's class?"

"I read it."

"Okay then." He spreads the blanket out again, pulls me down on it, and we make out some more, listening to the distant sound of thunder as it mixes with our heavy breathing.

A bolt of lightning flashes, illuminating the entire field momentarily. We stop kissing, both of us silently counting. By the time I hit twelve, droplets of rain pepper my face and thunder crackles.

"Way too close," he says. He stands, picks up the blanket, and hauls me onto his shoulder like a sack of potatoes before heading for cover.

I laugh as he walks us to the dugout, the rain coming down heavier now, soaking my rear end. But I don't care. I love being this close to him. It makes my body tingle in places I've only read about in Mom's romance novels.

He descends the three steps and sets me down next to the bench along the back wall. He pounds on the wooden structure. "Good thing this isn't made of metal, or we'd be toast."

"*Actually, that's a myth. The presence of metal makes absolutely no difference in where lightning strikes. Height, pointy shapes, and isolated structures are the dominant factors.*"

He spreads the blanket on the bench, and we sit, dim streetlights from the distant parking lot providing just enough light for us to see. "*How do you know so much about this stuff?*"

I shrug, embarrassed about my geeky tendencies. "*I watch The Weather Channel a lot. And I read books about meteorology.*"

"*Really?*"

I draw in a breath, ready to reveal something I've never told him before. "*I know it's stupid, but I think I want to be a meteorologist.*"

He pulls back. "*How have we been together almost a year and I didn't know this about you?*"

I lean against the wall. "*I guess I didn't want you seeing me as a science nerd.*"

His hand covers mine. "*Nicky, I'd never think that. In fact, I think it's great that you know what you want to do at fourteen. I do, too.*"

"*You do?*"

"*I want to be a teacher. In fact, I want to teach right here at CCHS.*"

His revelation doesn't surprise me. Jaxon gets along with everyone—well, except the McQuaids. He's patient. Smart. Empathetic. I cuddle next to him. "*I think you'd make a great teacher.*"

"*I think you'd make a great weather girl.*"

"*They aren't called that anymore, especially if they have a degree. They're called weather forecasters. Or just meteorologists.*"

He wraps his arm around me. "*My girlfriend is so cool.*"

I can't help my smile. Every time he calls me his girlfriend, I'm reminded of how lucky I am to be dating the nicest guy in Calloway Creek. "*You think it's cool that I want to study the weather?*"

Unfinished **EX**

"I think the probability of us ever getting struck by lightning just went way down," he jokes. He squeezes me. "And yes, it's very cool. Now how about we stop talking about sciency stuff and start making out again?"

Butterflies dance inside me. We've never done much more than make out and roam each other on top of our clothes, but the way he makes me feel with just those innocent moments makes me wonder what he could do to me when we take it further. And I know, right here, right now, that he's the one I want to go there with. He's the one I want to do everything with.

As if he can sense what I'm thinking, he looks into my eyes. His lips inch closer to mine. Just before his mouth lands on me, he stops and declares, "I'll never have another girlfriend, Nicky. You're the one for me."

And as his kiss detonates me, I know that someday, I want to marry Jaxon Calloway.

By the time three a.m. rolls around, my regret has turned into a sense of emptiness, and not just because Jaxon is gone. I fear I may have made a huge mistake. But it's one I can't take back. Yesterday, I saw Neil Pittman roaming the halls with Barry. Neil is the meteorologist for an NBC affiliate in New Jersey. And Barry looked happy. Barry's never happy.

I sip my coffee knowing I blew it to the extreme.

When I walk up to the XTN building before dawn, I find a familiar face in the lobby. Instantly, he's in my arms. "Marty!"

"I've missed you," he says. He pulls back and studies me. "As someone who hasn't seen you up close in almost four months, I can say you are dangerously close to being found out. Your face is rounder, not to mention the bump that was just squished between us."

"I know. We were supposed to tell everyone last night, but then…"

"I know what happened."

I narrow my eyes, confused. "Did Makenna Kendall call you?"

"Jaxon Calloway did."

"Jaxon? Why did *he* call you?"

"Maybe he thought I was the only one who could talk sense into you. He wanted me to beg you to come back to WRKT."

"But that's so far away. Why would he want that?"

"I kind of get the feeling that man would do anything to make you happy. Even if it means having you fifteen hundred miles away. Nicky, people like you, type A-ers who need to work like other people need to breathe, you'll never be happy unless you're going eighty miles per hour, wind in your hair. Jaxon gets that. And I have to tell you, not a lot of men would."

I nod, knowing how badly I screwed up. "Can you come up and stay for the broadcast?"

"I thought you'd never ask."

Clarice catches me on the way to my dressing room. "A word?"

I direct her inside and introduce her to Marty. "You can speak freely. He knows."

She hands me a blouse and pants. "You've pushed this about as far as you can, Nicole. Barry is oblivious. Or he simply doesn't care what with the candidates for Tim's job milling about. But Henri made a comment about your face looking heavier. And Jenny asked me if I thought you were okay after she caught you napping in your dressing room. And really, what does it matter if you make an announcement with you leaving in a few weeks and all?"

I drape the clothes over the back of my chair and sit. "You're right. I guess it doesn't make a bit of difference. I'll tell them after third hour."

Marty and I chat about nothing important while I get my hair and makeup done. The baby is really kicking today. Maybe even hard enough for Jaxon to feel. Thinking about him not being around to feel every kick, every milestone, makes me sad.

The room clears, and Marty and I are alone right before I go on.

"Thank you for coming. It's nice to know I still have a job with WRKT."

"You don't. We hired someone. I said Jaxon called me to ask me to take you back. I never said I agreed to."

"You hired someone? Without telling me?"

"Nicky, I know what we talked about before, but you don't want to go back there. We both know it's beneath you at this point. You've got other offers. Take one."

I shake my head. "I've already turned everything down."

He opens my door and pushes me toward the studio. "Looks like you've gotten yourself in a bit of a pickle then."

"Nicole, on in two," Barry says, passing in the hallway. He takes a moment and stares me down from head to toe, almost like he's finally noticing what he hadn't before, that I haven't worn a skin-tight dress in weeks.

"I'll wait here," Marty says, moving off in the corner behind the cameras. "Do your thing."

I go through the motions for my spots in the first two hours. By the time hour three rolls around, the guilt consumes me. The regret. The stupidity of my actions. I've painted myself into a corner I'm not sure I can get out of.

"Quit fiddling with your damn necklace," Barry's voice echoes through my earpiece. "And don't forget to announce Makenna's return."

I paste on a smile. "It's my pleasure to be the bearer of great news. Makenna Kendall, who graciously allowed me to fill in for her over the past several months, will be returning to XTN January third. I hope you'll all join me in welcoming her back." I pause before doing my usual sign-off. I inhale a shaky breath. "I have something I'd like to say before turning it back to Roman. There is someone out there I need to apologize to. You see, I was offered my dream job, and I turned it down for the man I love. But I've come to realize that the man I love wouldn't want a woman who turned down her dream job."

"What the fuck are you doing, Nicole?" Barry says in my ear.

I rub sweaty palms down the side of my slacks, then I flatten my blouse against my stomach and turn. "I'm pregnant." I ignore Barry's shouting and the gasps in the studio and focus directly into the camera hoping *he's* watching. "I don't know what's going to happen, Jaxon. But whatever happens, I know I want it to happen with you by my side. Even if it means being a thousand miles away until I can work my way back here. I get it now. I get that I can have you and our daughter and still go after my dreams. You were right." I cup my bump. "She needs me to set an example. So, if I promise to take the next offer that comes my way, no matter where it might be, will you take me back? Because being a family with you is something I've wanted since I was thirteen years old." I wipe the tears that have surely smeared my makeup, making me look utterly unprofessional. "And now, back to Roman."

The studio is silent except for Roman's voice. All eyes are on me. I see Barry having a conniption up in the booth. I race past Marty and everyone, needing to get to my dressing room before I collapse.

Xuan Le comes out of the booth and catches up to me.

Unfinished EX

"I'm sorry," I tell her. "I'll clear out my dressing room and be gone in an hour."

"The hell you will." She follows me in and shuts the door. "Who do you think kept the cameras rolling? Not Barry. He was having a coronary and ordered them to cut over to the news desk. *I* kept them rolling, Nicole." She points to my door. "What you did out there is exactly why I hired you. Do you know how many women and girls you just inspired?"

I catch a glimpse of myself in the mirror. Mascara tracks run down my face. I look like the living dead. "You still want me here for the next two weeks?"

"Nicole, I want you here for the next two decades. We haven't filled the position yet."

"But I saw Neil Pittman talking with Barry yesterday."

"Wishful thinking on Barry's part."

I swallow. Can I do this? Can I take this on and still be a good partner and mother?

I must hesitate for too long. Xuan Le paces. "Fine. I can offer you twenty percent more than before. And four months maternity leave. And a lighter travel schedule for eighteen months. What do you say, Nicole?"

Chapter Forty-one

Jaxon

My phone blows up with texts and emails. *Shit.* Someone must have spilled the beans. If it's Hudson McQuaid, I will thump the ever-living shit out of him. The doorbell rings, and I ignore it. I almost don't answer the phone when my mother calls, but I know how persistent she can be.

"What it is, Mom?"

"Answer your door, Jaxon. Your father and I are freezing out here."

How did news travel so quickly?

I open the door. Mom pulls me in for a hug. "My boy. Oh, what a situation you're in. Two babies? Why didn't you tell us? And what's this nonsense about Nicky wanting you back? I wasn't aware you were having trouble."

"I'm confused. How did you find out? We weren't telling anyone yet. Not until we told you, which was supposed to happen last night, but then, well, we just…" I walk into my living room and sit. "I screwed up. I kicked her out when she turned down a job at XTN. She said she did it for me, but all I saw was the past repeating itself. I called her old producer, and now he's probably going to take her back to Oklahoma, and that scares the shit out of me, too, but I didn't know what else to do. And now I don't know how to fix things."

"So you didn't see the eleven o'clock hour?" Dad asks.

"On XTN?"

He hands me the remote. "You DVR it, right? It was near the end."

Heisman settles next to me as I forward through.

"Stop there," Mom says. "It was right after that."

I sit glued to the TV while Nicky announces her pregnancy to the world, along with a plea for me to take her back.

"Holy crap." I look at Mom and Dad. "A hundred bucks says that Barry guy fired her on the spot after that."

"Now that's what I call a grand gesture," Mom says. "It takes a lot of courage to admit when we've done something wrong. To admit it to millions of people takes more guts than I've ever had. She put it all on the line for you, Jaxon. Is it safe to assume you're going to take her back?"

"Mom, I was always planning on it. I thought one of us would cave sooner or later. I guess I assumed it would be me."

The front door opens. Tag and Addy come in.

"I don't know what idiotic thing you did that would make her have to beg you to take her back on national TV," Addy says, "but if you don't marry that girl again, you'll be the stupidest person on the planet."

"I agree," I say.

Everyone goes silent. "You do?" Mom asks.

"Guys, I've wanted to marry her again since the day she walked back into Calloway Creek."

Addison claps. "How can we help?"

I laugh. "Addy, proposing to my ex-wife is something I need to do on my own. But thanks."

"Oh, no. She went on TV and cut herself open for you. You have to do something equally as spectacular. Do you still have the ring?"

"No. But I know where it is."

"You want to give her the *same* ring?" Tag asks. "Isn't that bad luck or something?"

"We never should have been divorced, so yeah, I want her to have the same one."

"It's so romantic," Addy says. "How will you do it? Where will you do it?" She turns to Tag. "Call Maddie. Tell her he'll need lots of flowers. I'll call Ava, Regan, and Paige. They'll want to be in on it. Oh, and you should get lights, Jaxon. It's Christmastime. Twinkly lights. Please say you'll do it tonight. It *has* to be tonight."

"I don't even know if she'll come over," I say.

"Then go to her."

"You want me to take flowers and twinkly lights to her? At her parents' house? How would that even work?"

Mom checks the time, obviously in on Addy's excitement. "We have almost ten hours. That's plenty of time to come up with something."

Nerves take hold. I'm going to ask her to marry me. *Again*. The love of my fucking life.

And this time, it's going to be forever.

~ ~ ~

People have caught on. A crowd has gathered. Phones are out and ready to record.

Maybe this wasn't such a good idea after all.

I glance around the train station. White lights have been strung on every post and between every pillar. Roses are intertwined with the lights. Bundles of flowers line a pathway under the awning and over to where I'm waiting.

My family is doing a good job keeping onlookers back. I really don't care if people record it. In fact, it might be fun to show our daughter one day, but I don't want anyone to ruin it. Like a McQuaid for instance. But among the dozens of spectators, I don't see one enemy in sight. And I have a feeling my big brother would take care of them if I did.

The train appears in the distance. My heart beats out of my chest. Suddenly, I'm terrified. What if she says no? What if she only wants to be together as partners and co-parents? We never talked about re-marriage. I'm making a hell of a lot of assumptions here.

I take my place among the flowers and lights. Addy tells everyone to shut up. Phones start recording. Brakes squeal as the train comes to a stop. People trickle out, their shoes scraping against the concrete pad. A crying baby gets comforted by his mother. A man emerges and a woman jumps into his arms. I wait with bated breath. Murmurs echo through the crowd. But the train pulls away. And Nicky isn't here.

Fuck.

Everyone knows there isn't another train for an hour. And I know she's never missed the eleven-p.m. train.

"Sorry folks," Tag says. "I guess there's nothing to see."

People dissipate, giving me looks of pity. I feel like the biggest idiot. Why didn't she come home? Is something wrong? With her? The baby? I pull out my phone. No messages. *Wait—I can track her.* I pull up the app. It says she's… *here?*

I glance around but don't see her. I do see Calista. I don't feel like talking to anyone. I just want to find Nicky. But Calista is emphatically waving me over. Then she points to a limousine in the street.

"She's in *there?*"

Calista smiles. "Go get your girl."

How things have changed from a few weeks ago. Who'd have thought the mother of one of my future children would be standing here encouraging me to go propose to the other mother of one of my future children. I mean, you can't make this shit up.

When I approach the limo, the driver gets out and opens the door for me. It's hard to hold in my surprise, and my laughter, when I look inside. Twinkly lights and roses are all over the interior of the limo. And Nicky is sitting among them, sporting a beautiful but nervous smile.

I climb in and motion outside. "I kind of did a thing out there."

"I kind of did a thing in here."

I pull her engagement ring out of my pocket. "But my thing includes this."

Tears coat her lashes. "Oh, god, Jaxon."

I scoot my way over to her. "Your thing is definitely better because your thing has me making love to my fiancée in a limo."

"It does?"

"I damn well hope so." I hold up the ring. "I swore I'd never get married again. But that was before I knew marrying the same woman was a possibility. I'd never marry anyone but you, Nicky. You're my soul mate. The person I want to grow old with." I touch her belly. "The mother of some of my children."

She chuckles.

"And if you want to stay home with the baby for now, who am I to say you can't? But you have to promise me that when you're ready, you'll go chase tornadoes. You'll drive into the path of a hurricane and stand on the edge of a volcano. Because no matter how much it worries me to watch you do those things, it's all part of why I love you."

"Are you sure? Are you absolutely sure, Jaxon?"

"More than I've ever been before."

"Good. Because you're looking at XTN's new weekday weather anchor."

"What? They still offered you the job? I thought they'd have banned you from the building after what you did earlier."

"Me too. Instead, they offered me more money, great maternity leave, limited travel time for eighteen months, and get this, I even talked them into bringing on Marty as my producer. Oh, and the use of the station limo for tonight." She swallows. "So I could propose."

I swear I feel my heart grow larger. *"You* were going to propose? And you're staying in New York?"

"If you'll have me." She eyes the ring I'm holding. "And I'm guessing you will."

"Yes."

She smiles sweetly, tears rimming her eyes. "Isn't that supposed to be my line?"

I get on a knee and work myself between her legs. "Nicole Forbes, will you marry me? Again?"

"Only if you start calling me Nicky Calloway."

My eyebrows shoot up.

"Professionally, I'll be Nicole Forbes, but for all other intents and purposes, I'll be Nicky Calloway, legally and otherwise."

"So that's a yes?"

She holds out her hand. "That's a yes."

I slip it on, noticing it's a tight fit.

She laughs. "I've put on a few pounds since we last did this."

I nuzzle her neck and cup her belly. "I love your extra pounds. And I love you."

"I love you, too. I always have."

I nudge further between her legs and trap her against the leather seat. Staring into her eyes, I see my future. It's not the same future I envisioned the last time we got engaged. This future is full of half-siblings, middle-of-the-night phone calls whisking her away to some natural disaster, ex-girlfriends who live next door, and otherwise pure chaos. But I'm not sure I'd have it any other way.

I lean in and capture her lips with mine. Our kiss starts out gently, like when we were teens, then turns more demanding, our tongues battling madly for dominance. I let her win. Then she lets me. I have a feeling this is how our whole relationship is going to go from here on out.

We've shared a million kisses over the years, but this one tops them all. Her flowery smell floats through the air, mixing with the aroma of the roses strewn about the limo. Her lips taste of butterscotch, her neck of salty tears. My heart flutters knowing this woman is going to be mine forever.

I pull away. "You're mine," I say with the will and determination of a gladiator.

She lets out a contented sigh. "Yes."

I kiss her cheek. "I'm never letting you go." I lick her neck. "No takebacks." I run my tongue along her throat. "We're talking forever here."

Looking up to see tears rolling down her cheek, I wipe them and stare at her beautiful face. Her pink lips turn into a slow smile. She pulls my hand to her belly and settles it in place. "Can you feel her?"

We're both completely still. Waiting. Hoping. My heart leaps when under my hand are faint movements I would never feel if I weren't concentrating intently. They come and go as softly as a feather blowing in the breeze, but they're there. I'm afraid to move, not wanting to break the spell. I want to stay rooted in this moment until the end of my days.

Now *she's* wiping *my* tears as we become bonded on a level we never have before.

The engine starts, ending our moment but not our night.

"Where do you want to go?" she asks. "We have the limo all night. And Xuan Le gave me the day off tomorrow."

"Anywhere?"

"Anywhere."

"Aren't you tired?"

"I slept in my dressing room all afternoon. I'm fine. And I'm yours for the night."

"Good. Because I want to make love to you all night and then go to Battery Park and watch the sun come up with you."

She pushes a chunk of hair out of my eyes. "Because last time we got engaged, we watched the sunset. This time, you want to watch it *rise*. Because this is the start of something new, something great, something different. Like an aurora. A dawn. A new beginning."

Now we're both crying. "See?" I say. "Soul mate."

I find the button for the driver. "We're ready to go. Drive anywhere. And leave the partition up."

"Yes, sir."

I push it again. "Wait one second." I go to the window and roll it down. There's still a small crowd: my family, Nicky's, and a few random friends. I stick my head out the window. "She said yes!"

Cheers erupt.

"Now go home. My fiancée and I are out of here."

Unfinished **EX**

Her arms come around me from behind. "Fiancée. I like the sound of that."

"Don't get too used to it. You won't be one for long. February eighth is right around the corner."

She smiles at the idea of getting remarried on our original wedding date. "And I'll be your wife for the rest of my life."

"You bet your hot weather anchor ass you will be."

Chapter Forty-two

Nicky

Four months later...

"Nicky, you okay?" Marty asks through my earpiece.

I look to the booth and give him a thumbs-up.

"If you need anything..."

Annoyed, I offer the OK sign.

I lean against a wall and stretch my aching back. I know people are only looking out for me, but I'm growing tired of giving constant reassurances that, at just over thirty-six weeks along, I'm not going to squat and drop the baby here on the studio floor.

The Braxton-Hicks contractions have been getting stronger over the past few weeks. Jaxon even drove me to the hospital twice, sure I was in labor. It's hard not to smile when I think of him. The poor man is in a constant state of worry and excitement having two babies due in the next three and a half weeks. He really should be more concerned with Calista, though. She has eleven days left, and it was obvious to me last week that her belly had dropped—a sure sign labor will come sooner rather than later.

We've had nothing but encouraging news from our many ultrasounds. There's been no indication of my scarring interfering with the placenta, and I couldn't have asked for an easier pregnancy. Physically, anyway.

Sitting in a chair they brought for me right next to the set, I rub my belly, hoping to calm it down. Like me, the baby seems on edge. All day, I've been reporting on the outbreak of tornadoes across the Midwest. If I weren't feeling a hundred weeks pregnant, I'd actually be sad that I wasn't out in the field.

One of the assistant producers hands me a fact sheet with new stats about the destruction in a small Kansas town. "Back in twenty," Marty informs me as I memorize the numbers on the piece of paper. "We've got art to go with those stats."

I nod and try not to grunt as another Braxton-Hicks temporarily consumes me. I breathe through it and go over to my mark.

"Three, two, one…" Marty counts in my ear.

"Coffeyville is a small town in southeastern Kansas, about two and a half hours from Wichita and eighty miles from Tulsa, Oklahoma. Its population is just under 9,000." I point to the screen behind me. "And I can only hope those 9,000 residents were all in a safe place when this F3 tornado with wind speeds estimated at 180 miles per hour blew through moments ago. XTN has been able to acquire drone footage thanks to—"

I feel a pop. I stop talking and inspect the floor beneath me.

"Nicky?" Marty asks through my earpiece.

I look at the booth, then back at the camera. "I'm sorry, folks, it seems my water has broken." I glance at the graphic, seeing the horrific damage caused by the tornado, and go into autopilot. "Thanks to, uh, Judd Neilson of nearby Independence, we have rare footage of the immediate aftermath—"

Unfinished EX

Marty does something a producer has never done. He walks out onto the set and interrupts my broadcast.

"I'm almost finished," I tell him (and three-quarters of a million viewers).

He laughs. "Sweetheart, you're done."

"Are we still rolling?"

"This is you, Nicole. Of course we are."

I stare into the camera. "Dr. Peterman, if you're watching, meet me at the hospital. Oh, and Jaxon, it looks like our baby girl wants an April birthday!"

Marty nods to the cameraman. The tally light goes off, and I hear Landon Miller take over my story.

I'm escorted to the nearest chair. I cup my belly. "You couldn't have waited until *after* the tornado outbreak?"

A dozen people are bustling around me, asking if it hurts or if I feel pressure down there. Xuan Le plows a path to me. "Give her space, people. This is your first baby. It may take hours. The limo is outside. Marty will ride with you in case things get dicey along the way. Kenny says traffic is light between here and Calloway Creek." She glances at Marty. "What are you waiting for? Get her to the hospital!"

An assistant producer gives me my phone—which is understandably blowing up with texts. I wait until I'm inside the limo to call Jaxon back.

"Are you crazy?" he answers.

"I'd be remiss if I didn't mention it's not in good form to call a pregnant woman crazy."

"Nicky, Jesus, were you really going to continue on air?"

"Have you seen how bad the outbreak is? They're predicting F4s and F5s. This could be the next super outbreak. I can't believe I'm going to miss it."

"Who the hell cares about that when you're in labor?"

"The people of Coffeyville, that's who."

"We'll send a big donation," he says. "Can we just focus on you now? Please tell me someone is with you."

I put him on speaker. "Marty and I are headed back to Calloway Creek now."

"What if you have her in the car?" His voice cracks, two octaves higher than usual.

"I'm not going to have her in the car, Jaxon. Delivery can happen as long as twenty-four hours after water breaking."

"Yeah, without contractions. Have you had any?"

I'm silent.

"She has," Marty says.

"I thought they were Braxton-Hicks." I close my eyes, feeling all kinds of stupid.

"How long?" Jaxon asks. "How far apart?"

I wince and grab the door handle. Marty checks the time. "I'd say less than ten minutes."

"Okay," Jaxon says. "Then no need to panic."

"You're the only one who's panicking," I say when it passes. "We'll meet you at the hospital in about forty-five minutes."

"I'm staying on the phone with you. I'm not going to miss a second of this, Nic."

Calista's face appears on my phone. "I have another call. I'll switch over and be right back."

"Ni—"

"Hey."

"Are you seriously in labor, Nicky?" Calista asks.

"Looks like it."

She squeals. "I can't believe you're going first. Are you scared? What if you don't make it to the hospital? Where are you? On the train? Nicky, how exciting would it be if you had the baby on the train? You'd be front page news for sure! Have you had any contractions? Oh my god, have you spoken with Jaxon? Is he freaking out?"

I laugh. My best friend and my husband are two sides of the same coin. "He's on the other line."

She giggles. "He must be livid that you put him on hold for me."

"What can I say? Sometimes hoes trump bros."

"I'm going to tell him you said that."

"No you're not."

"You're right, I'm not. Nicky, I can't believe this is happening."

"Me neither. I'm in a limo on the way back to Calloway Creek. I promise I'll call you from the hospital."

"You better."

"Love you."

"Love you too." I switch over. "Jaxon?"

"Was the president calling? Or maybe God? You put me on hold!"

"Calm down, it was Calista."

"If you tell me her water broke too, I'm going straight to the psych ward when I get to the hospital."

I start laughing, but it quickly turns into a grimace.

"Nic? Are you having a contraction? Marty?"

"I'm on it," Marty says. "Timer started."

I breathe through it. They're becoming stronger, and this one radiates all the way to my thighs.

"Four minutes twenty seconds since the last one," Jaxon says. "They're getting much closer."

"Forty-five seconds long," Marty says.

"Any update on the storms?" I ask.

Marty shoots me a scolding look. "Perhaps you could take the day off."

"Bad weather doesn't only happen when it's convenient for meteorologists."

"There are plenty of people to handle it. There's only one thing you need to do right now."

My other line rings. "Jaxon, my mom is calling. If I don't take it, she'll worry."

"Quickly, please."

I reassure my mother and switch back over. "She'll meet us at the hospital."

"Somehow I get the idea *everyone* will meet us there," Jaxon says. "I wouldn't be surprised if XTN already had a team there to cover the birth."

Marty shrugs. "You did announce your water breaking on national TV."

"Oh, ow, ow…"

"Shit," Jaxon says. "They're coming faster. How long until you get here?"

Marty shouts to the driver, then tells Jaxon, "Twenty minutes."

Something changes inside me. Pressure is building. I grab Marty's hand. "Oh, god. I feel like I have to push."

"Drive faster!" Marty yells.

"Hold on, Nicky," Jaxon begs.

I close my eyes and concentrate. The feeling has subsided for the moment. Please don't let me have this baby in the car. "Tell me something to distract me."

"Names," Jaxon says. "Let's pick a name."

He's been trying to get me to do it for months. I've refused. How can I possibly name my child without seeing her? Not to mention I wasn't about to do anything to jinx this. "Something else."

Marty shoves his phone in my face. "The storms spared Kansas City; they've moved into a largely rural area of Missouri. And they're dissipating. Looks like you aren't going to miss the next super outbreak after all."

"Pictures?"

He scrolls and finds some. He zooms in on a housing development. I take the phone and survey the damage. "See here, there is surface damage to the roofs. A few overturned vehicles and downed trees. Probably an F1. They *are* weakening."

"Uh, hello?" Jaxon says. "Are you two being serious right now?"

"Your wife did ask us to distract her," Marty says. "Well, she's distracted."

Another contraction strikes, and with it, immense pressure. I push Marty's phone away and grip the seat.

"She's having another," Marty says. "Driver! How long?"

"Less than five."

"Marty, I feel really strange. I think the baby is coming now."

"Nic, hold on, please," Jaxon cries. "I'm here at the hospital. I'm waiting for you. Hold on."

"I'm trying," I say once the contraction has passed. "But I'm not sure your daughter is listening. She wants to come, Jaxon. I'm not sure I can stop. I have to push."

I hear Jaxon yelling to someone.

"Almost there!" the driver bellows.

"I see you," Jaxon shouts. "I see the limo. Hold on, babe!"

I squeeze Marty's hand. "Marty, it hurts."

"I know, Nicky. We're pulling up now. You can do this."

The limo rolls to a stop. The doors open. Marty gets out and people rush in. Jaxon. A nurse. And… *Hudson McQuaid?*

"Where the hell is Dr. Peterman?" Jaxon asks, blocking him.

"Fishing," Hudson says. "He's on his way, but by the looks of things, he may not make it."

"You are not delivering my baby," Jaxon says. "There has to be someone else."

I wave a hand. "While you two are arguing, I have a human coming out of me."

"Get over yourself, Calloway," Hudson says. "Your wife is having a baby. You're about to become a father. Now we can sit here and argue, or we can deliver your fucking kid. I'm a trained physician, Jaxon. I got her. I promise."

Jaxon moves aside and sits next to me.

"Nicky, I need to check you," Hudson says. The nurse helps me with my underwear and shines a bright light while he examines me between the legs. "No time to transport. She's crowning. Nicky, go ahead and push."

"Here?" Jaxon shouts.

"Jaxon, take her hand. Nicole, give me a big push."

I squeeze Jaxon's hand and bear down hard. It feels good to push, even though it still hurts.

"Okay, stop. Keep breathing, but don't push," Hudson says. He talks to the nurse, something about the umbilical. I feel his hands down there. "Now, push again. Give it all you've got. Jaxon, you'll want to watch."

I scream and feel like I'm being torn in two, then almost instantly, relief comes. Then I hear my baby cry. Then I hear cheers from what sounds like hundreds of people outside the limo.

"Is she okay?"

"She appears healthy," Hudson says. "Now let's get you up to the floor so we can cut the cord and get you both cleaned up and checked out. Mark the time. 4:42 p.m."

He lays my daughter on my chest, and the nurse covers us with a blanket. "Happy birthday," I tell the beautiful, perfect tiny human.

Jaxon leans down and kisses her, then me. Then his ring. "I didn't know I had this much love to give. My god, Nicky, my heart is so incredibly full."

With a lot of help, I scoot out of the limo, and we're placed on a gurney. Applause surrounds us, and phone cameras are recording.

Marty comes over and congratulates us. "Why do I have the feeling you're going to be the leading story on tonight's news?"

Jaxon thanks Marty, and then we're whisked to the maternity ward.

Thirty minutes later, after our daughter is examined and bathed, she's wheeled over to me in a rolling bassinet. Jaxon picks her up and places her in my arms. "Now can we discuss names?"

I gaze at my beautiful baby. My miracle. And instantly, I know that no discussion is necessary. "Aurora," I say. "It means—"

"I know what it means." He blinks tears out of his eyes. "My wife is a meteorologist, you know. And I can't think of a more fitting name." He places a kiss on her tiny knit cap. "Welcome to the world, Aurora Calloway."

The next thing I know, it's dark out and I'm waking up, looking at Jaxon on the couch admiring our daughter in the bassinet next to him. If Aurora only knew how lucky she is to have him as her father. There's no better man. He's not perfect, by any means, and we've both made mistakes along the way, but somehow

I feel if it weren't for those mistakes, we wouldn't be right here right now.

"What time is it?" I ask sleepily.

"Almost one a.m. Yesterday really wiped it out of you. You've been sleeping for hours." Aurora cries and he stands. It's when he rises that I see he's holding a baby. *Another* baby.

My heart races. "Jaxon?"

"Calista was rushed in a few hours ago. She had an emergency C-section. She's going to be fine. She's in recovery. Eric is with her." He pushes the bassinet over by my bed and sits on the edge. "I was just introducing Aurora to her sister, Ashley."

Tears stream down my face. "Another girl? You always thought you'd have two girls."

"That's not all," he says. He motions to the clock. "She was born at 11:59 p.m."

My jaw drops. "On the same day?" I shake my head at the unbelievability of it all. Then something occurs to me. "Oh my gosh, Jaxon. Does this mean the girls are half twins?"

The two of us look between them, stunned. "Is that even a thing?" he says.

"You have two daughters born on the same day. What would *you* call it?"

"Half twins," he says, musing over the term. "I think I like it. Although poor Aurora and Ashley will have some major explaining to do."

I laugh. "We all will."

We stare at the girls, both knowing our lives have forever changed.

"Nine months ago, I was lost," he says. "I never thought I'd find love again, let alone with the only woman I could ever love. I thought my dream of having children was gone. And now I sit here with the love of my life and the daughters who I already love so fiercely. I pity any boy that even comes near them." I giggle and capture one of his tears with my thumb. He looks into my eyes. "How did I ever get this lucky?"

 I pull his head toward mine. "No," I say. "How did *I?*"

Epilogue

Jaxon

Five years later...

How I love the first few weeks of summer break. I have unlimited time with the kids, football conditioning hasn't started yet, and I get to watch Nicky on television every morning.

"Daddy!" Ashley calls from the backyard.

Heisman darts through the open slider, going to her before I do. Apparently, he thinks his name is Daddy.

"What is it, sweetie?"

"Watch me!"

She hangs upside down from the trapeze bar on the massive play structure we installed last year.

"Look at you."

"Daddy!" Aurora shouts. "I can do it too."

"Let's see."

Heisman licks her from below, making her giggle endlessly.

"Me, me, me, me," Ashley's two-year-old brother says as he toddles over.

Calista and Eric adopted Matthew as a baby. He was the perfect addition to their family and has become like a son to Nic and me.

I run over and pick him up. "Not quite yet, little buddy." I walk him over to Eric, who's supervising as he does some gardening. "Maybe help your pop pull some weeds."

"Gee, thanks," Eric says.

"Just trying to catch the last hour of Nic's show."

Nicky has been co-hosting the third morning hour for years. She's so good that I sometimes forget she got hired as a meteorologist instead of a news anchor.

Back inside, it's a commercial, so I stare out the window and watch the girls. They're not only half twins; they're also best friends. Technically, they are half-siblings who happened to be born on the same day. But they certainly look like they could be twins, both of them resembling me with their dark, wavy hair, blue eyes, and propensity toward athletics. The only difference between the two is that Aurora has Ashley by two whole inches—something she gets from Nicky, for sure.

Shortly after the girls were born, we removed the fence separating our two yards. Half of it got destroyed by the tree falling that Christmas, so it only made sense to remove the rest. Besides, it makes it much easier to go back and forth. And we do. *Often.*

Calista never went back to teaching. She's not only a stay-at-home mom but also Aurora's nanny. We're one big happy family. My focus goes back to the TV when the show comes back on. And our family is about to get bigger.

Seven and a half months ago, Heisman alerted us to the fact that Nicky was expecting. We weren't necessarily trying, but we weren't preventing it from happening. Nicky let her viewers in on the pregnancy right after the first trimester. She even told them the

Unfinished EX

name we picked. *Autumn.* Actually, it's the name Aurora and Ashley chose. After Nic's surgery to remove the scar tissue three years ago, this pregnancy has been nothing if not uneventful, for which I'm eternally grateful.

On the show, it's almost comical how Nicky struggles to get up from the couch when she goes over to do the weather. Why don't they have her go over during the commercial break? I swear Xuan Le loves the fact that Nicky's pregnancies have both been watched and followed by XTN's adoring fans. Viewership increased twenty percent after Nicky announced her pregnancy with Aurora and has stayed up ten percent ever since. Nicky has earned every penny they pay her, even if she tells me constantly that she's overpaid. Knowing Nic, she'd do the job for free.

I watch her in awe. Even after all this time, she's still passionate about reporting the weather. I'm not sure how many different spins you can put on a snowstorm or a waterspout, but she keeps coming up with more interesting ways to do it. She's doing what she was born to do.

The girls run inside, Matthew and Heisman trailing behind. "Daddy, we're thirsty," Aurora and Ashley say at the same time.

I keep one eye on the TV and walk to the fridge, getting three juice boxes. I hand one to each of the girls and pierce Matthew's straw through the box for him.

"There they are." Calista comes through the back door. She eyes the show. "Nicky looks pretty today. I love that color on her."

The blue maternity dress she's wearing flatters her large belly and matches the pendant she still wears to this day. I still wear my ring, too, a constant reminder of what we lost, yet what somehow bonded us back together.

385

"She's beautiful," I say, unable to take my eyes off her. She's as gorgeous as the day we married. Correction—the *two* days we married.

"Hi, Mommy," Aurora shouts at the TV as she dances out the back door.

Everyone else follows. "I'll be out in a minute," I say. "Show's almost over."

"Grab that sunscreen," Nicky says. "And if you have a friend with a boat, today might be a good day to—" She stops mid-sentence and looks down. I have déjà vu as I can clearly see the puddle forming beneath her. They don't cut. Of course they don't, this is Nicole Forbes, weather darling of XTN.

"Oh, boy," she says. "Or should I say *girl?*" Nicky's mouth turns up into a grin, and she stares right into the camera as if the camera is me. "Here we go again."

Acknowledgements

Unfinished Ex is my twenty-third book. Whoa!

As always, there are so many people whose hard work went into making it happen. Without my incredible team of supporters, experts, editors, and beta readers, I would have quit after three books.

My amazing list of beta readers is long: Joelle Yates, Shauna Salley, Laura Conley, Heather Carver, Ann Peters, Michelle Fewer, and Tammy Dixon. The honest critiques I get from you only make my books better, and for that I'm eternally grateful.

Thank you to my copy editor, Amanda Cuff, and my PR peeps at Social Butterfly.

Details matter, so my sincere appreciation goes out to Kimberly Kernek, M.D. FACOG (fellow of the American college of obstetrics and gynecology) for schooling me on Asherman's syndrome. Although I'm sure I took some creative liberties, your guidance helped immensely.

Last, but certainly not least, thank you to my wonderful assistant, Julie Collier, who makes me feel like she's at my beck and call 24/7.

I'm in love with these trash-talking Calloway Brothers, and I can't wait for you to dive into Cooper's very personal and painful story. But you know me—you can always expect an HEA!

About the author

Samantha Christy's passion for writing started long before her first novel was published. Graduating from the University of Nebraska with a degree in Criminal Justice, she held the title of Computer Systems Analyst for The Supreme Court of Wisconsin and several major universities around the United States. Raised mainly in Indianapolis, she holds the Midwest and its homegrown values dear to her heart and upon the birth of her third child devoted herself to raising her family full time. While it took time to get from there to here, writing has remained her utmost passion and being a stay-at-home mom facilitated her ability to follow that dream. When she is not writing, she keeps busy cruising to every Caribbean island where ships sail. Samantha Christy currently resides in St. Augustine, Florida with her husband and four children.

You can reach Samantha Christy at any of these wonderful places:

Website: www.samanthachristy.com

Facebook: https://www.facebook.com/SamanthaChristyAuthor

Instagram: @authorsamanthachristy

E-mail: samanthachristy@comcast.net

Printed in Great Britain
by Amazon